# SARAWAK

by
Jerry D. Mohrlang

PublishAmerica
Baltimore

©Copyright 2002 by Jerry D. Mohrlang.

All rights reserved. No part of this book may be reproduced in any form without written permission from the publishers, except by a reviewer who may quote brief passages in a review to be printed in a newspaper or magazine.

First printing

ISBN: 1-59129-336-7
PUBLISHED BY PUBLISHAMERICA BOOK PUBLISHERS
www.publishamerica.com
Baltimore

Printed in the United States of America

*For my wife, Mary Lee, whose cup is always half full;*
*and for the indigenous people of Sarawak who treated*
*me with kindness and whose ancestors, history*
*and culture were the inspiration for this novel.*

Mike:
May all of the adventures
in your life be filled
with joy & beauty. Enjoy
the adventure of "Sarawak"!

Best Always
Jerry D. Malmberg
8/19/02

## AUTHOR'S NOTE

Certain places, names, geographical references
and time-frames have been altered,
condensed and/or fictionalized

# Prologue

"The Island of Borneo (so called from the city of that name) lies on the North of Java, and on the East of Sumatra, and of the Peninsula of Malacca. It is situated between the 7 degrees 30 minutes of North Latitude, and the 4 degrees 10 minutes Of South, under the Equinoctial, which divides it into two unequal parts so that it is in length 700 miles, in breadth 480, and in circuit about 2,000. It is counted the biggest island, not only in the Indian Sea, but in the whole world, except perhaps California in the South Sea. Many score miles near the sea the country looks like a dark forest, being full of prodigious tall trees, between which is nothing but vast swamps of mud. At high water you may sail in a great way among these trees in several places, seeing nothing but biting Insects of enormous size and poisonous serpents of a kind unknown to man, but at low water it is all mud, upon which the sun (especially in the Equinox) darting his scorching beams perpendicularly, raises noisome vapors, fogs, etc., which afterwards turn into most violent showers that fall more like cataracts than rain. The land and the naked savages which inhabit it are ill disposed to contact with ships or men and voyagers are forewarned to avoid, if humanly possible, this most inhospitable and treacherous of all lands known to the civilized world."[1]

Captain Nathanial Beekman
HMS Discovery
October 16, 1627

[1] Beekman, D. *A Voyage to and from the Island of Borneo in the East Indies*, London, 1718.

# CHAPTER ONE

## I

*Circa* 1824 A.D.
The Jungle
Borneo

His name was stone. Batu. When he ducked behind a *nipa* palm beneath the dark folds of jungle canopy above him and remained motionless, the five members of his tiny Punan clan following several strides behind him, melted noiselessly into the cover of the dense forest and crouched silently, observing only the tensed and well-defined muscles of their leader's naked back for a sign.

It was early dawn and only singular blades of sunlight pierced the forest canopy high above the clan. The emerging warmth of the new day began to scatter wisps of a lingering fog and evaporate dewdrops clinging tenaciously to each leaf of vegetation surrounding the tiny group.

Batu's band of jungle nomads awakened long before dawn from their temporary shelters of raised platforms constructed of nothing more than bamboo and palm thatch and had begun their daily trek through the dense interior of their jungle homeland to hunt and forage. Typical of their nomadic race, Batu's band was small in numbers, consisting of a girl no more than ten years of age, a boy not much older, Batu's brother who, at the age of sixteen, was only two years younger than the clan's leader, and Batu's fourteen-year-old wife and four-month-old child.

Small in stature, the Punan were, nevertheless, muscular and strong. Their Mongoloid features were less than defined as if thousands of years of intense isolation from the rest of mankind gave nature the respite it needed to sculpt a new race of man. Although the Punan were genetically related to the various tribes who shared their island habitat, their skin was chalk white as a result of self imposed isolation within the deepest recesses of the dark jungle by generations of Batu's Punan ancestors.

Batu's band were a shy and timid people, preferring the less accessible highland jungle within the interior of the huge island to the more open terrain near the coast where countless watersheds sliced through the less dense lowlands as they transported their cargo of stolen water and silt from the inland mountains of the interior and dumped it amid the ugly mud flats along the coast. Unlike his sea-going neighbors, the Iban, Kayan and Kenyan, the

Punan never adapted to travel by water and Batu was careful not to lead his clan on foraging expeditions near the lowland regions particularly during *landas*, an annual event of nature that freed enormous volumes of water from moisture laden clouds which transformed the lowlands into impassable snake-infested swamps and changed the normally docile watersheds into raging mud-filled torrents.

The Punan clan remained silent and alert for a sign from their leader. Even Batu's young child stopped suckling at his mother's breast and fixed his eyes on his father, inherently aware that an event of some magnitude was about to occur. It was as if the same nature which had provided this race of people with such an abundance of temerity compensated and balanced the scales by bestowing upon even the youngest of their clan the instinct to hold his quiet for the survival of the band. Whether Batu had spotted game or danger didn't matter to Batu's tiny family. Their reaction would have been the same in either situation. Their survival depended upon each of them maintaining a cloistered silence and an ability to react instantaneously to any sign given by their leader.

As his name implied, Batu remained motionless, a pillar of rock in the thick of the jungle, a solid monument to a vanishing race of the island's original inhabitants. Only his eyes shifted to follow the movements of the object of his attention some fifty meters beyond the cover of a *nipa* palm. Batu's right hand clutched the long, smooth shaft of his blowpipe. A bamboo sheath fit snugly into the folds of his bark-beaten loin cloth. The sheath contained stiletto-thin darts fashioned from slivers of bamboo and freshly dipped in a mixture of lime and the deadly juice of the *ipoh* nut. If threatened, Batu was confident that he could easily hit the target to save his band.

But Batu hoped there would be no hostile encounter with the lone Kayan warrior passing before him. It was the way of the Punan to limit contact with others and to avoid confrontation whenever possible. Batu's keen eyes told him that it was unlikely that the Kayan had detected Batu's band because the young Kayan warrior appeared to be moving with some urgency and his movements informed Batu that the Kayan's attention was diverted elsewhere, behind him, in the direction from which he had come.

Batu observed the interloper move quickly but cautiously along the leading edge of the forest where it had been cleft by one of the many feeder stream's which fed the mighty Rajang River some distance below. The Kayan continued to move along the streams rocky bank in a series of hurried steps followed by a succession of stops while he turned his head and appeared to listen for sounds other than the steady ripple of the stream or the sporadic cries of awakening forest creatures.

Twenty meters from where Batu hid, the lone Kayan paused, glanced nervously behind him one final time and then disappeared into the protective womb of the thick forest. It was then that Batu recognized the young Kayan as Jau, son of the elderly Headman of the Kayan longhouse of Long Selah'at near the treacherous headwaters of the Barum River some distance northeast of where the Punans hid. Jau wore the distinctive fangs of the clouded leopard inserted securely in the cartilage of his ear lobes and like all Kayan, his facial hair, including his eyelashes and brows, were plucked clean, giving the youthful Kayan a smooth and placid appearance that belied his naturally fierce nature.

The young warrior's hair was jet black and cut in the distinctive style of his tribe, in a straight line high around his forehead and along the sides of his head. The hair on the back of his head grew to a long, flowing mane held together by an unadorned knot at the middle of his naked back.

Jau carried a thick bladed knife, a *parang*, unsheathed and at the ready as if he expected to be set upon at any moment. His *chawat*, a length of black cloth enveloping his waist and covering his youthful manhood, flowed gracefully between his legs and didn't hinder his movement through the underbrush beyond the stream.

Under normal circumstances, neither Jau nor the Punan clan would be a threat to one another. The Kayan treated their rare contact with the Punan much like a civilized parent might treat a feral child; with curiosity, detachment and tolerance. Only on rare occasions would the secretive Punan reveal themselves to their Kayan neighbors, and then only to trade the horns of the pigmy rhinoceros or the gall bladders of the honey bears which lived in the deep recesses of the highlands where the superstitious Kayan dared not enter. In return, the Punan received iron spear points which they affixed to the tips of their blowpipes having discovered that the combination of blowpipe and spear made a most formidable hunting weapon. Batu never understood why it was that the Kayan placed such a high premium upon horns and gall bladders; neither could be worn, eaten or used in a hunt. He was not aware that the Kayan, in turn, traded these precious jungle commodities to coastal Malay and Chinese merchants who coveted the objects as cures for all manner of ailments. In return, the Kayan obtained large earthenware jars, brass gongs and iron implements.

But Jau carried more than a *parang* in his hands and when Batu saw the object, he understood why the young Kayan moved with such obvious caution. Jau had completed his hunt for the day. But it wasn't the game of the forest that he clutched so tightly in his hand but, rather, the severed head of an Iban child.

When Batu safely determined that the Kayan had distanced himself from the Punan clan and was no longer a potential threat, the tensed, long muscles of his back relaxed, and gave a silent signal to his tiny band that the danger or opportunity to hunt had passed. Without a word spoken among them, the Punan stepped from their hiding places and tacitly followed their leader in single file as he led them into the thickest and most remote part of the surrounding forest.

Batu picked his way slowly and soundlessly through the underbrush of the forest floor, his keen senses elevated as always to carefully monitor any sight or sound that would alert him to the two elements his environment provided in abundance—food and danger. As he walked he thought of his close encounter with the young Kayan warrior, Jau, and the grotesque trophy he carried with him. Like the pigmy rhinoceros tusks and the honey bear bladders, it made no sense to him that the Kayan should prize such things. Even more perplexing to Batu were the newest arrivals to the lowlands, the people who called themselves, Iban or Sea Dyaks and whom the Kayan called, 'wanderers.' Like the sudden fury of the *landas,* the Iban had flooded the narrow river valleys near the Kayan lands in great numbers. They too, valued severed heads above all else but unlike their more refined neighbors and enemies, the Kayan and Kenyan, the Iban took heads wherever they found an opportunity—even from their own kind or from a careless Punan who strayed too close to the lowland territories.

Batu's mental stirrings of the strange practices of these neighboring tribes resulted in no judgments, no moral outrage or condemnation of any of them. Thousands of years of survival-honed instinct simply confirmed to Batu that outsiders must be avoided.

With that knowledge certain, Batu led his small band deeper into the safety of the highland forest.

## II

### Pre-Dawn
### Kampong Batang
### Borneo

Chopak pounded a brass gong with unusual vigor. Although the Iban residents of the longhouse of Kampong Batang had long awakened, he knew his incessant pounding grated on Rentab's nerves and he enjoyed every second of it.

"Enough, Chopak!" Rentab shouted. "It is not necessary to awaken the spirits as well as the village!" Rentab pressed his fingers to his temples and tried to rub away the lingering effects of a *tuak* induced hangover.

"Yes, *Tua Kampong*." Satisfied that he had caused sufficient agony to the village's Headman, Chopak set aside the gong and joined the rank of Iban warriors who were scurrying down a hewn log stairway from the longhouse to the forest floor.

Unlike the other Iban warriors clutching *parangs*, spears and brightly painted war shields, Chopak held no weapons. He was a *saperti perempuan*, an effeminate. As such, he wore a woman's black sarong which extended from his armpits to below his knees and his long black hair was tied in a compact bun at the base of his neck in the manner of all Iban women. Chopak's only other adornment was a beaded necklace that suspended a feathered leather pouch containing pig's knuckles. To the Iban, Chopak was an anomaly, a female spirit harbored in the body of a man. No one understood why the spirits did such things, but the superstitious Iban considered Chopak blessed, one who could make the whims of the spirit world known to man by casting the small bones of a pig and divining their meaning.

"Chopak!" Rentab called before the effeminate descended the stairway. "Wait a moment," he said. "I would have you toss the pig's knuckles for me before I depart with my warriors."

Chopak stopped his descent from the longhouse and returned to the *ruii* where Rentab stood. "If that is your wish, *Tua Kampong*," he said, opening the feathered pouch around his neck and removing the pig's knuckles.

*Tua Kampong*, Headman, how good those words sounded to Rentab. He had waited a long time to be addressed by that title. Yesterday, there were those in his village who were of the opinion that Rentab was too old to be elected as the new *Tua Kampong* of Kampong Batang and Chopak was

11

among them. But Rentab's promise to lead his warriors on a successful raid to obtain heads—which the young warriors coveted to prove their manhood and the older warriors needed to reaffirm theirs—won the day for Rentab and he was elected *Tua Kampong* despite his wrinkle plastered face and graying hair.

Surrounded by a curious contingent of women, children and young warriors who would be among those left behind to protect the village in the absence of his raiding party, Rentab and Chopak squatted face to face on the bamboo floor of the *ruii*.

"Toss the bones for me, Chopak," Rentab said. "I would know what the spirits know."

"The spirits are not always kind in the telling," Chopak warned. "Sometimes the desires of man are played upon by those in the nether world, *Tua*."

Rentab was certain that Chopak's use of the word, *"tua,"* which simply means 'old,' as opposed to Rentab's full title was just another attempt by the effeminate to irritate him. And it did, but he didn't let it show. "Scatter the bones, Chopak," Rentab ordered. "I'm certain that the spirits will find my desires less easily played upon than most."

"As you command," Chopak said and scattered the knuckles in front of Rentab. Chopak closed his eyes as if listening to distant voices and asked, dreamily, "What is it you ask of the nether world, Rentab?"

Rentab realized that he risked the success of the impending raid and his recent election as *Tua Kampong* with the question he was about to ask, but the right answer from the spirit world would cement his leadership and his title for a long time to come. And the spirits wouldn't be so fickle as to assist in his confirmation as *Tua Kampong* one day only to turn upon him the next, would they? With the hushed assembly of villagers pressed close to hear the words of the spirits from the mouth of the *saperti perempuan*, Rentab asked his question. "Will the blessings of the spirits be upon the warriors of Kampong Batang at the moment of our battle?" Rentab asked. Rentab swallowed hard and held his breath.

Chopak opened his eyes and gazed upon the bones. "I see fire in the darkness...Iban and others...a battle...the taking of many heads..."

Rentab brightened. "The raid? It will be a success, then?"

"Yes," Chopak said. "I see many heads hanging from the rafters of Kampong Batang...and..."

Rentab eased forward. "And what else do you see, Chopak?" he eagerly asked.

"...a *gawai* in honor of..."

"Of course a *gawai*," Rentab interrupted. "A huge celebration of our

12

victory!" he exclaimed to the onlookers.

"...the victorious raid and one..." Chopak continued, now in deep trance and oblivious to Rentab's interruption.

"There is more?" Rentab asked. The reading was more than he hoped for. Victory. Honor. And yet more?

"...and one," Chopak repeated, "of the young will be mourned..."

*Only one of the young will be mourned?* Only *one* casualty, Rentab reasoned. *Such a minuscule price to pay for such a huge victory!*

"...and the spirits will bless Kampong Batang...until the..."

Rentab could barely contain his elation. *The spirits are truly with me. They are with me!*

"...coming...of...the one with a...long...shadow."

"Wha...What is that you say?" Rentab asked. "What is meant by this? What is the 'coming of a long shadow,' Chopak?"

Chopak gazed dumbfounded at the splay of bones and began to shake away the effects of his trance. "I...I...don't know," Chopak said. "I don't understand...."

Confused, Rentab stared at the bones in a vain attempt to extract some meaning from them. But any story that remained to be told eluded him and the bones appeared as they always had to him before entering the world of the spirits-simply the scattered skeletal remains of a pig.

Suddenly, Rentab stood and faced the small group of remaining warriors and others who had witnessed Chopak's reading of the bones. "The oracle is finished!" Rentab boomed. "You all heard. Chopak has spoken for the spirits and they are with the warriors of Kampong Batang. The spirits have assured us of a great victory and much honor for our warriors and our village!"

With Rentab's pronouncement, the women cheered and the warriors beat upon their wooden war shields with their spears and *parangs* and shouted their newly elected leader's name, "Rentab! Rentab! Rentab!"

Although still puzzled by Chopak's final pronouncement, Rentab pushed the thought from his mind and absorbed the accolades of his people. When the din ebbed, Rentab ordered one of the young warriors to fetch his weapons and then announced to the warriors, "You are entrusted with the task of protecting our village while we are gone. I know that each of you would rather be with me on this raid, but there will be other raids and other opportunities for you. This I promise."

"When shall we expect your return, *Tua Kampong*?" one of them asked.

Once again Rentab consciously absorbed the power in the words that the title, 'Tua Kampong' bestowed upon him. Now, with both the title *and* the blessings of the spirits conferred, he was truly Headman of Kampong Batang and he fully intended to use the power of his station from this day forward.

"We should return within three days time," he said, then puffed his thin chest and added, "But regardless of when I return, let it be known that I, Rentab, *Tua Kampong* of Batang, shall not return until my warriors' *praus* are filled with the heads of our enemies. Soon, the rafters of Kampong Batang," he said, casting a dramatic toss of his hand to the *bilian* beams that stretched between the individual rooms of the longhouse and the *ruii*, will be filled with the skulls of our enemies and Kampong Batang will be the most feared village in all of Sarawak!"

Chopak gathered the pig knuckles and replaced them in the leather poach hanging from his neck and listened in dismay as Rentab spoke. He had not changed his mind about Rentab. For Chopak, Rentab was not a good choice to be Headman. He believed that Rentab's thirst for blood would lead to more and more raids. Too many raids most certainly meant reprisals and many Iban would die protecting their village. And yet, the spirits' story, through him, had augured well for Rentab and Kampong Batang. Still, his reading filled him with apprehension. He tried to fathom the meaning of the spirits' message about the coming of a long shadow. Had he misread the bones? But the answer was as much of a mystery to him now as it had been earlier.

"Come, Chopak," Rentab said. "The warriors await. I would have you bless my departure." Rentab took his war shield and *parang* from the young warrior who had retrieved it for him, turned and, somewhat unsteadily, stepped down the log stairway of the longhouse and headed toward the river with Chopak following close behind.

When the two of them reached the river, twenty *praus*-sleek canoes each hewn from a single massive log—had already been filled with warriors and weapons. Excitement hung in the air as thick and palpable as the rising river mist because news of Chopak's auspicious reading had spread among the war party and they were anxious to fulfill the spirits' prophesy of a successful raid and the taking of many heads.

Rentab stopped at the river's edge and surveyed the site before him. The dull throb in his head returned and he wished he had consumed less *tuak* the previous evening. But the anticipation of leading the largest war party ever assembled in his lifetime to a great victory was balm enough for his temporary discomfort.

All eyes fixed upon Rentab when he raised his arms for silence and announced, "Yesterday, I, Rentab, was chosen above all others as *Tua Kampong*. Today I will lead you to glory. Soon, each of you will wear the marks of courage that I, Rentab, have earned through my own bravery and daring!" Rentab thrust his envied fists into the air and raised his chin so that all could see the finely etched tattoo that covered his throat and marked him as a killer.

Chopak watched in silence. Even he could not deny Rentab's courage. No one did. The purple tattoos etched upon Rentab's hands, wrists, shoulders and throat attested to his bravery. They were the marks allowed only to those who had proven their courage against an enemy and who had taken heads. And Rentab had taken many heads—more than anyone in the village. Still, Chopak remained suspicious of Rentab's motives and was not yet convinced that Rentab's election as *Tua Kampong* would augur favorably for Kampong Batang despite the vote of the people or the prognostications of the spirit world.

"Rentab! Rentab! Rentab!" the war party chanted. The clamor of weapons beating against wooden war shields was deafening as the sound reverberated between the forested walls of the river.

Rentab swelled his narrow chest and sucked in his warriors' accolade like a blood starved leech and boarded the nearest *prau*. "Your blessing, Chopak. I would have it now," he said to the *saperti perempuan* before reaching for an oar and pushing the *prau* from its sandy mooring.

"You have no need for my blessing, *tua*," Chopak said as the leading edge of Rentab's *prau* caught the river's current and slipped away. "You have heard the words of the spirits and perhaps that will be blessing enough."

*Perhaps? What did Chopak mean by that?* Chopak annoyed him as much as the lingering effects of his hangover did. Rentab closed his eyes and settled back into the stern of the *prau* content to let the others do the paddling while he tried to retrieve the sleep that escaped him the night before. *No matter. With or without Chopak's blessing, my victory is assured,* he thought. And Rentab had reason to feel confident. On the eve of his impending election as *Tua Kampong*, Rentab had met clandestinely in a remote cove along the Batang River far below Kampong Batang with *Awang* Api, younger son of the powerful *Dayang* Udang and nephew to the Sultan of Brunei. There, Rentab and the ambitious Malay prince conspired in a plan that would assure an Iban victory and eventually to Rentab's own rise to power and prominence in the Malay dominated region of Sarawak.

Rentab fell into a deep, restful sleep, secure in the knowledge that the meager influence he held today was a mere shadow of the power he was certain to wield in the future. In his slumber, Rentab had little reason to suspect that one element of Chopak's reading of the bones was about to be fulfilled for at that moment Rentab's six year old son was entering the forest near Kampong Batang and the Kayan, Jau, was waiting for him.

*"...and one of the young will be mourned..."*

## III

Near Kampong Long Selah'at
The Lowlands
Borneo

Jau, too, trusted his instincts when he felt hidden eyes of the Punan observing him. Although he could not determine to whom the eyes belonged or from where they watched, he *knew* he was being observed from a close distance. He also knew that it was unlikely that the voyeurs were Iban warriors or other enemies or they would have fallen upon him by now. An animal, perhaps? Electing caution as an ally, Jau decided to leave the relatively open terrain along the stream's rocky bank where he made good time in his escape from the Iban village and duck into the protective folds of the forest where his movement would be slowed but infinitely safer. He proceeded in a meandering northerly course through the forest for the better part of an hour. Eventually, the jungle thinned and merged with a narrow band of thick *lalang* grass between two dense stands of forest. A narrow footpath slithered through the center of the *lalang* field to a rise several meters beyond where Jau stood and then the path fell away on the far side of a hill rising directly in front of him and beyond the march of the *lalang* grass.

Jau hurried through the field of *lalang* and stepped onto the narrow foot path leading to the hill before him. There he paused momentarily and looked behind him one final time. He hadn't felt the eyes of whoever or whatever it was that watched him since he left the bank of the stream and for the first time since his pre-dawn exit from his village of Long Selah'at, his feeling of apprehension began to fade. He was safe now. It was unlikely that even the fierce Iban would dare pursue him this close to his own village. When his senses confirmed his thought that it was safe to proceed, Jau sheathed his father's *parang*, sliding it carefully into an intricately carved wooden sheath lined with monkey hair. Then Jau straightened, filled his lungs with cool morning air, lifted his chin proudly and walked with long confident strides toward the top of the hill. His village of Long Selah'at lay just beyond the hill within a small valley adjacent to an inordinately wide and remarkably clear runnel, similar to all the streams in this region, which eventually spilled its contents into the mighty Barum River some two miles below the village of Long Selah'at.

Before cresting the hill, Jau slowed his pace and began to savor this moment of personal triumph and his coming of age. His feeling of pride for his accomplishment coursed through his lithe young body like the mighty Barum itself and Jau's stride changed to a purposeful self-assured strut. Jau thought of the *gawai* his tribesmen would hold in his honor as a communal celebration of his triumph. There would be dancing, the playing of gongs, singing and consumption of huge quantities of *borak*, a bitter, rice-fermented beer made by the Kayan women. More importantly, his trophy of the Iban child's head would hang in a place of honor in the village's headhouse and confer upon him the tribal right to marry and have children—hopefully many sons who would succeed him as Headman of Long Selah'at just as he would succeed his own aging father one day—and would forever be a reminder to the story tellers of Long Selah'at as they would chant of the bravery and daring of Jau, son of Mong from this day forward.

Before reaching the crest of the hill, Jau raised the head of the Iban boy in front of his eyes and beamed. Admittedly, the taking of this child's head was easier than he anticipated, but even so, nothing could diminish the thrill of this, his first kill. And Jau made a vow to himself that this head would be the first of many he would take in his lifetime.

Having moved beyond the crown of the hill Jau began his descent to the awakened village of Long Selah'at below. The word spread quickly among his people that Jau had returned and soon each villager put aside whatever morning task they were doing and watched the approach of the Headman's son with interest. Seeing that all eyes were fixed upon his approach, Jau hoisted the Iban child's head high in the air and broke into a loud, melodious song which boasted of his brave deed that day. Hearing the chant, the villagers streamed forward from the longhouse to more clearly hear Jau's story.

Jau sang of how he arose long before the break of day, before the cocks began to crow. He told them how he had taken his father's sharpest *parang*—the one with the orang-hutang hair imbedded in its hilt and sheathed in a finely carved *bilian* scabbard lined with monkey hair—and then made his way to the stream to bathe and pray to the spirits to protect him from the *hantus*, the fickle jungle spirits that killed men by setting traps that appeared as accidents so that a man's soul would be forced to wander forever, never to know the eternal peace of a warrior's death. Jau sang of how the moonlight guided him several miles along the banks of a feeder stream and then through the forest until he reached the outskirts of the Iban village known as Kampong Batang because it lay along the Batang River and housed the fiercest enemies of the Kayan. Even after the emerging dawn swallowed the moon, Jau sang of how his courage and resolve never deserted him although he was one against many.

Jau didn't sing of the surge of fear that gripped him shortly after he hid himself among the thickets of *nibong* palms near the Iban longhouse. His resolve was tested when a cacophony of brass gongs erupted from the longhouse and shattered the morning calm. Jau was certain he had been detected, but his fear rooted him to his hiding place and he was only capable of watching dozens of armed Iban warriors pour from the longhouse and race to the river on the far side of the village. Jau reasoned that the Iban were mustering for a raid, perhaps on some hapless Bidayuh village further downstream and he slowly exhaled the breath he unconsciously held in his fright and calmed the beat of his heart. Jau gulped in new air and then nestled himself further into the safety of the *nibong* thicket.

Soon, hungry morning sunlight ate away the darkness of the forest and consumed the remains of pre-dawn shadows lingering about the Iban village. Now, Jau could clearly see the Iban women begin their early morning chores along the *tanju*, the exposed, open verandah which spanned the front of the longhouse. Many of the women and a few young girls pounded rice with a long shaft of hardwood held between each pair of them, a method used by Jau's own people to remove the grain from the husk. Other women used flat rattan baskets to toss the broken grain into the air so that the early morning breeze could whisk away the chaff while the heavier, edible grain remained.

But Jau's attention focused mainly upon the small contingent of Iban warriors who had not accompanied the raiding party. Most of them gathered in a cluster along with others of the village and appeared to be listening to a conversation between two men seated face-to-face on the *ruii*. Others chewed beetle nut, talked and honed spear points and *parangs*. The Iban morning ritual was not unfamiliar to Jau. The women of his own village would be performing similar labors and the Kayan men would be preparing for the morning hunt just as the Iban seemed to be doing. Moments later, an older Iban and an effeminate exited the longhouse and headed for the river. Shortly, Jau knew, children would be sent from the longhouse to collect water from the river and firewood from the forest. That would be his chance, he thought.

Jau's patience was soon rewarded. Several children, five girls and a boy no more than six years old, climbed down the log-hewn steps of the longhouse and began tossing food scraps to a flock of scrawny chickens and a host of squealing pigs. When the animals were fed, the children separated. Three of the girls picked up round lengths of bamboo and headed toward the river, away from Jau. The two remaining girls removed woven baskets hanging from one of the poles which elevated the longhouse above the forest floor and with the lone boy in tow, moved unsuspectingly to the edge of the forest where Jau had hidden himself.

Jau recognized his good fortune. It would not be necessary to leave his hiding place to collect his head. He scanned the longhouse one final time before he placed his hand around the hilt of his father's *parang*. Jau then fixed his eyes on the approaching children and his excitement grew. Taking the head of a woman or child was more than he could have hoped for. It would be received with more honor by his Kayan tribesmen because it would prove that he had the courage to enter the perimeter of an enemy village where the women and children would surely be protected by a contingent of warriors.

Jau's chant rose above the congratulatory murmurs of his kinsmen and he continued his song. "I waited like my brother, the clouded leopard, until the children separated themselves before I singled out the Iban boy's head to decorate the rafters of the headhouse of Long Selah'at. I moved low on the forest floor-silently, swiftly like the deadly kryte and took up a position behind a *jilangtan* tree. There I remained as motionless as the tiny *rusa*, the elusive forest deer while the two Iban girls passed by without detecting me."

Jau's song raised in volume as he reached the climax of his story. "When the boy passed I struck as quickly as the coiled cobra and slew my enemy with one swift strike of my father's *parang*." Jau raised the severed head and mimicked how he grabbed the boy, pulled him skyward and separated the boy's head from his body. "My enemy's body twitched and thrashed at my feet when it released its spirit to the nether world," he sang. "But no sound reached the ears of the Iban girls or the village because of the silence and speed of my attack."

Jau's voice slowed in timbre as he completed his song. "With the head of my vanquished enemy clutched in my hand, I made my escape with the speed of the wild pig. I, Jau the victor, Jau the warrior, Jau the man, return with honor to my father's village of Long Selah'at where my deed this day will be told by the singers of songs now and forevermore."

IV

## Kampong Bau
## Sarawak

Kameja, a fourteen-year-old Melanau slave girl, watched with fearful eyes through a crack in the bamboo wall of her master's *bilek*. Her arms encircled two of her master's children.

"Shhhh," she whispered while she rocked them in her arms to soothe their trembling and tried desperately not to convey her own fear to them.

Fear always gripped the normally tranquil village of the Bidayuh whenever the Malay prince, *Awang* Api arrived to collect taxes. Api, whose name meant 'fire,' was as volatile and hot-tempered as his name implied and he was often implacable and cruel. He wore a finely woven sarong of scarlet and gold with a *kris* inserted in the folds of cloth about his waist. His chest and arms were bare and unadorned except for bands of gold wrapped around his biceps. His closely cropped midnight black hair was partially covered by a folded band of scarlet cloth tied in a knot above his right ear. Api's handsome face bore high cheekbones, a sharply defined nose and a strong, jutting jaw that combined to convey the message that this was a man of noble birth and superior to all others. Unusually tall for his race, Api's height and his arrogant bearing often proved as intimidating as his rancorous reputation and a single stare of Api's cobra-black eyes could gut a man of his strength and will. At the age of twenty-seven, Api was in the prime of his manhood and he considered no man his equal.

With mounting anxiety, Kameja watched and listened to the exchange between the Malay Lord and her master, Endap, Headman of Bau.

Careful to keep his shoulders slumped and his head lowered in submission, Endap said with a voice cracking in fear, "We have no more to give, Lord Api. Your men have taken it all."

"Nothing more to give, you say? Nothing more in this entire village?" Api said with a sweep of his arm. "Why is that, Headman? Why is it that you have failed to raise the amount of *serah* owed me?"

"We are a poor people, Lord Api. My village works hard just to find enough food to quiet the rumblings of our children's bellies. There has not been enough time to collect the *serah* you demand of us, my Lord. Perhaps, if you would allow us more time, we could—"

"Time? You have the audacity to ask me for more time? Are you telling me that your filthy village needs more *time* to raise the *serah* due me?" Api stepped close to Endap and allowed his taller frame to dwarf the Bidayuh spokesman. He took Endap's chin between his thumb and fingers and raised it, squeezing tighter as he forced Endap's eyes upward to meet his own. "Tell me, Endap," Api said, "What do you propose if I consent to this foolish request and grant your village more *time* to raise the *serah*?" A cruel, twisted smile formed on Api's lips and his eyes radiated with pleasure from tormenting the smaller Bidayuh.

Endap knew that deadly fangs lurked behind Api's false grin and if provoked further, Api would strike. He considered his words carefully when he spoke. "We will have the full measure of *serah* by the next full moon, Lord Api. This I vow."

"Fool!" Api's patience snapped and with a lightning stroke of his open hand, he slapped Endap to the ground. "Your constant pleas for more time annoy me, Endap! The full measure of *serah* will be paid *now*, not a full moon from now not even one hour from now. Do you understand me, Endap? Fail and I shall torch this stinking sty of a village to the ground. It only serves to aggravate me anyway."

Kameja winced when Api struck her Bidayuh master and sent him sprawling to the ground. Endap was a kind and benevolent man and treated her like one of his own daughters and it saddened her deeply to witness his humiliation. Until Api's rise to power in Sarawak, the system of *serah,* of taxation, had been an equitable one between the Malay and the various indigenous tribes living near the coast of Sarawak. In return for a portion of the wealth these coastal tribes extracted from the sea or forest or fashioned with the skill of their own hands, the Malay overlords settled disputes among them and willingly protected them from pirates and Dyak raiders who prowled the rivers and coastal waters in search of easy prey. But Api's voracious appetite for more and more *serah* had so debilitated Bau and other villages of the region, that the people found it increasingly difficult to accommodate their own basic needs and some Bidayuh villages had already chosen to move inland, preferring the savagery of the Iban, Kayan and Kenyan to the torment and starvation induced by the demands of their cruel Malay lord.

Api straddled the fallen Headman, grabbed him by the hair and twisted his head until their eyes met and hissed, "What shall it be, old man, a full measure of *serah* or ashes?"

As much as it pained him, Endap realized what he must do to save Bau from Api's torch. "I...I have *serah* in full measure, Lord Api."

"Hah! I thought as much!" Api pasted a fake grin on his face and said, "I knew you could be reasoned with, old man." Api extended his open hand to Endap and guided him to his feet. "There now," Api said, pretending to wipe the dust from Endap's shoulders. "See how pleasant things can be when you chose to cooperate?"

Endap bowed his head and nodded an assent.

Api placed his hand on the hilt of his *kris*. "The *serah*," Api prompted. "Now!"

Endap turned his head to face his *bilek* and called in a hoarse whisper filled with pain, "Ka...Kameja. Come here, girl."

Kameja's heart sank and her eyes drowned in fear. She cast a pleading glance to Endap's wife who only shook her head to convey the message that there was nothing she could do. Kameja hugged each of the children one final time and touched them lightly on their cheeks and then gently pushed them from her arms. Kameja stood and with uncertain legs exited the *bilek* and approached her master and the Lord Api.

"Ahhh...so this is your compensation, my friend." Api swallowed the beauty of the bare-breasted slave with one gulp of his eyes and conveyed his pleasure with a wide, lustful grin. He motioned for Kameja to approach him. "Come closer, girl" he ordered. "Api will not bite such a fine gift. Your new lord and master will know how to treat one so fair," he teased.

With trembling legs, Kameja stepped forward to accept whatever fate her new lord and master would determine for her. Her short life had now come full circle. Before her sale to Endap and the Bidayuh, she had been a slave to a Malay village after coastal raiders had torn her from her mother's dead arms and traded her to them for an ingot of iron. Even now, after five pleasant years with the gentle Bidayuh, she still awakened at night with nightmares of the brutality she suffered at the hands of her former masters.

Api placed his hand on the girl's chin and lifted her head. Kameja flushed at Api's touch and passively raised her head but her large almond eyes remained closed. Api felt the girl shudder beneath his fingertips and it delighted him. "Very nice," Api breathed. "Yes, very nice indeed." Api circled Kameja slowly, surveying her every feature. The slave girl wore a faded blue sarong that covered her body from her navel to her calves and was wrapped, tucked and neatly folded at her waist. A single brass ring surrounded her right ankle. Her arms and torso were bare, revealing smooth, light-toned skin and small breasts with unusually pink nipples still in the formative stage of development. The girl's hair was cropped just below her shoulders and had tones of brown in it that lacked the luster and sheen of the more common jet-black hair. A smoothly rounded face, plucked eyebrows, long dark lashes and full lips set upon the same light toned skin that sheltered the rest of her body hinted at the beauty she would become one day. "This one is Melanau, is she not?" Api asked.

"Yes...Melanau," Endap replied, sadly.

22

"This Melanau slave is a fine gift, old man," Api said, placing his hands on Endap's shoulders and holding him at arms length. "You have chosen well, this day, my friend. For that, I will not torch your pathetic village but," he added, digging his fingers into Endap's shallow shoulders, "when I next return, I will expect my tribute in full measure. Is that understood, Headman?"

"Yes, *serah* in full measure," Endap said, rubbing the residue of pain from his shoulders.

As Kameja was led away she cast one final backward glance at the poor Bidayuh village and read the despair on Endap's face. But it was nothing compared to the hopelessness she felt inside and she shuddered to think how her life was about to change.

# V

## Sin Bok
## Sarawak

In contrast to the recently founded coastal Malay village of Kuching that lay along the low, muddy banks of the Sarawak River, the Chinese community of Sin Bok-situated on high ground some ten miles upriver from Kuching-was well drained, relatively free of pests and biting insects and efficiently organized through the industry of its Hakka Chinese inhabitants. A single cambered street complete with parallel drainage ditches and surfaced with hand-hauled and hand-crushed granite from a distant quarry bisected two rows of facing wooden buildings and led directly to a small dock adjacent to the west bank of the Sarawak River. At its eastern-most point, the street faded into the jungle beyond the small settlement, eventually shrinking to nothing more than a rock encrusted trail that meandered a full two miles through the forest before exhausting itself at the base of a series of granite outcroppings that bore the multiple scars of the Hakka's mining activities.

The granite outcroppings were the primary source of Sin Bok's prosperity. The small hills contained gold and although the mines were not overly rich in the precious metal, the diligent Chinese miners extracted every possible ounce of the yellow glitter with their sweat and the incessant pokes and prods of their picks and shovels until the rock surrendered its bounty. In addition to the gold mining, trade and opium smuggling rounded out Sin Bok's flourishing economy. Sin Bok thrived like no other village in Sarawak and one man was responsible for it.

As was his daily habit, Loi Pek, founder and undisputed leader of Sin Bok, stood at an open window in the inner office of his shop and surveyed his accomplishment. His *kongsi* had grown from a fledgling thatch and bamboo village of fewer than fifty Hakka immigrants, to a prosperous and thriving community of more than five hundred in the span of ten years. It was *he* who discovered the gold-bearing granite outcroppings and it was *he* who extracted a mining concession from the Sultan of Brunei and it was *he* who determined the final building site for Sin Bok, nestling it safely between the friendly Bidayuh village of Bau further upriver and Kuching, the Rajah of Sarawak's principle city down river from Sin Bok. And it was *he* who saw to it that each of the Iban leaders located within threatening distance of his *kongsi* were well supplied with opium and other gifts to assuage any thoughts they may have to take Chinese heads or to otherwise disrupt the gentle business of Chinese profit making.

On a normal day, Loi Pek's observation of Sin Bok's prosperity would have filled him with pride, but today the *Kapitan* had more pressing thoughts on his mind.

"Lord Api has arrived, *Kapitan,* and he awaits you at his launch." The announcement came from a young Hakka who entered Loi Pek's darkened inner chamber. The boy kept his head and torso lowered as a sign of respect for the elderly leader of the community and awaited his reply.

"Yes, thank you, Wen. I have been watching the Malay's arrival from the window for some minutes now. See to it that Lord Api is made comfortable in the *bilek* by the dock.

Shaking off his former thoughts, Loi Pek turned from the window and motioned for the boy to leave. "Inform Lord Api that I will be along shortly. There is one final detail I must attend to first."

"Yes, *Kapitan.*" The boy proffered a succession of bows and backed through the doorway of the inner office, drawing closed the silk curtains separating the two rooms as he exited.

Loi Pek waited until he heard Wen leave the front of the shop and close the door before moved to the far corner of the room. With a habit of caution borne of an innate distrust of others, Loi Pek listened quietly for a moment before placing his thin arms around a highly ornate five-foot porcelain vase. With some effort, he managed to lean the vase against his torso and roll it away from the corner of the room. Loi Pek lowered himself to his hands and knees and rolled back the thick edge of carpet covering the wooden floor of the inner room. There, cut in the plank flooring, was a small door. A smooth hollow had been carved from the door and a metal ring inserted within. Loi Pek grasped the ring and with a single tug, removed the door from its mooring and placed it on top of the folded carpet. He extended his hand into the dark hole beneath the floor and, one-by-one, touched each of the many leather pouches he had previously placed there, and counted. Satisfied that his cache remained inviolate, he selected a single pouch and bounced it in the palm of his hand. *Too heavy*, he thought and repeated the process with a second pouch and then a third. Satisfied that the third pouch was near the weight he desired, he set it at his knee, replaced the small door onto the flooring and rolled the carpet back into place. He grasped the pouch and slowly pushed himself to his feet while his seventy-year-old joints, arthritic and weak, protested his movement upward with a dull and aching pain.

For the moment, Loi Pek ignored the growing throb in his joints and carefully rocked the porcelain vase back to its sentinel spot above his hidden treasure. Satisfied that all was as it had been, Loi Pek shuffled to an ornately carved desk in the center of the room and eased his aching frame into the desk's matching hard-backed chair. He placed the leather pouch to one side of the desk and with his gnarled fingers slid a small ginger jar to the center of the desk and removed its lid. He extracted a small silver spoon from the jar, then tipped the jar toward him so that he could more clearly see the white powder it contained. Loi Pek dipped the spoon into the jar, removed a heaping spoonful of the white powder from it and then placed the spoon in his mouth and extracted the powder. He mixed the powder with his own saliva for a few seconds before swallowing. Then he leaned back against the hard-backed chair, closed his eyes and waited for the opium to course through his body and drive away the pain from his disease ravaged joints.

Within moments, the opium completed its intended task and Loi Pek returned the silver spoon to the ginger jar, covered it, pushed it to its normal resting place on his desk and turned his attention to the leather pouch.

His fingers, more nimble now, easily untied the leather strap securing the pouch. Loi Pek scribed his finger through the glistening flakes of gold dust contained in the pouch as if he were tenderly touching the face of a small child. Mentally he calculated its worth, sighed heavily and then re-tied the precious bundle and stuffed it within the voluminous sleeve of his jacket.

*The price of Lord Api's favor remains high*, he thought as he exited the front of his shop and shuffled along the granite encrusted street toward the dock to meet with the Malay Lord. He shook his head at the thought of parting with his precious bundle of gold dust thinking, *I can only hope that it continues to be worth it.*

# IV

## Boat Dock Bilek
## Sin Bok

"We cannot wait for the Chinaman much longer, *Awang* Api. Not if we are to meet Rentab's Iban before night falls."

"I will be the judge of how long we wait," Api spat irritably. Api stood up and pushed his chair away from the table with such force that it fell to the floor and caromed against the wall of the *bilek* several feet beyond the table. "Fetch the Melanau slave girl," he ordered. "Perhaps she can amuse me while I await the Chinaman."

Haji, Api's cousin and chief lieutenant, hesitated and then said, "But, Lord Api, we haven't the time. We must be in Brunei by midnight otherwise the plan..."

Haji's voice trailed off when he felt Api's hot eyes bore into him. Api's irritability was rapidly morphing to anger and if there was one thing Haji had learned during his tenure of service with *Awang* Api, it was to avoid Api's wrath at all costs. Wisely, Haji bowed his head and said, "As you wish, my Lord. I will summon the slave." With head lowered, Haji backed through the entrance of the *bilek* and called for the girl.

Api turned and walked to an open window. Vacantly, he stared into the forest beyond the *bilek* and considered the event that would transpire that night. A wry smile tickled his lips. *Soon*, he thought, *all Sarawak and Brunei will be mine*. Satisfied that his plan to usurp power in Borneo was without flaw, Api allowed his thoughts to stray to the pretty Melanau slave girl. Her light skin and smooth, round features were characteristic of the tribe from which she had descended and their beautiful women were highly coveted as concubines by the Malay nobility.

Api felt his passion stir and then boil like molten lava within him. He had felt the rumblings of desire when he first laid eyes upon the girl at the Bidayuh village. *Perhaps this time it will be different*, he thought. Api's internal fire emblazoned hopes that he might, for the first time in his life, consume a woman and release the power of passion that smoldered and burned like hot embers within him.

Api turned to face the doorway when he heard his cousin enter the *bilek* with the slave girl in tow. "Leave us," Api said without glancing at his cousin. His eyes remained fixed upon the small breasts of the Melanau slave. "And close the door behind you," he commanded. "I do not wish to be disturbed."

With effort, Kameja quieted her fear and trembling. She forced herself to keep her eyes lowered to avert Api's penetrating stare. She sensed Api's desires and understood that resistance would only make the pain worse.

"So shy is my little Melanau beauty." Api spoke the words in a half-mocking, half-soothing tone of voice. "Come...come to me, child. Don't be afraid. I wish to look more closely upon my new and most valuable possession."

Api extended his hand and arm to Kameja and guided her to the center of the room and touched her face. "There, that's better. Now I can almost see your pretty eyes." He placed his hands on each side of her hips and whispered, "And now I will see all of you."

Api felt a shudder ripple through the girl as he pulled the tuck from her sarong and slid it slowly from her hips. Her docile acceptance of his hands excited him further and his expectations heightened. His hands released the folds of Kameja's sarong and he let it fall to the floor. Api emitted a long sigh of pleasure and grasped the girls hips with his strong hands while his eyes explored the whole of her. "Ahh...the beauty of your face is but a small sample of the beauty you possess elsewhere, my little one," he breathed.

With one hand, Api rubbed the smooth, flat surface of Kameja's abdomen for a moment and then allowed his hand to stray below her navel and caress the soft sparse triangle of her pubic hair while his other hand touched her small, developing breasts. He squeezed the nipple of her left breast between his thumb and forefinger and felt it harden. His other hand continued to stroke the fine, silky strands of her pubic hair before his fingers found the raised mound leading to Kameja's emerging womanhood.

Kameja gasped, tightly closed her eyes and willed herself to endure the violation.

Like so many times before, Api felt the passion steam and seethe within him, but he could not feel his manhood rise and throb beneath his sarong. Desperate, Api roughly pulled the girl to him and savagely began to caress her breasts with his mouth. Finding his passion again smothered by his impotence, Api squeezed his fingers into the flesh surrounding Kameja's hips and pressed her abdomen against his moist lips.

Kameja winced from the pain of Api's grasp. She opened her eyes and watched in disgust as Api roughly placed his mouth on her abdomen and worked his way downward.

Frantically Api tried to maintain his hold on the waning vestiges of his arousal, but he could not and once again he felt the passion dissipate from within. He pressed his forehead tightly against the slave girl's stomach and remained in the warm fold of her soft skin for a long moment before he sighed mournfully and once again accepted this mystery of nature which he could not comprehend. Somehow, Api thought it would be different this time, but it wasn't.

Kameja's arms slackened at her side and she breathed a sigh of relief for she sensed that Api was incapable of violating her this day or any other.

Api released the girl, rose from his knees and turned his head away. "Go. Leave me," he whispered. Api's voice was not angry, merely hollow and defeated.

Silently, but hastily, Kameja pulled her sarong to her hips and retreated from the *bilek* without a backward glance toward her new master. She too, did not understand these things, but she was grateful that it ended the way it had.

Haji, squatting on his haunches at the base of the steps to the *bilek*, allowed the fleeing slave girl to rush by him. He smiled lustfully after her and watched her tiny breasts bounce in rhythm as she ran down the dock and scrambled aboard Api's launch. He imagined the pleasure she must have given his cousin and entertained the thought that he might offer to buy her after the evening's work was completed.

But before Haji could begin to imagine the many delights he might enjoy with the Melanau slave girl as his own, he saw that the *Kapitan*, Loi Pek had arrived and was slowly making his way along Sin Bok's long dock where he was to meet with the Malay Lord.

Haji trudged up the stairs leading to the *bilek* and peeked into the open doorway. "The Chinaman, Loi Pek has arrived. He is awaiting you at the dock."

"Good," Api replied. The thought of Loi Pek's gold was a balm which quickly salved Api's previous disappointment.

As the two cousins made their way to the dock to join Loi Pek, Haji asked with a lascivious grin, "Was she good?"

"Better than most," Api replied without emotion.

"*Selamat Pagi*," Loi Pek, said, greeting the two approaching Malay lords in their language.

"*Selamat datang* my old friend," Api said magnanimously.

Loi Pek bowed courteously and said, "It is a pleasure to see you once again, Lord Api."

"And you too, *Kapitan*. Does Sin Bok continue to prosper?" It was a ritualistic question that Api always asked because he delighted in hearing the Chinaman's stock answer.

Loi Pek shook his head gravely and stroked the long hairs growing from a dime-sized mole on the right side of his chin. "Things have been better," he sighed. "Trade with the Bidayuh has not been good. They have very little of value these days and the Iban are not reliable providers of the goods we need to make a profit."

Api chuckled at the Chinaman's familiar words. Always it was the same with the cagey old Chinaman. He pretended to convey the impression that business was bad and profits were down in order to reduce his tax obligation to the Sultan. But Api didn't mind because he had his own arrangement with the *Kapitan*. As long as Loi Pek provided him with an occasional gift of gold dust, Api never collected more than the minimum *serah* required to satisfy the Sultan's mining concession to the Chinese at Sin Bok. Api also saw to it that the Chinese community was not harassed by any of the other Malay princes or the more warlike indigenous tribes he had suzerainty over. It was an arrangement that worked well for both of them.

"And the mines? How goes it there, Loi Pek?" Api had learned to read the Chinaman's every expression, as staid and placid as they seemed to be to others. He knew Loi Pek was as anxious to hang on to his mining concession as Api was anxious to relieve Loi Pek of a portion of the gold he extracted.

"Not so productive," Loi Pek moaned, continuing his charade. "My people work very hard to take only a few miserable granules from the hills each week."

"I'm sorry to hear that, *Kapitan*." Api managed an expression somewhere between concern and cynicism before he said, "But I trust that the mines have yielded enough to satisfy our *new* arrangement?"

Discussion of the "new" arrangement made the Chinaman nervous and Loi Pek began twirling the hair on his chin with renewed vigor. Previously, Api had told the *Kapitan* of plans to replace Saifudin, the current Sultan of Borneo, with Api's moronic uncle, Buntor. For an extra measure of gold, Api promised the old Hakka that he would see to it that Loi Pek's mining concession would be extended, not only in time, but also in territory. Loi Pek was led to believe that the additional gold was necessary to pay the Iban tribesmen for their part in assisting Api's family usurp the Sultan's throne. What Api didn't tell him was that Api planned to keep the gold for himself, knowing full well that the ignorant natives would be more than willing to assist him simply to fill their *praus* with human heads.

"Oh, yes, Lord Api. My men had to work extra hard, but we managed to extract the agreed upon amount."

"And I trust you have it with you, Loi Pek?"

"Yes, yes." Loi Pek reached into the sleeve of his jacket and withdrew the leather pouch containing the gold. When he handed it to Api he said, "You can feel by the weight of it that it is more than the agreed upon amount."

Greedily, Api tossed the leather pouch in the palm of his hand, sensing the value of it. "And what do I owe this unexpected generosity to, my friend?"

he asked.

"We Chinese have a saying, Lord Api. If one measure of gold can buy one time happiness, then an extra measure of gold should buy happiness forever. Is it not true, Lord Api?"

Api laughed. "True, and appropriate. You will have your happiness, old man. When I have returned from Brunei with the blessings of the new Sultan, my uncle, you shall have your new concessions just as I promised."

"I wish you well, Lord Api." Loi Pek bowed politely and added, "Both on your endeavor tonight and in the years to come."

"I accept your good wishes, *Kapitan*. I'm certain that our new arrangement will help us both to prosper." Api tossed the gold-filled pouch once more in the air before he tucked it into the folds of his sarong. "There is one more thing, my friend," he said as he hopped from the dock to board his launch. "I have a gift for you as well." Api shouted a command to one of his men and within moments the slave girl, Kameja was brought before him.

"For you, Loi Pek." Effusively, Api appraised the Melanau girl with his arms and said, "Have you ever seen a more beautiful creature, my friend? She has the cream colored skin of her ancestors and I guarantee that her passion will keep you young, Loi Pek. Use her as you will. She belongs to you now," Api said as he roughly pushed Kameja from the launch to the dock where she sprawled near the feet of the old Chinaman.

Loi Pek didn't bother to help the girl to her feet. At Loi Pek's age, he had no use for a slave of any kind. He considered slaves to be a bad investment. Seldom did they produce more than it cost to feed and clothe them. But to avoid angering the Malay prince, Loi Pek bowed politely and said, "A thousand thanks for your generosity, Lord Api."

Api shouted orders to his men to embark and as the launch caught the current and slowly moved away from the dock, Api cast a final glance toward the Melanau girl. The pity he felt was for himself.

# VII

Sultan's Palace
Brunei, Borneo

"Drink this, Exalted One, it will ease your pain and suffering." The *Dayang* Udang forced a bowl containing a bitter liquid to the dying Sultan's mouth.

Wearily, Saifudin opened his eyes and asked weakly, "What is it?"

"*Gadong*, the pain killing medicine from the climbing plant."

The old Sultan clamped his wrinkled lips shut and turned his head away from the bowl.

"Has my treatment not eased your pain before, Great Sultan?" *Dayang* Udang gave the dying man a placating smile and put her thick fingers on his chin, forcing his head toward the bowl.

Sultan Saifudin was too weak to resist. He opened his eyes and gazed suspiciously toward his niece. He didn't trust her and never had. She was cunning and shrewd, but when he felt discomfort in his chest several months ago, she was the only one who could provide the concoctions which eased the pain. Some called her a sorceress, but her knowledge of herbal medicine surpassed that of anyone else at his court. It was true her potions calmed his increasing agony, but with each passing day, the old Sultan found himself becoming weaker and he feared he might soon die.

"Take it. My medicine will ease your suffering, Uncle." *Dayang* Udang's chubby hand pushed the wooden bowl to the Sultan's lips and her other hand lifted his head from the pillow.

Reluctantly, Saifudin opened his mouth and swallowed the bitter tasting brew.

"All of it," she said. He tried to avert his head from the bowl, but she held his head firmly in place with her large hand and forced him to drink. When he finished draining the bowl, she let his head drop to the pillow and wiped the beads of sweat from his forehead. "There now, Uncle, don't you feel much better?"

Saifudin ignored her question and closed his tired eyes. Within moments the drug had its effect and he fell into a deep sleep.

*Dayang* Udang waited until the Sultan's breathing slowed and became more shallow before she arose from his bedside. Standing near the bed, she looked at the dying old man and whispered sarcastically, "Tonight, dear Uncle, you shall sleep the long sleep and tomorrow there shall be a new

Sultan to rule Brunei and Sarawak. She chuckled at the cleverness of her plan as she unfastened the strings that held a finely woven mosquito net above the Sultan's bed. She began to hum to herself as she spread the netting above the sleeping Sultan and then she broke out in laughter.

*Dayang* Udang was an opportunist. The wife of a *Datu*, a Malay nobleman who was the Sultan's brother, the *Dayang* Udang stayed close to the ruling elite following her husband's death many years earlier. Some held the belief that her magic had caused her husband's early demise-a rumor she never openly denied-preferring to allow the Brunei nobility to think what they would. There existed a certain cautious awe in the way the nobility perceived her, even fear. And that meant control—and power. And power was the thing *Dayang* Udang coveted most.

When she first became aware of the Sultan's illness, she saw it as her opportunity to usurp the throne and vest it with her own family. By guile and cunning–traits of *Dayang* Udang's which came as naturally to her as the monsoon storms came to Borneo–she cajoled the old Sultan to allow her to treat his illness. Distrusting her as he did, he most likely would have refused, but he was in great pain and none of his own magicians could ease his discomfort.

At first, her concoctions, mostly a mild narcotic extracted from the *gadong* tuber, eased the old Sultan's suffering and he developed a faith that her treatment would cure his illness. Gradually, however, she began to add larger quantities of poison from the *ipoh* nut, the same toxin used by the mysterious tribes of the interior, the Punan, who tipped their hunting darts in it. Before long, the mixture had the effect she sought and the Sultan became a complete invalid, totally dependent upon her treatment to ease the pain in his chest and stomach which was more a result of the increasing dosage of *ipoh* poison than the tuberculosis that ravished his lungs.

A woman of ponderous bulk, dark shiny skin and weasel-sized eyes, small and beady, the *Dayang* Udang didn't walk, she shuffled. And when she did, her elaborately embroidered silk sarong rippled in enormous waves as if it was struggling to contain the corpulence bulging within.

She waddled to a chair next to the bed and squeezed her enormous bulk into it, breathing heavily from the effort. She made a half-turn with her neck and called toward the entry. "You can come in now, Hasim."

Immediately the door flew open and Hasim, the *Dayang* Udang's eldest son stepped inside and closed the door tightly behind him, but not before he nervously peered down the hallway behind him. Physically, Hasim was the antitheses of his younger brother, Api. Whereas Api was tall and muscular, Hasim was short and fragile. Like a coat hanger, Hasim's narrow shoulders appeared merely to suspend his sagging flesh to his frail frame and his abdomen bulged in a gelatinous paunch as if it were attempting to flee the rest of him. Hasim had the same facial features as his mother, but where her eyes were intelligent and poignant, Hasim's eyes were often glazed with fear, futility and a lack of vitality.

"Is it done?" Hasim whispered. He gazed apprehensively at the bowl in his mother's hand.

"There is no need to whisper, Hasim," she chided. "No one can hear us. Within a few hours, the throne of Brunei and Sarawak will be ours." She tossed her rotund head to the sleeping Sultan and said, "See for yourself, Hasim. Even now the old man sucks in the last breaths of life."

Tentatively, Hasim stepped to the side of the Sultan's bed and lifted the mosquito netting with his thin fingers. He observed the old man's chest heave and sink with an uneven rhythm. Even now he could see a host of gray shadows creep around the hollows of the Sultan's eyes, signaling his imminent death. His mother was right. Death for the Sultan was near.

But it didn't calm Hasim. He worried that death would reach out and grab him too if his mother's plot failed. He dropped the netting back in place and turned to the *Dayang*.

"What if his death is discovered before Api and the Iban arrive?" he asked, anxiously. "What if Api is unable to take the stockade, Mother? What if..."

"You worry too much, Hasim." The *Dayang* Udang's eyes hardened beneath her brows. "Nothing will go wrong! I have taken care of everything."

The *Dayang's* eldest son's cowardice annoyed her, but she needed him if she was to place her half-wit brother, Buntor, on the throne. Once the childless Buntor became Sultan, her own sons, Hasim and Api would become the legitimate heirs to the throne and she would become regent to Buntor. In fact, given Buntor's moronic condition, she and her sons would be the real power behind the throne.

Hasim sulked and his mouth drooped to a pout.

"My son, did I not promise that one day you would become Sultan of Brunei and Sarawak?" The *Dayang* opened her massive arms and feigned an expression of motherly love. "Believe me when I say that I have taken great care to make certain that our moment of triumph will not be jeopardized."

"Yes, but..." Before Hasim could finish, his mother's familiar arms invited him and he went to her. He needed the strength of her embrace if he was to overcome his fear.

The *Dayang* Udang enveloped Hasim in her arms and pulled him close to her ample chest and said soothingly, "The hour is near, my son. Everything is set in motion. Everything is ready, *exactly* as I have planned it. Before *bulan sa'tinga*, midnight, Api and the Iban warriors will have taken the stockade. There will be very little resistance, I have seen to that."

She stroked Hasim's shortly cropped hair and cooed, "But you, Hasim, my favorite child, must also do your part. You must be brave and show that you are worthy of becoming Sultan."

Reluctantly, Hasim pushed himself away from the warmth and comfort of his mother's chest. He paced anxiously in a small circle in front of her. "Yes, my part..." he muttered as he thought of his role in his mother's plan to usurp the throne.

He and a cousin, Langau, a renegade *Pangirin*, a high ranking nobleman who supported the *Dayang*, but had been banished by the Sultan Saifudin, was to return clandestinely to Brunei and assist Hasim in capturing the Sultan's son, Tundjok, the legitimate heir to the throne. Tundjok, or the Sultan *Mudah* as was his formal title, was a formidable opponent and capturing him greatly concerned the cowardly Hasim.

"But what if the *Pangirin* Langau doesn't arrive in time?" Hasim asked, suddenly stopping his pacing. "What will I do then, Mother? Who will help me capture Tundjok then? What if the Sultan *Mudah* escapes? What will we do then, Mother?"

Hasim was near tears. He wrung his fingers and hands together, trying unsuccessfully to wipe away the clamminess in them. Again, be paced the floor, his mind imagining everything that could possibly go wrong.

The *Dayang* Udang masked the revulsion she felt for the cowardice of her eldest son. But for the coup to succeed, she needed him. The *Pangirin* Langau was capable of taking the Sultan *Mudah*, but it was important that Hasim be involved if for no other reason than to show the unaligned Malay nobility that Hasim was capable of action and leadership.

"You must trust me, my son. Langau will meet you as planned by the pepper field near Tundjok's *rumah*."

"But what if something goes wrong?" Hasim whined. "What if Langau doesn't arrive in time? What will I do then, Mother?"

A wry smile cracked along the *Dayang's* lips. "Not to worry, my son. Langau has already arrived from his exile in Labuan."

Hasim's mouth dropped open in surprise. "Why didn't you tell me before?"

"In these matters, it is best that secrets be kept until it becomes absolutely necessary to reveal them," she replied.

"Where is he?"

"He is hiding in a safe place for now. I assure you, Hasim, that Langau will meet you at the pepper garden at the appointed hour tonight."

The knowledge that Langau had arrived comforted Hasim to some extent. Langau reminded Hasim of his brother, Api. Both were fearless. Still, Hasim couldn't quiet the uneasiness that stirred within him.

"What if Tundjok puts up a fight?"

With difficulty, the *Dayang* Udang held her exasperation in check. "Do you think I would forget to apply a potion to Tundjok's evening meal? I assure you, Hasim, Tundjok will not resist."

"You drugged him?" Hasim almost collapsed with relief.

"It has been arranged. After Tundjok takes his evening meal, he will fall asleep. He will offer no resistance when you arrive."

"I should have known you would take care of it, Mother," he said, relieved.

"Don't I always take care of my sons?" The *Dayang* Udang smiled magnanimously. "Now you must go and prepare to meet with Langau. Remember, when you see the walls of the stockade burning, it will be the signal to attack Tundjok's *rumah*. Is that clear?"

Hasim nodded. His confidence in the coup had been partially restored, but he wouldn't relax completely until the night was over.

"One final thing, Hasim," the *Dayang* cautioned. "Do *exactly* as Langau instructs you to do. He has experience in these matters, understand?"

"Yes, Mother, I understand." Hasim was more than willing to let Langau take the lead. Even a drugged Sultan *Mudah* could be a formidable foe for the cravenly Hasim, and he knew it. Hasim bowed courteously to the *Dayang* Udang and exited the room, closing the door tightly behind him.

With effort, *Dayang* Udang pushed herself from the chair and shuffled her obese body to the side of the old Sultan's bed and lifted a corner of the netting. She smiled to herself when she perceived that his breathing was strained and shallow. "Soon, dear Uncle," she whispered as her thick lips erupted into a grin. "Soon Brunei and Sarawak shall have a new Sultan."

# VIII

## The Stockade
## Brunei, Borneo

As planned, Api and his Malay force of nearly two hundred men, mostly from the families of the *Datus* and *Pangirins* who supported the *Dayang* Udang's coup for greed and the promise of elevation to higher positions in the new regime, joined Rentab's band of Iban near the insignificant coastal community of Belait where the waters of the Barum and Tinjar Rivers emptied into the South China Sea. In launches and *praus*, the combined force of insurgents made their way along the coast from Belait and landed near an isolated cove south of Muara and then trekked overland through uninhabited forests and mud flats to reach the Sultan's stockade which protected Saifuden's palace on the landward side.

A crescent moon, high on the horizon, pierced the black blanket of the night sky by the time Api, Rentab and the leading elements of their combined force reached the edge of the jungle. Api ordered his men to stay hidden while he and Rentab crept to the edge of the forest for a closer look at the fortification. A single glance at the stockade below them was all it took for Rentab to understand why Api had chosen to approach from the landward side. Between where they hid and the stockade was a wide, flat clearing leading to the stockade's only entrance, a huge gate elaborately decorated with carvings of hornbills and other jungle creatures. Within the three-sided stockade, Rentab could barely discern the Sultan's palace. No more than an elaborately built wooden structure raised on stilts, the palace jutted into the open and heavily defended coastal waters adjacent to the town of Brunei. Rentab took note of the stockade's imposing walls that soared twenty feet upward and watched the shadows of the Sultan's sentries move upon the ramparts between a phalanx of torches.

"How shall we take such a thing?" Rentab asked, suddenly less confident than he had been on the trip to join forces with the Malay prince. He had promised his Iban warriors a great victory, but he didn't relish the idea of rushing the high stockade walls for it.

"We have arranged for the fort to be supplied tonight. When the gates are opened to allow the carts to enter, we will rush the entrance and get inside before the guards can remove the carts and close the gates."

"Ahh," Rentab smiled with relief. "A much better plan than trying to scale the walls."

"But remember what I told you, Rentab," Api cautioned. "Once we are inside, you and your men must confine yourselves to the fort itself. Take whatever heads and anything else you can find, but leave the palace to me and my men."

Without acknowledging Api, Rentab touched the hilt of his *parang* and glanced greedily beyond the stockade to the undefended town of Brunei sleeping in the distance.

The Iban leader's covetous stare did not escape Api. He grasped Rentab's bare shoulder and spat, "I warn you, Rentab, do not be tempted to raid Brunei or the palace. Not this time...there will be other opportunities, do I make myself clear?" Api dug his fingernails into the *Tua Kampong's* clavicle for emphasis.

"As you wish, *Awang* Api," Rentab replied. To do otherwise would bring swift retribution from the Malay lord and Rentab knew it. Besides, there was no reason to risk destroying a relationship which augured well for the future of both of them.

"There, coming down the road from Brunei...the supply carts! Spread the word, Rentab. We will rush the stockade as soon as the gates swing open!"

Two heavily laden carts drawn by plodding caribou lumbered toward the stockade and stopped near the gate. Several richly dressed Malay lords loyal to the *Dayang*, flanked either side of the carts. "Open the gate! We bring supplies by order of the Sultan Saifudin," one of them yelled.

Several sentries peered over the rampart. "At this hour?" a guard questioned. "The Sultan is ill. He cannot be disturbed. Come back in the morning."

"Impossible. We bring medicines ordered by the *Dayang* Udang to ease the Sultan's suffering."

The sentry hesitated and then appeared to consult with the other guards on the ramparts when the Malay lord added, "Check with the Sultan if you must, you fool. But be quick about it or the Sultan's wrath will be upon both our heads!"

The guard talked animatedly with the other sentries before they turned from him, apparently unwilling to share in the decision. "Open the gates!" he finally shouted.

Api, crowded on one side by his Malay force and on the other by Rentab's Iban, watched as the stockade's gate swung open and the carts were in position to block its closure before leaping to his feet and shouting, "Take the stockade!"

Api, brandishing his *parang* above his head, led the attack in a sprint across the clearing. His long knife glistened bare and naked in the minimal moonlight. Soon it would be coated with the gore of the Sultan's men.

Rentab and his Iban warriors followed quickly behind the Malay leader. Their shouts and war cries shattered the still of the night and echoed beyond the town of Brunei and into the jungle from which their savage charge had begun.

In their eagerness to take heads, the Iban warriors caught up with Api and sprinted past him like a frenzied mob of assassins. More disciplined, the Malay force held near their leader and followed the Iban through the gates.

The Sultan's men rushed to the gates to seal them, but the carts and caribou blocked the gates from closing. The impact of the Iban charge overwhelmed the nearest guards and the insurgents poured into the compound, cutting down anything that moved including the Malay lords who had delivered the carts to the gate. Even before Api and his Malay force entered the stockade, some of the Iban had stopped to claim their trophies, separating heads from bodies, holding their crimson prizes aloft and shouting chants that praised their manhood. Those Iban warriors whose *parangs* remained unbloodied, raced on, their wild and primitive eyes searching for anyone, man woman or child who would sate their *parangs'* thirst for blood.

While Rentab and his Iban slaughtered the fort's outnumbered defenders, Api and the Malay force reached the ramparts along the fort's northern-most wall and quickly dispatched the surprised defenders. Like wild-eyed scavengers, some of Rentab's Iban followed Api's Malay along the ramparts, chopping off the heads of the guards killed by Api's men.

"Burn the walls!" Api screamed before leaping from the rampart and sprinting to the Sultan's palace. Reaching the palace doors, Api stopped and gathered several dozen warriors around him. "Spread out and cover the palace," he commanded. "Let no one pass!"

Api waited until he saw the stockade walls ignite and the flames pierce the night sky. Satisfied that Langau and Hasim could see the signal beyond Brunei town, Api tossed open the palace doors and ran inside, alone. Two confused and frightened palace guards appeared suddenly, but Api easily cut them down with furious, hacking blows of his *parang*.

Like a rip tide, adrenaline surged through Api's veins and hammered every muscle in his sweat-glistened body. Api burst into the Sultan's throne room, his wild eyes rapidly searching the room for any who might oppose him. His bare chest heaved with the fury of his excitement. He held his blood drenched *parang* tightly in his strong arm, ready to strike down anyone who appeared. There was no one. The Sultan's throne room was empty.

Only now, following the ecstasy of battle, did Api become aware of the swelling and throb between his legs. Why it was that battle and bloodshed were the only things that allowed him to escape his sexual bondage and release his passions, Api never understood. For as long as he could remember, to kill and risk being killed were the only things that could succor the fire that raged within him.

Briefly, Api relaxed the grip on his *parang* and trembled while a colossal shudder overwhelmed him and his ardor burst forth in a sequence of powerful, ebbing explosions which dropped him to his knees in ecstacy. Within seconds of his dry and solitary coupling, Api felt the fire of his tormented soul subside and he shuddered once more before composing himself enough to sprint through the empty throne room toward a doorway leading to a long corridor beyond the far wall of the throne room.

# IX

## Tundjok's *Rumah*
## Brunei Town

"Who is it?" Hasim whispered in the direction of a rustling of palm fronds at the edge of Tundjok's pepper garden. He slid closer to the security of the six armed guards with him and stared through the darkness at the movement coming toward them.

"Quiet, you fool! Do you wish to awaken Tundjok's men?" Langau, the exiled Malay *Pangirin*, crawled to the group of huddled conspirators.

"Langau! I was afraid you weren't coming," Hasim whispered.

"I'm sure you were," Langau said. He made no attempt to hide the disdain he had for Hasim. Langau's arrangement was with Hasim's mother, the *Dayang* Udang and as far as Langau was concerned, Hasim was only a pawn to be used at a time such as this.

"How many men does Tundjok have in the *rumah*?" Landau asked.

"Only two that we have seen," one of Hasim's men replied. "One is on the *ruii* on the far side of the *rumah* and the other is inside."

"And Tundjok?"

"We watched him retire to his *rumah tidor*, his sleeping quarters, several hours ago," another of Hasim's men said.

"Good. The *Dayang's* potion must have worked. Are there others in the house...wife, children, servants?" Landau asked.

Hasim looked to his men for an answer. When they didn't respond, he shrugged and said, "We saw no others."

Langau grunted and frowned at Hasim's less than ample report. He would prefer to be with Api, storming the palace stockade, but they all knew that the incompetent Hasim could not be trusted to capture the Sultan *Mudah* by himself.

"Shall I order my men to take Tundjok now, Langau?"

"No, you idiot! We must wait for Api to take the stockade. When Api torches the stockade, that will be our signal to attack."

Hasim grew sullen following his cousin's rebuke. He wondered why it was that his mother arranged to have Langau return from his banishment with the promise to restore his titles. Why did they need Langau anyway? His own men could capture the drugged Sultan *Mudah*, he thought, unwilling to admit that he was not as capable as he believed himself to be. Hasim always disliked Langau and now he remembered why. Langau had always favored

41

Hasim's younger brother, Api, to him. *The two of them are alike in so many ways*, Hasim thought. *Both hotheads!*

"Look! Near the Sultan's palace. Fire!" one of Hasim's men whispered excitedly.

Langau craned his neck to see above the shelter of a tall pepper plant. "That's the signal. Api's men have taken the stockade. We must move fast before Tundjok is warned and has a chance to rally the Sultan's forces in Brunei town. Hasim, take four of your men to the *ruii* of Tundjok's house and take care of the guard there. The rest of us will enter the *rumah* and eliminate the guard inside and anyone else who interferes. Go, be quick! And above all, be silent!"

Hasim tapped four of his men on the shoulders—the four whom he considered to be the best of his group of six—and motioned for them to lead the way through the pepper garden to Tundjok's *ruii*.

Langau waited until the Malays led their incompetent prince to the side of Tundjok's house. When he saw that they were in position to rush the lone guard on the porch, he turned to the others and said, "Follow me."

Langau led his men through the garden noiselessly. Seconds later they approached a stairway leading from the ground to the main level of the stilt-supported home. With a finger to his lips, Langau cautioned silence and motioned for the two men to follow him up the stairway. Encased in shadow, they filed to the top of the stairs and gathered at the closed doorway leading to the *rumah's* main living room.

Langau waited until he heard commotion from the *ruii* on the far side of the *rumah*. Satisfied that Hasim's men had overpowered the guard there, Langau drew a teak-hilted *kris* from his sarong and shouted, "Now! Break in the door! Kill any who stand in your way, but leave Tundjok to me!"

Startled from his near-sleep, the guard inside leaped to his feet and reached for his *kris*. But he was too late. No sooner had he grasped the hilt of his wavy-bladed knife than he saw a flash of steel just as Langau's snakelike blade bit into his chest. The guard felt the sharp steel slither deep into his heart and was dead before his body hit the floor.

Langau extracted his blade from the guard's body and rushed down the narrow corridor which led to the *rumah tidor* where he expected to find the Sultan *Mudah*.

Meanwhile, Hasim's men burst through the rear entrance of the house with Hasim trailing behind just as Langau and his two men disappeared down the corridor. The guard stationed on the *ruii* had proven his mettle and had killed one of Hasim's men and severely wounded another before he had been slain.

"Follow Langau," Hasim ordered. "Tundjok must not escape!"

When his men raced into the corridor, Hasim approached the dead sentry sprawled in a pool of blood near the rear entry of the *rumah*. Hasim rolled the hilt of his clean and bare kris in the palm of his hand and glared at the vacant eyes of the body staring up at him. The dead man's face was frozen in an expression of surprise, but to Hasim, it appeared to be a sneer. "I could have taken you," Hasim muttered to the blood drenched corpse. "I'm not a coward...I'm as brave as Langau...as brave as Api," he whispered between tightly clenched teeth.

Suddenly, with a maniacal grimace on his face, Hasim lost control. He raised his kris and plunged it into the dead man's chest...again...and again...and again.

# X

### The Sultan's Palace
### Brunei, Borneo

Two hours following the successful coup, Tundjok knelt in the center of the Sultan's private quarters with his hands bound tightly behind him. Api, Hasim and Langau flanked the captured Sultan *Mudah*. Sitting in the Sultan's gold embossed chair was the *Dayang* Udang's brother, the *Pangirin* Buntor. Buntor sat as he went through life, with his mouth agape and his mind thinking confused thoughts which even he could not understand.

The *Dayang* Udang stood closely by the side of her half-wit brother. She held her sausage-like arms folded in front of her and raised her multi-layered chin in a regal manner. Her dense lips were drawn into a smile of satisfaction. "The coup has been a complete success," she announced. "Most of the *Datus* and *Pangirin's* in Brunei now support the new Sultan."

"And those that don't?" Langau asked.

"Those few that have not yet fled will be dealt with shortly," the *Dayang* replied simply.

"The Sultan, you are certain he is dead?" Api asked as he gazed at the shrouded figure lying beneath the cotton netting. There were no signs of blood.

"Poisoned," the *Dayang* said, "as I told you he would be. As of this moment, the Sultanate is ours. We will make the formal announcement in the morning."

An electric smile passed unnoticed between Api and his mother. They were of the same mold, but of a different dye lot. Where Api was courageous, *Dayang* Udang was calculating; where Api was bold, his mother was shrewd; where Api was cruel, the *Dayang* was manipulative. Together, mother and son were a deadly combination.

"And what of him?" Api strutted to the Sultan *Mudah* and rested his blood encrusted *parang* on Tundjok's shoulder. As heir apparent, Api knew that the Sultan *Mudah* must die and he was more than willing to be the one to end Tundjok's life.

Tundjok raised his head slowly and tried desperately to shake away the remnants of the *Dayang* Udang's drug that fogged his brain. A trickle of dried blood lay matted against his left cheek, the result of a heavy blow from Langau's fist when Tundjok attempted to resist his captor. Tundjok's eyes attempted to blink away his shroud of lethargy and he glared defiantly at his cousin, Api, whom he hated above all others.

Seeing this, Api raised his *parang* and said, "I shall kill him now!"

"No!" his mother shouted. "He will be dealt with in the proper way. The life of a Malay prince can only be taken by strangulation. It is the law and the law is what the people will accept. We must not begin our reign by violating the law."

When she observed Api relax his arm and lower his *parang*, she turned to Langau and asked, "The Malay *Pangirins* have agreed to support us as long as we follow the law, is it not so, Langau?" The question was asked for Api's benefit.

"It is so, *Dayang*. We must show them Tundjok's unmutilated body tomorrow to prove that he died in the manner befitting the execution of a Malay prince."

"Then *I* will strangle him," Api blurted between clenched teeth. He was anxious to wipe the defiance from Tundjok's face.

"I think not," the *Dayang* Udang said. "By rights, the honor should go to the new Sultan, my brother, Buntor." Her fat jowls rippled when she tossed her chin disparagingly in Buntor's direction. She emitted a deprecating sigh and said, "But it is obvious to all that he would be incapable of performing the deed for it is even a task for him to remove the drool from his chin." Her moronic brother disgusted her, but it was his lineage which gave her power and she intended to use it wisely. "Therefore, the honor must fall upon the eldest male in the Sultan Buntor's line...to you, Hasim." The *Dayang* tossed her eldest son a benevolent smile. "Hasim, you are now Rajah of Sarawak and principle heir to the throne of Brunei."

Hasim straightened pompously at the pronouncement. However, his attempt at elevating his ego faltered when he realized that he would also be required to strangle the hapless Sultan *Mudah*.

Api gazed with disdain upon his incompetent elder brother. He knew with certainty that he was the better man. But for a quirk in their birth order, it would be he, Api, who would be the Rajah of Sarawak and heir to the throne of Brunei. But Api was no fool. He would make his opportunity. For now, however, he would bide his time and be patient. And for Api, that was not an easy thing to do.

"Here is the cord." Langau handed Hasim a length of woven rope. "Finish him, Hasim. The honor is yours."

Reluctantly, Hasim accepted the cord and wrapped it around Tundjok's neck. Hasim's hands trembled and a band of perspiration appeared on his forehead as he tightened the rope.

Tundjok, knowing his end was near, summoned his remaining strength and shouted, "Let my words be a warning to all of you who deny me my rightful place as Sultan of Brunei. Should my lifeless form fall to the right, all shall be well for the rulers of Brunei. But should my soul pull my body to the left, ill winds shall blow upon the throne of Brunei and disaster will strike each of you and all you possess. This I vow with my dying breath!"

Hasim dropped the noose and skittered away from the Sultan *Mudah*. "A curse! He has cursed us!" he cried.

"End the pretender's nonsensical babbling, Hasim!" the *Dayang* commanded. "Do it now!"

"I can't...I can't," Hasim sobbed.

Api didn't hesitate. He snatched the cord from the floor and roughly pushed his brother aside. With one swift motion he placed his knee tightly behind Tundjok's back and whipped the cord around his neck. He yanked the cord taught and pulled until Tundjok's body lifted from the floor. Tundjok gagged and his eyes bulged and his face turned crimson for the brief moment before he caved beneath Api's grasp and fell back to his knees.

Api felt the life escape Tundjok's body and released the cord from Tundjok's neck. Tundjok's lifeless body wavered momentarily and then it slumped to the floor and toppled to the left.

## XI

## The Jungle
## Above Brunei

From a forested hill high above the lowlands and far removed from Brunei, Batu, the Punan, cradled his young son in his arms and watched a plume of smoke rise in the early morning sky from a distant fire near Brunei town. So many strange things were happening on the fringes of his homeland that he couldn't comprehend. Batu had sensed that changes were coming to his native land. *Perhaps the distant fire was an omen foretelling of such an event*, he thought. And for the descendants of a race of people who had lived in the same way as their ancestors had for thousands of years, changes were not considered a good thing.

Silently, Batu turned his back upon the distant clouds of smoke and returned to his clan. He decided to move his small band further into the depths of the jungle. Perhaps there, his people might avoid the changes Batu's primitive precognitive senses were warning him of.

Indeed, changes would come to Borneo, but unknown to Batu, these changes would be the result of events transpiring oceans and continents away and they would transform all of Sarawak and Brunei forever.

# CHAPTER TWO

## I

November, 1824
British Regimental Headquarters
Madras, India

Lieutenant James Brooke handed the garrison commander a dispatch containing his orders and snapped to attention in front of Colonel Southwell's desk. The twenty-two-year-old officer knew the contents of the packet were likely to elicit an incredulous response from the colonel, but it didn't matter to him; the orders gave him what he wanted.

Halfway through reading the orders, Colonel Southwell gazed up at the lieutenant, seeming to take his measure. He cleared his throat, but didn't say a word before he returned to reading the remainder of the document which bore the seal and signature of General Banton-Brown's office in Calcutta. Upon finishing, the colonel picked up a quill pen, leaned back in his chair, and rubbed the tip of the feather pen beneath his chin and said, "At ease, Lieutenant."

"Thank you, sir."

"Are you aware of the contents of these orders, Lieutenant Brooke?" he asked.

"Only in essence, sir. Not the specifics."

"I see." Colonel Southwell leaned forward, rolled the quill slowly between his thumb and finger and peered up at the young officer. "How long have you been in the cavalry, Lieutenant?"

"I was attached to the 6th Bengal Light Cavalry on September 17th of this year, sir."

Colonel Southwell raised his eyebrows. "That long? Nearly two whole months," he said, sarcastically. "And where were you attached before that, Lieutenant Brooke?"

"Sir! I received my commission on November 2nd, 1821 and was assigned to the 2nd Regimental Foot, Calcutta, sir!"

"And in what capacity did you serve, Lieutenant?"

Lieutenant Brook hesitated, cleared his throat and answered with some embarrassment, "I served as Sub-Assistant Commissary-General, sir."

"A quartermaster, eh? I thought as much."

The colonel's face remained placid. Since the Burmese War had broken

49

out the previous March, he was accustomed to receiving orders from the East India Company that made little or no sense at all to him and this particular instance was no different. It was incomprehensible to him that the Bengal Army would put an inexperienced officer like Lieutenant Brooke in charge of a detachment of cavalry scouts, regardless of how pressed the army was for men and officers.

"Are you aware, Lieutenant, that I am ordered to provide you with a half dozen able bodied men to form the nucleus of a detachment of cavalry scouts...complete with horses, arms and supplies?"

"Yes, sir."

"And are you also aware, Lieutenant, of the source from which I am ordered to obtain this contingent of so-called, 'able bodied' men for you?"

"No, sir. I would assume the colonel would wish to detach men from one of the Lancer Regiments stationed here..."

"You assume incorrectly, Lieutenant. My orders are to allow you to pick your own detachment."

"Sir?"

"That's correct, Lieutenant. General Banton-Brown's orders specifically state..." Colonel Southwell picked up the document and read verbatim, "...Lieutenant Brooke is to hand pick six able bodied men, all of whom will serve to form a special detachment of cavalry scouts to be attached to the Bengal Army in its operations against Burmese insurgents near Assam. The men selected for duty by Lieutenant Brooke shall be selected from the garrison prison at Madras and a full King's Pardon given to each man serving honorably with this temporary command for a period of six months from the commencement of operations..."

"Prisoners, sir?" The news stunned James. It had taken him months of submitting requests to be transferred from his position as quartermaster—a job by temperament he was ill-suited for—to obtain this assignment. He was one of the few officers in Calcutta who breathed a sigh of hope when the Burmese War broke out early in the year, sensing in it an opportunity to transfer to a more glamorous and adventurous position in a combat unit. James even evoked the considerable influence of his father, Sir Thomas Brooke, a former officer with the East India Company and now retired in England, who had written letters in his son's behalf imploring that his son be reassigned.

But James hadn't expected this. Somebody in Calcutta was having a hearty laugh at his expense, he thought. It didn't surprise him. An outspoken man, James often spoke derogatorily against the policies of the East India Company, and of the army. And now they were paying him back for his insubordination. The East India Company removed a relatively insignificant thorn in their side and placated James' influential father, Sir Thomas Brooke, at the same time.

"That's correct, Lieutenant. Prisoners. You have the authority to select your contingent of Horse from among the finest assortment of thieves, murderers and brigands this post has to offer."

Colonel Southwell contained a chuckle, dipped the quill pen in an ink well, signed the orders and handed them back to James. "Take these to the sergeant-major outside," he said. "He will escort you to the garrison prison, Lieutenant."

"Yes, sir!" James snapped to attention and held his salute properly. He'd be damned if he'd let the bloody bastards see his disappointment. "Thank you, sir!"

The colonel didn't rise. He tossed James a casual salute and said, "Don't thank me, Lieutenant. Thank the Company and General Banton-Brown. Dismissed."

# II

## Regimental Prison
## Madras, India

Si Tundok sat singular and alone beneath the room's lone, barred window set high against the back wall of the small prison cell. His knees were drawn up to his chest and his huge, dark arms—arms nearly as wide as his thighs—draped powerfully over his knees.

Of the remaining eleven prisoners who crowded the cell's sweat and excrement tinged interior, only Si Tundok sat with space on either side of him. It was precious space, the kind of space a powerful man like Si Tundok could carve out for himself.

A hot breeze wafted through the window and upon colliding with the stultifying air within the cell, sank as if defeated, enveloping the half-breed's bare head and enormous shoulders. Si Tundok kept his eyes half closed and savored the brief, refreshing scent of fresh, warm air. The fight to obtain this coveted spot below the window had been worth it, he thought.

As the cell's newest occupant and well trained in the schools of other prisons in other places, Si Tundok realized that whatever chances he had for survival in a place such as this depended upon his ability to establish himself at the top of the cell's pecking order. It hadn't taken much this time.

Tossed into the cell earlier that morning, Si Tundok took little time surveying his filthy environment and the ten prisoners who shared it. Ignoring their curious glances, Si Tundok stepped toward a big Englishman who sat beneath the cell's window and motioned for him to move.

"Get away you black duffer," the Englishman growled. "You're muckin' up my fresh air."

Without a word Si Tundok's right arm shot out as quickly as a striking cobra and he grabbed the Englishman by the collar and jerked him to his feet. With lightning speed, Si Tundok wheeled the Englishman around and pulled his arm behind his back while he circled the man's neck with his free arm. He grasped the big Englishman's hand and squeezed his fingers.

"Don't! You can have the bloody window!" the Englishman bellowed as he felt his thumb snap.

Si Tundok shoved the Englishman to the floor like a piece of worthless coconut husk and then, in turn, his flashing gray eyes pierced each of the cell's occupants as if to ask, *anyone else?*

One by one, each of the prisoners resumed their positions against the walls away from the window and away from the dangerous Oriental.

But one man, Henry Steele, a Welshman of numerous experiences and few talents continued to observe the newcomer as Si Tundok took his space below the coveted window and closed his eyes. Henry wore a soiled and tattered uniform with the brass buttons distinguishing him as a former soldier in the King's 77th Foot. He was short and wiry and his straight blonde hair had thinned prematurely, and his large green eyes and smooth, round face conveyed a look of innocence.

But innocent, Henry was not. Orphaned at an early age, Henry signed on as a cabin boy on an English merchant ship. Soon disillusioned with the seafaring life, young Henry jumped ship in Singapore and meandered through a series of misadventures throughout the Malay peninsula. After a dozen years, he found himself penniless in India where he discovered that the Colonials there were less willing to be bilked of their coin. Hungry and desperate, he joined the East India Company's Army with the full intention of deserting as soon as his belly was full and other prospects presented themselves.

An indiscretion with an officer's wife forced Henry to prematurely depart the King's service but, unfortunately, Henry was captured, tried as a deserter and tossed into his current circumstance to await execution.

Henry's subtle observation of Si Tundok told him nothing of the man. He couldn't determine the man's lineage, nor could he tell if the man could speak English or, for that matter, speak at all. One thing for certain, Henry thought, the man doesn't appear to have any weaknesses. *I think he'll retain the space below the window without challenge.* With that thought, Henry eased his head back against the wall and shut his eyes.

Momentarily, Henry felt two Indian prisoners on either side of him stir. He cracked his eyes into mere slits and observed the Indians sneaking toward the sleeping Oriental. One of the Indians had removed his turban and fashioned it into a garrote. Without thinking, Henry shouted, "Watch out!"

But his warning was too late. One of the Indians grabbed Si Tundok's hair and slammed his head against the wall of the cell while his partner drove his foot into Si Tundok's chest with such force that it sounded like a squash had been dropped from the top of a high building. Two more blows in quick succession and Si Tundok went limp giving the Indian the opportunity to wrap the garrote around the Oriental's neck.

Reflexively, Si Tundok raised his hands to his throat but his strength had momentarily abandoned him. He thought he was a dead man.

But as quickly as the attack had begun, Si Tundok felt the garrote fall away from his throat. He shook the fog from his eyes and saw one of his attackers carom off a side wall and stagger to the center of the crowded cell.

A scrawny white man rode the bigger Indian's back, pummeling him with his fists as the Indian tried to toss him off. His other assailant turned his back on Si Tundok and moved to stave off the sudden attack by the scrawny Welshman who, by now, lay sprawled on the cell's floor and in no position to defend himself.

Now aware of the situation, Si Tundok's rage released him from his grogginess and he leapt to his feet. He raised his arms above his head and entwined his hands into a single mace of flesh and with all the strength he could muster, slammed it onto the back of the nearest assailant. With the breath knocked from him, the Indian fell, rasping and heaving at Si Tundok's feet. Si Tundok leaped over the body of the fallen Indian and charged the other assailant. It only took a single blow from Si Tundok's fist to end the fight. He drove his powerful arm straight into the side of the Indian's jaw, splitting his cheek and smashing his nose. The Indian fell backwards against the cell door and wilted to the floor.

Henry started to pull himself to his feet, but before he could, he felt the hand of the Oriental grasp him and lift him upright. "Thanks," Henry said.

"It is I who should thank you," Si Tundok said. He guided Henry to a spot next to him beneath the window and then his empicanthic eyes quickly surveyed his fellow cell mates to see if more trouble was in the making. Satisfied that there was none, Si Tundok sat down, pulling Henry beside him.

"You speak English," Henry said, surprised.

"My father was part Anglo," Si Tundok said. "And part Spanish."

"And your mother?" Henry probed.

"Sulu Malay."

*That explains it,* Henry thought. His broad chested companion was a melange of genetic hybridization. It explained the man's unique eye color, a soft gray, and his skin which was dark and smooth, and it explained the man's ability to speak English.

"The name's Steele, Henry Steele," Henry said, offering his hand.

Si Tundok had long since given up on the need for friendship, particularly from a white man, but perhaps given his current circumstances, such an ally would be beneficial. Reluctantly, Si Tundok shook Henry's hand.

"And your name?" Henry persisted.

"Si Tundok," the Malay said and closed his eyes to signal that the conversation was over.

"On your feet, gentlemen," the sergeant-major ordered as he swung open the door to the cell. "The lieutenant here would have a look at you."

James stepped into the cell behind the sergeant-major, ducking his head when he entered. Immediately, the stench of the fetid air assailed his senses and he shortened his breath to avoid inhaling any more of the rank air than necessary. He watched the prisoners rise sullenly to their feet and slouch indifferently against the walls of the cell. A big Malay, sitting beneath the window opposite James was the last to stand, and then only after giving James a loathsome, defiant glare.

"Stand tall, lads," the sergeant-major said. His voice placated rather than commanded. "Try to look the men you once were." The sergeant-major puffed his chest and rocked on the heels of his boots. He held a swagger stick in his hands behind his back. Then he turned to James and said, "This is what's available, sir. Should I have the pris...er...*men* step outside, sir?"

"That won't be necessary, Sergeant-Major." James stepped to the center of the cell. Never before had he seen such a grim and motley assemblage of men. The cell contained only two white men, English, he presumed, three Sikhs, six Indians-two of which were bleeding-and a powerfully built man of unknown origin.

"Those of you who have military experience, raise your hands," James ordered.

Some of the prisoners shifted their feet, but no hands went up.

"Who among you can ride a horse?"

Still no response.

James turned to the Sergeant-Major. "Do they understand English, Sergeant-Major?" he asked.

"I'm certain they do, sir. Perhaps this band of rabble needs a wee bit of encouragement to loosen their tongues, if I might be so bold as to suggest, sir." The sergeant-major tapped his swagger stick against the palm of his hand to emphasize his suggestion.

"That won't be necessary, Sergeant-Major." James casually placed his arms behind his back and strolled up and down the center of the cell, appraising each of the prisoners as he paced. He was easily the tallest among them, extraordinarily tall for the times, but he was also inexperienced in the ways of their world and it showed.

James strutted when he paced through the cell and his bearing and speech, mannered and refined, signaled the brigands within that the young lieutenant was a man of breeding and privilege, an aristocrat and they resented him for it.

But other things were also apparent. As James evaluated each of the men with his unfaltering dark blue eyes, he left each of them with the impression that their very souls, as shallow as they might be, were touched. As young as the lieutenant appeared to be, and as inexperienced as he obviously was, his sagacious probe left no doubts that the man had confidence; confidence in his judgment of other men and confidence in his ability to control and lead them.

But it had always been like that for the young lieutenant. As a schoolboy at a predominantly upper class boarding school, the Norwich Grammar School near Bath, he displayed a force of character and leadership which, although often misdirected, was present in abundance. James often led his classmates away from the confining walls of the boarding school and took them to the River Wensum where they would spend their truancy sailing skiffs and playing Barbary pirates and all manner of adventurous games. Quite naturally, James' vivid imagination and thirst for adventure cast him in the role of sea heroes like Nelson, Drake and Raleigh.

An individualist, James was not suited to the strict codes of discipline required by the school and he was punished often. As a consequence, James ran away at the age of twelve. When his absence was discovered he was sent to live with his paternal grandmother. He disliked the new arrangement intensely. His grandmother's austerity and silly rules seemed no better than those he rebelled against at the boarding school. Again, James found himself in constant trouble when he chose to play his games of high adventure in lieu of his studies.

It was at about this age that James discovered that he possessed qualities which endeared him to his peers. No doubt part of it was physical. James was fully two heads taller than other boys his age, a characteristic he maintained into adulthood. He possessed a strong, lean body and his face, although not shockingly handsome, was endowed with enough components to make it pleasing. His bone structure was sharp and angular, giving him a solid appearance which was accentuated by a pronounced cleft-chin and strong jaw. His thin nose sloped gracefully below inquisitive blue eyes. Locks of strawberry-blonde curls surrounded his head in a disorganized array of tresses and, as an adult, James wore his sideburns long and thick to cover a mass of unsightly smallpox scars along the sides of his cheeks.

Amiable and intelligent, James found it particularly easy to sway his contemporaries to his way of thinking, particularly when it came to the more esoteric subjects such as virtue, justice and morality. In these, he fostered a personal philosophy which was a melange of his conservative upbringing and the liberal views of the age in which he lived.

Finally, in 1818, James' father retired from the service of the East India Company and his parents returned to their estate near Bath. It was not easy for James to cajole his father into not forcing him to return to the boarding school. James promised to continue his studies at home under his father's tutelage and to enroll as a cadet in the East India Company when he was eligible at the age of sixteen. Sir Thomas Brooke got what he wanted, a son to follow in his footsteps. All the more important to him because Sir Thomas' only other son, James' older brother, Henry Vyner, had died ten years previously as a result of wounds sustained in battle while serving as a commissioned officer with the Bengal Lancers.

And James got what he wanted—the removal of constraints of a formal education and eventually the opportunity to live his fantasy of adventure in the Far East. But now, after six years in the military, James found that he was not particularly adapted to the constraints of military life. Often he disagreed with his superiors and was frustrated by not being assigned to a combat regiment. On occasion, James considered resigning his commission and seeking his fortune in other ways, but he didn't. Above all else, James Brooke was an honorable man. He gave his promise to his father and he resolved to keep it.

Soon, James finished his hard evaluation of each of the prisoners and said, "Listen carefully, men. I shall select six of you to serve in my command. I care not what your crimes have been, nor do I care what crimes you are likely to perpetrate in the future. I am only interested in six men who can give me their word that they will faithfully perform their duty for a period of six months..."

"Haarumph!" The sergeant-major cleared his throat. "Begging the lieutenant's pardon, sir, but if I may be so bold to interject, sir?"

"What is it, Sergeant-Major?"

"To trust the word of any of these scum, sir, would be a mistake...sir."

"Ordinarily I would agree with you, Sergeant-Major but I have something more to offer than simple naivete."

"Of course, sir. Sorry to interrupt, sir."

James turned to the prisoners and raised his voice. "In return, I am empowered to grant each of those six men a King's Pardon. A complete and unconditional pardon for any and all crimes of which you may be accused, providing of course, that you keep your word and complete the six months of satisfactory service."

One by one the prisoners straightened and glanced from one to the other. A King's Pardon was more than any could have hoped for.

"Now then, I shall ask once again. How many of you have military experience?"

All of the prisoners raised their hands except one, Si Tundok.

"And of those with your hands raised, how many of you can ride?"

All hands remained raised. Some of the prisoners had never ridden a horse, but they weren't about to squander their chance to be released.

"Very well, then," James said. "Sergeant-Major, I'll have that man..."

James pointed to the big Englishman with the broken thumb.

"...that one..."

James pointed to an angular Indian.

"...those two..."

James nodded to two full-bearded Sikhs.

"...that man..." James said, pointing to Henry Steele.

"And the fellow next to him."

Si Tundok's heavy gray eyes lifted in surprise. Of all the prisoners, he was the only one who didn't raise his hand. "Why do you pick me?" Si Tundok asked. "My hand was not raised." Si Tundok didn't care one way or another about a King's Pardon. He had enough of the world, particularly the white man's world. Everywhere he went, misery followed and he was tired of searching to find his place in the order of things. He had few hopes that this time would be different.

James faced the broad shouldered Malay and peered down at him and said, "Because you didn't lie like the rest of this rabble. If you were willing to stay here and accept whatever punishment is waiting for you for whatever crime you have committed, I would suspect that you would be just as willing to take whatever orders I might give you. It couldn't be worse now, could it?"

James didn't wait for a reply. He turned abruptly on his heels and said to the Sergeant-Major as he passed by him and exited the cell, "See to it that those six men are cleaned, fed and in uniform, Sergeant-Major. We leave at dawn."

# IV

March, 1825
Brooke Manor
Near Bath, England

Sir Thomas Brooke's country estate, northwest of Bath, was as neatly ordered as the man's own life. A carriage road led straight to the Brooke Manor from the newly constructed Turnpike Trust toll road created by an act of Parliament in 1815. Lining each side of the carriage road were the remnants of the previous autumn's display of late-blooming flowers; begonias, aster daisies and marigolds, all neatly pruned and dormant, awaiting the coming of a new spring.

On either side of the path were spacious fields and pastures, divided into sections within a precise array of perpendicular fences. Sheep and dairy cows occupied several of the grass covered fields and fed upon freshly dropped bundles of winter fodder. Fallow fields extended beyond the pastures and below the smoothly manicured hills behind the manor.

In the spacious great room of the manor, two men sat beneath a high, mahogany etched ceiling. They faced one another and each man reclined comfortably in richly upholstered, high backed chairs and sipped port from elegant hand-blown crystal glasses, and talked.

"It's been a long time, Thomas," Sir Stamford Raffles said. He looked about the finely decorated room and admired its orderly elegance. The filigreed wall panels and French furniture were much too refined for his taste, but he recognized his friend's touch of pretense in both the room's elegance and in the way the furniture was arranged so that, regardless of where one sat, he could easily be in a position to not only admire the beautiful furniture and trimmings but, in fact, study them and in so doing, learn a great deal about the owner of the estate.

Sir Thomas Brooke, like his progeny, James, was tall for his time. Handsome by pre-Victorian standards, Sir Thomas carried himself stiffly as if his every physical action was thoroughly debated before he gave his body permission to carry out the movement. His was an old-fashioned, courtly manner. What Sir Thomas lacked in wit and spontaneity, he made up for by being well read and he was an affable conversationalist.

"Nearly twenty years as I recall," Sir Thomas replied.

"Twenty years since I've been to Brooke Manor, but not nearly so long since I last saw you, Sir Thomas."

"Yes, Singapore, I believe. 1816. About two years before I retired from His Majesty's service."

"Ah, yes, Singapore."

Sir Stamford's thoughts drifted to that far away island which sat like a sentry facing the strategically important Malacca straits. Fondly he thought of the island and how he had been instrumental in purchasing it for the Crown in 1819. As Governor of many of the Crown colonies, Sir Stamford Raffles had spent his lifetime organizing and securing British interests in the Far East. Considered a political visionary by some, including Sir Thomas, others considered him a meddler and purveyor of unfounded predictions of what was to become of British interests in the Far East if his recommendations were not carefully followed after his retirement early in 1824.

Already, only a short year following his return to England, Parliament had ignored his suggestions and Raffles' dream of a united, British controlled archipelago of East Indian territories appeared to have been crushed. Undaunted, Raffles continued to bend the ears of any who would listen to his opinions on Far Eastern affairs, particularly men of influence such as Sir Thomas.

"I read your latest treatise, Sir Stamford."

Raffles leaned forward on the plush chair and rested his glass of port on a small table separating the two men. "And what did you think, Thomas?" he asked.

"Interesting, a very interesting commentary. But I dare say, Sir Stamford, that it is not likely to endear you with the Company or certain members of Parliament."

"Balderdash! Had I wanted to endear myself to them, I would have written a sonnet. My intent was to lift them out of their lethargy before it was too late. Surely there must be some who feel that the treaty with the Dutch is a monumental mistake?"

"Perfectly so. But I doubt if they shall be heard with the times the way they are."

"Surely you are not one of those who thinks England's current prosperity will last forever, Sir Thomas?"

"On the contrary. I believe we are both astute enough to realize that it is a temporary thing. My point is, people have an aversion to sweeping change when we are in the midst of an economic boom, particularly changes involving treaties and territorial determinations."

Sir Stamford's face flushed. "That's *precisely* when these critical decisions must be made," he spewed. "Now England has the economic clout and military might to make demands upon the Dutch in the Far East. By this recent treaty, we have given in to them. Moreover, England has squandered its chance of any further growth and prosperity arising from future opportunities in the Asian Archipelago."

"But the treaty did define the spheres of influence between ourselves and the Dutch which have been a source of aggravation and friction for a number of years."

Sir Thomas could see the fury building in Sir Stamford. His own view prevented him from discussing the efficacy of the treaty further. Although he agreed with Raffles' assessment of the treaty, he doubted if the consequences would be as dire as Sir Stamford seemed to indicate.

"Another port, Sir Stamford?" he asked, hoping to change the subject.

"Thank you, no, Thomas. I must be going." Sir Stamford fumbled for his watch fob, popped open the cover and said, rising to his feet, "I have scheduled a meeting with Lord Gray in the hopes that I can garner some support to define the Borneo question."

Sir Thomas stood up and inquired, "The Borneo question?"

Raffles' wilted face grinned slyly. "Yes, Thomas. The politicians have not entirely given away British suzerainty to the Dutch. The treaty includes a minor ambiguity which I intend to exploit."

The two men made their way through the Great Room and into the hallway leading to the front door. Sir Thomas listened attentively as Raffles continued to expound.

"The treaty provides for British control of all territories in the archipelago which fall north of the line of demarcation. Only one island falls in that category, Borneo. But only the northern part which includes territories known as Brunei and Sarawak."

"But the Dutch have already formed stations on the southern tip of Borneo, at Pontianak."

"True, but the real power on the island is the Sultan of Brunei. And the Sultan has his palace on the *north* side of the island. He is the lord and master of the territory assigned to Britain in the treaty."

"But has it not been determined that the island offers very little in terms of resources? What would be the advantage of British interference there? Besides, I doubt if Parliament would be interested in challenging Dutch influence on the island, treaty or not."

Raffles smiled. "First, let me assure you, Thomas, the value of the island has not been thoroughly determined. With the exception of a few minor expeditions, little is known of the land, the people or the wealth it may contain. But its size alone makes me believe that it is potentially the richest treasure in the Far East."

Raffles plucked his coat and hat from the clothes tree next to the door and continued saying, "As far as challenging Dutch authority, that is why I am meeting with Lord Gray. It is my contention that Britain must secure a treaty with the Sultan of Brunei post haste to show the Dutch that we fully intend to protect British interests in northern Borneo before the entire region falls to the Dutch by default."

"I see..." Sir Thomas had a feeling that Lord Gray, a powerful Liberal Party leader would not share Raffles' point of view.

"Well, it was a delight seeing you again, Thomas." Raffles extended his hand and the two men shook hands. "Please convey my disappointment to your lovely wife, Anne. Sorry to have missed her."

"Indeed I will," Sir Thomas said, and opened the door. He called for Raffles' carriage to be brought to the front of the manor. While the two men awaited Raffles' carriage, Sir Stamford asked, "By the way, Thomas. Don't you have a son in the service of the Company?"

"Yes, my youngest, James," Sir Thomas responded proudly. "His commission is with the Bengal Army."

"Imagine that," Raffles chuckled. "And to think he was a mere babe the last time I saw him."

"They do have a way of becoming men, Sir Stamford."

"Indeed they do, Thomas. Indeed they do."

The carriage pulled to the front of the manor and Sir Thomas' servant opened the door for Raffles and assisted the elderly gentleman into the coach. Inside, with the carriage door closed, Raffles leaned out the window and added, "Nasty business this is with the Burmese. I trust your boy will be safe."

"Thank you, Sir Stamford. James has always been able to take care of himself. A most talented boy, my James."

Before Raffles gave the order to the driver to whip the horse into action, he said, "I should be pleased to meet this young man of yours should he return to England one day."

"He would be delighted, I'm sure. Good luck with Lord Gray," Sir Thomas added as the carriage jolted away from the manor.

The news that his only surviving son lay dying in an Army hospital near Rungpore, Burma had not yet reached Sir Thomas.

# V

January 25, 1825
Near Rungpore, Burma

On orders from General Banton-Brown's headquarters, James and his contingent of cavalry scouts had circled behind the Burmese lines with instructions to search out Burmese reinforcements. James had his men dismount and rest their horses while he explained the task at hand to them. Although his small unit lacked horsemanship, so far, James felt that the former prisoners had performed adequately. The big Englishman, Geoff, complained often about the pain in his thumb and although it had healed sufficiently, it had not been properly set and now stood at an awkward angle to the man's wrist. James determined that the abrasive man would have found other things to agonize about even without the thumb as an excuse. Geoff was incorrigible to the point of insubordination and James was forced to keep a close eye on him.

The two Sikhs performed their duties adequately although reluctantly as did the lone Indian. The Welshman, Henry Steele, proved himself to be resourceful, competent and friendly. James liked the man who, he was surprised to learn, was nearly eight years his senior. James believed the feeling was mutual.

But the big Sulu Malay remained an enigma. He preferred his own company, but was not adverse to Henry or James' presence. He seldom spoke, but performed his duties with methodical precision and in James' judgment was probably the most capable of the six.

James peered into a telescope and scanned the wide valley below them. In the far, hazy distance was Rungpore and rising clouds of smoke told James that General Banton-Brown had begun his assault against the Burmese.

"Men," James told them, "it is our task to scout this valley for signs of enemy reinforcements and report our findings back to headquarters. It looks clear enough, but we'll check out the other side of that smaller ridge..." James pointed to a ripple in the land on the north side of the valley, "...and that small canyon just south of it. If there are any enemy troops waiting, that's where they will most likely be."

"I don't see a bloody thing," Geoff countered irritably.

"I don't see anything either, Lieutenant," Henry concurred.

"That may be," James said, "but we're going to ride down there anyway to make certain. The general doesn't need any surprises waiting for him after he pushes through Rungpore."

Geoff gave James a sour look and spit on the ground. He was not an experienced horseman and his backside was sore. "Probably a waste of time, Lieutenant," he complained. His broad, ugly face wrinkled sourly to emphasize the lodging of his complaint.

"I'll be the judge of that, trooper." James drew himself to his full height and faced the older, rougher looking man. "Now all of you, mount up!" he ordered.

Geoff's Neanderthal eyes narrowed. *Possibly this is the time to challenge the lieutenant,* he thought. He had been waiting for an opportune time to make good his escape for he had no intention of dying for King and Empire. But the young officer seemed prepared to meet his challenge and when the big Malay and wiry Welshman stepped close to the lieutenant, Geoff realized that the balance was not in his favor. He shrugged and backed off. "Just letting you know how I see things, Lieutenant, that's all. No harm done." Geoff spit to the side of James' boots and mounted his horse.

After his troop was saddled, James said, "Si Tundok, you and Henry ride down to that groove south of the ridge and check it out. I'll take the rest of the men with me and have a look at the other side of the ridge. Let's stay in visual contact with one another, just in case one of us runs into something."

"Yes, sir, Lieutenant," Henry said and led Si Tundok down the slope toward the south end of the valley. James led his men to a ridge northwest of them. Both groups moved at a steady pace parallel to one another so that they could keep the other group within eyesight.

Reaching the top of the ridge, James' men had a clear view of an empty slice of valley. "Nothing here," James said and ordered his men to turn about and rejoin Henry and Si Tundok who had momentarily disappeared from view.

"I thought as much," Geoff muttered softly enough that James couldn't hear.

Just as they began their descent, gunfire erupted in the direction of Si Tundok and Henry. "To the ravine!" James yelled. He raked his horses flanks and galloped down the side of the ridge. He was halfway down when he realized he was alone. He pulled in his mount and looked behind him. Geoff and the Indian were nowhere in sight and the two Sikhs were galloping away from the ravine and the sound of gunfire.

"Stop, come back, you bloody fools!" he screamed, but the Sikhs kept riding away from him.

The sound of more gunfire snapped James' attention back to the ravine. He didn't hesitate. He dug his heels into the sides of his horse and galloped at breakneck speed to the ravine, drawing his saber as he charged.

When James entered the narrow chasm, he saw Henry and Si Tundok staving off the attack of a dozen Burmese footmen. Si Tundok's horse had been shot out from under him, but he held a broken lance taken from the enemy and was fighting on foot like a madman. Henry, still mounted was slashing furiously with his saber.

Again, James didn't hesitate. Without slowing his horse, James raised his sword and charged directly into the thick of the melee.

The lone officer's presence surprised the remaining Burmese. Thinking British reinforcements had arrived, the Burmese scattered in retreat. James pursued them, striking two of them to the ground with slashing blows of his saber. Henry followed and impaled a third.

Si Tundok finished off a wounded Burmese by thrusting the tip of the broken Burmese lance into the fallen man's throat. Exhausted, he collapsed to his knees and wiped the sweat and dirt from his face. When he looked up after clearing his eyes, he saw James and Henry rout the last of the enemy. He turned and looked toward the northwest ridge. Seeing nothing, he realized that the young lieutenant had saved him and Henry while the others had abandoned them. Si Tundok's gray eyes hardened to granite. Silently, he vowed to catch up with Geoff and the deserters one day and cut their throats for their cowardice.

But as much as Si Tundok felt hate for the four deserters, his heart softened for the tall white man who had risked his life to save them. Until now, Si Tundok had learned to hate all white men, including his own father. Si Tundok's father was a cruel and abusive man, prone to vicious fits of temper that led to savage beatings of his wife and children at the slightest provocation. Si Tundok, only fifteen at the time, attacked his father during a particularly violent encounter and without the least bit of remorse, Si Tundok wrapped his powerful arms around his father's neck and squeezed until he heard the man's neck snap. Si Tundok escaped before the Spanish authorities could catch him and he had roamed between the islands and continents of Asia ever since, carrying his hate and his guilt with him wherever he went.

"Break it off!" James called to Henry. "We can't follow them any farther."

James watched the last of the surviving Burmese climb beyond the horse's ability to reach them so he wheeled his horse around and trotted back to Si Tundok.

Henry joined him just as they reached the big Malay and the pile of bodies which littered the ground near Si Tundok's feet. Henry had lost his helmet and his face and uniform were coated with sweat and gore, but his boyish grin showed through the grime on his face. "Showed those bloody bastards a thing or two, eh, Lieutenant?" he said.

James, his spirits high with his small victory said, "Indeed we did, Henry.

Are you all right, Si Tundok?"

Si Tundok nodded that he was.

Neither Henry or James saw the wounded Burmese rifleman raise his musket, but his movement caught Si Tundok's eye. "Watch out!" he yelled and leapt toward the wounded man.

But Si Tundok was too late. The Burmese bullet found its mark, penetrating James' back below his right shoulder blade and knocking him from his mount.

# VI

## Bengal Army Field Hospital
## Rungpore, Burma

"Lieutenant Brooke, how is he Doctor? Will he make it?" Henry held the surgeon by the sleeve of his blood soaked smock. Si Tundok stepped close, blocking the doctor's attempt to reach a wash basin filled with gore.

"He's young...strong," the doctor said, wearily. "He's got a good chance." The doctor pulled away from Henry's grip on his coat and stepped around Si Tundok and began to wash the blood from his hands in the tainted water. "Couldn't extract the bullet though," he said. "Too dangerous. He lost too much blood. He'll have to carry it until a surgeon in England can see to it."

"England?"

"Of course," the surgeon said matter-of-factly. "Lieutenant Brooke will have more of a chance to recover in England than he would if he stays here. This bloody climate takes its toll on the wounded."

"Can we see him?" Henry asked

The doctor shook his head. "He's out. Wouldn't do him any good to try to talk anyway, not with that hole in his lung and all."

"I understand," Henry said, not attempting to mask his disappointment. "You'll take good care of him, won't you, Doctor?"

"It's my job," the surgeon said and returned to the surgical tent.

Henry and Si Tundok walked to a nearby banyan tree and rested beneath its shade. "What do you think?" Henry asked.

"He'll make it," Si Tundok replied.

"No, I mean about what we ought to do...you know, about the blokes who ran out on us."

"I'm going after them, make them pay with their lives," Si Tundok said.

"All right if I tag along? I've got the same score to settle. One for the lieutenant, too."

Si Tundok shrugged. "It's up to you."

"I've been thinking, Si Tundok. Maybe it would be a good idea to stick it out here until our tour is up. We've only got a couple of months left. Once we have the King's Pardon in our pocket, we won't need to worry about the army sniffing after us."

Si Tundok was ready to ride out of camp that very day, so deep was his anger for Geoff and the others. But what Henry said made sense. With a King's Pardon he could start his life all over—at least in British held territory.

And he could watch after James until he was sent to England. Si Tundok owed James his life and he wouldn't forget it.

"You're probably right, Henry," Si Tundok finally said. "Their kind won't be hard to find. We'll catch up to them soon enough."

Henry surprised Si Tundok when he said, "I think I'll write to the lieutenant's father, let him know how he's doing. Didn't he say his parents lived near Bath somewhere?"

"You can write?" Si Tundok was very impressed.

"One of my many hidden talents," Henry laughed. "Besides, it might be the last thing I'll get to do for the lieutenant before he sails for England. Probably won't see him again after that and I feel I owe him for coming in after us the way he did."

Henry thought often about the lieutenant's wild charge that saved their lives. He also thought about Geoff and the other deserters. *If the situation had been reversed, would I have joined the deserters and ran away too?* he wondered. The thought bothered him more than he was willing to admit.

May 1, 1825
Brooke Manor
Near Bath, England

"Anne! Anne, come quickly!" Sir Thomas Brooke held a letter in his hand dated February 20, 1825 and stamped with the seal of the East India Company. It had to contain news of his son. Anxiously, he tore open the letter with trembling hands.

"What is it, dear?"

"A letter, about James." Sir Thomas didn't look up and his dour expression signaled his wife that the news was not good.

"What does it say, Thomas? Tell me..."

Anne Brooke, a petite and attractive woman in her late fifties clutched her husband's arm and braced herself for the possibility that she had lost her only surviving son. "What is it? Is James, is he...?"

She couldn't say the word, 'dead.' By mutual agreement neither of James' parents would discuss the Burmese War or the danger their son might find himself in. Superstitiously, perhaps, they felt that to broach the subject would somehow imperil the life of their youngest son.

"James has been wounded," Sir Thomas said with some relief.

"No!" Anne gasped and covered her mouth with her palms. "How badly?"

"Seriously, but he is recovering...bullet in the back...happened in January, near Rungpore, it says." Suddenly Sir Thomas brightened and said enthusiastically, "James is returning to England for a period of recovery as soon as he's well enough to travel."

Sir Thomas didn't have a chance to finish the letter. The news was good enough. Anne enveloped him around the neck and kissed him on the cheek. "Oh, thank God he's all right, Thomas. I can't imagine what we'd do if something were to happen...."

Tears of relief welled in his wife's eyes and her husband held her close. His throat was drawn and tight, but he did not weep although he felt as joyous as his wife.

After a moment, Thomas gently pushed Anne away saying, "There's more to the letter. Let me finish reading it, dear."

Anne dried her tears and listened attentively to every word he read.

When Sir Thomas finished, he said, "The letter is signed by someone by the name of Henry Steele. Apparently he was with James when it all happened."

"Henry?" The name evoked bittersweet memories of her long lost eldest son. "Read it to me again, Thomas. Please, read all of it."

# CHAPTER THREE

## I

May 1, 1825
*HMS Cecilia*
Near Santabong, Sarawak

For five days the *HMS Cecilia*, a 700 ton British East Indiaman, had been locked in the jaws of a sandbar off the coast of west Borneo near the mouth of the Sarawak River. The ship listed badly to her starboard side forcing the ship's first officer, Timothy Irons, to hold onto the standing rigging while he made his way along the main deck. He brushed by two of the ship's crew, opened the forecastle hatch, hurried down the steps and pounded on the door of the wardroom of Captain John Templar.

"Who is it?"

"First Officer Irons, Captain."

"Enter," the captain said.

Timothy took a deep breath and opened the cabin door, resolved to try one final time to convince the inexperienced captain of the danger the *Cecilia* was in.

The captain was busy perusing a stack of maps and charts and didn't bother to look up. "What is it, Mister Irons?" he asked.

"Request permission to lead a landing party ashore, Captain."

"For what purpose, Mister Irons?"

"To seek out the assistance of friendly natives, Captain. With their help we could unload the cargo and some of the guns...lighten the ship and perhaps the tide will lift her off the sandbar, sir."

"There are no friendly natives on the island, Mister Irons," the captain countered. Captain Templar lifted his head from the pile of maps for the first time and looked directly at his first officer. "As I have told you on numerous occasions, Mister Irons, I have no intention of sending a single man of this ship's company ashore. I intend to remain exactly as we are until the Admiralty sends a search ship for us."

"Begging your pardon, sir, but the *Cecilia* is in a most vulnerable position." Timothy squeezed his fingers against the seams of his trousers and hoped he could make his case before the captain dismissed him as he had each of the previous five days. Timothy had more experience sailing the South China Sea than the captain and he knew of the many dangers that

71

lurked along these coastal waterways. "If we are spotted by marauders, Captain, the *Cecilia* would be indefensible. She lists so badly that both the port and starboard guns would be useless in her defense."

"You overestimate the ability of these ignorant savages, Mister Irons. And you underestimate the ability of the ship's crew to defend her in the unlikely event that they would need to."

"No, sir. I just think it's imperative that we..."

"That's enough, Mister Irons! We've had this discussion before and it serves absolutely no purpose to have it again! Do I make myself perfectly clear?"

"Aye, sir, but if I could just add..."

"*Mister* Irons!" The captain's face flushed with anger and he slammed his fist on the table, scattering charts and maps to the deck. "You, sir, are dangerously close to insubordination! If you are so concerned about this ship's welfare then you can stand the night watch. That is all, Mister Irons. You are dismissed!"

"Aye, Captain." Timothy turned on his heels and closed the cabin door harder than he intended.

Once he reached the main deck, Timothy's anger subsided somewhat, but not his concern. He observed the port side guns pointing uselessly upward toward the Southern Cross while the eighteen pound guns lining the starboard side of the ship leaned helplessly into the sea. He shook his head, clenched his jaw and made his way to the forestay mast, climbed halfway up the ratline and swung himself onto the yardarm. He sat there and watched the ocean consume the setting sun along the western horizon and wondered if there was anything more he could do.

## II

### Sultan's Palace
### Brunei, Borneo

"I disagree!" Api fumed at his mother's decision to rescue the stranded British ship. "These white foreigners are becoming too numerous. They prowl our shores constantly. They trouble me," he said.

"And you, Langau, what do you think?" The *Dayang* Udang had called the meeting with her son and the *Pengirin* Langau after escorting her moronic brother, Sultan Buntor, to his bed chambers. She sat in the Sultan's throne as regal as a queen, knowing full well that, as a woman, she would never be allowed to hold the exalted title of 'Sultan' herself, but she relished the opportunity to pretend, knowing she was as close to absolute power as she would ever get.

"I too am troubled by these white men, *Dayang*," Langau said. "When I was in exile in Labuan, the Spanish whites only brought death, disease and a lust for wealth. I agree with Api. We should kill these stranded foreigners, take their cargo and burn their ship. Let it be a warning to all foreigners to stay away from our shores."

"Under normal circumstances I would agree with both of you," the *Dayang* said. "But these are unusual times. We already know that the Sultan of Sulu has granted concessions to the Spanish and I have recently learned that the Sultan of Pontianak has made a similar agreement with the Dutch. These treaties have increased their power many times. Brunei has always been surrounded by these enemies but now the Sultans of Sulu and Pontianak have powerful allies and that creates a very dangerous situation for us."

"And how is it that the rescue of a single ship will solve the problem for us?" Langau asked.

"My dear *Pangirin*," the *Dayang* answered, "a simple gesture of friendship costs us nothing, but the reward may be great."

"Reward?" Api scoffed. "Allow me to seize the ship and we will have our reward in the form of the ship's cargo. No doubt it is worth many gold ingots."

"No, Api, I forbid it. I have already dispatched a messenger to Kuching ordering Hasim to immediately rescue the ship."

This was not good news to Api. When he had learned of the stranded ship two days earlier, he devised a plan of his own and it didn't involve a rescue.

The *Dayang* Udang continued. "The stranded ship flies the British flag.

Once rescued, I will forward a message to the ship's captain to be conveyed to the British authorities that the Sultan of Brunei wishes to discuss a possible concession with them. Once we reach an agreement with the British and have English guns and sea power as allies, the Sultans of Pontianak and Sulu will not dare encroach upon our sovereign territory."

"What makes you think the English will be interested in a concession?" Langau asked.

"Greed," *Dayang* Udang responded simply.

"But surely you don't intend granting the British the right to exploit Brunei as the Sultans of Sulu and Pontianak have done with their territories," Langau gasped.

"Not Brunei, Sarawak," the *Dayang* said.

Api was taken aback by his mother's revelation. Heredity divined that he would succeed Hasim as Rajah of Sarawak and Hasim would be elevated to the throne of Brunei after his mother's poisonous brews disposed of Buntor. But his mother's plan to grant concessions to the English were troublesome. Api had his own plans for Sarawak and Brunei and British ships and cannon were not a part of those plans.

"But what of Hasim?" Api protested. "He is Rajah of Sarawak. Your plan is certain to anger him."

*Dayang* Udang dismissed the question with a shrug of her shoulders and said, "I am gratified to learn of your concern for your brother's welfare, Api," she said sarcastically. "But, as both of you know, I have more important plans for Hasim. Besides, Sarawak is a troublesome territory." Then she bored her eyes into her son and said, "And I have been disappointed with the amount of *serah* the Sultan receives from Sarawak. As the Sultan's tax collector, perhaps you can explain the problem, Api?"

*She suspects me of keeping a portion of the* serah, Api thought. *Or does she know?*

"The meager gold mines at Sin Bok have been depleted, Mother," he said, speaking on the assumption that the *Dayang* had no proof of his theft. "But I have advised Hasim to grant additional concessions to the *Kapitan* there. Perhaps Loi Pek's Hakkas will discover other sources of gold in the new concession."

"And the natives?" she probed. "Why is it that their contributions to the Sultan's treasury have diminished?"

"The wretched Bidayuh have nothing and the coastal tribes produce very little to– "

"Enough!" *Dayang* Udang cut Api's excuse off in mid-sentence with a wave of her trunk-like arm. "The problem is not the natives, it is instability! This...this...what is the name of that *Tua Kampong* of the Iban in Sarawak?"

"Rentab," Api replied.

"Yes, Rentab. His raids are becoming more frequent. Without peace there is little hope for increased production among the other tribes." The *Dayang* leaned her ponderous bulk forward and the throne creaked. "You know this Iban leader well, don't you, Api?"

"Yes, his warriors were instrumental in our success against the stockade," Api said.

"For that, he has my gratitude but inform him, Api, that further raids will not be tolerated and if you can't stop him now, perhaps British guns will stop his insurrection in the future.

## III

Rajah's Palace
Kuching, Sarawak

Hasim paced the floor of his small courtroom like a frightened mouse. He had been Rajah of Sarawak for nearly a year, but neither the title nor the power that went with it increased his self-confidence or decreased his temerity.

Why had his mother, the *Dayang* Udang, chosen to remain in Brunei and leave him to rule this unmanageable and rebellious territory? And where was Api? He relied upon Api's counsel and yet he still had not returned from Brunei. What was taking his mother so long to reply to his message informing her of the crippled British ship and asking for instructions on what he should do about it? Perhaps he should have heeded Api's advice and ordered an attack on the foreigners.

Suddenly a courtier appeared and prostrated himself at the Rajah's feet. "Rajah Hasim, a messenger has arrived from Brunei," he said.

"Finally! Send him in...be quick!"

Shortly, the messenger entered, dropped to his knees and kissed the Rajah's feet. With his eyes glued to the floor he extended a parchment to Hasim. "From the Sultan, Rajah Hasim."

Eagerly, Hasim snatched the rolled document from the man's hand and ripped off the royal seal. Hasim's countenance visibly soared when he finished reading the contents of it. The letter, although it had the Sultan Buntor's stamp, was from his mother. In it, she praised him for his foresight and ordered him to rescue the British ship and accommodate its crew. Hasim was further gratified with the thought that Api had given him faulty advice and perhaps his brother wasn't as infallible as Hasim thought him to be.

Hasim dismissed the messenger and to his courtier commanded, "Summon the *Datu* Temanggong. I will have words with him."

Hasim ordered his servants to prepare refreshments and then sat in his crudely carved bilian throne and re-read his mother's letter. For the first time, he actually felt like a Rajah.

When the *Datu* Temanggong arrived, Hasim received him magnanimously with a broad smile and open arms. "Ahh...*Datu*, how good it is to see you again. Please be seated, there is a small task I wish you to take care of for me."

The *Datu* Temanggong was a paunchy, middle-aged lowly prince of lethargic but affable disposition. In former times he had been a trusted underling of the previous Sultan, Saifudin. Although his title made him the principle war chief of the Sarawak Malay, his duties had largely been assumed by *Awang* Api.

"Of course, Rajah Hasim. Whatever you command, I will do," he said, grateful to once again have the chance to prove his worthiness.

The Rajah's servants brought the two men fresh coconut milk and fried bananas and while they ate Hasim explained that he wanted the *Datu* Temanggong to gather a force and rescue the British ship.

"I will make ready immediately, Rajah Hasim," *Datu* Temanggong said. "And we will depart in the morning."

"No, *Datu*, you will leave tonight," Hasim commanded.

IV

## Santabong, Sarawak

"See how the English ship leans to its side, Lutu?" Api said, pointing to the *Cecilia* from a mangrove cove where he and Lutu could not be seen by the ship's crew.

Lutu, an unscrupulous cutthroat and Illuan pirate from Mindanau grunted and said, "As you said, *Awang* Api, the ship's guns will be useless against my triremes. We will take it easily." Lutu and his band of Malay corsairs had made their reputation attacking trading vessels from Borneo to the Indonesian Islands, but even as fearless as he was, Lutu had learned to respect the fire power of the European ships. "Are you certain the Rajah Hasim will not interfere?"

Api knew he was playing a dangerous game. The *Dayang* Udang had expressly forbidden him to harm the English ship and she had sent Hasim instructions to rescue it, but his plan had been put in motion before he learned either of these things. *Besides,* he thought, *the destruction of the English ship would thwart Mother's plan to grant the British a concession to Sarawak.* The *Dayang* would be furious, of course, but then again, Api could always blame the ship's demise on Lutu.

Api chuckled, "My brother is as cautious as a water buffalo. Even if he has received the *Dayang's* instructions, he won't send a rescue party until daylight."

"Good," Lutu grunted. "Then we will attack before midnight."

The two men returned to where Lutu's three triremes were beached. A motley band of well-armed renegades and savages manned the large outriggers, over fifty men to a craft. *More than enough to complete the task,* Api thought.

"You won't forget who told you of this prize, will you, Lutu?" Api asked with a hint of warning on his voice.

Lutu considered that he could easily cut down Api and his small retinue of warriors and take the British ship's treasure for himself, but his dealings with the Malay prince had proven lucrative for both of them in the past and there was no reason to believe the same relationship wouldn't continue into the future, especially now that Api's family was in control of the Sultanate of Brunei.

Lutu feigned shock and said, "I won't forget. Your share will be given to you as always."

Api smiled and placed his arm jovially around the old pirate's shoulders. "And a *generous* share it will be, I trust?"

"Of course," Lutu grumbled.

"Just one more thing before I leave you to your night's work, Lutu. Make certain that you kill all of the English dogs. No one must survive, is that clear?"

Lutu tossed his head toward his band of cutthroats and said, "Don't worry, killing is never a problem for them."

# V

## Near Midnight
### *HMS Cecilia*

From his perch high upon the mainsail halyard, the *Cecilia's* first officer, Timothy Irons was first to spot Lutu's triremes.

Lutu used the high waves and the night-blackened horizon to his advantage. His ships approached the *Cecilia* from her listing seaward side, riding the deep folds of the ocean's waves and the endless dark horizon to skillfully keep their sixty-man crafts hidden in the hollows of the slow breaking waves.

"Pirates!" Timothy shouted to the forecastle night watchman. "Sound the alarm!" By the time Timothy shouted his warning and heard the clang of the ship's bell awakening the *Cecilia's* sleeping crew, the Illuan pirates reached the British ship and were scaling its starboard hull.

Weaponless, Timothy barely had time to scamper down the ratline and grab a belay pin before the first of Lutu's pirates leaped upon the main deck in front of him. Timothy didn't wait. With his belay pin gripped tightly in his fist he charged the savage, a ferocious looking black with bones plugged into his ears and the septum of his nose. The pirate met Timothy's charge with a blood-curdling scream and a slash of his short sword. Timothy ducked the blow and slammed into the pirate with his shoulder. The pirate reeled, stumbling sideways and before he could regain his balance, Timothy's belay pin caught the savage's head with a crunching blow and the pirate crashed to the deck. No sooner had Timothy dispatched the first invader when a host of Lutu's cut-throats poured unimpeded onto the ship's deck.

Timothy heard the shouts of his shipmates rallying somewhere behind him, but he could do nothing but hold his ground and try to fend off the attackers who swarmed the deck in front of him. Furiously, he swung the belay pin and met his attackers with the desperation of a cornered tiger. His first blow caught a pirate on the shoulder, breaking his arm and dropping him to the deck. A second blow caught another savage on the hip and sent him vaulting over the ship's side and into the sea.

But as viciously as Timothy fought, it was only moments before the pirate horde overwhelmed him. A glancing blow from a war club smashed him on the side of the head and neck and sent him sprawling unconscious on the deck. The swarm of wildly screaming savages leaped Timothy's body and pressed their attack toward the outnumbered ship's crew.

The battle lasted less than thirty minutes. Of the *Cecilia's* sixty crew, only sixteen survived the pirate attack. Bound and huddled around the mainsail mast, the defeated crew watched Lutu's savages ravage the ship. When they finished looting everything of value except the main cargo of cinnabar, antimony and cloves, the non-Malay members of Lutu's band began the grisly task of separating the *Cecilia's* dead crewmen's heads from their bodies and dumping the headless corpses over the ship's side. The pirates had found the ship's store of rum and drank heavily, making them doubly dangerous to the ship's survivors.

"What shall we do with these captured *orang puteh*, these white men, Lutu?" The question came from a mildly intoxicated Kedayan warrior who had three white heads tied to his *chawat* by their own hair. The Kedayan gleefully waved his blood stained *parang* in the faces of the captured crew, taunting them.

Lutu took a long draft of rum from a silver tankard he had stolen from the captain's cabin. It had been a good raid and would be a profitable one once they removed the main cargo. For that task, he planned to use the *Cecilia's* captured crew. Beyond that, the ship's crew had no future and his warriors could do with them what they would. Lutu only grunted in response to the Kedayan's question, took another pull of rum from the tankard and approached the captives with a drunken swagger.

"Yes, what shall I do with you pathetic white dogs?" Lutu taunted. "No suggestions?" he mocked. "My friend here wants to add your heads to his belt." Lutu grabbed the nearest captive by the hair and spat, "Would you like your head to decorate the rafters of his longhouse, eh, white man? Shall Lutu let his men have you and the others?"

Timothy merely gasped at the pain of Lutu's hold on his hair and then slumped against the mainsail mast. The blow that he sustained earlier intercepted any commands he tried to give to his body to force it to function and he fell into unconsciousness.

Reading the ship's crew's silence as fear and the fact that they probably didn't understand his language, Lutu laughed and took another long draught of rum.

Clad only in his nightshirt, Captain John Templer, with a river of blood flowing along the side of his head, understood enough of Lutu's words and gestures to know that the remnants of his crew were dead men unless he intervened.

"You barbarian!" Captain Templer struggled to his feet and shouted at the pirate leader. "I demand that my men be released immediately," he fumed. "In the name of His Majesty, King George, and all that is civilized, I demand that these atrocities– "

Lutu's face soured and he tossed the half-emptied tankard of rum into the captain's face. He glared at the upstart captive, not understanding what the man was saying but angered by the beaten man's audacity to speak at all. No one ever spoke to Lutu in such a tone of voice and lived and this white man would be no exception. Lutu snatched the Kedayan's gore-stained *parang* from him and with a single, swift stroke of the blade, split open the captain's abdomen, spilling his innards to the deck. "This noisy white man is yours, Muka," he said to the Kedayan and tossed the bloody *parang* back to him.

With a gleeful war whoop, the Kedayan pounced upon the dead captain's body and crudely hacked the captain's head from his shoulders and added it to the others dangling at his waist. Finished, Muka's wild, bloodthirsty eyes enveloped the surviving members of the crew. He wanted more.

"Lutu, Look!" someone near the starboard railing shouted. "War *praus*!"

Lutu spun around and looked shoreward to where the man was pointing. Against slivers of moonlight reflecting off the water, Lutu saw a flotilla of *praus* approaching rapidly towards them. "The Rajah!" Lutu spewed. Api had assured him that the Rajah Hasim wouldn't attempt to rescue the British ship until daylight, but Api apparently had underestimated his brother. There was no time to transfer the cargo, kill the captives, or fire the ship, and since he concluded that there was little chance to negotiate the spoils of the ship with the Rajah's warriors he yelled, "To the boats! Make for the open sea!"

Lutu's men scrambled over the *Cecilia's* starboard side, hastily boarded the triremes and frantically paddled seaward, knowing that the Rajah's boats, designed for cruising the calm and relatively shallow coastal waters, would be unable to pursue them in the open sea.

*HMS Rainbow*
Off The Coast Of West Africa

The same morning that the survivors of the *Cecilia's* crew were being rescued by Hasim's men under the command of the *Datu* Temanggong, James Brooke labored to exercise his damaged lung by inhaling a breath of fresh, salty sea air aboard the *HMS Rainbow* which was making its way northward along the calm coastal waters of the dark continent on its final leg of the journey from India to England.

James stood on the forecastle deck of the lumbering East Indiaman brigatine and continued his morning breathing exercise. Due to his vigor, youth and will to heal, James' wound had mended itself reasonably well although the Burmese musket ball still lodged behind his rib cage taxed his ability to breath deeply. James planned to have the ball removed immediately upon reaching England as the military physician's in Calcutta had advised. Following recovery, he planned to explore his future options with his father.

"Ah, Lieutenant. You're up and about early this morning. Feeling better, I trust."

"Indeed I am, Doctor," James replied, turning to meet the face of the man who addressed him. "Thanks to your treatments more than anything else."

"Your medicine is out there," said the man, nodding to the open expanse of sea which led to the shores of England. "The fresh sea air and the prospects of being reunited with your family are better medicine than anything I have buried in my medical bag."

"You're probably right," James chuckled. "It has been nearly six years since I last visited England. I dare say, I am looking forward to it."

"As we all are, Lieutenant." Arthur Claygate, ship's surgeon, laid his forearms on top of the ship's railing and leaned against it. Both men gazed quietly into the vast expanse of open sea for a moment, reflecting upon their imminent reunion with their native land.

James had taken a particular liking to the *Rainbow's* surgeon although Arthur was nearly twenty years James' senior and James was certain that the feeling was mutual. After only a few days at sea, the two men found each other's company to be interesting and engaging. James amused the older man with his long discourses on the way he thought things were and the way he thought things should be. Quick to laugh and sharing many of James' opinions and philosophy, Arthur Claygate responded favorably to the affable young army officer and soon a strong bond of friendship evolved between the two of them. In the mornings, Arthur tended to James' wound. In the afternoons, they idled away the time playing chess and cribbage and discussed the way of the world. And to the young Brooke's delight, Arthur Claygate knew a great deal of the world.

As a young physician, Arthur had "itching powder for brains" as he put it, and longed to see the world. For over twenty years, he had traversed the globe, visiting lands which James had only recently begun to imagine. The tales of his travels piqued James' own sense of adventure and even Arthur's propensity to embellish his stories only served to increase James' passion to hear more.

Arthur Claygate looked nothing like a doctor. He had broad hands and thick, stubby fingers—not the physical attributes one expects to find in a man who uses his hands to delicately tend the flesh of the ill and dying. Arthur's average frame supported a full-barreled chest and matching stomach. Long curls of red hair, never properly groomed, hung in a riotous array across his forehead and down the side of his round face drawing attention to his ruddy complexion and a brigade of freckles that covered him since birth. The doctor had a jovial disposition, talkative and quick of wit—even to the point of being bellicose at times. Whatever characteristics Arthur Claygate may have lacked as a surgeon, he more than compensated for with his amiable personality.

Through his bushy red brows and his twinkling green eyes, Arthur studied the lanky lieutenant for a moment before asking, "Do you intend to return to the Far East after your recovery, James?"

"Indeed, I do, Arthur. Your stories have intrigued me, made me consider my own future."

"How so?"

James turned and faced the surgeon. His deep blue eyes sparkled when he said, "A man can make his fortune in the Far East. There are treasures there beyond imagining. Of that, I am convinced. I intend to return someday and have my share of it."

"But what of your commission with the East India Company? I doubt if they will be amenable to one of their fine, young officers interfering with their own business of profit-taking in the East?" he chuckled with a throaty laugh from deep within his massive chest.

"Quite true, Arthur," James said. "I won't be able to retain my commission while I seek my fortune, but I hope to solve that problem after I return to England."

James understood that the plans he had formulated for his future depended upon convincing his father to allow him to resign his commission and persuading his father to finance the plan he had to develop a merchant trade business in the Far East. It would be the most difficult part of his return home, James knew. He understood how his father felt about James' military career and how he wanted James to follow in his own footsteps. And James had not forgotten the promise he made to his father. Perhaps Sir Thomas had mellowed in the past six years. James hoped it was so.

"Forgive me for saying so, James, but you appear to be a gentleman of some means. Do you mind if I ask you why you find it necessary to risk your fortune and possibly your life seeking treasures which may not exist? It seems obvious to me that you could live...uh...comfortably on your own wealth."

James cocked his head and grinned. "Arthur, are you saying that your tales of fortunes to be made in the Orient were exaggerated?"

Arthur bellowed out a hearty laugh. "No, no, James. Embellished a bit, perhaps, but not totally false. But it isn't as easy as plucking apples from a tree either. The risks can break a man physically and ruin him financially. I've seen it happen many times, James. The whim of a becalmed sea, an accident, disease, pirates...any number of things can go wrong."

"Is that why you have chosen to remain a ship's surgeon, Arthur?"

"For fear of failure?" Arthur placed his hand dramatically over his heart. "Never! And that's the God's truth, James. Had I been so disposed, I could have picked the Orient clean of her treasures by now. But I am a simple man, James, more content to observe the foibles of other men than I am in accumulating personal wealth."

James shook his head. It was difficult for him to understand someone who didn't want more out of life than simply observing the follies of others, so he asked, "Then what do you hope to eventually accomplish with your life, Arthur?"

"Oh, other than treat lieutenants who catch musket balls with their bodies and stoke their impressionable heads with tales of the Far East, I intend to marry."

"Marry?"

"You sound surprised, James." Arthur said with a twinkle in his eye. "I may not be as good of a catch as a certain handsome lieutenant I know, but I have a beautiful woman who's been waiting a long time for me to return and place a band of gold about her finger. Believe me when I say that she is worth all the treasure to be had in the East or anywhere else for that matter."

James slapped the shorter man playfully on the shoulders and said with a big grin, "Well, you old rooster! I didn't peg you for the marrying kind."

"The only man who is not the marrying kind, is the man who has yet to feel the sweet sting of Cupid's arrow."

"Well, congratulations, Arthur. I am happy for you, but I dare say, I will not let the temptation of a woman interfere with my plans."

"Don't be too sure of yourself, James," Arthur said. "Cupid probably has an arrow in his quiver just waiting for you and, I warn you, he can sneak up on you at the most damnable time."

They both laughed and then James said, "Let's go to the galley and fetch something to eat. Then you can tell me all about her. I also want you to tell me more about Singapore and Malaya, Arthur."

# VII

## May 16, 1825
## Penang, Malaya

The British held island of Penang northeast of the Malay peninsula never slept for it was much too busy providing round-the-clock drink and pleasure to the world's seamen and transients. Even at four in the morning, a tumult of activity sounded within the inns, pubs and brothels along the waterfront. Drunken sailors, some with their arms smothering Oriental prostitutes, others looking for whores or other amusements, strolled unsteadily along the walkway separating the row of crumbling buildings from the waterfront. From one of the inns, a man emerged and waited for a group of intoxicated sailors to pass by before he quickly ducked around the corner of the inn and disappeared among the shadows.

"Well?" Si Tundok asked.

"The blokes are settling their account with the innkeeper now. They'll be coming out soon."

"Good," Si Tundok said and started to move away from the side of the building before Henry grabbed his arm.

"Wait," Henry whispered. "Better to follow them...have a go at them when there are fewer people around."

Since leaving the Bengal Army with a King's Pardon in their pockets, Si Tundok and Henry Steele were making good on their vow to find and kill the four members of Lieutenant Brooke's cavalry scouts who deserted them outside Rungpore several months earlier. The Indian had been easy.

Evidently the Indian thought the three of them had been killed by the Burmese and so he separated himself from Geoff and the two Sikhs and returned to the British base in Madras, obviously thinking of fulfilling his six-month obligation and collecting a King's Pardon as the lieutenant had promised. But Henry spotted him and after counseling Si Tundok in the virtues of patience, he and Si Tundok watched and waited for an opportunity to take the Indian. Finally, late one evening, the Indian exited his tent and walked to the edge of a brush shrouded ravine, dropped his pants amid the foliage and began to relieve himself. Si Tundok saw his opportunity and without stealth or Henry, the big Malay simply crashed through the brush, grabbed the startled Indian around the head with his powerful arms and snapped his neck. Henry arrived in time to help Si Tundok toss the man-sans trousers-into the ravine so that his demise looked every bit like the man had wandered off the edge of the cliff during the night while vacating his bowels.

Although the Englishman, Geoff, continued to elude them, Henry and Si-Tundok picked up the Sikhs' trail in Calcutta on a tip from a merchant who had purchased two of His Majesty's finest cavalry steeds from 'two Sikhs who seemed to be in a hurry to reach Penang and needed the money.' Six weeks later, Henry and Si Tundok finally had the Sikhs cornered.

Impatiently, Si Tundok grunted an assent and fell back into the shadows and carefully peeked around the corner to the door of the inn. "Are you sure they didn't spot you?" he whispered.

"Not a chance," Henry replied. "They were much to busy paying the mama-san and saying their last good bye's to a couple of Siamese whores."

Suddenly, Si Tundok reached back and touched Henry on the shoulder. "They are coming out now," he whispered with anticipation on his voice.

"Which way are they heading?"

"This way."

Henry could hear muffled sounds of merriment and the bellicose voices of sailors espousing their prowess or disparaging another's, but none of the commotion sounded too close by.

Si Tundok pressed himself harder into the shadows and pulled Henry to him whispering, "No need to follow them, we will take them here."

Henry started to protest, but it was too late. He heard the Sikhs laugh lasciviously and became aware of the sound of their footsteps drumming along the wooden walkway toward them. Si Tundok unsheathed a *kris* from his belt and raised it to shoulder height, preparing to strike. Henry followed Si Tundok's lead and pulled a dagger from its sheath beneath his tunic. Henry didn't like to kill with a knife. It always seemed so personal in a way he couldn't explain. But Si Tundok had made the decision for them and it was now best to do it quickly and silently.

As the Sikhs appeared, Si Tundok grabbed the nearest one by the tunic and yanked him into the alleyway and tossed him towards Henry. Without hesitation he grabbed the second surprised Sikh around the head and with one quick motion, sliced his throat with the *kris*. The man emitted a gurgling sound and then slumped to the ground. Quickly, Si Tundok released the dead man and turned to assist Henry.

But Henry needed no help. The first Sikh was already on the ground. The force with which Si Tundok had tossed him had left the man unbalanced and he had impaled himself upon Henry's waiting dagger. The dying Sikh began to moan.

"Finish him," Si Tundok said.

Henry muttered, "This is the part I don't like." He swallowed hard, withdrew his dagger from the man's chest and, holding the man's mouth with his free hand, slashed the Sikh's throat.

"That one's for the lieutenant," Henry whispered as he wiped his blade on the man's clothing.

Si Tundok muttered something similar and then drug the body of the Sikh he killed deeper into the shadows of the building and then helped Henry stack the second corpse on top of the first.

"C'mon, let's get out of here, Henry," Si Tundok said, as he moved with giant strides from the alley and onto the walkway.

Henry surveyed the area while he scrambled to catch up. No one seemed to have been aware of the disturbance and Henry's steps lightened. "Three down and one to go," he said, returning to his normal cherubic self. "Not a bad night's work if I say so myself."

Si Tundok scowled and said, "Yes, one to go. I should have killed him in Madras when I had the chance instead of just breaking his thumb."

"We'll find him someday," Henry said

"Yes, someday," Si Tundok confirmed.

"Come on then," Henry said jovially. "This deserves a celebration. I'll buy."

When they reached the same inn the Sikhs departed earlier, Henry opened the door for his friend and with a bow and a sweeping flourish of his arm, beckoned Si Tundok inside.

# VIII

## *HMS Cecilia*
## Singapore

"Drop anchor!" First Officer, Timothy Irons called from the *Cecilia's* bridge. He had captained the *Cecilia* safely into Singapore harbor escorted by the *HMS Quicksilver* which had been dispatched by the Admiralty to search for the missing Indiaman and came across her midway between Borneo and Singapore.

The second half of the return trip had been easy sailing once Timothy's skeleton crew of survivors were complimented with sailors from the *Quicksilver*, but even without the rescuers help, Timothy was confident that even with his small crew they would have made the voyage, so anxious were the men to leave Borneo.

But it wasn't the end of the matter. The Admiralty would hold a board of inquiry and examine every detail of the *Cecilia's* disaster. But Timothy was confident that the inquiry would exonerate both him and the crew. After all, his attempts to apprise Captain Templer of the situation he felt the *Cecilia* was in was well documented in the ship's log, although not as accurately as he would have hoped. In addition, he had saved the ship, its crew and its valuable cargo, thanks to the help of the Rajah of Sarawak.

Following their timely rescue by the *Datu* Temanggong, Timothy and his crew were taken to Kuching where they were fed and housed and had their wounds attended to. The Rajah Hasim was pleasantly accommodating, although he often seemed to be nervous in the presence of the British sailors. With some difficulty, Timothy managed to convey his wish to the Rajah to enlist his assistance and provide men to help right the listing *Cecilia*. It took several days of heavy work to unload the ship's cargo and float her from the sandbar and several more days to re-load the cargo and make ready to set sail for Singapore.

Even as Timothy called out his final commands for the *Cecilia's* mooring, he couldn't help but think that once the Admiralty made its final accounting, he might finally be assigned a ship of his own to command. It was a dream he had for a very long time.

# CHAPTER FOUR

## I

June 21, 1825
Brooke Manor
Near Bath, England

"Most commendable. I believe you handled the situation splendidly, James." Sir Thomas Brooke beamed with pride.

At his father's insistence, James once again recounted how he had maneuvered his small unit of cavalry scouts behind enemy lines on the day he was wounded. It was the first time since James' surgery to remove the Burmese bullet from his chest that James felt up to giving a detailed account of his life in India and the small part he played in the Burmese War.

"Simply an abhorrent display of cowardice," Sir Thomas said in a huff after James told of the desertion of the four members of his patrol. "Can't imagine that British trained troops would behave in such a cowardly fashion."

"They weren't regular soldiers, Father," James said.

"No need to defend them, James. Any man worth his salt, British trained or not, would have held his ground."

Sir Thomas started to sip from his cup of tea, but a coughing spasm cut him short.

"Goodness, dear!" Anne cried. "Are you all right?" Anne set her cup upon a sitting table set between the three of them and approached her husband. She touched him tenderly upon his broad shoulders. Concern etched her face. "We simply must follow Doctor Barrington's instructions and keep your chest wrapped in mustard poultices during the night."

Sir Thomas stifled another cough and waved off his wife. He pulled a handkerchief from the inside pocket of his coat, held it to his mouth and hacked up a dose of phlegm. Quickly, he folded the handkerchief and replaced it in his pocket before his wife could see the flecks of blood on it.

"No need to worry, Anne," Sir Thomas labored to say. "It's simply that time of the year. All that damnable cottonwood fluff in the air, you know."

"Nevertheless, Thomas, I insist that we apply the poultices to your chest tonight and keep applying them as the doctor ordered." Anne returned to her seat, but not before casting a solicitous glance at James.

"Mother's right, Father. You should follow the doctor's advice if you expect to cure that cough."

Sir Thomas raised his palms in submission and said, "Very well, the two of you can prepare that smelly contraption for me later, but for now, I want to hear more of what James has to say." Thomas settled back into his chair. "Go on, James, tell us about the young man who sent us the letter advising us of your wound. What was his name? Henry...Henry something or other, wasn't it?"

"Oh, yes, James," his mother chimed, "Do tell us all about that nice young man."

James smiled tolerantly at his mother. In her view everyone was a nice young man or woman. It was a flaw in her judgment of people that, fortunately, James had not inherited. "I can't say I know much about him," James said. "I do know, however, that Henry was as reliable as any line soldier and he had a splendid disposition. An easy fellow to get on with, actually."

James' eyes twinkled when he added, "But I don't know how nice a fellow Henry really was, Mother. I suspect I would not have found him in the predicament he was in if he was the epitome of moral piety."

"Oh, James," Anne said with a toss of her head, "it was more than likely a misunderstanding. I hardly think the young man would have been so kind as to write to us if he was less than morally responsible. And he fought bravely, didn't you say so, James?"

James nodded.

"You forget, Anne," Sir Thomas interjected, "that it was James who rescued him. Who knows what he might have done had the situation been reversed?"

"I believe he would have come to my assistance, Father," James responded. "I am certain Si Tundok would have."

"More tea, James?" Anne asked.

"Please," James said, lifting his cup.

Sir Thomas waved off his wife's offering and asked, "How can you be so certain of this other fellow, James?"

James shrugged. "I'm just guessing really. But there was something about Si Tundok...I don't know exactly what it was, but I had a feeling he trusted me and I think trust meant a great deal to him." James placed a hand to his chin and thought for a moment, then added, " I even think he took a liking to me, so did Henry."

James set his cup down and continued. "After they hauled me back to our lines and had me patched up, they stayed close by until I was well enough to sail home. During that time, we got to know each other quite well."

"This Malay chap, what was he like, James?" Sir Thomas asked.

"An extraordinary fellow," James replied. "At first, I thought I might have made a mistake selecting him for the troop, but he soon proved his mettle." James chuckled and then continued, saying, "In the beginning, I had the feeling that Si Tundok was weighing me like a lamb chop to ascertain whether I measured up. Evidently I passed his standard because his performance to duty was easily the best of the lot. Si Tundok never said much, but I did get to know him during the many times when he and Henry visited me in the field hospital."

"What did you talk about, dear?" Anne asked.

"Everything. Si Tundok was honest and open about his life. From what he told me, he was somewhat a lost soul, wandering in and out of most every port in the Far East. He was even a pirate at one time, if you can imagine."

"A pirate?" Sir Thomas gasped.

Anne placed her delicate fingers to her mouth in surprise.

James laughed at his parents' shocked expressions. "Yes, a buccaneer. Si Tundok told me he sailed with a band of cutthroats somewhere around Murudu Bay in North Borneo for a short time."

"Si Tundok, what an unusual name," his mother deflected, trying to change the subject, uncomfortable with the thought that her son included a pirate among his circle of friends.

"It's a Malay name," James said. "It means to bow one's head."

"A rather inappropriate name for a pirate, wouldn't you say?" Sir Thomas asked.

"Former pirate," James corrected.

"You said he told you a great deal about the Far East, James," his mother said, remembering their earlier conversations.

"Yes, he did, but mostly the rougher side of the Orient." James had no intention delving into that aspect of Oriental life with his mother so he said, "Actually, it was the ship's surgeon, Arthur Claygate—the man I told you about earlier—who proved most informative of the possibilities available in the East."

"And what possibilities are those?" his father asked.

Sir Thomas suppressed another cough and wiped his mouth with a fresh linen.

"Yes, Father, numerous possibilities," James said, leaning forward on his chair and gazing directly into his father's eyes. James had avoided discussing his thoughts about his own future with his father, but time was short and now that his father had broached the subject, James was determined to see it through. "I am considering my options, Father. With your blessing, of course, I intend to purchase a small frigate and visit the islands Si Tundok and Arthur told me about. From what I understand, there is a fortune to be had for the person with the proper incentive and enterprise."

Shocked, Sir Thomas stiffened in his chair. His bushy brows wrinkled along his forehead. "Are you telling me that you are considering resigning your commission to become a...a *merchant*?"

"I'm considering the possibilities that such a change might offer, certainly, Father."

"Unacceptable!" his father nearly shouted. "Absolutely absurd!" Sir Thomas sprang from his chair and leaned over the sitting table close to his son. He slammed his palms on the table, scattering the tea cups. "Absolutely out of the question!" he fumed. "Resign your commission to become a fortune seeker? Madness! No Brooke in the history of our family has ever lowered himself to such a preposterous notion!"

James expected an argument from his father, but not such a vehement display as this. In silence, he leaned back in his chair and waited for his father's temper to diffuse.

Sir Thomas pushed himself from the small table and paced back and forth between his wife and James like a caged tiger. "I will not permit it!" he said. "Your duty is to this family and to the East India Company!" Then he pointed to his son, and although his voice had softened, his message had not. "Years ago you made a promise to me, James. I suspended your formal education and purchased a commission for you in the King's Army. In return, you vowed to follow in my footsteps with the Company. I expect you to be a man of your word and keep to it."

James contained his anger, but not his disappointment. He knew he should hold his tongue, but he couldn't. "Father, the future you envision for me was Henry's, not mine. In case you've forgotten, my brother's dead." James regretted his words as soon as they were spoken.

Stunned, his father wheezed, "This subject is closed." And then he stormed from the room.

"You shouldn't have upset your father with surprise pronouncements like that, James," Anne said, busily straightening the tea cups on the table. "Especially since your father's not been well of late."

"I know, Mother," James sighed and reached over to touch her hand, "I apologize."

"You should apologize to your father," she said, offering him more tea.

James waved off the offering. "I have nothing to apologize for, Mother. As I've stated honestly, a career with the East India Company is not for me."

"I can understand your apprehension about the Army and all, James, particularly with all you've been through, but– "

"It's not that, Mother," James interjected. "It's just that I'm not cut out to take orders for the rest of my life. Don't you understand? I want to make my own decisions, make my own way in life."

*So unlike his older brother,* Anne thought. Whereas Henry was firmly grounded in reality, her youngest son was a dreamer. She realized that the intervening years had not changed him. "You have always chosen your own path, James," she said in all seriousness. "I suspect you will this time, too." Anne sighed and smiled tolerantly in a way James recognized from earlier times. "Be patient, James, all I ask is a little patience."

## II

Lord Gray's Estate
Bath, England

"Lord Gray shall be mortified when he finds out what you've been up to mistress," Mollie chastised. The nanny's dumpy fingers snatched a cluster of wet and soiled skirts and underclothes lying over the top of the dressing room divider and tossed them in a pile.

"Nonsense, Mollie," exclaimed a youthful voice behind the divider. "Not unless you tell him, that is." Elizabeth Wethington's sixteen-year-old face peered around the divider. The girl's eyes were large and brown and as deceptively innocent as the eyes of a dove. A long, slender neck supported tresses of auburn curls which tumbled below the girl's thin and naked shoulders. "And you won't tell him will you, Mollie?" The thin brows above the girl's pretty face lifted and her head cocked in a questioning manner. "Will you?"

Mollie simply rolled her eyes and clucked her tongue. The nanny had seen the same look a thousand times since Elizabeth was taken in by her uncle, Lord Gray, following the death of Elizabeth's family who were shipwrecked off the coast of Virginia a dozen years earlier. The beguiling way Elizabeth cocked her head when she wanted an affirmative was truly enchanting and it never failed to melt the plump old nanny's heart.

"Besides," Elizabeth went on to say while she removed the remainder of her wet clothing, "Nothing happened, not really."

"I certainly should hope not!" Mollie scolded. The nanny waddled quickly back and forth from one wall to another in the spacious bedroom like a Christmas goose avoiding the ax. Each time she bent over to pick up one item of Elizabeth's scattered clothing, she spotted another. "I'm certain that your uncle would disinherit you if he knew you were seeing that awful Ansley boy," she said, shaking her head with disapproval. "I simply can't imagine what his Lordship would do if he even *suspected* that something untoward occurred," she chided, adding more clothes to the growing pile of soiled clothing on the floor.

Elizabeth giggled. "Oh Mollie, you are so prudish, really you are. Perhaps you haven't noticed, but I'm a grown woman now and I'm perfectly capable of making my own decisions when it comes to whom I chose to see."

Mollie bustled to the closet and pulled open the doors. "Not tonight," she said over her shoulder as she rifled Elizabeth's extensive wardrobe. "Or have you forgotten?"

"Forgotten what?"

Mollie rolled her eyes and pulled a green, high-necked chintz dress from the closet. She examined the sheen of the dress and it's magnificent embroidery and judged it appropriate. "You are to accompany Lord and Lady Gray to dine with the Brookes this evening and unless you hurry, you are sure to be late. Now wash up and I'll hand you your clothes."

"Oh, God, how I absolutely *hate* these stuffy old dinner parties," Elizabeth moaned as she sponged herself in a bowl of warm water.

Drying herself, Elizabeth glimpsed the image of her nakedness in the dressing room mirror. She didn't look at the reflection of her face. She already knew she was pretty. She could tell by the way the young men, and even many of the older men among her uncle's associates stared at her. Instead, her eyes centered on the reflection of her breasts. They were smaller than she thought becoming, but she believed they would continue to blossom because she was still young. She held her breasts in the palm of her hands and massaged them until the small, pink nipples stood full and erect. Satisfied, she gave the remainder of the front of her body only a cursory glance and then turned so that she could see her hips and buttocks. She smiled at what she saw. Her small buttocks held high at the back of her waist and her hips had widened. If Mollie could be believed, it would mean that she would be a very fertile mother. The thought of her emerging womanhood filled Elizabeth with delight.

"Mollie, where are my clothes? I'm freezing to death."

"Here," Mollie said, and tossed an armful of petticoats and the chintz dress atop the divider. "And it would serve you right, mistress Elizabeth, if you did freeze to death," she scolded. "Imagine, wading like two ducks in a pond with that...that commoner with no thought to his Lordship's good name or your own reputation." Mollie clicked her tongue and shook her head. "What ever would people think?"

"I don't care what people think," Elizabeth replied, petulantly. "And Phillip Ansley is not a commoner. He comes from a very fine family and he's a very nice young man."

*Too nice*, she thought, stepping into her undergarments. She had given the young man every opportunity to seduce her, yet he hadn't. Sometimes she just couldn't understand men at all.

# III

## Brooke Manor

As always, Anne Brooke's dinner party was a success, bringing her praises from all of her appreciative guests.

Following dinner, the men adjourned to the library for brandy and cigars while the women congregated together in the manor's spacious parlor.

"Excellent brandy, Sir Thomas." The compliment was spoken by Lord Gray, neighbor to the Brookes' and a powerful member of the House Of Lords. Of the five men, only he and Sir Thomas puffed on hand-rolled tubes of American tobacco.

"French, I presume?" The innocuous question was uttered by George Barton, the Brookes' solicitor.

"Actually, it's Italian," Sir Thomas replied.

"Oh, I wouldn't have guessed." George Barton studied the amber liquor in his glass and wondered how he could make such a mistake. To the men in the room, the solicitor's comment was benign enough, but to George, it was a major blunder. Through will and determination, Barton had done well for himself, rising from the ranks of commoner to handling the legal affairs of some of the most prominent families in Bath, including the Brookes'. But try as he might to convey the impression that he, too, was a man of taste and breeding, he always seemed to fall short of the mark and believed that he would never truly be accepted as a social equal by the powerful men in the room and people like them.

"Italian? I would have thought it to be French brandy also," James said, sensing Barton's discomfort. During the course of the dinner conversation, James had come to admire the introverted man not so much because of his impressive legal triumphs, but because George was a self-made man in a society where class distinctions were very much an impediment to success.

"So, James, your father tells me you had a bit of a run-in with a Burmese bullet, eh?" Lord Gray said, standing alongside George Barton near the fireplace.

"Only a minor incident," James replied.

"Well, you appear fit enough, fully recovered are you?" Sir Raffles asked, nestled in a stuffed chair next to Sir Thomas and opposite from where James sat.

"For the most part," James said. "I'm still a bit sore from the surgery, but I suspect I'll be fine once I get out and about a bit more."

"Anne insisted on keeping the musket ball as a memento," Sir Thomas said. He pointed to an object above the fireplace. "It's in the bell-jar there on the mantle."

Lord Gray and George turned to examine the jar. Sir Stamford looked up, but only to assess Lord Gray. His previous meeting with Lord Gray had not been conclusive and he debated with himself whether or not it would be appropriate to pursue the discussion at this time.

"Well," Lord Gray said when he turned back to face the seated men, "let's hope you don't intend to fill this jar by the time you end your commission in the East, James."

They all chuckled and James said, "It's certainly not my intention, but it would have been more comforting if Mother had used a smaller jar."

The men laughed and then Raffles shook his head and added, "Women do the most peculiar things at times."

"Indeed they do," Lord Gray chimed. "When we were young and courting, we thought we knew everything there was to know about women only to discover later that they are different creatures entirely."

Sir Thomas nodded assent, "Blinded by the romance, I suspect," he said.

"And the passion," Sir Stamford added.

"Gentlemen, gentlemen," Lord Gray interjected feigning seriousness. "We mustn't reveal so much of our knowledge about women to the room's only eligible bachelor. After all, it is incumbent upon James to discover the mystery of the fair sex for himself."

"Hear! Hear!" the men said in unison and raised their glasses to James.

James smiled and returned the toast acknowledging each of them in turn and while Lord Gray and the others discussed other mysteries of the fair sex, James' mind strayed to thoughts of Lord Gray's ward, Elizabeth Wethington. He was still trying to sort out the effect her beauty and charm had upon him. Normally at ease with members of the opposite sex, he found it disconcerting that he had to struggle to find the proper things to say when she directed her attentions to him during the course of the dinner that evening and wondered why it was so.

James was pulled from his reverie when Sir Stamford said, "I presume you will be returning to your post in India soon, James. Might I ask what you intend to do after you have fulfilled your commission there?"

James glanced at his father, then to the glass of brandy he held in his hand. He swirled it in his palm a moment before he answered. "There is still some indecision in that regard."

Sir Thomas coughed. He withdrew the thick cigar from his mouth and snuffed it out. "Damnable tobacco they use in these things nowadays," he muttered. He coughed again and pulled a linen from his vest and held it to his lips.

Raffles noted the red flecks upon Sir Thomas' linen, but chose not to draw attention to it. "Indecision, you say? How so, James?" he asked.

Sir Thomas did not want to re-visit the conversation he and James had earlier. Before James could answer Raffles' question he said, "James has decided to stay on with the East India Company after he fulfills his commission, haven't you, James?"

"Most probably," James said, in an attempt to placate his father and at the same time indicate to him that the matter between them was far from settled. "However, Sir Stamford, I understand that there may be other opportunities in the Far East as well." James had read a great deal Sir Stamford had written on the Orient. Certainly the opinions of a man who spent a lifetime in Asia would have some credence with his father.

"Indeed there are," Raffles said. "Fortunes have been made, but Barton here would know more about that than I do, right, George?"

Barton cleared his throat, surprised to be pulled into the conversation. "Well, I..."

"Tell James about some of the clients you represent, George," Raffles prodded.

"Oh, yes. A number of my clients have made substantial fortunes in trading endeavors of one kind or the other," the shy man said. "Particularly in India and Singapore. Of course, a few of them have also lost fortunes as well," he added.

"Always that risk," Raffles said, unfazed. "But what bothers me more than the risk is that opportunities may be rather limited in the future," Raffles said.

"Why is that?" James asked, disappointed with the remark.

"Britain recently signed a treaty with the Dutch which will limit British influence in many parts of the Orient, particularly the East Indies," Sir Stamford answered. "Simply stated, the treaty specifies that lands to the north of the equator; India, Malaya, Penang, Singapore and Hong Kong, will be recognized to be in the British sphere, while those lands lying south of the line of demarcation are in the Dutch sphere of influence. Unfortunately the treaty now gives the Dutch complete sovereignty over the Spice Islands and practically the entire East Indies. That's why I say that future opportunities in the Far East will be limited."

"Personally, I believe Britain is well served by the agreement with the Dutch," Lord Gray said somewhat defensively. "Britain has been at odds with the Dutch in the region for some time and now we have a treaty that defines each sphere of influence, keeping us at arm's length from one another so to speak."

"True, but it also put Britain at arm's length from exploiting the wealth of many of the unexplored islands of the region," Sir Stamford countered.

"It's doubtful the islands have resources worth exploiting," Sir Gray said. "Besides, many of the islands are no more than rocks protruding from the sea. I doubt if they would justify the expense to explore or protect them even for a sea power such as Britain. And from all accounts, most of these islands are inhabited by the most inhospitable and uncivilized savages on the face of the earth, thus making them unsuitable for colonization."

Raffles shook his head. "I still hold the position that the treaty was premature. We should have learned more of these islands before agreeing to such conditions. I fear Britain will regret signing this treaty with the Dutch one day."

"Well, regret it or not," Sir Thomas said, "Parliament has ratified the treaty and so it appears that England will make do with what it has left. In my opinion, our interests in India, Malaya and China are much more valuable to us than anything the Dutch have retained."

"I quite agree, Thomas," Lord Gray affirmed. Then, as to put finality on the discussion he asked, "Another brandy perhaps, Sir Thomas?"

"Of course." Thomas rose and poured each of the men brandy from a hand cut decanter.

But Raffles wouldn't let the subject die. "Parliament may have finalized the treaty, but they have yet to deal with the sticky problem of Borneo."

"Borneo? Isn't that the large island previously claimed by both Britain and the Dutch?" George Barton asked.

*Borneo!* The very name held magic for James. He thought of Si Tundok and the many stories he and Arthur Claygate had told him about Borneo and the lands surrounding it. Intent to learn more, James pressed himself forward in his chair and listened to Sir Stamford's response.

"Yes," Raffles said, smiling somewhat smugly. "Fortunately, Parliament knows less of latitude lines than it thinks it knows of treaties."

"Really, Sir Stamford," Lord Gray protested. "One minor oversight certainly doesn't mean the entire treaty is a waste."

"I'm not certain I understand," James said.

"As I stated previously, James, the treaty divides the region into two distinct spheres of influence defined by the line of the Equinoctial. Anything north of the line is Britain's to control, south of the line belongs to the Dutch—except those areas already settled by other sovereign nations such as the Spanish in the Philippines, of course."

"Then where is the problem?" James asked.

Raffles almost gleamed with delight. He noticed Lord Gray shifting uncomfortably. "Because Borneo, the largest island in the archipelago, partially lies within the British sphere! And although the Dutch have gained concessions from the Sultan of Pontianak and have already established trading stations on the southwest coast of Borneo, imagine their surprise when they get around to the north coast of the island and see the Union Jack flapping in the breeze."

"Posh!" Lord Gray replied. "I doubt Parliament would challenge the Dutch even if they wanted to settle the whole damnable island. Of what consequence is one small territory to His Majesty's Empire anyway?"

"Of what consequence, indeed?" Raffles parroted. "You seem to forget, your Lordship, that western and northern Borneo is located between China and the Malacca Straits. In my estimation that makes Borneo strategically vital to the British interests in the area. I might add that there may be coal deposits on many of these islands. If coal is found on Borneo, then these new ships—'steamers,' I believe they are called—will revolutionize control of the sea."

"Steamers? Hah! About as important to sea travel as the stock you put in the strategic value of Borneo, I'm afraid, Sir Stamford," Lord Gray countered. "Wouldn't you agree, Sir Thomas?"

"I'm inclined to think it quite impossible to replace the English tall ships. I can't imagine a British frigate cruising around the world dependent upon carrying its own fuel," Thomas answered. "Mother Nature's winds have always been sufficient to propel British ships around the globe faster and with less mishap than any of the Continentals. I simply can't see coal-burning ships replacing the reliability of a solidly built, sail-rigged frigate. What say you, George?"

All eyes strayed to the quiet man who had not taken part in the debate. "Oh, well, I..." he stammered, trying to stay above the controversy and not risking the chance he might offend any of these important people, "...I agree with you, Sir Thomas, but then again, perhaps these steamers have possibilities."

James, cognizant of George's discomfort, said, "Another brandy, anyone?"

"Not I, thank you, James. Actually it's time Lady Gray and I take our leave. It's been a most enjoyable evening, Sir Thomas, but we really must attend to our ward, Elizabeth. We try not to keep one her age out too late, you understand?"

As if Lord Gray's pronouncement was a signal to the others, both Sir Stamford and George Barton also announced they were leaving and conveyed their gratitude to Sir Thomas for the enjoyable evening. As the men trailed through the hallway to collect their wives, coats and hats, Sir Stamford lagged behind and touched James on the arm.

"I'm afraid we really didn't get around to specifically answering the question you proposed earlier, James—about potential opportunity in the Orient," Sir Stamford said, almost conspiratorially. "However, if you feel up to listening to the opinions of an old man...some say, an old fool..." Raffles nodded curtly in the direction of Lord Gray, "...then I would be most pleased to discuss the matter further if you so desire."

"I would be delighted and honored, sir," James said graciously. "When would it be convenient?"

"Tomorrow, afternoon tea. I'm currently staying in my summer cottage. Your father or any of your household staff can give you directions, I'm sure."

"Tomorrow afternoon, then. I'll look forward to it."

The conversation in the parlor among the women had been more mundane than the men's had been. Lady Gray was a tall stuffy woman with sweeping gray hair and a porcelain complexion. Her countenance was as stiff as her skinny frame was tall and her manner was insufferable, haughty and aloof.

Harriet Barton, although expensively dressed, was a woman of simple tastes and simple pleasures. Affairs of this sort bordered on the intolerable for her, but she generally managed to endure her discomfort with aplomb, knowing that such gatherings were important to her husband's success.

If it hadn't have been for the gracious hospitality of Anne Brooke and the enchantingly delightful wit of the Gray's niece, Elizabeth, the women would have found themselves with nothing in common to discuss.

"Perhaps I shall reside at Wethington castle when I come of age," Elizabeth answered in response to a question about what her future held for her.

"That dreary place? I can't imagine you would even consider it, Elizabeth," Lady Gray said with a sour curl of her lips.

"I think castles are charming," Elizabeth countered.

"And so big," Anne Brooke offered.

"And cold...I would guess," said Mrs. Barton. Her eyes flitted to each of the older women for confirmation that castles were, as Harriet suspected, cold.

"Oh, I don't intend to live alone," Elizabeth said. She shook her head emphatically and as she did so, her curls bounced delightfully around her pretty face. "Heavens no," she laughed. "A castle is much too big for one person. I intend to have a husband by then. Children too, perhaps."

"Elizabeth! Your are much too young to be talking of such things," Lady Gray chastened.

"I'll soon be seventeen. More than old enough to know my own mind." Elizabeth smiled at her aunt but her deep brown eyes had defiance written on them. "Besides," she chuckled, "a castle is cold, as Harriet said, and I shall need someone to keep me warm."

Lady Gray gasped, looked askance and fanned herself furiously with a lace handkerchief.

Harriet Barton chuckled to herself and admitted that she liked this brassy ward of the Grays'—even if it was only because she put a barb in Lady Gray's overstuffed ego.

Anne Brooke merely smiled pleasantly and said, "More tea, ladies?"

Elizabeth smiled inwardly. She delighted in shocking her staid aunt more than anything else. But her remark wasn't altogether flippant. At eighteen, she would inherit her family estates and a substantial sum of money which was held in trust for her and she had made up her mind that she wouldn't stay with the Gray's one minute longer than was necessary by the term's of her father's will.

She hadn't been entirely joking about having a man by then either. She often fantasized about Phillip Ansley; he was reasonably good looking and Elizabeth knew he was infatuated with her. But next to the dashing son of the Brookes', James, whom she had met for the first time that evening, Phillip Ansley was a dullard. James was seven years her senior but, unlike Phillip and the other young men she had known, James was a man. James was extraordinarily tall and ruggedly handsome and she was enchanted by his easy smile which responded synchronously to the flash of his deep blue eyes. *And he was brave and so exciting! Imagine, wounded in combat by naked savages*—as Elizabeth presumed the Burmese to be-*while rescuing his men.* Such a man would definitely need further consideration.

Already Elizabeth schemed of a way to get to know the dashing Lieutenant Brooke better. She smiled easily the remainder of the evening, no matter what boring things the old ladies discussed, pleased with how her thoughts of James Brooke made her feel.

IV

A Country Lane
Near Raffles' Cottage

Rain had fallen during the night and an unseasonably cold afternoon drizzle sliced through a thick, lingering fog along the path where James rode. The air was thick and humid and both horse and rider emitted puffs of phantom-like vapors from their nostrils.

James, filled with enthusiasm following his scheduled meeting with Raffles earlier that afternoon, was tempted to give his mount his head and sprint the remaining few kilometers to Brooke Manor. Instead, he chose to tolerate the cold and damp and slowed his pace to ponder the exciting things he had learned from Sir Stamford about the Far East.

"The Sultan of Brunei controls all of this area along the north and west coasts of Borneo, including the territory of Sarawak," Raffles said. He had displayed an assortment of maps and documents to illustrate the points he was making and he spoke with rapid-fire enthusiasm. "And the Sultan of Sulu controls this section of north Borneo and most of this area of the Philippines, Raffles said, pointing to a map. "And the Sultan of Pontianak controls this large area of south Borneo. Actually the territories contract and expand from time to time because the three Sultans are constantly squabbling with one another."

"I have read many of your treatise on the islands of the East Indies, Sir Stamford," James said. "You indicate that they abound with spices and minerals, but I've not read anything specifically about Borneo."

Sir Stamford drew James' attention to the blank interior of the map of Borneo. "As you can see, James, we know little of the coastline of the island and practically nothing about the interior. Borneo has not yet been explored. But, I strongly suspect that if it follows suite with the other islands in the area, the Spice Islands, as they are called, then it *must* contain tremendous resources."

James' mind raced with excitement. *Imagine, a virgin land, possibly abounding in riches, awaiting to be explored!*

"And what of the people? Is anything known about them?"

"The Malay rule the coastal areas and have a nebulous suzerainty over the indigenous population whom they refer to as 'Dayaks'. To the best of my knowledge the Dayaks are actually comprised of many distinct tribes of savages, headhunters, I'm told, but no one knows for certain. It's also my understanding that some of the Dayaks are involved in piracy, probably with the blessings of the Sultans or some of the more powerful Malay princes."

"Sounds inhospitable," James said.

"It is," Raffles confirmed. "But the real reason His Majesty's government hasn't had much interest in Borneo is its position in the South China Sea. As you can see from the map, the island is rather far removed from the generally acceptable trade routes from Southeast Asia to China. That, and, of course, the unusually heavy activity of piracy in the region."

"I gathered from the discussion last night that Lord Gray is of the opinion that England would cede its claim to Brunei and Sarawak if the Dutch pushed for it," James said.

"As much as I hate to say it, he's right on that matter." Raffles sighed deeply and said, "All of my protestations have been for nothing, I'm afraid. Without an active English presence in the area, Brunei and Sarawak will eventually become Dutch colonies and, I predict, one day England will regret the opportunity it squandered."

"Although the Crown has no interest in Borneo, wouldn't it be possible for a private enterprise to explore possibilities within the English sector?" James asked.

Raffles was hoping for the question. He suspected James' intentions all along and had invited James to his cottage that day specifically to encourage him. Sir Stamford was not interested so much in anyone making his fortune from the exploitation of the island as he was convinced that British interests would best be served if an English enterprise forced Britain to maintain control of Brunei and Sarawak.

"It would not be an easy task," Raffles said in all honesty. "His Majesty's government is not currently disposed to protect private endeavors outside of currently established colonies, but if I were a young man with such interests, I would seek an agreement with the Sultan of Brunei for concessions to trading and mining rights."

"Wouldn't the Crown frown on such a pact by a private concern?" James asked.

"Most probably," Raffles grinned. "But they can't prevent it. As bad as the treaty with the Dutch is, Brunei and Sarawak still belong in the British sphere and I would suspect that if such a document is granted by the Sultan of Brunei to a private concern, His Majesty's government would be forced to accept it." Sir Stamford then tossed James a wizened eye and asked, "You wouldn't be considering such an enterprise, would you, James?"

James smiled his easy smile and walked around the table containing the maps and documents and absorbed as many of the details of them as he could. "I intend to make my fortune in the Far East, Sir Stamford. The East India

Company controls all of the British territories there with the exception of Borneo. It appears to me that Borneo would be a particularly good place to start." James glanced up from the array of maps and his deep blue eyes twinkled, signaling his inner excitement.

Watching James' enthusiasm exude, Raffles wondered if his encouragement was a disservice to the young man so he said, "You haven't chosen to ignore the dangers such an enterprise poses, have you, James?"

"Life is full of danger, Sir Stamford," James responded. "But it is my contention that only those who dare greatly will be rewarded in proportion to their courage."

"Well said, James, but I feel it is my duty as a friend of your father's to point these things out to you."

"I appreciate your candor, Sir Stamford."

"And since I'm being so candid, might I not add that I believe your father would not be supportive if you pursued your interests in Borneo? I think he has pinned his hopes on your career with the East India Company."

James sighed. "Yes, my father," he said slowly. "He adamantly opposes any suggestion that I resign my commission. He's determined that I continue a career with the Company."

"I detect that you are not totally enamored with the prospects of such a career?"

"Not at all," James said, placing his palm on the map of Borneo. "This will be my career...one day."

"I see..." Sir Stamford placed a wrinkled hand to his mutton-chop whiskers and rubbed them thoughtfully. "And how do you intend to resolve this conflict between your desires and your father's wishes?" he asked.

James shrugged and said, "I have two years remaining on my commission. I have given my word that I will complete my tour. After that, well..." Again James shrugged.

"Your father is a fine man, James. I would hate to see him disappointed. But I can also understand your point of view. Regardless of the outcome, I wish you well."

Then as an afterthought, Raffles reached into his coat pocket and extracted a sealed envelope and handed it to James. "I almost forgot. I prepared this letter for you."

"Oh, what is it?"

"It's a letter of introduction for you to present to Samuel McDonald."

"The Governor-General of Singapore?"

"The very same. Samuel's an old friend of mine. If you ever make your way to Singapore, Samuel may be of assistance to you."

James thanked Sir Stamford for the meeting and the letter of introduction and then shook his hand. It was the last time the two men would see each other, and as the fire of life diminished in one, it blazed in the other.

The weather had not improved by the time James exited Sir Stamford's cottage and rode towards home. But he was in no hurry to get out of the drizzle and cold. He pulled his cape tightly around his neck, mounted his horse and rode towards Brooke Manor at a leisurely pace all the while contemplating what he had learned from Raffles and the irresolvable dilemma between himself and his father. So engrossed in thought was he, that he almost passed by a riderless horse and a person seated on a nearby fallen log.

"James! Thank goodness you happened along!"

"Miss Wethington! What on earth are you doing out here in this weather?" He dismounted and led his horse to the side of the road and looked down in puzzlement at Elizabeth. "Is something the matter?" He surveyed the area with some concern.

With a brazenness which was part of her nature, Elizabeth wrapped her arm around James' and led him to her horse. She smiled effusively, satisfied that her plan had worked.

"Whatever are you doing so far from home on a day like this, Miss Wethington?" James asked, still confused by Elizabeth's surprise appearance. James' baffled face peered down at the petite young lady as she led him to her horse. Her auburn curls bounced gaily from beneath her hooded cape and her smooth, white face was ringed with pink kisses from the chilly air which nipped her nose and the ridges of her cheeks and chin. Her easy smile and dancing eyes were almost too much for him and he reluctantly looked away.

Elizabeth shrugged and said, "I just felt like riding, James," she lied. "I didn't realize how far I had strayed or that the weather was going to remain so nasty. I started to return home, but my saddle kept slipping. I tried to tighten the cinch, but I guess I'm not strong enough."

Elizabeth overheard Sir Stamford's invitation to James the previous evening and knew James would be returning this way after his meeting with Raffles and she had ridden out in the early afternoon with the intention of meeting with him. She was chilled to the bone, but now that the tall man was by her side, she willingly let his closeness flood her with inner warmth.

"Here, hold my horse's reins and I'll see what I can do," James said when they approached Elizabeth's horse. James passed the reins to her and patted the neck of Elizabeth's mare. He could tell by the lack of vapor from the horses nostrils and the cool of its hide that the horse had been standing, unridden for quite some time. "The cinch, you say?" James ducked under the horse's flank and checked the cinch. It was lose, but not unfastened. He pulled on the leather belt and easily fastened the cinch beneath the horse's broad belly nearly two notches from where it had been. He was surprised at how easily the belt tightened, but he didn't suspect that it was part of Elizabeth's ruse to meet with him.

"There, that should do it," James said, patting the big mare on the side of the neck. He turned back to Elizabeth and added, "I had better see you home. It will be dark soon and I'm certain that Lord and Lady Gray will be concerned with your whereabouts."

"Oh, how thoughtful of you, James. I really don't know what I would have done if you hadn't happened along."

"You're chilled. Here, take my cape." Without waiting for Elizabeth to protest, James unfastened his cape and draped it around her thin shoulders. Elizabeth covered his hands beneath her neck for a moment and flashed him a grateful smile.

"Thank you, James. That is so kind of you. But you will catch a chill of your own, I fear."

Suddenly conscious that Elizabeth's hands held his close to her bosom, James, somewhat embarrassed, pulled his hands away and said, "I'll be fine. Let me help you onto your horse."

Elizabeth felt James' strong hands encircle her waist and hoist her onto the side-saddle. He was several heads taller than her horse and she considered bending down and kissing him, but she controlled her impulse to be indiscrete. James Brooke was truly more of a man than Phillip Ansley or any of the other young men she knew and she decided to bide her time and nurture him well.

James swung himself gracefully into his own saddle and the two of them turned their horses and headed down the road to the Gray Estate. As they rode, Elizabeth talked rapidly, she laughed easily and her eyes seldom strayed long from James.

Before long, James found he was no longer thinking of his conversation with Raffles or the anticipation of exploring Borneo. His thoughts riveted solely on this pretty and spirited ward of the Grays and soon James began thinking of other adventures.

# V

## Northwest of London

Arthur Claygate and his new bride of six months, Margaret Johnson rode together in the back of a chaise on their way to London where Arthur had rented a small flat, temporary living quarters for them until they received their assignment from the Anglican Missionary Society.

As the only two passengers in the carriage, they sat close to one another, Arthur with his burley arm around his wife's sloping shoulders and she with her head and hat tucked lovingly against the side of his broad chest, both content to simply watch the late summer landscape roll by.

"Are you happy, Arthur?" Margaret asked, not for the first time. Margaret needed the reassurance. At twenty-nine years of age, Margaret had almost given up her prospects for marriage before her father's long time acquaintance proposed to her following his most recent return from the Far East. Margaret was aware that she was not an attractive woman; scarecrow thin and fragile, with an ashen complexion that shrouded small, innocuous brown eyes and gaunt lips that perpetually turned upwards in a Madonna-like grin. She wore her straight, light brown hair curled in a tight knot at the top of her head and generally covered her head with an unpretentious hat without color, ornamentation or flair. All in all, observers would consider Margaret drab.

Arthur squeezed his wife firmly on her shoulders. "I couldn't be happier," he said, and pecked her lightly on the cheek.

Arthur saw beyond his wife's limited physical attributes and found a kind and gentle soul who radiated an inner peace that touched the hearts and spirit of those around her. And Margaret was tolerant, too. She ignored Arthur's many shortcomings, attributing them to his having spent so much time in the company of seamen. But as odd as the two of them appeared to be at first glance, it wouldn't be long before even a casual observer would ascertain that they had a deep and abiding affection for one another.

She patted him on his knee with her gloved hand. "I'm so excited with the prospect of the work we have ahead of us." Margaret nuzzled her head against his chest, nestling her face in the warmth of his embrace.

"I only hope you don't find our assignment too taxing for you, my dear. The trip alone can sometimes wear one down."

"I'm not worried," she said, smiling. "My husband is a doctor. He will take care of me."

110

"Correction, madam. Your husband *was* a doctor. He is now a missionary." Margaret's father, Bishop Andrew Johnson was known by reputation to be one of the most pious and God-fearing churchmen in all of England and even though he realized that his eldest daughter had few prospects for marriage, he insisted that she marry only a clergyman or missionary. For Arthur, becoming a missionary was a small price to pay for a wife such as he considered Margaret to be. And so far, he had no regrets.

"I love the sound of that word, *missionary*," Margaret said. "Where do you suppose the Society will send us, Arthur?"

Although Arthur hoped they would be sent to the Far East, perhaps China, he said, "Wherever we can be together for the rest of our lives."

Margaret snuggled closer and thanked God for sending such a man to her so that, together, they could do His work. "Really, Arthur, don't you have a preference? Africa perhaps or maybe the New World, South America?"

"No, I really don't, darling. You forget that I have seen most of this magnificent globe and as far as I am concerned one place is as good as another. However, a warm climate would be nice."

"Yes, the tropics, somewhere in the tropics," Margaret said with enthusiasm. "That *would* be nice, wouldn't it?"

Arthur's eyes sparkled. "Yes, the tropics would be nice, but it would take a great deal of getting used to for you, I'm afraid to say."

"Oh, why is that, Arthur? The heat?"

"No, not exactly. You see, most tropical natives generally go about their business in the buff."

"You mean-?" Shocked, Margaret couldn't make herself say the word.

"That's right, my dear, naked. As naked as red-bottomed newborns. Do you think your sense of decorum could handle that?" he teased.

Margaret slapped him lightly on the chest when she finally realized that he was joking. "Oh, you tease, you!" she said. "But even if it was the custom, it would be precisely the reason our work is so important. We must civilize and educate them, teach them the proper way God expects His children to conduct themselves."

Arthur had no illusions as to his wife's naivete, but he elected to let her discover what the world offered for herself. "Yes, I'm certain God would prefer that His children be civilized and properly clothed," he said.

"Oh, Arthur, the very thought of our mission excites me so!"

Arthur tightened his embrace about his wife and said, "It excites me too, darling." He kissed her full on her small lips, knowing that it wasn't the thought of missionary work which excited him, but rather the thought of making love when they reached London.

# VI

## The River Wensum
## Near Bath, England

James spent the few remaining weeks before he was scheduled to depart from England for Madras reading and copying all the information he could gather which pertained to the islands of Southeast Asia, particularly Borneo. The more he read, the more convinced he became that Raffles was correct in his assessment of Borneo. Largely ignoring the political entanglements, James focused his attention on the financial rewards such an endeavor might provide.

But James worried a great deal too. His father had suffered greatly during the past few weeks. Sir Thomas had lost weight and the coughing spells had increased. No matter what their differences were in regard to James' future, James loved and respected his father and concern for his father's well-being affected him greatly.

But there was a pleasant side to his final weeks in England—Elizabeth Wethington. James conceded that the woman was well worth pursuing and he had seen her often since his chance encounter with her following his meeting with Sir Stamford. He shared with her his ambitions and his dreams and also his disappointment on having to wait to seek his fortune until his commission expired. James told Elizabeth of his own family and the death of his brother, Henry.

And once, curious to see what her reaction would be, he discussed life in the Far East with her. He spoke of the climate, living conditions and regaled her with the many things he had seen and done.

But while Elizabeth feigned interest in James' desire for adventure in the Orient, Elizabeth was far from enthusiastic about life in a land which she imagined to be uncivilized and brutal. To James' disappointment, she commented that she would find living in any foreign land other than France to be an intolerable nuisance and she couldn't imagine why anyone would deliberately choose such a life. But she was aware that James would be leaving soon and the thought of losing him was beginning to weigh heavily on her heart and signaling to her how much she was in love with him.

She understood that she could not bear having him leave her now and she regaled him with stories of her impending inheritance and how she intended to take up her residence at Wethington castle and alluded to how two people in love could find comfort in such a place and raise children and be happy ever after. Elizabeth bubbled with enthusiasm when she spoke of marrying an English gentleman, intending to make James jealous, hoping he would go against his father's wishes, resign his commission and stay with her. She would find a way to make him forget his thoughts of adventure and fortune-seeking in far off lands if she had the time. She was sure of it.

And time weighed heavily on James also. He was infatuated with Elizabeth and he couldn't stand the thought of returning to India and risk losing her to an 'English gentleman'. But he couldn't break his promise to his father or give up his dream of adventure in the Far East either. After days of pondering his options, James made a decision. He would ask her to marry him and take her to India with him. When his commission expired, he would fulfill his plan of exploration with Elizabeth accompanying him. James had already booked his return passage aboard the *Castle Huntley* and he would be departing shortly. If Elizabeth was to join him on the voyage as his wife, he would have to ask her hand in marriage soon.

It was a gorgeous early autumn day, sunny and warm as James expertly maneuvered the skiff's rudder and sailed the skiff along the west bank of the River Wensum.

Elizabeth snuggled closely to him and maintained a lively conversation about the landmarks they passed along the river's edges. "Where did you learn to sail so skillfully, James?"

"When I was a boy. Sailing had a special fascination for me—more so than attending boarding school on a regular basis," he chuckled mirthfully. "When the day was warm and there was a breeze in the air, I often came to the river and sailed up and down, sometimes by myself, occasionally with a friend or two who I managed to persuade to come along. Those were grand times."

"You naughty boy, James. Neglecting your studies like that. I guess you knew your own mind then as well as you do now."

"What do you mean by that?"

"You seem so confident about everything you do. Like the way you sail this boat. It's as if everything about you is under control."

James laughed and said, "It is just an illusion. Actually, I'm mad as a hatter, you just haven't noticed."

"Should I be worried?"

"Worried? Why?"

"You being mad and all. Certainly you must have entertained thoughts of taking advantage of me and my innocence by now?" she said, her eyes fluttering suggestively.

At times, Elizabeth was too brash and her suggestive comments often made James uncomfortable. Not that he didn't entertain such ideas, but his sense of propriety had kept his passions in check.

But James chuckled anyway and said, "A gentleman doesn't take advantage of another's innocence, mad or not."

Elizabeth drew away from him and pretended to pout. Shortly she pointed to a secluded cove along the far bank and said with excitement, "There, James. Sail the boat to that cove. It will be a beautiful spot for our picnic."

James turned the rudder and the skiff instantly darted across the river's current and slid into the isolated cove. James dropped the sail and secured the craft to the shore while Elizabeth found a small clearing between a grove of ancient oak trees and spread out a blanket.

After they had eaten the ample picnic lunch Elizabeth had packed and were sipping the remnants of a bottle of white wine, Elizabeth asked, "You have been awfully quiet today, James. Is something the matter?"

James shifted uncomfortably on the blanket. "I'll be returning to my post in India shortly and—"

The news shocked Elizabeth. "I didn't realize it would be so soon. Why didn't you tell me earlier, James?"

"I had other things on my mind, I guess. I was hoping things might turn out differently by now...for us, I mean."

Elizabeth edged closer to him and put her hands in his. "What ever do you mean to say, James?"

James gazed into her inquiring eyes and brushed his hand through her curls. She was the loveliest creature he had ever seen. "I believe I'm in love with you, Elizabeth. I wish for you to be my wife." The words he worried about saying flowed easily from his mouth and all thoughts of his commission, of India and of adventure vanished when he beheld her beauty.

"Oh, James," she said, softly. She threw her arms around his neck and pulled him to her. "How I have longed for you to say those words. I love you and I *will* be your wife."

Elizabeth drew him closer to her and placed her full, moist lips to his cheek before he could say another word. She circled her tongue around his ear and lightly bit his earlobe. Their passions were aroused simultaneously and neither failed to respond to the other's caress or kiss.

For Elizabeth, her lovemaking was the culmination of a carefully designed plan to sample a real man and take him for her husband. Her affair with young Phillip Ansley and the others had been stimulating, but it didn't arouse the fire and passion she now felt. This moment was the culmination of her desire and her fantasy. In her mind she was no longer a girl content to entertain mere boys and simple pleasures. She was a woman now and she longed to taste the delights that only a grown man like James had aroused in her.

James was consumed by her. Whatever sense of propriety he had vanished with the press of her lips to his and he wanted her now more than he ever wanted anything in his life.

Elizabeth guided him into her and within minutes they both lay exhausted and satisfied, entwined in each other's embrace. Elizabeth smiled sweetly and touched him tenderly along the side of his face with her fingers. Neither of them spoke. She ran her fingers through his red-blonde curls. She was satisfied. She had conquered the man she most wanted to possess and it had been more wonderful than she imagined it could be. "What are you thinking, my darling?" she asked, softly.

James averted his eyes from her nakedness and said, despondently, "I'm so sorry, Elizabeth."

"James, dearest, whatever for do you have reason to apologize? Didn't you find the experience to your liking? Didn't I please you?"

"Yes, yes," he said, quickly. "You were wonderful. But I shouldn't have taken advantage of you the way I did. For that I apologize."

Suddenly James became aware of his own nakedness and he reached for his trousers. "Perhaps you should dress and we should leave," he said.

Elizabeth raised her naked arm and pulled her to him once again. She laughed. "Oh, James, don't be such a ninny. We were only expressing our love to one another, that's all. I want you to see me as I am, and I want to see you. Kiss me, James. Kiss me again...please." She closed her eyes and pressed her full lips to him. As before, James felt his resolve melt away by the heat of her touch. How happy they would be in India, he thought as he kissed her passionately and lowered her slowly to the blanket where he allowed her to consume him once again.

# VII

*HMS Castle Huntley*
London, England

James stood on the dock near the *Castle Huntley* amid the throngs of departing passengers and the bustle of the longshoremen and said his final farewell to his father and mother. Sir Thomas' solicitor, George Barton, had graciously offered to escort them to the ship in his own carriage and James shook the quiet man's hand and told him how much he appreciated the kind gesture.

"Think nothing of it, Mister Brooke," George said. "If there is anything I can ever do, please do not hesitate to write." Already James had expressed his concern over his father's health and had asked George to watch over him and inform James of Sir Thomas' progress.

James turned to his parents and embraced each of them in turn and then joined the crowd boarding the ship. He found an open space near a railing and waved to George and his parents and then cast a melancholy glance toward the congregated crowd, hoping to catch a glimpse of Elizabeth. But, as he expected, she had not come to see him off and his heart sank to previously unknown depths with the certainty that he had lost her forever.

When they discussed marriage that day on the bank of the Wensum River, Elizabeth imposed conditions. She offered her consent only if James resigned his commission and stayed in England. She explained that she could not endure the hardships and deprivations the Colonial life offered and cajoled him with her impending inheritance and the life of leisure and luxury it would provide the two of them.

James agonized over what to do. Should he resign his commission, marry Elizabeth and settle into the easy life of an English aristocrat? Could he break his oath to his father? Could he forget the dreams he had of finding his fortune in the Far East, of becoming a self-made man?

Finally, on the day before his scheduled departure, James explained to Elizabeth the oath he had made to his father and how he was honor bound to keep it. He asked her to wait for him for the two years he had remaining on his commission, but she turned petulant and informed him that although she loved him deeply, he could not expect her to wait. She too, had promises to keep—the promises she had made to herself, to marry early, reside at Wethington Castle and have children. As James would keep his promises, she would keep hers.

Now, as James stood staring vacantly into the throngs along the wharf, he wished he had agreed to Elizabeth's demands. What kind of life would he have without her? he wondered. For a brief, insane instant, James considered rushing down the gangplank, finding Elizabeth, and agreeing to her conditions. But it was too late. The *Castle Huntley* eased away from the harbor and James waved a final farewell to his parents and somberly turned his back on England and the life he might have had.

### HMS Castle Huntley

The *Castle Huntley* loomed like a prehistoric beast as it lumbered into the open sea beyond the sight of land. The twelve-hundred ton frigate was as much a cargo ship as she was a warship. Fifty-two eighteen pound guns lined her upper deck. Below, her cargo holds brimmed full with English trade goods, mostly pig iron and manufactured products which would be exchanged for the produce of the Orient and the pound notes of the English colonists in India, Malaya and Hong Kong. Because of her weight and draft, the *Castle Huntley* was literally the slow boat to China, her final destination.

Saddened, James went directly to his small quarters aft of the captain's cabin. He saw to it that his luggage and personal effects had all been attended to and carefully stored in the cabin's shallow locker before he sullenly sprawled upon a built-in cot which was several inches too short for his long frame. He tried to escape his misery in sleep, but his thoughts continually strayed to Elizabeth and their final moments together. Finally, gloomy and morose and without sleep to rescue him, James hoisted himself from the cot and went topside with the hope that the scent of fresh air would mellow his memories and quiet his aching heart.

"Lieutenant! Lieutenant Brooke! James, is that you?"

Abruptly, James turned to the sound of his name being called from the starboard railing. It was Arthur Claygate and he was dragging a twig of a woman behind him as he hastily approached.

"Arthur! My God, what a pleasant surprise!" James exclaimed. He couldn't have asked for a better remedy to soothe his growing depression than reuniting with the affable surgeon.

The two men shook hands vigorously and clasped one another on the shoulders. "Forgive me, James," Arthur said, withdrawing. "Allow me to introduce my wife, Margaret John...I mean, Margaret *Claygate*." Arthur beamed with pride as he pulled his wife forward to greet James.

"Mrs. Claygate. I'm honored to meet you. Arthur told me a great deal about you."

Margaret glanced quizzically at her husband and Arthur shuffled his feet like an embarrassed schoolboy and quickly explained. "James and I returned to England together on the *Rainbow*. It was my last voyage as ship's surgeon and James' first trip as a wounded Army officer, right, James?"

Before James could answer, Margaret said, "Oh, dear, I do hope it wasn't serious Lieutenant Brooke."

"No, my lady, your husband is as masterful a physician as he is a chess player. Not only was Arthur responsible for restoring my health, but he was also responsible for making an otherwise tedious voyage most tolerable."

"I assume you are returning to your post in India, James?" Arthur asked.

James sighed, revealing his disappointment and said, "Unfortunately, yes. I am to report to headquarters in Calcutta by the end of December."

"Do I detect from the tone of your voice that you would much prefer pursuing your plans for adventure instead?" Arthur inquired.

James almost revealed the depths of his heartache and the mistake he felt he made leaving Elizabeth and England behind, but he didn't. Instead, he forced a smile and said, "I couldn't keep your stories out of my mind, Arthur. I'm still intent to follow my stars but, for the time being at least, I'll have to remain content in the Company's service."

"Don't take it too hard, my boy," Arthur said, clasping James' shoulder. "You are still young. There is plenty of time for you to fulfill your dreams, believe me when I say that." Arthur winked and pulled his wife affectionately close to him.

"Arthur and I are on our way to Towchi. That's in China, Lieutenant Brooke." Margaret chimed.

James observed that when Margaret smiled, her face appeared more pained than pleasant, but nevertheless, she radiated a sense of peace and calm that James found delightful. "China? Whatever for?"

"Arthur and I will be opening a missionary station there. We're so very excited, aren't we, Arthur?"

"Indeed we are," Arthur replied.

"A mission? You are giving up medicine, Arthur?" James asked, perplexed.

"Oh, no, James. Simply combining the two professions. It is my understanding that doctoring is as much a part of missionary work as spreading the Word of God."

Margaret gazed proudly upon her husband. She knew Arthur was not a devoutly religious man, but she was convinced that he was a good man. And for a good man, there was hope that he would be given the gift of understanding God's joy one day. "As you are most probably aware, Lieutenant, Arthur is not a formally trained clergyman," she said, "but I know that it is God's will that once we begin our work with the poor and deprived, God will work His miracle upon my husband. I expect he will become as good a missionary as you have indicated he is a surgeon and chess player."

"I'm confident that you are right, Mrs. Claygate." But James had his doubts based upon earlier conversations between he and Arthur. It was

James' contention—and Arthur agreed—that native races should be allowed to retain the religion of their culture. It presented fewer administrative problems and reduced the friction between natives and colonists. They both agreed, however, that there was nothing wrong with missions providing the native races with an education and a sense of Christian morality. At least in their view, it caused no harm.

As they continued their dialogue, it became increasingly obvious to James, judging by what was said and the manner in which Arthur doted upon his wife, that Arthur had made concessions to gain the woman he loved. James could respect that and, at that moment, wished he had made similar concessions.

Although nothing erased the ache in his heart and his thoughts of lost love, James was pleased to have the company of the Claygates on the long voyage to India. They would help him pass the time and, perhaps more importantly, help ease the memory of Elizabeth which haunted him every waking moment.

# CHAPTER FIVE

## I

December 28, 1825
Madras, India

Fickle winds and fierce storms delayed the *Castle Huntley's* arrival in Madras by nearly four weeks and James realized it would be impossible to report to his regiment, now stationed in Calcutta, before his leave expired on the last day of the month. As much as he hated the prospect of returning to duty, James hated parting company with the Claygates even more. Both Margaret and Arthur had proven to be pleasant and entertaining company on the long voyage and the three of them had formed a bond of friendship that James found difficult to sever as they conveyed their final farewells.

"I do hope the Army will consider the circumstances of your late arrival, James," Arthur said as he and Margaret escorted James to the departure gangplank.

James shrugged and said, "I don't think it will be a problem. I'll just report to the post here in Madras and request a change of orders." It sounded simple enough, but James wasn't too sure. He knew how the Army felt about those who were absent without leave—often leaping to the conclusion that they had deserted—and the fetid cell where he first found Si Tundok and Henry was still fresh in his mind.

"God willing, I'm sure everything will work out fine for you James," Margaret chimed, with the same pained, but ebullient smile that James had come to know so well during the course of the voyage.

"I'm sure you're right, Margaret." James turned at the railing adjacent to the gangplank and faced them both. "Well, I guess it's time to say good-bye. You both have made what might otherwise have been a lonely and tedious voyage most enjoyable and I will miss each of you very much."

"Likewise, James," Arthur said and then surprised James by throwing his arms about James' shoulders and embracing him tightly to his barrel chest. "You take care of yourself, my friend," he whispered in James' ear.

"I will. You too, Arthur." A lump welled up in James' throat and he found himself struggling to contain his emotions. James disengaged himself from Arthur's embrace and leaned over and hugged Margaret and kissed her gently on the cheek.

"Goodbye, James," she said. "Our prayers will always be with you."

James said a final farewell to each of them and sadly walked down the gangplank without turning to wave and without revealing the single tear that rolled down his cheek.

## II

### Regimental Headquarters
### Madras, India

After leaving the *Castle Huntley* and the Claygates, James made hasty arrangements to have himself and his luggage taken by carriage to the East Indian Army garrison located several kilometers north of Madras. His intention was to request the Adjutant-General to issue orders temporarily assigning him to duty in Madras until he could be transferred to his unit now stationed in Calcutta.

"The Adjutant-General will see you now, Lieutenant Brooke."

"Thank you, Corporal." James had been waiting in the Adjutant-General's hot office for nearly two hours. He was in uniform, but the dusty ride from the seaport to the Army base gave James the mussed appearance of having returned from a long patrol.

Quickly, he wiped a plume of dust from the silver braid along the sleeves of his uniform and straightened the folds of his blue dress jacket. He tucked his cap beneath his left arm and marched into the Adjutant-General's office and in front of the post-officer's tidy desk, snapped to attention and saluted smartly.

"Lieutenant James Brooke, 6$^{th}$ Bengal Light, reporting for duty and permission to speak, sir!" James' eyes fixed themselves to a spot on the wall above the head of the Adjutant-General.

The Adjutant-General looked up at James and studied him for a moment before he tossed his quill pen to the table, leaned back in his chair and said, "At ease, Lieutenant. What can I do for you?"

"Sir, I'm afraid I'm in a bit of a pickle to be honest, sir. I am returning from convalescence leave in England and am to report to my unit by the last day of the month, sir."

The officer behind the desk frowned beneath his heavy white sideburns and matching mustache. "I fail to see your point, Lieutenant. The 6$^{th}$ Bengal Light Horse is assigned to His Majesty's service in Calcutta, is it not?"

"Yes, sir, it is, but..."

"Then why are you reporting for duty here?"

James explained how his return to India had been delayed and then added, "Given my late arrival, I will be unable to reach Calcutta before the date specified in my orders, sir. Therefore, I am requesting temporary assignment here, in Madras, until I can affect a transfer to my regiment, sir."

The Adjutant-General cocked his head and stared into James' face until James began to shift uncomfortably under the man's scrutiny. Finally, the Adjutant-General dropped his eyes and pulled at his whiskers and said, with finality, "Quite impossible, Lieutenant Brooke."

"Sir?"

"A simple matter of procedure, Lieutenant. If your orders are to report to the 6th Bengal Light Horse in Calcutta, then that's where you must report. Surely you must be aware that I cannot issue contradictory orders without a request from your commanding officer?"

"Yes, sir, I realize that, but I thought...given the circumstances– "

"I'm sorry, Lieutenant. There is nothing I can do for you. I suggest you be on your way to Calcutta. There's nothing that can be done for you here."

"But, sir, I will be considered absent without leave and—"

The Adjutant-General rose from his chair and leaned across the table and glared up at the protesting lieutenant. He raised his voice and spat, "Procedure is quite clear, Lieutenant Brooke! Without orders from your commanding officer, I cannot assign you to a temporary position here or anywhere else for that matter! I suggest you make haste to Calcutta and hope that the Army doesn't try you for desertion!" The Adjutant-General reclaimed his chair, looked back to his desk, picked up his pen and said with finality, "There is nothing more to discuss. You are dismissed, Lieutenant."

James didn't move. He glared at the top of the Adjutant-General's head and he flushed red with anger through the white layer of dust covering his face. His jaw tightened and he began to speak through clenched teeth, accentuating each word slowly and distinctly as if he were releasing his fury in stages.

"Sir, may I prevail upon you for a sheet of paper and a pen?"

James' strange request and his reluctance to turn on his heels and disappear momentarily confused the Adjutant-General. He tossed James a befuddled look and muttered, "Whatever for, Lieutenant?"

"I wish to resign my commission, sir!"

James regretted the statement as soon as he made it, but his frustration had been building since events in England made him feel more and more like he was losing control over his own life. He knew he had dishonored himself by breaking his vow with his father, but as he signed the letter of resignation, a sense of relief flooded through him and for the first time in as long as he could remember, James felt that he was once again in control of his own future.

# III

December 28, 1825
Singapore

On the same evening that James resigned his commission, Timothy Irons sat alone at a dirty, ale-stained table in the corner of a sleazy wharf-side bar called *the Golden Hoof* and tossed down the remnants of a locally brewed ale. Timothy Irons was just beginning to celebrate.

A court of inquiry had convened in September and had finally made its ruling exonerating the crew of the *Cecilia* for any wrongful conduct which might have led to her maritime disaster. Additionally, the ruling specifically cited '*...Timothy Irons, First Officer of the Cecilia for brave and meritorious service under the most difficult of circumstances...*' and generally credited him for the salvage and return of the ship, its cargo, and her surviving crew to Singapore. The commendation, timely as it was, led to his appointment just that morning as Captain of *HMS Skimalong*, a 175 ton schooner which carried a minimal armament of 24 eighteen-pound guns and four eight pound-guns, and was used primarily as a fleet communications vessel between Singapore and other British ports-of-call along the shores of the South China Sea.

Timothy was happy. More, he was elated. He wouldn't assume command of the *Skimalong* for another two weeks. By then the ship would return from her final patrol from Penang under the command of her retiring captain and then Timothy would take charge of her. He had waited seventeen years for his first command and now that he finally had it, he planned to celebrate. He drank heartily from the dark bottle of ale, not bothering to pour the bitter brew in a film-stained mug resting on the table. He savored every swallow and was beginning to feel the soothing effects of the alcohol and the satisfaction that he had nothing better to do in the next two weeks than drink and sample the flesh of the Oriental prostitutes who approached his table every few minutes.

When Timothy called for another bottle of beer and brushed off the solicitations of two Malay whores, he noticed that the grungy pub was beginning to fill up with seamen and bluejackets. It was all the same to Timothy. Every bar in every port was an exact duplicate of every other after seventeen years as a seaman. The men were the same; loud, boisterous, inebriated, and more than willing to part with what few shillings they had saved for a gut of ale and a drunken lay with a whore. And, after seventeen years, the whores looked the same too. Some young, some old. Some fat, some thin. Few of them ever spoke more than a few words of any sailor's language, but they were all experts in the language of selling their wares. They plastered toothy smiles on their faces and stroked the sailors in just the right places and uttered words like, "Hey, sailor man, you want buy good time?" in eight or nine different languages. What they made from selling their bodies was usually enough to provide the whores with a better life than they would have had in the starving villages most of them had migrated from and it satisfied a sailor's need for release and, in some cases, temporary love before they shipped out only to visit a similar bar and similar whores in another part of the world. Only the complexion of the women changed, and the taste of the beer. Nothing else.

"Hello, Tim-ho-ti." A cute Chinese whore greeted Timothy with a broad smile and set the bottle of beer he ordered on the table. She sat on his lap and rubbed him lightly between his legs. "You want go upstairs? Make big bang-bang now?"

Timothy gently pushed her away. "In a few minutes, Kim Chai. Soon as I finish this beer. Here, for big bang-bang later," he said, fishing a generous handful of coins out of his pocket and handing them to her.

*"Terima Kasi"*, thank you, she said in Malay and her fake smile turned genuine. "Finish beer, Tim-ho-ti. I go work. Then we go up stairs and do big bang-bang."

Kim Chai was one of Timothy's favorites whores. He fondly watched her small rump, which was round and compact, shift rhythmically side to side under her tight chongsan as she pushed through the growing crowd and made her way back to the bar. He took a long draft of beer from the bottle and decided he would finish his drink quickly and take Kim Chai upstairs while he was still sober enough to enjoy it. Afterwards, he would drink the night away, he decided.

Kim Chai reached the bar and rubbed her hip provocatively against a wiry-looking white man who was standing next to a dour, broad-shouldered half-breed with muscular arms. They were unaware that they were being observed.

Geoff pressed himself tightly against the upstairs stairway landing and held a beaded curtain parted open just enough to allow the man standing behind him, a round-faced one-eyed man of Chinese and Eurasian mix, to catch a glimpse of the two men his partner pointed out to him.

"That's them! See that skinny blonde Englishman and the big duffer standin' at the end of the bar talkin' to that whore? That's them alright!"

The Chinaman poked his big face near the opening in the curtain and grunted. "We cut them here?" he asked.

Geoff peered into the sightless pupil of his companion's right eye. The reminder of a knife blade lingered on the Chinaman's face from his forehead to his chin, leaving the man's eyelid to heal in two, separately swollen patches of skin that never completely closed over the opaque orb which blindly tracked whatever his good eye was seeing. "Damned, right!" Geoff spat. "Time's come to rid myself of those two buggers!"

The Chinaman grinned sinisterly. There was nothing he enjoyed more than cutting on human flesh. It was his perverse way of obtaining retribution for what had been done to him years earlier.

Geoff peered down at the two men standing at the bar and watched as the Chinese whore put the touch on the Englishman and began to formulate his plan. The Englishman and the Malay half-breed had been following Geoff's tracks for months now and Geoff felt it was time to get rid of them permanently. Only by the narrowest of margins had he been able to stay ahead of them, but now he had his chance. For once, Geoff had the advantage and he knew it. They were unsuspecting and he had Chin, a bilious half-breed Chinaman with him. Geoff continued to spy on the two men at the bar until he saw the Englishman slip the whore some money. She took the Englishman's hand and pulled him to the stairway. This was his chance.

There were eight clap-trap rooms lining the corridor at the top of the steps, four on each side of the hallway. One room had the door ajar, anticipating the next customer.

Geoff pushed the beaded curtain closed and led the Chinaman to the open door of the room. "In here, Chin."

Geoff and the Chinaman stepped into the room and pressed themselves against the wall behind the door, keeping the door itself cracked open. Geoff pulled a belay pin from under his coat and the Chinaman withdrew a broad-bladed knife from a bronze sheath hidden beneath the folds of a wide sash that suspended his three-quarter length trousers.

Henry Steele wore a bright smile of anticipation as Kim Chai pulled him away from the bar. "I'll be back in a few minutes," he told Si Tundok.

Si Tundok nodded and returned to sipping his beer.

Kim Chai led Henry up the flight of stairs and through the beaded curtain that divided the hallway to the rooms from the stairwell. The muffled sounds of rutting sailors and the fetid stench of sweat and sex greeted Henry when he and Kim Chai reached the corridor. "This room good," Kim Chai said, leading Henry to the room with the open door.

Timothy Irons followed Kim Chai and the wiry Englishman with his eyes as the two of them moved from the bar and up the stairs. Timothy took another pull on his beer, pushed himself away from the table and made his way towards the end of the bar near the bottom of the staircase and leaned against the banister. Thoughts of Kim Chai performing sexual gymnastics with him as she had in the past aroused him and he decided he would have her as soon as she was finished with the Englishman.

Kim Chai entered the room ahead of Henry. No sooner had Henry stepped into the room behind her, than Geoff slammed the door shut and sent the Englishman sprawling to the floor with a vicious blow to the side of Henry's head with his belay pin. Chin had his heavy arms around the whore's mouth before she could scream and was about to draw the bare blade of his knife across her throat.

"Hold it, Chin! Not yet!" Geoff bent over and grabbed Henry by a sleeve and rolled him over and examined Henry for signs of life. Seeing none, Geoff hoisted Henry by the belt and tossed him face down upon the room's lone cot and then turned to face the frightened whore.

Immobilized by Chin's grasp, Kim Chai's terrified eyes peered above the hand of the Chinaman and she felt the cold blade of Chin's knife against her bare throat.

Geoff smiled menacingly, exposing his yellow teeth and said, "Now China doll, I want you to do something for me. You will, won't you?"

Kim Chai's fearful expression gave him every indication that she would cooperate, do whatever Geoff wished, but Chin's strong grip and her awareness of the knife at her throat prevented her from acknowledging her willingness.

Geoff reached out and slowly unbuttoned the whore's chongsan until her small, pear-shaped breasts were completely exposed. "I know how much she wants to be of help to old Geoff," he teased, "but maybe she needs a reminder of what will happen if she doesn't do exactly as I say. What do you think, Chin?"

Chin moved his knife from Kim Chai's throat to her chest and scraped the blade against her left breast, slowly back and forth, not breaking the skin, but with enough pressure that the girl stopped breathing. After the skin of her breast flushed red from the abrasion, Chin placed the tip of his knife to her nipple and flicked it.

Kim Chai winced and emitted a muffled cry of fear through Chin's hand gripping her mouth.

Geoff flashed his yellow teeth saying, "I think she get's the point so-to-speak, don't you, Chin? Now my little China doll, I want you to go back down those stairs and fetch the big Malay half-breed who was standing next to this little English bugger. Tell him his friend wants to see him and bring him up here." Geoff scowled and pressed his face close to the whore. "Understand what I'm telling you to do?"

Chin released his hold on the girl just enough to allow Kim Chai to take a deep breath and nod her comprehension.

"Good, very good. But just to make sure there's no misunderstanding, you know what my friend will do to you if you decide to bugger out on me, don't you?" Geoff lifted his massive brows quizzically while Chin pressed the tip of his blade against Kim Chai's nipple, expertly puncturing the skin until a single drop of blood appeared.

Kim Chai twitched and tears of fear welled up in her eyes. Even against Chin's firm grasp, she managed to affirm that she understood what would happen if she failed to do as Geoff asked.

"That's a smart girl," Geoff said. "A whore without tits just won't be making much of a living no more, will she?" Geoff chuckled and began to button the girl's chongsan. "Chin, you can let our little partner go now. I think she understands what we expect her to do, am I right, honey?"

When Chin released his grip and removed the blade from her chest, Kim Chai pressed her arms across her breasts in relief. "I do what want. No worry, you see," she gushed.

"I just knew I could count on you," Geoff chuckled. "But just to make sure, Chin here will go on down to the bar and keep an eye on you—make sure you don't have second thoughts and try to run out on us." Geoff cast a sinister nod toward Chin and said, "You know what he'll do to you if you muck up what you've been told to do, don't you, China doll?"

Kim Chai flitted her terrified eyes to Chin and back to Geoff and shook her head vociferously. "I do what told! No worry! I do what you say!"

Chin stared at Geoff with his one good eye, his jagged brows furrowed. It was Chin's way of questioning his companion.

"I'll take the half-breed the same way as I did the Englishman, Chin," Geoff explained. "You go on down to the bar and keep an eye on our little whore here and make sure she does what she's been told to do."

Chin nodded that he understood and hurried out of the room to take up a position in the downstairs tavern.

Geoff squeezed Kim Chai's arm for emphasis and said, "All right, China doll, time to do your number on the Malay wog." He pulled her close to his face, grinned wickedly and added, "Maybe when we're all finished, if you do the job right, old Geoff here will give you a special treat tonight." With that said, Geoff slapped her on the rump and pushed her through the doorway.

Timothy Irons straightened when the one-eyed Chinaman brushed by him. He watched the Chinaman push through the crowd and saunter to the front of the tavern where the man leaned against the wall near the front entry with his arms folded across his chest. To Timothy, even amid the current crowd of tough and rugged men, the Chinaman seemed tougher, meaner somehow.

When Kim Chai approached the landing, Timothy pushed himself away from the handrail and clasped her on the arm before she reached the bottom landing of the stairs.

"We'll go upstairs now, Kim Chai," he said, motioning with a toss of his chin to the upstairs rooms.

"No can do, Tim-oh-ti. Other sailor man first." She tried to pull away, but Timothy held tightly to her arm.

"He'll need to wait," Timothy said, turning Kim Chai and guiding her up the stairs. "You've already been bought and paid for, remember?"

In near panic, Kim Chai turned her head and her eyes flitted across the floor of the crowded bar seeing first the big Malay and then the Chinaman who was watching her from the doorway. Kim Chai knew it was useless to protest. If she started a scene, the Chinaman was liable to do worse than cut her. She tossed Chin a fearful glance and hoped he understood what had happened and then reluctantly allowed Timothy to guide her up the steps.

Timothy felt Kim Chai's body tighten. It wasn't like her to be so reticent, he thought. Timothy had always treated his whores right and usually Kim Chai was happy to see him as she was earlier, but now she seemed tense, almost fearful. *Perhaps she had a bad lay with the Englishman*, he thought fleetingly. And where was the small Englishman? Surely Timothy would have passed him on the staircase, wouldn't he?

As the two of them approached the partially opened doorway leading to the room, Kim Chai hesitated momentarily before entering and Timothy felt her body tense. In his seventeen years of seamanship, Timothy had been rolled, mugged and beaten and those many experiences had given him a second sense to recognize when things were not altogether right. And his senses warned him now that something or somebody was lurking just beyond the threshold of the room.

Timothy didn't bother to consider if the whore was part of the set-up or not. When she stepped through the doorway, he pushed her into the room and threw his body hard against the door, swinging the door inwardly and slamming it against the body of the man hiding there and pinning him to the wall. Timothy used the door like a battering ram. He slammed it time and time again against the trapped body of his would be assailant until the door began to rip from its hinges.

Kim Chai screamed, alerting Timothy to the presence of a second man coming through the doorway. Without releasing the door, Timothy turned his head and caught a glimpse of the one-eyed Chinaman he had seen earlier. He also caught the glint of the knife in the Chinaman's hand.

Instantly, Timothy pulled the door toward himself and swung it back to the entryway. The door tore from its hinges but managed to clip Chin on the shoulder, momentarily throwing him off balance.

Weaponless, Timothy rushed the Chinaman with his shoulders and caught him flush in the rib cage. Timothy's momentum carried the two men across the floor like drunken dancers until they slammed against the far wall. Timothy grabbed for the Chinaman's wrist holding the knife and the two men grappled for control of the weapon.

Meanwhile, Geoff, slumped on the floor, was shaking off the vestiges of the battering he had taken from the pounding of the door. Unsteadily, he pushed himself to his knees and searched for his belay pin. It had fallen from his hand and rolled beneath the cot where Henry Steele lay lifeless. Geoff spotted it and scrambled on all fours to reach it. He snatched the weapon from under the cot and leapt to his feet. Only then did he realize that the man struggling with Chin was not the big Malay half-breed.

Kim Chai had squeezed herself into a corner of the tiny room. When she saw Geoff pick up the hardwood weapon, she screamed again and dashed for the doorway. Geoff lunged for her, but she managed to duck under his outstreached arms and sprinted down the hallway, screaming as she ran.

The Chinaman was strong, but Timothy managed to keep him pressed against the wall where he couldn't maneuver his knife. With an effort born of his instinct for survival, Timothy twisted the Chinaman's wrist and fingers until the pressure forced Chin to release his grip on the knife. Timothy heard the blade fall harmlessly to the floor. Timothy continued to drive the full weight of his stocky body into the Chinaman's chest, keeping Chin pinned against the wall. Timothy managed to free his forearm and slammed it against the Chinaman's head. The blow bounced Chin's head against the wall so hard that the plaster on the wall crumbled behind Chin's skull and scattered to the floor.

Timothy was about to reach for the knife and shove it into the Chinaman's guts when a shadow appeared across the wall and alerted him that his first assailant was behind him. Timothy reeled to his right side, but he was too late.

The blow from Geoff's belay pin caught Timothy with a glancing blow on the left side of his ear and smashed into his left shoulder. He heard his clavicle snap like a piece of dry tinder before he crashed unconscious to the floor.

"He's coming around." Si Tundok removed a damp cloth from Timothy Irons' head and handed it to the Chinese whore, Kim Chai. Dutifully, she rinsed it in a basin of water normally reserved for douching and handed it back to Si Tundok who replaced it on Timothy's forehead. Timothy groaned and pushed Si Tundok's hand away.

Henry sat at the foot of the cot. "The bloke saved my life," he muttered as he held his throbbing skull in his hands.

Timothy moaned. He tried to lift his head from the cot, but the effort was too much and he slumped back down. Grimacing in pain, he cracked open his eyes. His eyelids felt as if lead weights had been stitched into them and he felt streaks of fire spread from his left ear to his shoulder and down through his arm. Gingerly, he started to reach the source of the pain with his good arm.

"You're shoulder is broken," Si Tundok said, and stopped Timothy from touching his wound.

Timothy blinked and tried to erase the fog clouding his head and eyes. Momentarily his vision cleared and he was able to see the man who spoke to him. Beyond him, sitting on the cot at Timothy's feet was a second man. Timothy recognized them as the two men whom he had seen earlier standing at the end of the bar. Kim Chai stood near the wash basin, disheveled and frightened.

Si Tundok assisted Timothy in sitting up on the cot with his head and shoulders leaning against the wall. "What happened?" Timothy asked, trying to sort out the confusion that muddled his brain.

Henry spoke first. "You'll have to ask her, mate," he said, tossing his chin towards Kim Chai. "I was in la-la land, same as you." Gingerly, Henry touched the bandage Si Tundok had wrapped around his head.

"Oh, yeah, now I remember. Some guy was behind the door when I came in and then the one-eyed Chinaman with the knife...who the hell were they?" Timothy asked.

"One's a rogue me and Si Tundok have been tracking for a long time. Don't know who the squint-eyed bugger was though," Henry replied. "I didn't see him. Sorry to get you involved, mate."

"I heard the whore scream," Si Tundok said. "That's when I ran up the stairs, but by the time I got here, they were gone."

"After they did you in and heard the whore sounding the alarm, they probably thought it best to bugger off. Looks like they went out through that window," Henry said, motioning towards the room's only window.

Timothy nodded that he understood.

"I'll put a sling on that arm of yours," Si Tundok said.

"Christ!" Timothy muttered between clenched teeth. It wasn't the pain that bothered him so much as realizing how close he came to never commanding his own ship.

# IV

## January, 1826
## Singapore

James arrived in Singapore from Madras aboard the *Carn Brae* in late January. His intention was to return to England and seek forgiveness from his father for breaking his promise and to attempt a reconciliation with Elizabeth. He booked passage on the only ship available, the *Carn Brae,* knowing that it would complete its westward journey to Singapore before turning eastward toward England. But a fierce storm had battered the frigate severely on its passage through the Straits of Malacca and it was only by the skill of the captain and good fortune that the ship managed to limp into the harbor at Singapore. James and the other passengers were informed that their passage to England would be delayed four to six weeks while necessary repairs were made to the ship.

Unable to book alternative passage, James rented a one-room flat facing Gumbar Street, a middle class residential district between the harbor and the commercial center of Singapore. Remembering the letter of introduction given to him by Sir Stamford Raffles and with time on his hands, James decided to present himself to the Governor-General of Singapore, Samuel McDonald.

He made his way by foot through the bustling crowds of the thriving community to the British administrative offices. In the midst of the many more modest structures was a recently constructed building of grand proportions and magnificently beautiful landscaping and a sign designating it as the residence and offices of the Governor-General of Singapore. James admired the splendid architecture of the building for a moment before he climbed the broad granite steps that led to a pillared entrance.

Inside, James presented Raffles' letter of introduction to the clerk and waited patiently in the outer office while the clerk took the letter to the office of the Governor-General.

Shortly, the heavy mahogany doors leading to the Governor-General's office swung open and a distinguished looking man in his late fifties greeted James with a broad smile and an extended hand. "Mister Brooke, I'm delighted by your visit. Please step inside. You must tell me what that old war horse Raffles is up to these days," Samuel McDonald said, effusively.

The Governor-General was not a big man, but his animated gestures and strutting gait gave James the impression that the amiable Scot was confident and self-assured. Samuel was immaculately dressed in a fashionable gray topcoat with a high collar and broad lapels, worn open to display a fine satin waistcoat. A black cravat covered the front of his shirt. White nankeen trousers and topless black leather shoes, the fashion of the day, rounded out his attire.

"Please, make yourself comfortable, Mister Brooke." Samuel waved to a red-upholstered, cow-hocked chair made of beech, but grained and stained to mimic rosewood. He slid a second chair, similar to the other but with emerald upholstery, next to James' chair and reached for a crystal liquor bottle situated on a brass pedestal holding a silver platter and several stemmed crystal glasses. "Sherry?" he asked.

"Yes, thank you." James situated himself comfortably in the chair and accepted the proffered beverage.

With his own glass in hand, Samuel sat in the green chair across from James and said, "So, tell me, Mister Brooke, what brings you to Singapore?"

The Governor-General crossed his legs and continued to beam his relaxed and natural smile, a smile which wrinkled his face in permanent lines from the edges of his mouth to his pronounced cheek bones. Coupled with his thick, sandy colored hair and flashing green eyes, Samuel McDonald appeared more like a mischievous schoolboy than an emissary of His Majesty's government.

James explained that he was returning to England and the circumstances of the *Carn Brae* that necessitated his temporary stay in Singapore. Then he said, "Since I had Sir Stamford's introductory letter, I thought I'd pay you a visit and convey Sir Stamford's regards."

The Governor-General was eager to learn how his old friend, Sir Stamford was doing and how he was handling his retirement in England. James assured the Governor-General that Sir Stamford was in excellent health and added, "But he does seem to keep himself worked up over the recent treaty between Britain and the Dutch with regard to the demarcation line in the East Indies."

"Ahh, yes, the treaty. *That* is an issue Raffles and I agree upon fully. Unfortunately, my instructions are not to pursue British interests on the one island that partially remains in the British sphere of influence as a result of the treaty," he said with some disgust.

"Borneo?"

"Yes, Borneo. I take it that Raffles has discussed the matter with you, Mister Brooke?"

"In detail, Governor," James replied.

The Governor-General was an astute observer of human behavior and he detected James' rising interest in the subject being discussed. "Raffles alluded in his letter that you have an interest in pursuing opportunities here in the Far

East, Mister Brooke. Does that imply a specific interest in Borneo?" he asked.

"It did," James replied somewhat despondently. "But unfortunately there are matters in England that require my immediate attention."

"I see," the Governor-General responded, somewhat disappointed. "Well, Raffles and I think alike on the Borneo matter. We agree that Borneo may offer tremendous resources and neither of us want to see the Dutch exert their influence over the entire island. Unfortunately, His Majesty's government doesn't see things in the same way. Prior to his retirement, Raffles and I discussed the possibility that an enterprising British subject such as yourself might be enticed to represent British interests there. Perhaps after you have settled your affairs in England you will reconsider your interest in Borneo, eh, Mister Brooke?"

"Quite possibly," James said pensively. After resigning his commission, James accepted the fact that he would likely never fulfill his dream of pursuing his fortune in the Orient. Without his father's blessing and his financial support, it would be impossible. And, too, there was Elizabeth. His heart still ached for her and he knew that if she would still have him, he would consent to her wishes and forget all about the Far East. Still, it was difficult to shed the magical spell that his dreams held over him.

"Until recently, such an enterprise in Borneo would have been fraught with difficulty, even for His Majesty's fleet," the Governor-General went on to say.

"Until recently, you say?"

"Yes, several months ago, one of our ships ran aground near the Sarawak River. The ship was attacked by pirates and most of the crew was killed. Fortunately, the ship and her surviving crew were saved by a timely intervention from the Rajah of Sarawak, a fellow by the name of Hasim. The crew's First Officer gave a rather glowing report of the Rajah's accommodation of them," the Governor-General said.

"It was my understanding that the natives there were inhospitable," James said.

"Savages, actually," Samuel replied, "from what we've learned from previous accounts. That's why the ship's rescue was a most surprising development. Ordinarily we would expect the ship, its cargo and its crew to simply vanish as others have in the past when they ran into difficulty in those dangerous waters."

The Governor-General rose from his chair and freshened their drinks. He remained standing and continued speaking, "I sent word to the Rajah of Sarawak that I intend to dispatch an envoy to Sarawak to convey His Majesty's gratitude for his kind assistance to our ship's crew. Unfortunately, I've had to wait much too long to receive the report of the findings by the board of inquiry, but now that I have it, I'll dispatch a communications vessel as soon as one returns to Singapore in the next few days."

The Governor-General took a sip of his sherry and then almost offhandedly said, "Perhaps, Mister Brooke, you would consider going to Sarawak for me?"

"Me?" James was so surprised by the offer that he almost choked on his sherry.

"Yes, as an emissary of sorts. Nothing to do, really, just extend His Majesty's gratitude and present a few baubles and trinkets to the Rajah, that's all."

It would be weeks before the *Carn Brae* would be ready to leave for England. James had nothing to do in the interim and the Governor-General's sudden offer would give him the chance to at least witness the land he so often thought of.

"It would be a privilege to be of service, Governor," James said, without hesitation. "I accept your most generous offer."

"Good, very good!" Satisfied that he-with due consideration given to the influence of Raffles' glowing letter of introduction of James-had picked the right man for the task and that James had accepted, the Governor-General extended his arm and the two men shook hands.

Samuel led James to the door saying, "Please leave information with my clerk on where you can be reached and I'll send word to you when the *Skimalong* is ready to depart for Sarawak and we can make arrangements to meet and discuss the dispatch I wish to convey to the Rajah. Does that sound satisfactory, Mister Brooke?"

"Quite satisfactory, Governor," James said, barely containing his enthusiasm. "I'll look forward to hearing from you."

In the course of his short meeting with Samuel McDonald, James had climbed from the depths of despondency to the heights of exhilaration. He didn't know it yet, but events had transpired which would crush the elation he now felt.

# V

Gumbar Street
Singapore

Several days following his meeting with the Governor-General, James answered a knock at the door of his flat.

"Mister Brooke?" a smartly dressed Malay boy asked.

"Yes, I'm James Brooke."

"These are for you," the boy said in perfect English. "From the Governor-General's office."

James accepted an envelope stamped with the Governor-General's seal and a larger packet wrapped in oilskin, thanked the boy and tipped him generously before closing the door.

James walked across the room and sat on the bed and opened the letter from the Governor's office. As expected, the Governor-General's office informed him that the *HMS Skimalong* had arrived from Penang and asked if it would be convenient for James to meet with the Governor-General in a few days to discuss the impending trip to Sarawak. James put the letter aside and picked up the oilskin packet. James opened it and found that it contained two letters. He deduced from the inked stamps that the first of the two letters had been sent nearly a month following his departure from England the previous year and had followed him from Madras to Penang and finally, to Singapore. It was addressed in his mother's dainty scrawl.

The second letter was written in a bolder, heavier style. Because of the time it took for news to reach from one end of the Empire to the other, news from home was a rare and joyful event.

James fluffed the pillow on his bed, sprawled his long body on top of the bed, loosened his cravat, leaned comfortably against the pillow and carefully opened the wax seal of the envelope containing the letter from his mother.

'*Dearest James,*' it began. '*It is with the deepest Sorrow that I must inform You of Your Father's Death...*'

Stunned by the opening line of the letter, James leaped upright to the edge of the bed. "No, it can't be...dear God, no!"

His eyes raced through the remaining lines of the letter. When he finished, he read each line again, slower this time, hoping that somehow the words would mysteriously change. Even following a third and fourth reading, the words remained the same and he finally accepted the truth that his father was dead.

His mother informed him that James' father had died in his sleep shortly after James departed from England. Of the croup, she had written. James recalled the coughing spells his father had been subjected to, but he had no idea at the time that his father was seriously ill. Tears welled up in James' eyes. Images of his father, strong and robust, flitted through his mind. James loved his father. He always had. He just never realized how much until that very moment.

James dropped his head to his chest and wrapped his hands in front of his face and wept. His tears were for the loss of his father as well as the guilt he felt for having broken his oath to him. Now there could never be a reconciliation.

Several minutes passed before James wiped the back of his palms against his eyes, drying them so he could read his mother's letter another time. She mentioned other things; details of the funeral, how kind their friends and neighbors had been and other details surrounding his father's death. None of it was of interest to him.

Toward the end of her letter, however, James read again what his mother wrote about Elizabeth. She informed him that the Gray's ward, whom she knew James to be fond of, had taken seriously ill several weeks following his departure and was currently convalescing in a warmer climate in the south of France. His mother went on to say that she prayed everyday for the young lady's recovery and hoped that James would consider writing to her as she felt it would be of benefit to Elizabeth's health and well-being.

Elizabeth! James stared at the wall, seeing nothing but a vision of her pretty face, her coquettish smile and the auburn curls that lay upon her bare shoulders as softly as snowflakes. The thought of her and the intimate moment they shared raised his spirits, but as the image of her faded from his mind, James' melancholy returned.

Finally, he placed his mother's letter aside and broke open the seal of the second letter which, he noted, was actually dated several days later than his mother's letter. There were two pages. It was from his father's solicitor, George Barton.

*My dearest Mister Brooke,*

*I am certain that by now You have heard news of your Father's untimely Death. We are all deeply moved to Sorrow and share in your Grief. As your Father's trusted Solicitor, It is my Duty and Obligation to inform you of the provisions made by your Father for the Welfare of you and your Mother, his only surviving Heirs. I have enclosed a copy of your Father's Last Will and Testament for your perusal. Please advise me as to how you wish to receive said Disbursements and I shall comply post-haste. Should you require*

*additional services, please do not hesitate to inquire of me. It is my Sincere desire to be of further Service to you and your Mother. Again, my deepest Condolences in this time of your Grief.*
  *Your Most Humble and Obedient Servant,*

*George Barton, Esq.*

James read the second sheet of paper. It was a handwritten copy of his father's will, written and signed in his father's own hand. In it, he discovered that he had been given the sum of 30,000 Pounds, a small fortune. In addition, he was to receive a small cottage in Suffox for use as a retirement home. His mother would inherit the bulk of his father's estate and the remainder of his fortune. The inheritance, coming on the heels of the news of his father's death did not immediately lift James' spirits or ease the pain he felt in his heart.

He set both the will and George Barton's letter aside, shuffled mechanically to a basin filled with water and splashed his face and rubbed the back of his neck and tried to comprehend all he had been told in the letters.

The more James contemplated the letters, the more morose and depressed he became. Finally, he dried himself off, grabbed his great-coat, stuffed the letters in a side pocket and left the flat without bothering to bolt the door.

VI

The Jolly Bachelor Inn
Singapore

Inside the Jolly Bachelor Inn, two stubble-faced men sat at a corner table and surreptitiously eyed James who was drowning his sorrow, alone, at a far table.

"Another drink and we'll make our move on the drunken sot," the smaller of the two men whispered through the corner of his mouth.

"Aye," the larger man replied. He scratched at the pock marks on the sides of his face and leered wickedly at James. In a voice as coarse as sandpaper he whispered, "This bloke's going to be as easy as pluckin' berries, mate."

"Aye, as easy as berry pluckin'," his friend concurred.

"Barkeep! Another flagon!" James waved his tankard above his head and slumped slightly forward onto the table.

Momentarily, a dumpy barmaid approached and set another tankard of ale on the table. "Had about enough ain't you? Ain't hardly proper for a gentleman such as yourself to carry on so," she said with some disgust.

James gave the woman a crooked smile and tossed her a sloppy salute. "Yes, sir...er...madam...hardly...proper...."

James fished a handful of coins from his pocket and squeezed them in the woman's hand, dropping several of them in the process. "For you...general," he slurred. "Take 'em all, doesn't matter..." and then waved the barmaid and her recriminations away and reached for the fresh tankard of ale.

James had made the rounds of every tavern within staggering distance of Gumbar Street that afternoon before discovering the unusually quiet, Jolly Bachelor Inn. Finding that the name appealed to his sense of irony, he entered and continued drinking late into the night in a feeble attempt to drown his sorrow.

The two miscreants eyeing James from across the room didn't have to wait long. Within moments after the barmaid picked up the scattered coins and returned to the bar, James slumped forward, sprawling his torso, arms and head across the top of the table. He had finally passed out.

The smaller of the two thugs lifted his tankard and said, "Drink up, mate. Time's come to pluck them berries we been talkin' about, heh?"

The two men pushed themselves away from their table and strolled over to James' table. The bigger man, the one with the pock-marked face, picked up the unfinished tankard of ale at James' table. He grinned conspiratorially at his partner, raised the mug as if to toast their good fortune and slurped the ale down in one draft, spilling only a fraction of it down his chin. He wiped the suds from his stubble, slammed the tankard to the table and winked to his partner that he was ready.

The shorter brigand reached his arms under James' shoulders and began to hoist him to his feet. "C'mon, mate," he said loud enough for the sparse crowd to hear, "time to get you back to the ship. You've had enough grog to last the next voyage or two."

Three West Indian seamen sitting nearby watched the two men lift James to his feet and sling his arms around their necks. They laughed at the familiar scene and one of them shouted out, "He's a long one, mates. You'll need to bring a ship's riggin' to haul that sot outta here!"

The two muggers laughed heartily and the larger one retorted, "Happens every time. Can't pass a damned inn without getting himself loaded fuller than Neptune's own locker."

"This is the last time we salvage his arse for him," added the shorter man. "You can bet your last sixpence on that, mates."

The West Indians guffawed along with the rest of the inn's spectators as the two men half-carried, half-drug James' body from the tavern.

"Around the side of the building. We'll take care of him there," the pock-marked man instructed when they exited the inn.

James muttered incoherently as the two muggers carried him into the shadows at the side of the building and dropped him to the ground.

"What's he sayin?"

"I think he's sayin' he's delighted to make our acquaintance," the smaller man joked.

James tried to pull his knees under himself and regain his feet, but the large, pock-marked man kicked him in the ribs and knocked him flat to the ground. James moaned and began vomiting.

"He's a filthy bastard, ain't he mate?"

"Aye, and a drunk one too." The larger man kicked James again in the side and then once in the head. "That'll teach you to heave your filthy guts all over the bloody place!"

His partner chuckled and bent over James and began rifling James' pockets. "Let's see what the Christmas goose has for old Artey and me this evening, heh?"

They turned James' coat pockets inside out, removing everything they could find. Finally, the small man said, "That's all he's got on him. You want any of his clothes, Artey?"

"Naw, forget it. Blokes too bloody tall. Wouldn't fit anyway."

"Well then, let's see what you got?"

141

"Couple a letters...he tossed them to the ground. "Few coins..." he stuffed them into his pocket. "Ain't bloody much," the bigger man said.

The smaller mugger held up James' watch and fob. "This'll fetch a fair price..." and stuffed it into his pocket. "Well, now, what have we here?" He opened James' leather wallet and saw that it was stuffed with Pound notes as well as his receipt for return passage to England aboard the *Carn Brae*. He extracted the notes and tossed the wallet and receipt to the ground. "I believe we done harpooned us a fat one this time, mate." He fanned the bills out in front of his partner's face.

Seeing the bills, Artey's eyes opened as wide as a giant sea conch. "Whew, that'll keep us in ale and women for a fortnight or two, eh, mate?"

Ecstatic at their good fortune, the men clasped each other's shoulders and began to sing a sea ditty and dance a hornpipe but the sound of approaching footsteps cut their celebration short.

"C'mon, mate. Let's get the bloody hell outta here!" The smaller mugger pushed his partner to the back of the Jolly Bachelor and they disappeared among a tightly packed row of hovels.

The sound of the thieves' retreating footsteps caused the two interlopers rounding the corner of the inn to pause. Cautiously, the two of them peered around the corner, but they caught only a fleeting glimpse of the men running before they vanished behind the tavern. They glanced at one another, shrugged and walked on. But a painful groan from the shadows halted them.

"Someone's in there," the smaller man said, stopping and straining to see through the shadows. He saw movement and then heard more groaning. "Let's check it out," he said. "Sound's like some bloke's in trouble."

Cautiously the two men approached. James, vaguely aware of the approaching men, stirred once again and drew his hands to his face and felt the blood pasted to his scalp. He tried to rise, but pain bolted through his rib cage where he had been kicked and he collapsed with a shriek. Through the pain and the cloud of alcohol, James heard a familiar voice say, "Poor bastard looks about done in."

A second familiar voice said, "Let's drag him into the light...see how bad he's hurt."

# VII

## Gumbar Street
## Singapore

Carried between their shoulders, James was barely able to guide Si Tundok and Henry back to his flat. They placed him on the cot, removed his top coat and shirt and examined and treated his wounds. Si Tundok shredded a bed sheet and wrapped a bandage around James' bruised ribs while Henry dabbed at the oozing wound on James' scalp with a wet cloth.

"You're a mess, mate, if you don't mind me saying so, Lieutenant." It was unclear if Henry was referring to James' wounds or his drunken condition.

Sluggishly, James touched the wound on his scalp and winced. "I can't look half as bad as I feel," he said, wearily.

Henry removed James' hand from the head wound. "Better not touch it, Lieutenant. You have a nasty gash on your scalp and it'll just start bleeding again." As he wrapped a bandage around James' head, he wrinkled his nose and said, "Smell's like you tried to drink Singapore dry in a single sitting, Lieutenant."

"I feel like I got a good start on it anyway," James mumbled. His ribs ached and his head throbbed with every breath and every movement he made. "The letters...?" James started to touch the pocket of his great coat, but realized his chest was bare.

"I put them on the table, Lieutenant," Si Tundok said. "That's all I found other than a booking receipt."

"The buggers stripped you clean," Henry added.

Relieved that he still had the letters in his possession, he shook his head slowly and said, "The rest doesn't matter, just the letters."

"Wish we would've come along sooner, Lieutenant. Si Tundok and I might have been able to spare you a bit of agony," Henry said.

"Glad you came at all," James said, attempting a smile. "Thanks. Can't believe my luck...two of you...Singapore ...how?"

"Me and Si Tundok figured the bloody army was a good place to get ourselves killed, particularly without you to protect our behinds, Lieutenant," Henry responded. "So, we finished our tour with the army, got the King's Pardon just like you promised and then we sort of bounced around for a while doing odd jobs on the docks here and there until we eventually found ourselves here in Singapore. That's about the short of it, Lieutenant."

143

From the previous stories James remembered them telling him, he was sure Henry hadn't told him everything. Trouble had a way of following close on the heels of his two friends and he wasn't sure Henry had told him the whole truth of their exodus. "So, what's the *long* of it, Henry?"

Henry glanced quizzically at Si Tundok. The big Malay nodded, giving Henry permission to tell the whole story. "Truth is, Lieutenant, Si Tundok and I spent most of the time hunting down those four blokes who buggered out on us in Burma."

James was not surprised. "Did you find any of them?"

"Funny you should ask, Lieutenant. We caught up with the Indian and the two Sikhs and managed to even the score with them, if you know what I mean?"

"You killed them?" Personally, James did not feel the same sense of betrayal that his two companions felt. Had it been his choice, he would have let the British Army take care of it as they eventually would. But he understood his friends' backgrounds and the code of raw justice that sprang from it.

"Let's just say they won't be running out on a fight again," Henry replied.

"What about the big Englishman, the one with the crooked thumb? What was his name...?"

"Geoff!" Si Tundok spat out the name as if he was expectorating an insect. "Last month we tracked him here, to Singapore, but he got away. We'll catch up to him someday."

"There's truth in that, Lieutenant. We almost had him a short while ago, but that bastard, Geoff had a squint-eyed bloke with him. They had me drawn and was about to quarter me before some sea captain by the name of Irons happened along. The captain took a crack on the head meant for Si Tundok here. Hadn't been for the captain getting all horny when he did, me and Si Tundok would be floating belly side down in Singapore harbor about now and you would still be bleeding in that alley. But as Si Tundok says, we'll catch up to the bloody bastard someday. You can bet your last shilling on it."

"I don't doubt it for a moment," James said. He was finding it easier to talk. The throbbing in his head had subsided to a dull ache and he decided to take a chance and sit up. "I'm almost feeling half-human again," James said after he managed to rise with Si Tundok's help. "Except for the ribs and the ale still floating in my gullet, I think I might survive."

Si Tundok hands grazed the scar on James' chest when he helped steady him. It was a tactile reminder of the debt he owed this brave Englishman and he was glad to be in James' company once again.

"It appears that you got patched up all right in England, Lieutenant," Henry said after taking note of the scar as Si Tundok had. "Guess you're heading back to join up with the Regiment now?"

James shook his head and said, "No, I resigned my commission. I'm just another expatriate same as the two of you now. No need to call me 'Lieutenant' any longer either. I don't need any reminders of that part of my life."

Si Tundok and Henry glanced at each other, both wore expressions of surprise at hearing the news. Then Si Tundok said, "And what will you do now, Lieutenant?"

"James, call me James." James shrugged, and said, "I'm not sure, I really haven't had a chance to give it much thought."

"Maybe you could come with Henry and me, Lieu...I mean, James," Si Tundok suggested.

"Good idea," Henry chimed. "You could help us run down that bastard Geoff."

James shook his head. He studied his two friends for a moment and began to think clearly for the first time since early that afternoon. Suddenly, James felt that Providence had intervened in his life and his destiny was revealed to him. He didn't know if it was the remnants of the alcohol in his brain or the fact that he was reunited with his two friends, but it didn't matter. "No, I don't think so," he replied. He reached over and picked up the letters that Si Tundok had salvaged. "These letters are the start of a new life for me...for the two of you also, if you want."

Si Tundok and Henry exchanged puzzled expressions.

James told them of all the things Raffles had told him about Borneo, the treaty with the Dutch, and of his meeting with the Governor-General and of his impending trip to Sarawak. When he finished relating the background material to them, he said, "I am hopeful that I will be able to extract a concession from the Sultan or whoever is in charge in Borneo and open up trade with the British part of the island. If things work out as I expect them to, it could be well worth your while to come along."

Si Tundok wrinkled his forehead and frowned. "Borneo...I have been there, James. It is not a very friendly place."

"How do you mean?" James asked.

Si Tundok drew a finger across his throat and said simply, "Headhunters."

"Headhunters? Why in bloody hell would you want to try to trade in a place full of headhunters, James? Aren't there less dangerous places to trade?" Henry asked.

"Probably, but Borneo hasn't been explored and nobody has opened up trade with the island yet. Raffles and the Governor-General are of the opinion

145

that Borneo has the possibility of enormous riches and I'm inclined to agree with him." James tossed Henry a questioning smile and asked, "You're not afraid of a few headhunters are you, Henry?"

"Not bloody likely!" Henry replied, balling his hand into a fist and puffing his chest indignantly. "Any uncivilized savage tries to touch a hair on this Welsh head of mine and I'll reform him right into the next century with the knuckles of this here fist!"

James laughed and Si Tundok cracked a smile then asked, "How will you transport goods if you manage to gain a trading concession, James?"

James pointed once again to the letters. "I've recently come into a small inheritance. Enough to purchase a small ship and fit it for trade. Like I said earlier, this is the start of a new life for me and I'm offering you both a chance to come along. What do you say?"

James watched Henry's eyes track to Si Tundok, and realized that Henry expected the big Malay to make the decision for the two of them. "Si Tundok?"

Si Tundok shrugged his broad shoulders. He looked James straight in the eye and said, "I expect you will need someone who speaks Malay. Might as well be me."

Henry whooped and slapped Si Tundok on the shoulder. "Count us in, James!" he announced with an ear-to-ear grin.

James slapped his hands together. "Good! Well, no sense wasting time. Where can we find a ship?"

# VIII

## Singapore Harbor

Early the following morning, the three men separated. James sent Si Tundok and Henry to the harbor to search for a ship. He would join them later. In the meantime, he had important matters to attend to.

First, James paid a visit to the Charter Bank of England, Singapore Branch, and presented George Barton's letter and the copy of his father's will to secure a line of credit to finance his Borneo adventure. He easily established the account after using the Governor-General's name as a local reference.

That important detail taken care of, James purchased stationery, pen and ink from a street vendor and found a quiet table at a local *kedai*, a Malay restaurant which served beverages and steamed cakes, and ordered sweetened tea and two freshly made *kueh*, sweet buns. He composed three letters.

The first, to his mother, expressed his sadness upon hearing the news of his father's death and generally advised her of his current circumstances with the promise that he would write again soon and inform her of all developments.

The second letter was addressed to George Barton. In it, James thanked him for his timely letter, retained him as James' own solicitor, and instructed him to transfer the bulk of his inheritance to the Charter Bank in Singapore.

The third and final letter was much more difficult to compose. It was to Elizabeth and James deliberated a long while before he wrote:

*My Dearest Elizabeth,*

*My Mother has informed me of your illness. I Trust and Pray that by the time this Letter reaches you, you will have fully and completely recovered. As for me, Darling Elizabeth, Providence has found me as I knew it one day would. I am filled with the most profound Joy at the Prospects I have before me. At the present time, it would be imprudent for me to explain my situation further, but let me assure you, my Dearest, that the Fates have presented me with an Opportunity of incalculable Worth.*

*The only Sadness which creeps between me and my boundless Joy is my many thoughts of having lost you. I realize that your position regarding my proposal has most likely not changed, but my Circumstances are such that, God willing, I will be able to return to England sooner than expected and I Hope with all my Heart that you will wait for my return. I could be made*

*King of all the Spice Islands, but without you, my Heart will always remain a Pauper. Until we meet again, I shall remain Incomplete and my Joy less than Bountiful.*

*With all my Love in anticipation of receiving Word of your recovery, I remain your most Humble and Obedient Servant.*

*James Brooke*

James read the letter twice before folding and addressing it. James left the *kedai* and flagged down a rickshaw and had the runner convey him to the harbor where he transferred the letters to the Port Authority and then set out to find Si Tundok and Henry.

A few minutes of walking dockside was all the time it took to find his friends. Henry greeted him enthusiastically. "We've found one, James. We hear it's the only ship available between here and Hong Kong."

Henry and Si Tundok hurried James along the wharf until they stood facing a dry-docked Portuguese-made brigantine with the faded name, *Lisbon* scrolled on her bow.

James' initial optimism turned sour. Before him was a decrepit, barnacle-encrusted sea relic with tattered sails and frayed rigging. The *Lisbon's* hull was cracked and sun-bleached and her railings were damaged. All in all, the *Lisbon* looked like a refugee from Davy Jones' locker and James doubted if her deck timbers would even stand the weight of his own feet.

Henry perceived James' consternation and hastened to say, "I've combed every plank of her from bow to stern, James, and her timber's as sound as the day she was built."

James remained doubtful so Henry added, "Oh, I know she looks like she's been through every war since the Spanish Armada fought in English waters, but with some new planking, a bit of hull-scraping and a little tar here and there, and proper sails, she should be as fit a ship to ever sail the South China Sea."

"I suspect it may take a bit more than that, Henry," James sighed. "But we need a ship, and if she's the only one available, she'll probably have to do."

James led the two of them onto the main deck and the three of them spent some time examining the *Lisbon*. When they finished, James said, "Well, at least she still floats. Where can I find the owner?"

Si Tundok directed James to the forecastle cabin of an adjacent ship. Once aboard, Si Tundok touched James' arm and cautioned, "Drive a hard bargain, James. She's not worth much as she sits."

"You're right about that," James said.

The negotiations with the ship's owner, a Spaniard from Manila, went well, and before long they had agreed upon a fair price. James had been honest, telling the destitute Spaniard how he intended to use the ship and the Spaniard had been encouraging, although he privately thought James somewhat of a fool for attempting such an adventure.

The Spaniard saw some of his own youthful enthusiasm in James, ambitions now tempered by too many years, too many storms, and too many failures. Even the Spaniard's last voyage, the one designed to extricate himself from his burdensome debt by hauling spices from Indonesia to the Americas, had met with disaster. A storm forced the crippled *Lisbon* into port in Singapore where the Spaniard was obliged to sell off his cargo at a ridiculously low price in order to meet some of his debts and repair most of the major damage to the ship. Unable to obtain another underwriter, the Spaniard decided to sell the ship and give up his search for fortune. That was five years ago.

But if the young Englishman and his friends were willing to try their luck, that was their problem. As for him, he figured he was more than willing to take the young man's money, pay off his creditors, and purchase passage back to the Philippines. If he never heard another story of the fortunes to be made in Far Eastern trade, it would be fine with him.

James made arrangements to meet with the Spaniard at the Charter Bank of England the following day to consummate the purchase.

Before they left the ship, Henry asked, "What do you intend to name her, James?"

James stopped and reflected for a moment. "I've been thinking about that," he said. "Several names have come to mind, but last night I was in about the same shape as the *Lisbon* is now, yet I recovered. And it all began at the Jolly Bachelor Inn. Guess I'll call her the *Jolly Bachelor*, how does that sound?"

"Sound's like a damned fine name to me," Henry said with spirit.

Si Tundok nodded his agreement as well.

# CHAPTER SIX

## I

Sin Bok
Sarawak

"Enough food and drink, let's get down to business, old man." Chin tossed a half-eaten *bao*, a filled steamed dumpling, onto a serving tray and leaned over the table and into the room's only light, a single oil lamp set to the side of the table.

"Leave us girl," Loi Pek ordered with a wave of his hand.

Quickly, Kameja, the Melanau slave girl, removed the serving tray from the table and scurried out of Loi Pek's inner office. She pulled the doorway curtain behind her, relieved to have been dismissed. She had never seen Loi Pek's guests before this night, and both of them frightened her. The one-eyed Chinaman, the one called Chin, disconcerted her with his grotesquely scarred eye that seemed to track her every move. But the ugly white man called Geoff, he was worse. He leered at her lecherously and his crooked yellow teeth flashed menacingly in the light reflected from the oil lamp. She feared Loi Pek would sell her to the men or worse, force her to submit to certain indignities with them. It had happened before.

Kameja left through the front door of Loi Pek's shop and hurried down the quiet street until she arrived at Loi Pek's house where she had a small room near the back. Inside, she was careful not to awaken Loi Pek's family, a host of immediate relatives who lived with him. She tip-toed to her room, carrying the serving tray with her. It was late and she was tired. She decided she would clean the dishes and the tray in the morning.

"Do you have proof of who you say you are?" Loi Pek peered suspiciously at the one-eyed Chinaman sitting at the table opposite him. He ignored the white man seated to his left.

The light from the oil lamp flickered and created a macabre dance of light and shadow across Chin's tallow face. At first, Chin said nothing. He appraised Loi Pek's question for a moment and then leaned forward into the light of the solitary lamp. He pulled his shirt sleeve up and slid his broad arm across the table until it was bathed in the light of the lamp. Slowly, Chin rolled over his forearm and revealed a large, purple tattoo on the inside of his arm just below the elbow.

"This is my proof, old man," Chin said in Hakka.

Loi Pek's eyes were not what they once were, but he readily recognized the ancient sign of the *Tien-Ti Hueh*, the Heaven and Earth Society. Emblazoned on Chin's forearm was an oval circle with a tree in the center and Chinese characters on each side of it which identified Chin as a member of *Sam-Hup*, one of the three most powerful and ruthless triads in China.

Loi Pek extended his withered finger and touched the raised scar on Chin's forearm, satisfying himself that it had been burned into the flesh as tradition demanded.

Chin snickered and pulled his arm away. "Now you, old man."

Loi Pek nodded, pulled back the sleeve of his elaborately embroidered silk tunic and revealed a similar, but much more shriveled scar. "Satisfied, my brother?"

"We can do business," Chin replied flatly.

"Perhaps. But first I must ask you a question. I find it unusual that a brother of the Heaven and Earth Society would find it necessary to keep the company of a white devil." Loi Pek spoke in Hakka having previously determined that the white man was ignorant of the language.

"He is my friend. We work together. He has connections with the British white devils in China which make it easier to conduct business there."

"I see...and do you trust this white devil?"

"If I didn't, he would be dead."

Loi Pek had no doubts that Chin was telling the truth. Chin appeared to be the epitome of ruthlessness, but so were all who belonged to the *Sam-Hup*. Satisfied that his Heaven and Earth brother and his white friend could be trusted with the transaction, Loi Pek said, "Very well then, we will discuss business. How much opium can you supply?"

Chin snickered. "The question is, old man, how much can you pay...in gold?"

"Gold? That is a very rare commodity in Sarawak," Loi Pek lied. "Perhaps we can arrange to pay in– "

"Gold! Or we have nothing more to discuss, old man."

Loi Pek stared at Chin's hard face. The light of the oil lamp continued to dance along the side of Chin's head, highlighting his severed eyeball and giving him a ghoulish appearance. His Heaven and Earth brother was going to drive a hard bargain, Loi Pek thought. But he wasn't intimidated by the severity of the man's features, or his detestable manner.

Quickly, Loi Pek calculated what the worth of the opium would be to him. The drug was a rare commodity in Sarawak and commanded a high price. If he could strike a strong bargain with Chin, the opium would repay his investment in gold many times over. "You take advantage of me, my brother, but I agree to pay in gold."

"Good! I demand one *kati* of gold for every two *katis* of opium I supply," Chin said sharply.

Loi Pek maintained calm at Chin's exorbitant demand. Without changing expressions, he said without inflection, "That is too much. I offer you one *kati* of gold for each six *katis* of the drug."

Chin was insulted by the offer. Angrily, his one good eye bored into Loi Pek. "I am no fool, old man. Even with one eye, I can see that you intend to cheat me! I warn you, that would not be a wise thing to do," he cautioned.

Loi Pek, a master of tough negotiation, appeared to back down. He shrugged an apology and opened his empty palms. "We are a poor community," he said, "but I am an honorable man. Never would I attempt to cheat a fellow brother of the Heaven and Earth Society. There are, perhaps conditions I am unaware of which might cause you to feel the opium is worth far more than I have ever paid for it in the past?"

"You have been out of touch, old man, living as you do in this swamp infested land. Have you not learned that the white devils now control the opium traffic out of China. It is most difficult and very dangerous to smuggle the drug out of China now. The extra risk increases the price."

"I understand..." Loi Pek pretended to weigh what Chin had told him. He pulled at the long strands of hair growing from the mole at the edge of his chin. Surreptitiously, he observed Chin and the Englishman with his peripheral vision. When they exchanged quick glances with one another, it gave him the sign he was waiting for. As he hoped, they were becoming impatient. Loi Pek had avoided discussing the transaction until well after dark, choosing instead to regale his guest with stories of the marauding bands of headhunters and the dangers of traveling at night. Yes, they were becoming impatient, he thought, and impatient men will settle for less than they ask for. Slowly, Loi Pek began to shake his head from side to side, creating a deliberate impression that he was rejecting the offer.

Geoff turned anxiously to Chin. He remembered Chin's warning to keep his mouth shut during the negotiations, but after drinking countless cups of insipid tea and listening to gibberish he couldn't understand, he was becoming unsettled.

Geoff took Loi Pek's shaking head to mean the deal had been blown. "What the hell's he saying, Chin? Why is the old duffer shaking his head like that?"

"Patience," Chin said in English. "The old man's driving a hard bargain, that's all."

"Yeah? What's he want to give for the opium?"

"One kati of gold for each six katis of opium."

Geoff's larcenous mouth flopped open. "And you're not taking it? What the hell's the matter with you, Chin? That's twice what I figured we could get!"

"Keep your mouth shut," Chin threatened. "I can get more."

It was apparent that the two men were arguing. *I have them now,* Loi Pek thought. *Perhaps if I delay just a bit longer....*

"All right, Chin," Geoff said. "I'll keep my mouth shut. Just hurry up and make the deal. This place gives me the creeps."

Chin didn't like Sin Bok any more than Geoff did and the old man's stories of headhunters and other dangers in the unfamiliar jungle made him uneasy as well.

Finally, Loi Pek broke his silence. "As you have seen, my *kongsi* is but a poor village in a backward part of the world controlled by barbarians. We have little to sustain us," he lamented. "I'm sorry, regardless of the risk you must take, I am unable to meet your price. My offer of one *kati* of gold for each six *katis* of opium stands. Take it or leave it, my brother. It is the best I can do." Loi Pek made his offer in a pleasant voice, but it had a ring of finality to it.

"What did he say?" Geoff asked.

Although annoyed with Geoff for speaking, Chin was more annoyed with what he perceived to be Loi Pek's final offer. "He says his offer is final, but I think he lies. He will go higher."

"Dammit, Chin! Look around, man. This place is as barren as a barmaid's womb. The old goat is probably offering every bloody speck of gold he has."

Chin bored his one good eye into Loi Pek's placid face. *Could the old man pay more? Is he bluffing?*

"Agreed, old man!" Chin finally blurted. "One measure of gold for each six measures of the drug."

"When can I expect delivery?" Loi Pek's expression remained tranquil, but his old heart was pounding. He had made a most profitable transaction. If he could keep it a secret, even *Awang* Api would not have to be paid his *serah* and his own profits would be greater than he imagined.

"As soon as we can make the arrangements. Possibly within three or four months time."

"Very good." Loi Pek was only mildly disappointed. An earlier delivery would mean earlier profits, but for the sum he calculated in his mind, he could afford to wait. In closing, Loi Pek said, "The Rajah's warriors keep a close watch on the boat traffic along the Sarawak River. I trust you will be cautious."

Chin smiled evilly. "We will find a way to get the drug through. Just make certain you have the gold ready for us when we arrive, old man."

## II

Buntor's *Rumah*
Brunei, Borneo

Killing the Sultan Buntor was easy.

Api waited until well after midnight before he crept along the darkened corridors of the palace and entered the sleeping Sultan's quarters undetected. The Sultan's two personal bodyguards posed no problem; earlier they had received a half measure of Loi Pek's gold and were conveniently absent from the front of the doorway to the Sultan's *rumah tidor*, his bedroom, when Api emerged from the shadows.

A rank smell from burning fish oil greeted Api when he quietly closed the door behind him. The Sultan's room was awash with light from foul smelling cruzie lamps which the Sultan insisted be burned each night because of his childish fear of the dark.

Soundlessly, Api approached the Sultan's bed and lifted the canopy of mosquito netting which enveloped it. The imbecilic Sultan slept, his mouth agape and emitting long, rasping drafts of breath. Saliva dribbled from the corner of his mouth.

Api momentarily stared in disgust at his sleeping uncle. Aware of so little around him, the Sultan was equally oblivious of the mild poison that coursed through his bloodstream that was daily administered by his sister, the *Dayang* Udang. But Api couldn't wait for his mother's slow method of killing. He had other plans. And they were to begin now.

Api nudged the Sultan until Buntor lethargically opened his eyes. The Sultan recognized Api. But, unaware if he was awake or dreaming—his mental world much the same in either case—Buntor wrinkled his lips into a moronic grin like a crib-bound child focusing upon the movement of a brightly colored toy above its head. Buntor appeared delighted with Api's visit. He gurgled to clear the phlegm from his throat and began to lift his head and shoulders from the bed.

But before Buntor could rise up, Api snatched the Sultan's pillow from beneath him and slapped it to the Sultan's face and pinned Buntor's head against the bed. The retarded Buntor thrashed wildly, but years of inactivity had made him weak and he was unable to pull the pillow from his face.

Shortly, his body fell limp and Api removed the pillow and tucked it behind the dead Sultan's head. Api arranged the Sultan's arms across his body and smoothed his bed coverings to give the appearance that Buntor had died in his sleep. He dropped the mosquito netting over Buntor's bed as it had been before and stealthily exited the room.

The first part of Api's plan to make himself Sultan of Brunei and Sarawak was complete. But the next step, killing his mother, the *Dayang* Udang, would not be as easy.

III

## *Dayang* Udang's Private Quarters
## Brunei, Sarawak

The *Dayang* Udang's private quarters were located at the opposite end of the palace from Buntor's *rumah*. Once Api found himself in the familiar corridor that led to his mother's rooms, he didn't bother to hide himself from the palace guards who lined the narrow hallway. They were accustomed to his visits with the *Dayang*, even at this odd hour of the night.

Api hoped his mother would be asleep. It would make the kill easier. But when he eased open the door to her quarters, he saw her sitting on a pile of pillows in the far corner of the outer room, fully dressed and rifling through a mound of State documents beneath the light of a single oil lamp.

She glanced up when she heard the door open. "Api? What is it you want?" Her face only registered mild surprise at her son's nocturnal visit.

Api hesitated before stepping inside. He closed the door tightly behind him. He was committed now.

"I want to ask you something, Mother," he said and approached to where the *Dayang* sprawled like a fat sow nestled amid the cushions and parchments.

She invoked a sigh of frustration and waved her hands over the scattered documents. "Can't you see that I am busy? Come back in the morning."

Api knelt by his mother's side. "It can't wait until then." His hand slid beneath his *baju* and he grasped a garrote hidden beneath his tunic.

"Then what is it?" she snapped. "Make it quick I am extremely busy." With an expression of exasperation, she returned to perusing a document held in her hands.

Beads of sweat erupted along Api's forehead and in his hands. *All I need to do is wrap the garrote around her neck and pull—do it in the same way I did when I killed the Sultan Mudah, Tundjok. Simple.*

But it wasn't. Something held him back and his hand remained frozen to the garrote. He struggled to visualize the murderous act in an unconscious attempt to make it more ethereal, less personal.

When Api didn't respond to her question, the *Dayang* lowered the documents and raised her ponderous head towards him. Her son appeared to be in a trance. "Api? What is it? Are you not feeling well?"

The sound of the *Dayang's* words abruptly snapped Api from his reverie and without further hesitation, he ripped the garrote from beneath his tunic.

157

"No!" the *Dayang* gasped. Impulsively her massive arm struck at the garrote, knocking it from Api's hands and she made an attempt to roll her corpulent bulk away from him.

But Api pounced on her and mashed her into the cushions and wrapped his hands over her bulbous lips, preventing her from crying out.

The *Dayang's* eyes bulged with fear and surprise at the suddenness and treachery of Api's attack, but there was little she could do, so tightly had Api's body pinned her to the cushions.

Unable to use the garrote, Api's powerful hands slid from his mother's mouth to her neck and he squeezed with all his might, digging his fingers into her thick flesh until he felt the neck bones buried deep beneath the layers of flesh and flab and he squeezed tighter and tighter while his eyes burned with rage.

Unable to extricate herself from the weight of her son and his powerful grip on her throat, the *Dayang* grabbed desperately to Api's wrists and tried to pry them from her neck, but Api was too strong. Shortly, her thick tongue distended from her mouth and like a beached carp she mouthed at the air, but was unable to pull it into her lungs. Her protruding eyes stared with incomprehension at the maniacal face of her son, the spawn of her womb.

Api's eyes saw only blackness; a dark void only penetrated by rapid-fire images of his own past and his mother's dominance of his youth and control of his life. Each image provoked him to tighten his fingers deeper into his mother's neck. Long after the *Dayang* Udang's portly hands fell away from his arms in death, Api continued to squeeze forth his hate.

With violent strokes, Api shook the dead *Dayang's* head until her neck snapped and flopped between his hands like a broken *sago* branch. "I hate you!...always...hated you...hated..." he muttered over and over through froth covered lips.

Then, a second sensation, an emotion stronger than Api's own hatred for his mother rushed through his body, overwhelming him. He felt the fire grow in his loins and surge through him until he could no longer contain it.

He broke his deathly grip on his mother's neck and fell limp on top of her, allowing the powerful emotion to consume him completely. He moved his hips, rhythmically, up and down over his mother's warm corpse until the imprisoned passion in his groin burst forth in a series of enormous explosions. Api shuddered with each spasm and groaned through his clenched teeth.

Moments later, Api's passion abated and retreated to the depths of Api's unconscious mind where it would remain banished and imprisoned within Api's own psyche. Api, spent and exhausted, rolled from his dead mother's body. He lay amid the pile of pillows, breathing heavily. Slowly, he opened his eyes and stared at the blank ceiling above him. The light from the oil lamp cast accusatory shadows across the ceiling and Api thought he could see the faces of Kameja, the Melanau slave girl, and all the others he had tried so unsuccessfully to take in the past. Gradually, his fingers moved between his legs and for the first time in his life, he touched his own wetness through his sarong.

IV

Rajah's Palace
Kuching, Sarawak

The third part of Api's plan, the assassination of his brother, Hasim, did not go as planned. Previously, the *Dayang* Udang had received word that a British delegation was soon to arrive in Sarawak, and knowing that his mother was prepared to grant concessions to the foreigners, Api quickly planned the coup. It was the only way, he reasoned, that he could keep foreign influence out of Brunei and Sarawak and gain the throne to which he felt entitled. But the hereditary right to the throne was Hasim's as he was the eldest male in Sultan Buntor's line. Therefore, along with the Sultan, and the *Dayang* Udang, Hasim, too must die.

For that task, Api enlisted the eager aid of his cousin, Langau, with the promise that he would make Langau Rajah of Sarawak once Api assumed the throne in Brunei. So, the day previous to Api's murder of Buntor and his mother, Api had dispatched Langau to Kuching, ostensibly to relay information from the *Dayang* to Hasim concerning the anticipated arrival of the British. Api had no reason to fear that Langau would fail. After all, Hasim was a whimpering fool, and Langau, much of the same mold as Api himself, should find no lack of opportunity in taking Hasim's life.

Langau arrived in Kuching late in the evening and announced to the Rajah Hasim that he had been sent by the *Dayang* Udang to assist the Rajah in making preparations for the arrival of the British. But, because of the late hour, it was agreed to wait until the following morning to discuss this matter. But Langau had no intentions of allowing the Rajah Hasim to live that long.

Meanwhile, dispatched a week earlier by the Rajah to travel upriver and assess the strength of a marauding band of Iban who were gathering along the upper Sarawak River near a place called Siniawan, the *Datu* Temanggong was returning to Kuching with his report. Since being reinstated as the Rajah's war chief and becoming a permanent fixture within the walls of Hasim's palace following his rescue of the British vessel, the *Cecilia*, the self-effacing old warrior was grateful to be in the service of the Sultanate once again and he felt confident that the Rajah would greet his actions in Siniawan with favor. While in Siniawan, *Datu* Temanggong had his warriors build a stockade near the confluence of the two branches of the Sarawak River, the Sarawak Kanon and the Sarawak Kiri. He manned the fort with his best warriors and a contingent of Chinese musketeers from Sin Bok and ordered them to prevent the Iban from penetrating further into the coastal regions of Sarawak.

It was past midnight when the *Datu* Temanggong's *prau* reached Kuching. Fatigued and recognizing the lateness of the hour, *Datu* Temanggong elected not to awaken the Rajah Hasim with news of his arrival. Instead, he decided to retire to his bed chamber adjacent to the Rajah's private quarters.

Later that same night, at approximately the same time Api was disposing of the Sultan Buntor, Langau emerged from his room in the Rajah's unpretentious palace and stealthily made his way to Hasim's quarters. He didn't know he was being watched.

The *Datu* Temanggong had just entered his small room next to the Rajah's bed chamber, being unusually quiet so as not to disturb the sleeping Hasim, when he heard the door to the room across from his faintly creep open. The noise puzzled him. Other than himself and an occasional guest from Brunei, the fearful Rajah allowed no one else to reside in the palace. Even the palace guards were stationed outside the building.

Cautiously, the *Datu* Temanggong eased open the door just enough to catch sight of someone sneaking toward the Rajah's bed chamber. As the interloper reached for the door to the Rajah's chamber, he glanced around suspiciously. In that instant, *Datu* Temanggong recognized Langau and caught a glimpse of the *kris* he held in his hand.

Without delay, the loyal old warrior sprang into action. He snatched his *parang* and flung open the door to his room and charged across the short hall, screaming his war cry.

Startled, Langau turned at the charging shadow. He was barely able to raise his *kris* to defend himself before the *Datu* Temanggong was upon him. Langau's wavy-bladed knife was no match for the *Datu* Temanggong's heavy *parang*. With the first practiced slash of his weapon, the *Datu* Temanggong separated Langau's knife from his hand. The blow caught Langau above the wrist, severing bone and flesh cleanly. The *kris* and the hand holding it flew to the floor and Langau instinctively grabbed at the pain and gushing blood from his severed limb.

The *Datu* Temanggong showed no mercy. He brought his heavy *parang* down with a second vicious blow and caught the incredulous assassin flush at the juncture of his shoulder and neck. The force of the blow dug deep into Langau's neck, crushing bone and muscle until the blade reached his heart. Langau's face contorted in pain and he tried to emit a cry, but he was dead before his body collapsed to the floor.

## V

Rajah's Palace
Kuching, Sarawak

"What am I to do, now?" Hasim wailed. He paced the floor of his throne room and held his arms tightly around his chest in front of him like a frightened child. Earlier, news of the Sultan and his mother's murders had reached him and thrown him into hysteria. Coupled with Langau's assassination attempt the previous night, Hasim had completely panicked. He ordered the palace sealed off and refused to admit anyone with the exception of the faithful *Datu* Temanggong.

"Why, Api, Why?" he sobbed. Hasim had no one to turn to. His mother had made most of the decisions for him and Hasim often leaned upon Api for advice. But now his mother was dead, and Api was a traitor and was certain to try to kill him again before Hasim could reach Brunei and claim the throne and the protection of the Malay princes there. Whom could he trust? Who would advise him now? How could he escape Sarawak and avoid being killed by Api?

And the bad news continued to reach Hasim's ears. Only a short time ago, a messenger from Siniawan had informed the *Datu* that a strong renegade Malay force, rumored to be led by Api himself, was moving toward Siniawan to augment the Iban tribes massing near the fort.

"If the Iban overwhelm the stockade, Api will be in Kuching within hours," Hasim cried. He crossed his arms and patted his own shoulders, trying to comfort himself.

"Perhaps, Lord Rajah, it would be wise for you to flee to Brunei. You will be safe there until my warriors defeat Api's rebels." The *Datu* Temanggong remained quietly distressed. He had done his best to fortify Siniawan, but without his leadership and with reports of more rebels moving toward Siniawan, he doubted his warriors would be able to hold the stockade. So far, Hasim adamantly refused to let the *Datu* Temanggong out of his sight or allow him to return to Siniawan.

"No! I will not leave! Who knows who might be in league with Api and the traitors? I can't trust anyone," Hasim sobbed. "Api's spies are probably waiting for me to leave the protection of the palace right now. I will not leave. It is much too dangerous!"

Hasim pointed a trembling finger beyond the closed window of the throne room and wailed, "Out there I would be easy to kill. Here, with you, I am safe."

But he knew he wasn't.

Never before had the *Datu* Temanggong questioned the orders of those whom he had served. But Hasim was unlike any of the other Rajahs and time was becoming precariously short. He knew he had to convince Hasim to flee to Brunei and allow him to return to Siniawan or all of Sarawak, perhaps Brunei as well, would fall into the hands of Api and the rebels.

"My Lord," *Datu* Temanggong pleaded haltingly. "The stockade at Siniawan is strong and my best warriors are behind its walls. With my leadership, they have a good chance to defeat the Iban and Api's rebels."

Hasim froze in his tracks and swung his head to face the old war chief. "A *chance?*" he spewed angrily. "Only a chance, you say? Do you mean to say that my life hangs on the thread of a...a mere *chance?*"

"No, my Lord Rajah, I only meant—"

Hasim continued pacing and lifted his arms in supplication. "Oh, Allah, why is it that you are against me? What sin have I committed to deserve such a fate?"

The *Datu* Temanggong summoned his courage for one final attempt to change Hasim's mind. "My Lord Rajah, if you would only reconsider. Send me to Siniawan where I can lead my warriors to victory over your enemies. I will rout the Iban and bring you the head of your brother. This I promise!"

Hasim stopped pacing. His tear-stained eyes faced away from the *Datu* Temanggong and stared blankly at the far wall. "If you leave me, who will remain to protect me?" he asked, pathetically.

"I will leave some of my most trusted warriors. They will see to your safety, my Lord."

"No...no, you must not go." Hasim fell to his knees and covered his head with his hands. He sobbed uncontrollably. "You cannot slay Api. No one can." The thought of Api's invincibility fell on Hasim like a blow from a *parang*. He was doomed.

There was nothing more the *Datu* Temanggong could do or say. He slumped his shoulders in defeat and resigned himself to stay with Hasim until the end.

# VI

## Near Siniawan,
## Sarawak, Borneo

"Read the bones again, Chopak," Rentab ordered.

The *saperti perempuan*, Chopak, prissily fondled the silver necklace dangling from his neck and frowned in disgust as he watched Rentab burn the flesh from three severed heads. "The words of the spirits will not change, *Tua Kampong*, no matter how many times I read the pig knuckles for you."

Rentab shot Chopak an annoyed glance before picking up a stick and poking at the three skulls he had tossed into the coals of his small fire. His mood turned pensive, contemplative. He prodded at the burning heads until his stick caught one of the skulls in the eye socket. The eyeball popped, hissing and exuding a flaming gelatinous mass into the fire. Rentab flipped each of the skulls over, inspecting each with the tip of his stick. Soon the flesh, hair and soft organs would be burned away and he could remove them from the fire. Afterwards he would scrape the skulls clean and bleach them in the sun until they were suitable to hang in the rafters of his longhouse at Batang.

"Again," Rentab persisted. "You may have missed something the first time."

Rentab hoped that the words of the spirits through Chopak would become clearer with a second reading of the pig's knuckles. After all, things had been going well for him since he became *Tua Kampong* of Batang; his raids against the Kayan and others had been successful and already songs were being sung about his heroism and leadership. He was reluctant to return to Batang before he accomplished one final thing and received the reward that Api promised him for doing it.

"Again, Chopak!" Rentab commanded, his voice harsher than before.

With reluctance, Chopak sighed and tossed the bones a second time. He breathed deeply and rolled his eyes until only the whites showed. He began to rock back and forth and twitched his head from side to side as if listening to invisible voices. "The spirits give you two choices, Rentab. Encounter the one with the long shadow and misfortune will befall some or return now to Batang and misfortune will befall none." Chopak stopped his rocking and opened his eyes. "The spirits say no more," he said with finality.

"It is the same," Rentab sighed.

"Of course it is the same. I told you the spirits would not change their minds just because you wanted to hear something different."

"What can it mean, Chopak? Tell me."

Chopak shrugged and tightened his woman's sarong around his chest. "I have already told you—"

"Tell me again. Perhaps you missed something. It is not an easy decision for me to make."

"Very well," Chopak sighed in resignation. "I think *Awang* Api is the one with the long shadow that the spirits refer to. He is the tallest of the Malay princes, is he not?"

Rentab nodded that Api was, indeed, the tallest of the Malay lords. "How can you be so sure it is *Awang* Api the spirits refer to?"

"Because he has offered you the title of *Pengulu* if you stay with him and help him defeat the Rajah's forces. Certainly some will die when you attack Siniawan and Kuching which is most probably the misfortune the spirits refer to."

Rentab nodded his agreement and contemplated the initial choice the spirits had given him. For Rentab's assistance in taking control of the Sultanate, Api promised to confer the title of *Pengulu*, Lord of the all the regional tribes, upon him, an honor that had never before been bestowed by a Malay lord upon a native. Rentab desired the title and power of a *Pengulu* more than anything else in the world. Since Api's offer, his own title of *Tua Kampong* now seemed trivial and petty and he coveted more.

Rentab nodded and then said casually, "Yes, some will die. That is the way of war. It can not be helped." Rentab smeared a dab of wet lime on a *sireh* leaf and wrapped an areca nut in it. "But there is something I don't understand about the spirit's second choice, Chopak," he said, offering the prepared leaf to Chopak.

Chopak declined the offering and Rentab popped it into his own mouth and began chewing at it. "What part do you not understand, *Tua Kampong?*" Chopak watched Rentab munch away at the mild narcotic. In Chopak's view, it was a disgusting habit. Chewing the *areca* nut turned the teeth black and, in time, abraded the teeth, assuring future discomfort for habitual users.

Rentab spit a long stream of crimson juice into the fire and wiped his mouth. "If I return to Batang, naturally none of my warriors will die which would be fortunate for them. But if I return to Batang, I will not become *Pengulu* of all the tribes which would be unfortunate for me. This makes no sense to me."

"The spirits can only make us aware of the many paths available to us," Chopak replied. "It is our choice to select one and make sense of it later."

Rentab remained reflective. He rolled one of the skulls from the fire and tossed dirt on it to cool it down. *Pengulu!* The very thought of him having such a title was worth any sacrifice, any risk. He flicked the remaining two skulls from the fire and watched them smolder on the ground as they cooled. He would add more skulls to his growing collection, he decided. The skulls of the Malay warriors at Siniawan as well as those in Kuching. Perhaps even the Rajah's head as well, he thought.

"I have decided. We will meet *Awang* Api in Siniawan as previously planned."

# VII

## Kampong Batang

Jau barely turned nineteen when his father died of the fever and he became headman of the Kayan village of Long Selah'at. His manhood had long been proven; since the time, years earlier, when he had returned to the village with the head of Rentab's young son. In the intervening years, Jau had added to his collection of skulls and had gradually assumed hegemony over neighboring Kayan tribes as well as the tribes of their close kinsmen, the Kenyah and Kedayan.

When he received word that his enemies, the Iban living along the Rajang and Batang Rivers, had banded together for a raiding expedition along the Sarawak River, he saw it as an opportunity to crush them.

Now, as Jau watched his warriors burn Batang to the ground, he felt as if something almost mystical had happened to him since it was at Batang that the Kayan Chieftan had taken his first head.

"What would you have us do with these Iban dogs, Jau?" A Kedayan warrior pushed six Iban captives, an old woman, two younger women and three children, the youngest a girl no more than two years old, to the ground at Jau's feet.

"These would make good slaves," another warrior said, waving his *parang* at the two younger women.

Jau stared impassively at the defeated enemy. The Iban masked their fear well and Jau respected that. Even the two-year-old child seemed impassive to the fact that her fate was now being decided by the man with the leopard fangs inserted in the lobes of his ears.

"No, we need no more slaves, especially Iban slaves. Kill them."

No sooner had the command been spoken than Jau's warriors pounced upon the captives and hacked off their heads. Jau watched the executions without emotion. The older Iban woman seemed to have more life in her death than she had while alive. When Jau's warriors decapitated her, her wilted body jumped and kicked as it had been tossed on an ant hill. The others died without protest.

"The spirits of our enemy will walk the forest forever. They will never find peace!" Jau exclaimed after the grim task was completed. Then, Jau's warriors began to sing songs praising Jau's leadership and bravery.

# VIII

### Rajah's Palace
### Kuching, Sarawak

A loud pounding on the bared door to the throne room awakened Hasim from his two day fit of catatonia and self-pity. He turned his frightened eyes toward the door and waved a trembling finger at it. "Assassins!" he cried. "Assassins! Api has come to kill me!"

Bravely, the *Datu* Temanggong pulled his *parang* from its sheath and stood protectively between the door and his nearly insane Rajah. "Who is there? Speak up! Traitor or friend?"

"A message for the Lord Rajah," came the voice from behind the door.

"What is it?"

"An English ship is approaching Kuching. It is nearing Santabong at this moment."

# IX

## The Jungle
## Above Kampong Batang

"You saw these things?" Batu asked.

His brother nodded that he had. "Many fires, all along the Rajang and Batang Rivers. I saw many Iban, mostly women and children flee into the jungle to escape Jau and his warriors. There was much death and many Iban longhouses were burned."

Batu shook his head sadly. He had never heard of so much destruction before. *What could it mean?* He wondered.

"Perhaps these are bad omens," his brother offered.

"Yes, these are bad signs," Batu concurred. He recalled seeing the fire when Brunei had burned several years earlier and had heard rumors from the Kayan about what had transpired in Brunei that night.

"What does it mean, Batu?" his brother asked. "What spirit is it that causes such things to happen?"

"Perhaps it is not a spirit at all," Batu offered. "Maybe it is the one the Kayan told us about, the Malay prince, the one with the long shadow."

Batu's Punan clan murmured uneasily and they pressed closer to the warmth and safety of their small fire.

To comfort them, Batu said, "In the morning we will leave this place. It is not wise for us to remain so near this troubled land and the one with the long shadow."

# CHAPTER SEVEN

## I

*HMS Skimalong*

"So that's Sarawak," James said with awe and wonder on his voice. He stood at the rail near the stern of the *Skimalong* flanked on either side by Captain Irons and Si Tundok. The morning was bright and the sea surrounding the green coast of the land was calm and blue.

"We will round that point over there and make our way up the Sarawak River to Kuching. The river's navigable, but we will need to be careful because it's full of constantly shifting mud bars." Timothy pointed to the murky confluence of the river. The flow of river water created a brown fan-like projection into the coastal waters of the South China Sea. Timothy then drew James' and Si Tundok's attention to the port side of the ship and said, "That is where the *Cecilia* ran aground. Even from this distance, you can see the dangerous shallows."

Timothy had told James and Si Tundok the entire story of the *Cecilia's* disaster and the crew's narrow escape shortly after they had departed Singapore. James spotted the shallows easily and he understood why Captain Irons was so upset with Captain Templar for running the *Cecilia* aground.

Prior to the *Skimalong* setting sail for Sarawak, James met with the Governor-General, Samuel McDonald. James took Henry and Si Tundok with him to the meeting and it was there that he was introduced to the newly appointed captain of the *Skimalong*, Timothy Irons. It was then that James learned that the same man who had rescued Henry and Si Tundok from Geoff and the one-eyed Chinaman was the same man who would be conveying him to Borneo. It was a happy reunion for Timothy, Si Tundok and Henry, and James had a sense that the coincidence augured well for the expedition. With the Governor-General's permission, it was agreed that Si Tundok would accompany James and serve as interpreter while Henry remained in Singapore to oversee the fitting of the *Jolly Bachelor*.

"You say the Rajah's court is at the mouth of that river over there?" James asked, pointing to the wide, muddy mouth of the Sarawak River which was partially obscured by thick jungle that seemed to grow in the river itself without benefit of beach or land.

"That's right, about twelve to fifteen kilometers from here. But it's not much of a court—not much of a town either. Not in our way of thinking,

171

anyway," Captain Irons said. "Just a bunch of bamboo and thatch houses raised from the mud on stilts. I would guess maybe five or six hundred people live there, mostly Malay."

"You mentioned earlier that you met the Rajah. What was he like, Captain?" James asked.

"Seemed like a pleasant enough fellow to me. His name's Hasim, but he has a brother by the name of Api who I don't think was as willing to help us out as the Rajah was."

"Oh, how do you mean?"

Timothy shook his head. "Don't really know how to put it. He just seemed like an incorrigible sort of fellow. Arrogant too, always giving orders and never going out of his way to be solicitous. Had a mean look in his eye, if you know what I mean. One of my mates spoke a bit of the language and I had him pump the fellow who rescued us, a bloke they called the *Datu* Temanggong. Scuttlebutt has it that the Rajah's brother pretty much runs Sarawak. But I got the impression that he wasn't doing much of a job of it according to what the *Datu* Temanggong told us."

"Oh?"

"Yeah. Seems like this old fellow, the *Datu* Temanggong was some sort of advisor to the Rajah, maybe he was royalty or something, I don't really know, but he told us that this Api fellow took control of the Rajah's court and demoted most of Hasim's advisors after Hasim became Rajah of Sarawak. Since that time, the Rajah has had his hands full trying to control the Dyaks within the country and the pirates who prey upon the coastal territories of Sarawak."

James remembered Sir Stamford telling him about the Dyaks, the term designated by the Malay for the indigenous people of Borneo. "This fellow you call the *Datu* Temanggong, what was he like?"

"Friendly. Good bloke. Went out of his way to make sure we were properly cared for."

"I see..." James wanted to learn more about the Rajah and the men who were closest to him. He felt that the more he learned, the easier it would be to negotiate a trade concession. But before he could ask more questions of Captain Irons, Timothy excused himself and went to the bridge of the ship where he could oversee the tricky navigation of the *Skimalong* up the Sarawak River.

As Captain Irons walked away, Si Tundok said, "Captain Irons is a good man." For most of his life, Si Tundok had been at war with the Europeans. First, his father, then the Dutch and Spanish and finally, the British who incarcerated him. And now he was finding himself in their debt; to James for saving his life, to Henry who had proven himself a faithful and loyal companion, and to Captain Irons whose intervention most certainly saved Henry's life and probably his own. Si Tundok wondered how he could possibly repay these men whom he had come to respect.

"Yes, yes, he is. We are fortunate to have him commanding the ship," James agreed. "Not only is the captain a capable officer, but he will also be someone familiar to the Rajah." James knew that Captain Irons' role in the mission was limited, but the presence of Captain Irons and the *Skimalong* should give the impression that James himself had the power of the British navy behind him and that was something he hoped to use to his advantage.

"We might be glad to have the *Skimalong* under our feet too, James. If what Captain Irons tells us about there being trouble with the Dyaks is true, we may need the ship's guns before our trip is finished." Si Tundok turned his head and his gray eyes scanned the two rows of cannon lining the ship's mainsail deck behind them.

"Let us hope we don't need them. I've waited too long for this moment to let a few savages spoil it for me."

The two of them watched the slow progress of the *Skimalong* as Timothy eased her up the Sarawak River. Captain Irons had ordered the mainsail lowered and had placed seamen along the bow and sides of the ship with instructions to keep a sharp eye out for shallow water.

"What do you know of these people, the Dyaks, Si Tundok?"

Si Tundok shrugged. "Not much. Like Captain Irons said, the term refers to all the native tribes. I only know of one of the tribes."

"Oh, which one is that?" James asked.

"The Iban. They are headhunters. Some of them sailed with us when I lived in Marudu Bay."

"You mean when you were a pirate, don't you?" James chuckled, remembering the stories Si Tundok told him about his early years as a pirate sailing out of the Philippines and preying upon Chinese shipping.

Si Tundok grinned. "That was a long time ago, James."

"I know. So what can you tell me about the Iban?"

"They were tough, sometimes cruel and would often take great risks to take a head. They were good seamen though," Si Tundok said with some admiration.

"Well, let's hope the Iban are looking for heads somewhere else for the next few days. I don't want anything or anybody interfering with my chance to get a trade concession from the Rajah," James said.

"This concession, it means a great deal to you, doesn't it, James?"

James took note of the serious cast to Si Tundok's face when he asked the question. "It means everything to me," James said. "Since I was a boy, I dreamed of doing this very thing. Sailing off somewhere and seeking my fortune. This is the beginning of making that dream a reality. I gave up a great deal to make it happen." James thought of how he left Elizabeth and his broken vow to his father. "Yes, a very great deal," he emphasized somewhat dolefully.

Si Tundok had difficulty understanding what James was telling him. That the expedition was important to James was made clear to Si Tundok by James' demeanor when James explained his dream to him, with a voice and expression that seemed far, far away as if the past and present had congealed at this very moment in time. But the reason for James' dream, or any man's dream of the future still eluded Si Tundok. He couldn't fathom why a man of James' background, one of position and comfort, would seek to put his life in jeopardy to pursue such a dream. Si Tundok only remembered having one dream—to escape the tyranny of his own father, a dream he fulfilled by killing him. Since that time, there had been no dreams for Si Tundok, only a desire to do what he had to do to survive.

"I am hopeful that your dream will come true," Si Tundok said in all sincerity. His gray eyes stared pensively into the muddy waters of the river passing beneath the ship's bow and he silently vowed to do whatever he could to make James' dream a reality. He also hoped that he, too, might have such dreams some day.

"Boats off the beam, Captain!"

Si Tundok and James glanced upriver to where the crewman pointed. Coming around the next bend in the river were a dozen war canoes.

As the boats closed, it became apparent that they were not hostile. Each of the canoes displayed colorful banners and their hulls were lined with garlands of flowers and palm branches. A cacophony of discordant sound emanated from the *praus*.

"Gongs," Si Tundok explained. "And drums. It is a traditional greeting. The Rajah is welcoming us to Kuching."

Soon the Rajah's swift *praus* were darting along the side of the British man-of-war, their oarsman waving their arms and shouting greetings.

"This is truly a spectacular sight," James said to no one in particular. He was caught up in the moment as if the threads of his dream had finally stitched him to this one particular place and this one particular moment in time. He felt more than excitement, he felt as if his personal destiny was one step closer to fulfillment.

From the *Skimalong's* bridge, Captain Irons had his hands full directing his ship's cautious course up the river. The discordant noise from the clatter of gongs and the banging of drums made it difficult for him to hear the reports of the watchmen who shouted warnings of shallows or hidden mud banks.

"The bloke standin' up in the big craft off the starboard beam seems to be calling for you, Captain." The helmsman pointed to the largest of the Malay boats.

Timothy recognized the man waving his arms. It was the *Datu* Temanggong and he seemed to want something.

"Si Tundok," Captain Irons yelled, "can you hear him? What does he want?"

Si Tundok moved to the starboard side of the ship and shouted Timothy's question to the old war chief. "He wants you to follow his canoe. He will lead you through the shallow water to Kuching."

In less than an hour, the *Skimalong* dropped anchor in the middle of the wide river, opposite the sprawling village of Kuching.

It was just as Timothy told James, a village of bamboo and thatch houses raised above the mud flats on hardwood stilts. Other buildings, built in a similar manner, littered the grassy slopes leading to the river's edge. A single dock jutted into the river and was surrounded by sailing vessels of various sizes and shapes. Just beyond the dock, the largest of the village's buildings stood apart from the rest. James correctly guessed that it was the Rajah's palace. And Kuching seemed more populous than James imagined it would be.

As a pinnace was lowered to take the British landing party ashore, Timothy ordered a twenty-one gun salute to be fired in the Rajah's honor.

The sudden blast of the ship's guns startled the throng of curious spectators who had gathered along the narrow wharf and the river's edge to catch a glimpse of the foreigners. Some fell to the ground and covered their heads, certain they were being fired upon. Others scattered and ran to the safety of their *rumahs*. But a few, like the *Datu* Temanggong held their ground and made disparaging remarks about the bravery of those who fled.

Eight bluejackets from the *Skimalong's* crew rowed the small delegation to Kuching's boat dock where they were affably greeted by the *Datu* Temanggong who seemed particularly delighted when he recognized Captain Irons in the shore party.

Si Tundok interpreted Captain Irons' introduction of James to the *Datu* Temanggong. The old war chief seemed equally delighted to receive James who was introduced by Si Tundok as the *Tuan Besar*, the Big Lord. Flanked by a contingent of elaborately dressed Kuching nobility and a widening throng of curious spectators, Captain Irons, James and Si Tundok were escorted to Hasim's unpretentious palace.

James, head and shoulders taller than the encircling crowd, took in every detail of what he could see of the village on the short walk to the Rajah's palace. There were no great stone monuments or intricately carved statues such as he had seen in Burma and India. Nor did Kuching give the appearance of being an elaborately planned port village, simply a maze of randomly built huts sprawling between the mud flats along the river and the impenetrable jungle beyond.

But the villagers, particularly the notables, wore exquisitely woven sarongs and lace and silk tunics, many adorned in elaborately hand crafted jewelry of gold and silver. Their smooth, oval faces smiled curiously at the passing British delegation and James determined that the people of Sarawak, at least the Malay, were a cultured race, if not an overly civilized one by Western standards.

James was mildly disappointed when the delegation was momentarily halted at the base of a wide expanse of steps leading to the Rajah's palace. A 'palace' it was not, at least not in James' estimation. The only features which differentiated the Rajah's palace from the other buildings in Kuching were its size, which was more than three times larger than the largest of any other visible building, and its walls which were constructed of hand hewn planks instead of split bamboo. Like all of the other *rumahs*, the roof of the palace was fabricated with palm thatch.

"Why are we waiting here?" James asked when the entourage stopped at the base of the steps leading to the palace.

"The *Datu* is dismissing the crowd and the *pangirins*, the nobility," Si Tundok replied.

"Isn't that a bit unusual?"

Si Tundok only shrugged that he didn't know and continued to interpret the *Datu* Temanggong's instructions. "The *Datu* asks that you leave your men here, Captain Irons. He says also that only he, Captain Irons, you and I are permitted to enter the throne room."

Having no objection, Timothy ordered the bluejackets to remain at the front of the palace. Two of the sailors toted a large trunk containing gifts sent from the Governor-General to the Rajah Hasim. They placed the trunk at Si Tundok's feet and he and Captain Irons carried it to the top of the stairway after the *Datu* Temanggong motioned them forward.

The large, bilian carved door leading to the interior of the palace remained sealed until after the men mounted the steps and the *Datu* Temanggong whispered something through the door. James heard a bar behind the door being removed. Slowly the heavy portal eased open and the strained and perplexed face of Hasim, Rajah of Sarawak tenuously peered at them from behind the door.

After a few uncomfortable moments, Hasim opened the door and beckoned the men forward. Once inside, Hasim hurried to shut the door and replaced the heavy bilian bar across it. When he turned to face his somewhat

176

confused guests, Hasim's haggard face erupted in a warm and gracious smile and he held his hands wide open in a sign of greeting.

More like a servant than a prince, Hasim ushered the men into the throne room and offered them seats on an intricately woven rattan mat which faced a simple hardwood throne littered with silk pillows. Hasim sat on the throne and faced the foreign delegation.

James quickly surveyed the inside of the palace. Unlike the crude exterior, the throne room was finely decorated. Evenly spaced tapestries graced the walls, each splendidly woven with colorful collages of white, maroon and black. Painted wooden war shields, spears and *parangs* adorned the spaces between the tapestries. Even the floor was of hand polished hardwood.

"That's the Rajah?" James asked through the corner of his mouth.

When Timothy nodded that it was, James took a closer look at the man exhibiting such strange behavior. Hasim was attired in a gold embroidered sarong with a *baju* of white silk and lace. His head was bare, and unlike many of the people James saw while being escorted to the palace, Hasim's straight black hair was cropped short above his ears as if a bowl had been placed upon his head before trimming his hair. The Rajah lacked the musculature of the other Malay James had seen and his clothing seemed to contain him rather than cover him. Appearing to be in his mid-thirties, Hasim was not an altogether unattractive man except for a small, pointed jaw and nervous, glossy eyes which flitted from place to place.

At first, Hasim remained nervously silent, his head turning from his guest to the *Datu* Temanggong who had taken up a protective position at his lord's side. Then Hasim covered his mouth and whispered something to the *Datu* who only nodded and grunted a response.

Without saying anything to James or the others, the *Datu* hastened back to the doorway and shouted something through it. Puzzled by the inexplicable behavior, the British envoy craned their necks and watched the *Datu* shout commands through the closed entryway. Shortly, the *Datu* removed the bar from the door and admitted two Malay girls carrying trays of food. With solemn, downcast eyes, the girls placed the trays before the visitors and then quickly scampered from the room. The *Datu* Temanggong closed the door behind them and replaced the bar before crossing the room and resuming his position adjacent to the Rajah.

James and Timothy exchanged glances, both conveying bafflement at the strange reception. Then Hasim spoke and Si Tundok interpreted.

"He asks that we eat."

With Si Tundok initiating, Timothy and James sampled a variety of spiced rice, curry and fresh fruit which had been elaborately arranged on the trays. Young, green coconuts, their tops slashed open, proved to be a cool and refreshing drink. And James particularly liked the sweet pith of a hairy fruit Si Tundok called, *rambutan.*

Hasim studied the Europeans, only breaking into a toothy grin when one of them glanced up at him. He tried to recall all of what his mother, the *Dayang* Udang, had said with regard to the British. She had arranged for their return and he remembered that she wanted to grant them a concession in return for their protection. And protection was what Hasim most needed now.

When they had finished eating, James stood up and made a formal bow to the Rajah. Through Si Tundok he said, "Your Majesty, we are most pleased by your warm hospitality."

Hasim seemed genuinely flattered by James' words and his formal bow. James' height amazed Hasim. He mentioned it to the *Datu*, asking if all English lords were giants. The *Datu* said he didn't know but he would ask the interpreter if the Rajah wished it. Hasim shook his head watched James and listened to Si Tundok interpret James' words.

"In appreciation for the Rajah's show of friendship and his brave and timely rescue of His Majesty's ship, the *Cecilia*, and the kindness the lord of Sarawak had shown the crew of the ship, I bring gifts from my King, His Majesty King George."

James asked that Timothy open the trunk and display the contents to the Rajah. As Timothy complied, James continued his formal speech. "These gifts are a mere token of the esteem, His Majesty, the Rajah of Sarawak, is held by the government of Great Britain and the English people. May they forever be but a small reminder of the great friendship which exists between His Majesty, the Rajah of Sarawak and His Majesty, King George of Britain."

Hasim was pleased with James' words, but more so with the gifts. Without respect to deportment, Hasim groveled among the gifts, holding each of them up for the *Datu* Temanggong to admire. He unraveled several bolts of Indian broadcloth and Thai silk, the world's finest, and touched its cool smoothness to his face. There were several military swords in ornate scabbards and a brace of muskets, complete with shot and powder, set in a red velvet cask of English oak. But the last item pulled from the trunk seemed to fascinate Hasim the most. It was a complete set of formal English attire including a broadcloth great-coat which was cape-less, trousers with instep straps attached to the cuffs and fashioned from colored nankeen, an assortment of shirts with full sleeves, gathered cuffs and pleated armholes, satin waistcoats, and several fashionable coats with high collars and spreading lapels accompanied by an assortment of dark cravats and white slips.

But as Hasim completed his wading through of the bonanza of fabric, one item fascinated him the most, a broad-brimmed Napoleon hat with a rising crown. Carefully and with as much show of grandeur as he could muster, Hasim placed the hat upon his head. Slowly he rotated for all to admire.

It was all that Timothy could do to keep from laughing, but James proffered another deep bow and said, "It will warm my King's heart to know that his gifts are so well received by His Majesty."

Hasim tugged on the *Datu's* arm. When the *Datu* Temanggong leaned over, Hasim, covering his mouth as before, whispered into his ear. When Hasim finished, he turned back to James and the others and smiled. The *Datu* relayed Hasim's words to Si Tundok.

"His Majesty, Hasim, Rajah of Sarawak, is most pleased with the gifts from the *Tuan Besar's* King. Does the *Tuan Besar* now wish to discuss a trade concession with the Rajah?"

The question caught James by surprise. He was thinking how he might breech the subject of a concession with the Rajah when the *Datu* made his surprise pronouncement.

James remained standing and wiped the momentary lack of composure from his face. "Most certainly," he replied. "I am most anxious to discuss a trade arrangement with the Rajah."

"It is granted," the *Datu* said simply.

"What?" James was flabbergasted. *It couldn't be this easy,* he told himself. "But we need to discuss the terms of the agreement...," he stammered. "...what I shall be licensed to do and what the Rajah shall expect in return."

Although Hasim could clearly hear Si Tundok's interpretation of James' words, he waited for the *Datu* Temanggong to relay them to him and again spoke in a whisper to his confidant.

"The Rajah says that you may have what you want."

"But I don't understand, does that mean exclusive trade rights in Sarawak?"

"If that is what you want, then the Rajah says you may have it."

James was overwhelmed by the offer. *Exclusive rights to all of Sarawak?* He could see his fortune already made.

"And what percentage of the profits does the Rajah wish from me for this most generous concession?"

"No payment. The Rajah only asks that you protect him for the privilege of the concession."

"Protect him? I'm afraid I don't understand what His Majesty means."

James waited while the Hasim continued whispering in the ear of the *Datu.*

"I think the Rajah is under the impression that you have other ships like the *Skimalong* at your command." Si Tundok tried to stifle a grin, but couldn't when he added, "I think the Rajah believes you are more important than you really are, James."

Although amused, Timothy said in a serious tone, "James, it is my duty to caution you. What you do as a private citizen is your own affair. But I am under strict orders not to involve the British government in any way with the affairs of Borneo."

"I understand, Captain Irons," James replied. He pondered what exactly Hasim meant by his request for protection.

Shortly, he received his answer. "The Rajah says you must go to Siniawan and defeat the rebel Malay and Iban who are gathering there. You must also slay the leader of the insurgents, Api, brother of the Rajah Hasim. If you do these things, the Rajah of Sarawak and soon to be Sultan of Brunei will grant you the terms of a concession as you desire it to be."

"Now you know what he means by protection, James," Timothy said. "He wants you to solve his internal problem for him. He's not asking for much, only the impossible."

James ignored Timothy's assessment and blurted out, "Agreed! I will defeat the Rajah's enemies. In return he shall grant me an exclusive right to trade in all manner of goods I shall desire."

Timothy shot up from the floor. "James, have you gone bloody mad? How in the hell do you intend to stop a rebellion when even the Rajah can't do it?"

"I don't know yet. I'll figure that out when I get to this place they call Siniawan."

"I can't help you, you know that don't you? My orders are—"

"I know, Captain Irons, you can't involve the government but, like you said, what I do as a private citizen is my own affair, right?"

"True," Timothy agreed. "But think, man! There's nothing you can possibly do against the Iban. They're headhunters, remember? You'll get yourself killed and your handsome English head will be hanging in some longhouse in this God-forsaken land. It's not worth the risk, James. I implore you, retract your offer before it's too late."

"I appreciate your concern, Captain Irons, honestly I do, but it is my decision to make and I have already made it."

James stepped around Timothy and spoke to Si Tundok. "Tell the Rajah that I will draw up the document regarding the concession. I will expect it to be signed and honored when I return from this place they call Siniawan."

"When *we* return," Si Tundok said.

## II

## The Stockade
## Siniawan, Sarawak

The sun neared its zenith by the time James and Si Tundok, accompanied by the *Datu* Temanggong and several war canoes filled with Malay warriors, reached Siniawan aboard the *Skimalong's* pinnace. Captain Irons, concerned for James' safety, granted permission to use the ship's pinnace and asked for three volunteers from the ship's company to accompany James and his party to Siniawan. Two bluejackets and an eager young officer by the name of Harris with shimmering shocks of blonde hair protruding from beneath his cock-and-pinch cap, joined James and Si Tundok for the trip up the Sarawak River. To James' delight, Captain Irons had also ordered that a four pound cannon be mounted in the pinnaces' bow saying, 'to see to it that you all return with your heads intact.'

Captain Irons also extended an invitation to the Rajah to join him as a guest aboard the *Skimalong* until the situation in Siniawan was resolved. Eagerly Hasim accepted, preferring the safety of the *Skimalong's* gun-lined deck to the insecurity of his own capital. Assured of his own personal safety, Hasim consented to allow the *Datu* Temanggong to accompany James' party.

After the pinnace disembarked at Siniawan, the *Datu* Temanggong led James, Si Tundok and the three members of the *Skimalong's* crew up a steep embankment which ended at a hastily constructed redoubt built of skinned timber, earth and bamboo.

As unimpressive as the fortress was, James' trained military eye decided that the Malay war chief had selected a strategically advantageous spot to build the stockade. It sat on top of a small knoll which overlooked the main branch of the Sarawak River as well as its two feeder streams, the Sarawak Kanon and the Sarawak Kiri. From this position, the garrison had an unimpeded view of each of the three rivers and, because the knoll sat at the end of a narrow peninsula, the Malay forces were in a position to observe land-side movement as well.

James noted that the steep landward approach to the fortress had been stripped clean of forest cover and the downed trees and brush had been burned for a distance of some hundred and fifty kilometers. Anyone moving up the slope to the fortress from the landward side would be easily seen from the garrison.

The garrison's force greeted the arrival of the *Datu* Temanggong with enthusiastic whoops of welcome. It was obvious to James and Si Tundok that the old war chief was well thought of by his warriors. The same raucous warriors viewed James and the crew with open curiosity. Most had never seen a white man before and none of them had ever seen a man who cast such a long shadow as James did.

Once inside the fortress, the new arrivals were offered refreshments of coconut milk and fruit which James declined. He was anxious to further access the defenses.

"Si Tundok, ask the *Datu* Temanggong how many men he has manning the fort," James said as he led them to the ramparts facing the landward side of the fortress.

"He says he has nearly two hundred warriors here, also some Chinese."

"Chinese?"

"Over there, near the south wall."

About three dozen Chinese huddled together near the wall. Unlike the Malay who were mostly armed with *parangs* and spears, the Chinese were better equipped with muskets and cutlasses.

"Any cannon?"

"No cannon."

James and Si Tundok turned simultaneously to the sound of men cursing along the west ramparts. The *Datu* Temanggong sprinted to the wall and joined a few shouting warriors along the ramparts and added his own shouts of insults to theirs.

"What's that all about," James asked as they followed the *Datu* to the redoubt.

"I'm not sure," Si Tundok said as the two of them mounted the rampart and stood next to the old Malay war chief. The *Datu* pointed to the jungle below the slope leading to the fortress and explained while Si Tundok interpreted.

"The rebels are massing at the edge of the jungle, there...just beyond where the Malay have cleared the forest. The *Datu* and his warriors are shouting insults to them."

James shaded the sun from his eyes and peered into the jungle beyond the base of the knoll. He could see movement, but little else.

"The Iban have built a barricade at the edge of the big trees. You can see it if you look closely." Si Tundok pointed and James followed the direction of his arm.

At first James saw nothing but the placid green of the jungle, occasionally disrupted by a moving form. As his vision began to filter out the myriads of greens from the background, he was able to detect the Iban barricade. It was nothing more than a single stand of cut timbers approximately four feet high facing the slope which led to the Malay fortress. The enemy stockade seemed to be built in sections between stands of enormous trees.

As James concentrated on the site, he could see men moving from the shelter of the jungle to take up positions behind the barrier. Shortly, the trickle of men became a stream. "They're massing to attack!" he said.

The *Datu* drew his *parang* and waved it wildly above his head and uttered some angry words.

"He says he is ready to attack them," Si Tundok told James.

James shook his head. "No, they have us outnumbered. We don't stand a chance out in the open. We'll let them come to us."

The Malay war chief seemed disappointed when Si Tundok translated James' orders. He mumbled something to Si Tundok and went back to tossing taunts at the Iban.

"The *Datu* says it is cowardly to hide behind these walls."

"It may seem that way to him, but I don't intend losing my head." James turned and shouted into the stockade, "Mister Harris, would you come here a moment?"

The *Skimalong's* young officer was casually sipping coconut milk with his men against a shaded portion of the north wall when he heard his name called.

"Quickly, Mister Harris!" James shouted.

The officer tossed the coconut aside and leapt to his feet and rushed to the base of the rampart and looked up at James. "Yes, sir, Mister Brooke, what is it?"

"Mister Harris, I want you and your bluejackets to dismount the four pounder from the pinnace and bring it to the rampart. Take some of the Malay with you and bring up all the shot and powder you've got."

The ship's officer nervously shuffled his feet and remained standing in place, a perplexed look on his inexperienced face.

"What is the matter, Mister Harris?"

"My apology, Mister Brooke, but my orders are not to engage in hostile action unless our lives are threatened."

James knelt down and leaned forward to face the young officer squarely. "Mister Harris, I don't have time to explain our situation, but unless you order your men to bring that cannon up here immediately, five hundred screaming savages are going to take this fortress and kill us all. Unless you want your head hanging in an Iban longhouse by nightfall, you had best do as I suggest and do it quickly!"

"Head?...Oh, no, sir...I mean, aye sir, I'll get the gun." Holding his cap to his head, the young officer ran to his men, gathered a few Malay warriors and headed down the backside of the Malay fortress to comply with James' command.

"The *Datu* wants to know what you plan to do," Si Tundok said.

"We'll mount the four pounder here, in the middle of the rampart and lay down a barrage of shot when the rebels rush us." James was hopeful that most of the savages had never been under fire before. If they reacted the same way as the citizens of Kuching did during Timothy's twenty-one gun salute, then James' smaller force may be able to gain an advantage.

With a sense of urgency, James explained the remainder of his hastily made plan.

# III

## The Rebel Barricade
## Siniawan, Sarawak

"Rentab, come quickly!"

Rentab didn't look up. He recognized Chopak's high pitched voice and decided to ignore him. With renewed vigor he placed the blade of his *parang* against a basalt rock outcropping and continued to sharpen it. He still pondered Chopak's reading of the bones and debated with himself if he had made the right choice by staying at Siniawan. *Things will be better*, he tried to convince himself, *once the battle begins*. It was much easier to fight and kill than it was to make decisions, he decided. *Maybe it will be easier once I am Pengulu*, he thought.

Chopak came crashing through the forest and dropped at Rentab's feet. Excitedly, he pointed toward the Malay fort. "*Tua Kampong*," he blurted, "A white man is with the Malay!"

"A white man?" Rentab leaped to his feet. He had never seen a white man before and he wondered what it meant.

Rentab sprinted to the barricade. "Summon *Awang* Api!" he shouted over his shoulder to Chopak.

When Rentab reached the barricade he peered up the rise to the Malay fort. It was as Chopak said. He saw a tall white man moving on the facing rampart between the *Datu* Temanggong and a broad-shouldered Malay he had never before seen.

"What is it? What do you want, Rentab?" Api had been in a black mood since he learned of Langau's failure to assassinate Hasim.

"There! On the Rampart, a white man!"

Api realized as soon as he saw James that the British had returned to Sarawak as the *Dayang* Udang had planned. He ground his teeth together. *If only Langau had killed Hasim*, he thought.

"Aiyee..." Rentab wheezed. "I have never seen a white man before. What does this mean, *Awang* Api?"

"It means nothing!" Api spat. "My brother is so weak, he must beg foreigners to help him, that is all."

"Perhaps Chopak should cast the bones?" Rentab suggested.

Api grabbed Rentab's arm and turned him. He read the doubt in Rentab's face and knew he must act quickly to convince the Iban chieftain to follow his plan. "Can the bones make you a *Pengulu*, Rentab? No, only I can do that

185

for you. Don't let the sight of a single white man turn your blood to the blood of a woman or make you weak in the head like this *seperti perempuan* here!" Angrily, Api pushed Chopak away.

"But the white man, he has a long shadow," Rentab protested, remembering Chopak's prior reading of the bones and trying to sort out in his mind what it all meant.

Api pressed his angry face close to Rentab's. "Listen to me! Think of what it will mean to take the head of a white man, Rentab. You will be honored and praised by all the tribes in Sarawak. It would be a rare opportunity for a *Pengulu.*"

*Pengulu*! The very sound of the title resounded in Rentab's head. It meant power and prestige. Swayed by Api's argument, Rentab suddenly found himself thinking less of Chopak's spirits and more of his future life as *Pengulu.*

Api pressed his advantage. "We have three times as many warriors as the *Datu* Temanggong. What can one white man possibly do to keep us from our destinies?"

*Yes, destiny! That's what it is.* Awang *Api is right. It is my destiny to become* Pengulu *as much as it is his destiny to become* Sultan. Rentab stepped away from Api and struck a pose with his chest swelled and his chin held high, revealing the full length of the tattoo on his throat. He scowled ferociously and shouted for all to hear, "The white man's head is mine!"

IV

## The Malay Stockade
## Siniawan, Sarawak

"Here they come!" Si Tundok shouted.

Rentab's Iban and Api's renegade Malay warriors poured over the barricade like a swarm of army ants and charged headlong up the sloping knoll toward the Malay fortress. There was no strategy to Api's mass attack, he simply meant to overpower the fortress with his superior numbers.

Si Tundok stood silently to James' right with the Chinese musketeers kneeling on the rampart in front of him. Si Tundok held a musket pistol in one hand and a saber in the other. His gray eyes narrowed. Like a pier of iron, Si Tundok stood straight with his feet spread and firmly anchored to the rampart. The well-defined muscles of his chest and massive arms glistened bare in the heat of the late afternoon sun.

To James' left, the *Datu* Temanggong brandished his heavy *parang* at the attacking Iban and shouted taunts and obscenities at them.

James stood between them and beside the *Skimalong's* crewmen who were preparing to fire the pinnace's four pound gun. Having discarded his coat, cravat, and hose, James wore only white breeches and a ruffled silk shirt with the sleeves rolled tightly to his upper arms. His calves and forearms were bare. Rays of sunlight danced upon his mussed red-blonde hair and reflected from his white clothing and pale skin giving him the appearance of a phantasm in a sea of brown and green. James held a saber in his right hand and a brace of musket pistols were tucked into the front of his breeches.

"Easy lads...easy," James said calmly to the *Skimalong's* gun crew.

The young officer's eyes darted nervously between the charging savages and James. The mass of screaming savages racing towards them disconcerted him and without waiting for James' order, he yelled, "Fire!"

The premature shot from the pinnace's small gun landed far beyond the Iban barricade and exploded harmlessly deep in the jungle.

James locked his cold blue eyes on the frightened young officer. "Wait for my command, Mister Harris," he said in a surprisingly calm tone of voice.

Soothed by James' demeanor, the ship's officer swallowed his fear. "Aye, Mister Brooke."

With mechanical efficiency, the gun crew re-packed the small cannon with powder and rolled another four pound ball of steel into its barrel, primed it and waited for James' command.

"Lower your aim, Mister Harris," James commanded. "We want them to get a closer look at British steel than we did the last time."

"Aye!" Harris' crew elevated the rear of the gun.

"Fire!" James yelled.

The shell exploded several kilometers in front of the advancing rebels. The percussion toppled a half dozen warriors, including Api's cousin, Haji, and the fragments of exploding steel cut down another four or five.

"That's the range, lads. Keep your volley right in front of them. Take over Mister Harris, but keep the shot in front of the charge!"

"Aye, Mister Brooke, we'll feed them all the steel we've got!"

James moved closer to Si Tundok and watched the havoc reaped by the gun crew on the charging savages. The rebels charge was slowed not only by the cannon shot but also by the soft, marshy ground along the slope where the *Datu's* men had cleared the forest. Some of the rebels had stopped completely, stunned and confused by the sound of the explosion and the sight of their dead comrades. The Iban and renegade Malay were unaccustomed to death being administered from a distance and already many of them in the front ranks appeared to be wavering. The first part of James' plan was working.

But before the startled warriors could break and retreat to the safety of the forest, James saw two men emerge from the smoke. Both men were distinguishable from the others; one was a heavily tattooed Iban who physically pushed and prodded his warriors forward while the second, a tall, lighter skinned man with shortly cropped hair and dressed in a sarong similar to the *Datu* Temanggong's, raised his *parang* and threatened to cut down any who dared to retreat. The attack continued.

James locked his eyes on the Malay leader. He knew instinctively that it was Api, the man he must kill.

"*Awang* Api, the Rajah's treacherous brother," the *Datu* Temanggong yelled. And Rentab, the Dayak leader! I shall cut the rebel pigs down with my own *parang*!" The old war chief started to leap from the rampart.

"No! Hold your position until James gives the command!" Si Tundok yelled just in time to prevent the *Datu* from attacking prematurely.

Rentab and Api's exhortations rallied the savages and they closed the gap between themselves and the Malay rampart to a mere hundred meters.

Unable to adjust the ship's canon any lower, Harris' gun crew saw their shot fall harmlessly behind the charging Iban. But the small canon had been effective. The slope was littered with fallen savages. Some were dead and others, wounded and stunned, struggled to gain their feet and crawl towards the safety of the Iban barricade or the forest behind it.

"Mister Harris," James shouted, "elevate your fire and lay down a volley along the edge of their barricade. Cut off any who retreat."

The *Skimalong's* officer seemed bewildered. All he could see were hordes of naked savages brandishing spears, *parangs* and war shields. Within moments they would reach the rampart and slaughter the defenders. If they were in retreat, he didn't see it. His fear and panic began to surface once again, but his training and discipline prevailed.

Harris turned to his gun crew and yelled, "You heard Mister Brooke! Elevate the gun, lads!"

"Si Tundok! Are you ready?" James shouted with his sword raised above his head.

"Ready, James!"

"Now!" James shouted.

Si Tundok gave the order and half of the Chinese musketeers huddled behind the rampart stood up and aimed their ancient long barreled muskets towards the oncoming attackers.

"Fire!" Si Tundok cried and watched a line of Rentab's warriors drop from the fusillade. "Second group up! Make Ready...Fire!"

The second half of the Chinese musketeers scrambled to their feet as the first group primed and reloaded their weapons. Their fire was equally devastating. As rapidly as each group could reload, Si Tundok gave the command to fire.

James watched the effect the Chinese rifles had on the surprised Iban. Again their charge faltered and as some of the savages began to flee, they were met with explosions from the pinnace's gun. The rebels were trapped between the ripping bursts of cannon balls behind them and the almost continuous volley of musket fire in front of them. The enemy charge faltered and even Rentab and Api could not prompt their warriors forward.

James saw his opportunity.

"*Datu*!" James shouted with a forward swipe of his sword. "Charge!"

The *Datu* Temanggong was the first to leap from the rampart. With his *parang* waving above his head, he led the charge of his warriors down the slope toward the enemy as fast as his old legs would carry him. Soon, his younger warriors, screaming war cries, sprinted past him and smashed headlong into the front ranks of the rebels.

James and Si Tundok leaped from the rampart and joined the Malay counter-attack. The ear piercing Malay war cry rose above the screams of agony and death as men locked themselves together in deadly one-on-one combat.

As they joined the Malay charge, James yelled, "Si Tundok, to the Rajah's brother. We've got to get him!"

Si Tundok and James were shoulder to shoulder when the momentum of their downhill sprint carried them into the center of the fray. They didn't have a chance to be selective.

With confusion and death all around them, the Iban and Malay rebels fought with brave determination. Those who fled the field were met with a gauntlet of explosive fire from the pinnace's gun crew. Some made it to safety, but many did not.

James fired his musket pistol point-blank into the maniacal face of an Iban warrior who was about to gut him with the point of a short spear. James didn't have time to reload. Nor could he seek out the Rajah's brother or separate him from the masses of Iban warriors who were pressing around he and Si Tundok. James tossed his spent musket pistol to the ground and drew a second pistol from his breeches and slashed wildly with his sword, clearing a path around himself.

Si Tundok, having dropped a renegade Malay warrior with a musket shot, dropped the pistol and brutally hacked at the enemy with his sword. Several Iban warriors near him, backed away from Si Tundok's ferocious attack and then began to retreat down the slope towards the forest. Momentarily free of assailants, Si Tundok searched the battlefield for Api.

"James! There!" Si Tundok saw Api to the left of the melee through the dissipating wisps of smoke rising from the bursts of canon fire below the hill.

James forced an Iban warrior to retreat with a crushing blow of his sword which knocked the warrior's war shield from his hand. He ran to Si Tundok and followed him towards a contingent of *Datu* Temanggong's Malay warriors who had been cut off and surrounded by a larger group of Iban and Malay renegades. In the center of the fray, the *Datu* Temanggong exhorted his men to stand fast and fight for their lives while Api pressed his rebel force forward.

With Si Tundok at his side, James and the broad-shouldered Malay slashed and hacked their way toward Api and the *Datu* Temanggong. One by one, the Iban warriors nearest them began to melt away and retreat, unable to stand against the ferocious attack. Soon, the Iban retreat became contagious as more of the savages disengaged themselves from the battle and sprinted down the slope to the safety of the jungle or the death administered by the lone cannon's exploding shot.

The *Datu* Temanggong and his outnumbered Malay warriors fought bravely, but were being quickly overwhelmed by Api's men in the isolated battle. Without a thought to the consequences of his own life, the *Datu* snatched up a war shield from a downed warrior and pressed forward to meet Api face to face.

"Now you die, traitor!" the *Datu* screamed as his tired old legs and weary arms carried him into Api's path.

Api, a mask of ferocity wired to his sweating face, emitted a blood-curdling whoop and charged the old war chief. Killing the *Datu* Temanggong would turn the tide of the battle and Api attacked with all his strength and determination.

Api easily dislodged the *Datu's* war shield with a succession of ferocious blows of his heavy *parang*. The *Datu* staggered backward from the force of Api's assault and his feet, seeking firm and level ground, stumbled against the body of a decapitated Malay warrior, and the *Datu* toppled to the ground.

*Datu* Temanggong raised his *parang* in time to block a second blow, but before the *Datu* could recover, Api was in position to deliver the final, lethal blow to the downed old warrior.

James saw the Datu fall, but knew he couldn't reach him in time to save him. "Api!" he screamed.

Api snapped his head to the sound of James' piercing challenge. For a fraction of a second, their eyes met; James' steel blue eyes issuing the challenge and Api's black eyes flashing hate and defiance, accepting the challenge.

But Api was intent upon slaying the downed *Datu* Temanggong before he took on the white man. Swiftly he raised his *parang* above his head and began to bring it down with all the force his strong arm could muster.

Too exhausted to lift his own *parang* to defend himself, the *Datu* Temanggong defiantly awaited Api's death blow.

Hastily, James pulled the second musket pistol from his breeches and, without having time to aim, fired it towards Api.

Miraculously, James' musket ball grazed the muscle of Api's upper arm, forcing the downward swing of Api's *parang* to move off-line of its intended trajectory. Api's blow dashed the ground harmlessly near the *Datu* Temanggong's head.

Api grabbed at the torn flesh of his arm and spun angrily toward James and Si Tundok who were both rapidly closing the ground to him. Furious, he stepped to meet their charge, but when he tried to raise his *parang*, the pain from his wound shot through him like a hot flame and he was unable to lift the heavy weapon.

All around him, Api saw Rentab's warriors and his own renegade Malay combatants fleeing the battle field. Unable to raise his weapon to meet the white man's challenge and realizing the battle was lost, Api leaped over the fallen *Datu* Temanggong and ran towards the forest.

As soon as Api fled the battle, the remaining rebel force broke in mass and ran for their lives, pursued by the Rajah's victorious Malay force and the singular whine of cannon shot.

"See to the *Datu!*" James shouted to Si Tundok. James tossed aside his spent musket pistol and, wielding only his saber, chased after the fleeing Malay prince.

But even before he reached the base of the knoll, James realized he wouldn't be able to catch the fleet footed Malay lord. Already Api had leaped the barricade and had melted into the thick forest behind it.

James slumped against the edge of the barricade and massaged his weary saber arm. Rivulets of sweat streamed into his eyes from his forehead and he wiped them away with the sleeve of his shirt. His perspiration soaked shirt clung to his skin and he unfastened it to allow the evaporation to cool him.

"Are you all right, James?" Si Tundok asked when he reached James. Although his naked chest glistened with sweat, Si Tundok was not breathing heavily. Spatters of blood raked across his chest and arms, but the blood was not his own. When James nodded that he was not injured, Si Tundok reached out a broad hand and helped James to his feet.

"Lost him," James said regretfully. "He was too bloody fast for me." He peered into the dark wall of forest for a moment before asking, "The *Datu*, is he all right?"

"He is fine, James. Just a bit of wounded pride, I think."

James scanned the battlefield. It was littered with dead and wounded warriors from both sides. Already many of the *Datu's* men were gathering up the wounded and marching captives toward the fortress. Some were stripping the dead of their weapons and jewelry.

As they walked through the carnage toward the fortress, Si Tundok said, "It was a great victory, James."

"Yes, I suppose it was. But without Api, I'm afraid I haven't accomplished much."

When the two of them reached the fortress they were greeted with shouts of praise by the Malay warriors. Even the normally stoic Chinese musketeers offered utterances of appreciation.

James glanced up to the rampart to the *Skimalong's* gun crew. "Well done, Mister Harris," he called out.

The ship's officer doffed his cap. "You too, Mister Brooke." And then he added, "Three cheers for Mister Brooke, lads!"

"Hip Hip Hurray! Hip Hip Hurray! Hip Hip Hurray!" the bluejackets shouted in unison.

James acknowledged the cheer with a smile and then said to Si Tundok, "Ask one of the warriors where we can find *Datu* Temanggong."

Si Tundok raised his hand for quiet and asked the nearest man the question. "He says the *Datu* has taken the captives to the river. He is executing them there."

"What?" With the exception of the lost opportunity to capture or kill Api, the victory was complete as far as James was concerned. There was no need of further killing. "We've got to stop him!"

With Si Tundok leading the way, the two of them pushed their way through the *Datu's* warriors who were gathering close to offer their own personal congratulations to the white man whom they credited with leading them to victory.

Eventually, they extricated themselves from the jubilant crowd and reached the edge of the river where they saw the *Datu's* warriors leading a line of captives, one at a time, toward the *Datu* Temanggong who was systematically beheading each of the prisoners.

"Stop!" James screamed and ran straight to the *Datu* Temanggong, grabbed him by the arm and roughly twisted him away from his grisly task.

The *Datu's* faithful warriors murmured and moved towards James with their weapons ready to strike him down if the old war chief gave the command.

"Enough! There has been enough killing, no more!"

The *Datu* Temanggong jerked his arm away from James' grip and angrily shouted a litany of protest.

"He says you have no right to stop him, James," Si Tundok said. "He says it is his duty to kill all of the traitors."

Si Tundok's gray eyes flitted from James to the Malay warriors who were gathering menacingly close to the two of them. "Better do as he says, James or we could end up the same as the captives."

"No!" James clenched his jaw. His face flushed red as his blue eyes bored his resolve into the *Datu* Temanggong. "Tell him it is over! No more killing! Go ahead, Si Tundok, tell him!"

James fixed his determined eyes on the old war chief as Si Tundok interpreted his message.

The *Datu* would have none of it. He protested vehemently, pointing his blood stained *parang* to the line of hostages and spitting upon the headless corpses of the massacred rebels littered near his feet.

"He says all the traitors must die. He says to spare the lives of these worthless rebels would anger the Rajah Hasim and the *Datu* will be punished for not performing his duty properly."

"Tell him I will be responsible to the Rajah for sparing the lives of these men. Tell him we will take these prisoners back to Kuching with us and let the Rajah decide their fate. In Kuching, I will tell the Rajah of the *Datu*

Temanggong's courageous leadership in battle today and how he led the Rajah's warriors to a great victory. Tell him that, Si Tundok."

The *Datu* considered what he was being told. He preferred to continue with the executions. It was a balm for his wounded pride at having been felled and almost killed by *Awang* Api. But, after all, it had been the white man's intervention that saved his life and he respected James for his bravery. He also sensed that the Rajah seemed to favor the white man and if James was willing to give him credit for today's victory, it would most assuredly increase his own standing with the Rajah. After a few moments of reflection, the *Datu* spoke.

"He agrees to your wishes, James. He will take the prisoners to Kuching as you request."

James breathed a sigh of relief and reached out his arm and clasped the *Datu* Temanggong on the shoulder. "Tell him he has made a wise decision, Si Tundok."

Rentab, his arms bound behind his back with a rope tethered to a captive behind him, was kneeling near James and next in line to feel the cold steel from the *Datu* Temanggong's *parang*. He heard the conversation between his captors and wondered what spirits guided the white man with hair the color of the orang-hutan. Whatever spirits they might be, he was thankful for their intervention. At the same time, he wished he had heeded Chopak's spirits and had chosen to return to Batang when he had the chance.

# V

*HMS Skimalong*
Kuching, Sarawak

The Rajah Hasim was ecstatic upon hearing the news of the victory at Siniawan, but he was equally upset upon learning that his renegade brother had escaped.

Witnessing the Rajah's emotional outburst, James knew that his agreement with the Rajah for his trade concession was in jeopardy. "Perhaps, Captain Irons, you would allow us to convene in your quarters to continue our discussion?"

Captain Irons, amazed to see James and his crew alive, readily consented and led Hasim, the *Datu* Temanggong, James and Si Tundok to his quarters where the men were comfortably seated and served tea and biscuits by the ship's steward. Si Tundok interpreted the Rajah's concern over his brother's escape.

"Hasim says that he will not sign your papers granting the concession since you did not kill or capture Api as you promised, James."

James glanced at the papers he had hastily drawn up prior to leaving for Siniawan. They rested, unsigned by Hasim, on top of the table which separated Hasim and the *Datu* from the other three men in the room. James' attention turned to Hasim. He looked for any sign which would tell him what Hasim was thinking. James kept his composure. He had come too close to fulfilling his dream to lose it all now.

"Si Tundok, tell the Rajah that his brother's power has been broken. Without the Iban, his brother is no longer a threat to him or his rule in Sarawak. His war chief, the *Datu* Temanggong and I have seen to that."

James learned on the return trip to Kuching that one of the Iban prisoners, a heavily tattooed warrior who called himself Rentab was the notorious leader of the raiding Iban. Through the *Datu* and Si Tundok, James extracted a promise from the Iban chieftain that he would do what he could to convince the Rajah to spare his life and the lives of all the captives if Rentab would agree to live in peace. Without Rentab to support Api's quest for Hasim's throne, James was convinced Api's influence was broken.

"He says you underestimate his brother, James. As long as Api is alive, the Rajah fears for his life."

James stared at the intractable Rajah and gritted his teeth. Inside, James was seething, but he maintained an outward calm and tried to think of

195

something he could do or say to change Hasim's obstinate mind and cause him to sign the concession document.

Then he thought of it. If the Rajah was worried about saving his neck, why not play upon Hasim's fear and at the same time offer him something which would help protect him from his brother? It was a risky thought, but James decided to try it.

"Ask the Rajah what he intends to do when we put him ashore in the morning and leave Kuching with the ship and its cannon which now protect him?"

James watched Hasim's composure break upon hearing Si Tundok's interpretation. As James suspected since their very first meeting, Hasim was an insecure coward who would do almost anything to protect himself from both real and imagined enemies.

"The Rajah says that you promised to protect him. You cannot leave him alone in Kuching, he says."

"I only agreed to protect him if he granted the concession. Since he hasn't signed the document, tell him I intend to set sail with the morning tide. Tell him that, Si Tundok."

Timothy shuffled uneasily in his chair. "You're taking quite a liberty with my ship, aren't you, Mister Brooke?"

"I'm sorry, Captain Irons," James apologized from the corner of his mouth. "I beg you, Captain, let me play out my charade. As far as the Rajah knows, I'm the one in charge. Believe me, British interests as well as my own will be served."

Timothy settled back in his chair. "All right, Mister Brooke, it's your show just as long as we understand who is Captain of the *Skimalong*." Actually, Timothy was beginning to enjoy the interchange between the timid Rajah and his brazen countryman. Like a member of a theatrical audience, Timothy was curious to see how it would all be resolved.

"Thank you, Captain," James whispered as he listened to Si Tundok interpret the Rajah's response.

"The Rajah says he will not be safe in Kuching. He will only be safe when he reaches Brunei. When he reaches Brunei, he will become Sultan. Then he will have the power to banish his brother. The Rajah says he will be safe then."

James' optimism plummeted. He knew he would not be able to convince Captain Irons to stay and protect Hasim until the *Jolly Bachelor* was seaworthy or until Hasim became Sultan. It would be beyond the scope of the Captain's authority. And if Hasim became Sultan without the protection James promised, then there would be no reason for Hasim to grant the concession. James was almost ready to admit defeat, but not quite.

"Si Tundok, ask the Rajah when he intends to leave for Brunei?"

When Si Tundok asked the question, it elicited a flurry of dialogue between Hasim and the *Datu* Temanggong, Hasim apparently asking his only trusted advisor for advice, and the *Datu*, fresh from his victory at Siniawan feeling confident enough to give it.

"What are they saying?" James asked.

"The *Datu* is encouraging the Rajah to go directly to Brunei and be conferred as Sultan, but the Rajah is reluctant because he fears he will be intercepted by pirates. He suspects that Api has some influence over them."

"That's crazy," James said. "He's afraid to stay in Kuching and he's fearful of going to Brunei..."

Si Tundok held up his hand, silencing James. "The Rajah says he will sign the concession if you will have your ship take him to Brunei. He knows the pirates will not attack a ship so heavily armed."

James' hopes rebounded. He glanced at Captain Irons who only shrugged noncommittally. He felt certain he could convince the captain to honor Hasim's request. After all, it was in the British interest to grant such a simple request to a sovereign. He finally had his concession! But before he agreed to the request, James remembered a promise he made. "Tell the Rajah that I will except his offer on one condition."

Si Tundok looked at James quizzically. "Are you sure you want to—?"

"Tell him, Si Tundok... on one condition."

Si Tundok cleared his throat and relayed James words. Hasim appeared visibly surprised. "The Rajah wants to know what your condition is."

"Tell him I want him to release the captives taken at Siniawan. I have the Iban leader's word that he will convince his people to give up headhunting and live in peace."

Another frenzy of conversation occurred between Hasim and the *Datu* when Si Tundok conveyed James' condition. Quickly, the conversation seemed to turn into an argument.

"What are they saying?" James asked.

"The Rajah is fearful the Dayak will not keep their word. That Api will convince them to continue to cause trouble in Sarawak for the Rajah."

"What about the *Datu*, what is he saying?"

"He supports the condition you imposed, James, but he is presenting an additional argument as well. It's very interesting."

James was about to ask what it was when the Rajah and *Datu* Temanggong suddenly stopped their rapid-fire dialogue and Hasim raised his hand for silence. Hasim lifted his chin regally and spoke slowly and solemnly.

"The Rajah accepts your condition," Si Tundok said.

197

But before James could claim victory in the matter, Si Tundok added, "But the Rajah also has a condition."

Again James' hopes plummeted. "Well, what is it? What does he want?" he asked, somewhat frustrated.

Si Tundok decided to relay most of the prior conversation before he mentioned the condition. "The Datu Temanggong told the Rajah of your bravery and how you helped destroy the Iban warriors and Api's rebels. But he agreed with the Rajah that the Dyaks will be further trouble in Sarawak..."

"But I thought you said—"

Si Tundok interrupted. "Let me finish, James. I think you will find this all very interesting." He went on to say, "The *Datu* told the Rajah that since it is you that wants to release the rebels, then you should be responsible for them."

"I don't understand. What does that mean?"

Si Tundok said, "I don't know how to tell you this, James, but the *Datu* Temanggong has convinced Hasim to make you Rajah of Sarawak once Hasim becomes Sultan."

James was stunned. Moments earlier, he was about to lose his concession and now he was being offered suzerainty over a land he intended to exploit. It didn't seem possible. How could it be?

"I...I don't...why would he want..?" James stammered.

Captain Irons was equally shocked at the proposal, but he let the conversation play out to its conclusion.

"The *Datu* told Hasim that it would be to his benefit if you were made Rajah. As Sultan, Hasim could then count on your ships and guns to help protect him and his country. And, of course, you would have the responsibility of dealing with the problems in Sarawak. There is also one other reason Hasim desires for you to become Rajah of Sarawak," Si Tundok said.

"What would that be?" James asked, still numbly trying to understand what all of it meant.

"You are not a member of a royal family, therefore you could never become Sultan. Hasim would never need to worry about you staging a coup against him."

James glanced to the *Datu* Temanggong, who was wearing a smug grin on his face, delighted that he had suggested the solution to Hasim's problem. Hasim also appeared satisfied. He leaned over the table, picked up the concession papers and furiously wrote on them while he talked.

"The Rajah is amending the papers, James. He is including a section which makes you Rajah of Sarawak. He wants to know if you accept his condition?"

"Yes...yes, I accept." The words left James' mouth without any conscious thought. He was still contemplating what he had agreed to when Captain Irons spoke up.

"None of my business, really, Mister Brooke, but where do you intend to get the guns and ships the Rajah *assumes* you have under your command?" Timothy had a wrinkled grin pasted to his face. He had enjoyed watching the scene, but now it was time to become an active player.

"Well, for the time being, I am hoping to convince you to convey the Rajah to Brunei aboard the *Skimalong*. After that, I would hope you would return me here, to Kuching where I plan to wait until Henry can bring the *Jolly Bachelor* to Sarawak."

When Timothy didn't immediately respond, James cleared his throat and said, "It would be within the limits of your orders, of course, Captain."

Timothy pretended to be considering James' proposition. "And how would you interpret my orders, Mister Brooke?"

"As you mentioned yourself, Captain, you are not to engage in hostilities, but simply to convey British gratitude and good will to the Rajah. What better way to comply with your orders than to escort Hasim to Brunei? Think of what good it will do for British interests in the area, Captain."

Timothy could control himself no longer. He laughed and slapped his knee. "Damn, if you aren't a bold one, Mister Brooke! I wouldn't have believed it if I hadn't witnessed it all myself. You come sailing into this land of savages with the crazy notion of getting a concession for trading rights and walk away three days later with the whole bloody country in your hip pocket. Who would ever believe it?"

"Does that mean you will do it?"

"Do a favor for a Rajah? A *white* Rajah? Of course I will," Timothy said, just as Hasim finished amending the documents giving James control of Sarawak.

# VI

## The Jungle
## Above Siniawan

"Tell us again about the men with the white skin," Batu's brother asked solemnly.

Batu nodded that he would. He watched the members of his clan scrape away the sweet, gelatinous interior of the *kelapa mudah*, the green coconuts he had found for them.

The previous morning, Batu had left the safety of the deep forest and slipped away to the lowlands near the Sarawak River where the fruit grew in abundance. It was there that he caught sight of the strange men with the white skins. They were traveling up river with a few Malay in war canoes.

Burong, Batu's brother, seemed particularly fascinated with Batu's account of what he had seen and continued to ask questions long after the story had been told.

"These white men, they covered their skin?" Burong asked as he swallowed another mouthful of the sweet nut.

"Yes, only their hands and faces could be seen."

"The white men must be very strong to cover themselves in the heat of the day," Batu's wife suggested. The other clan member's murmured their agreement.

"All of them had coverings on their head, but one. His hair was the color of the orang-hutan."

The clan looked at their leader in disbelief. "How can that be?" one of them asked.

Batu shook his head that he didn't know. "I saw his shadow against the water. It was very long."

The members of the clan exchanged glances with one another and scooted a fraction closer to their small camp fire. Except for their leader, Batu, none of them had seen a man with white skin nor could they imagine a man with hair the color of the great jungle ape which they considered as human as themselves.

"The one with the long shadow, he was not an animal?"

"Not an animal," Batu stated emphatically. "I could see him talk with those in the boat with him."

"The white man's shadow, it was longer than the Malay?"

"Yes," Batu said softly as he tossed a few sticks of kindling into the fire. "Even longer than the Kayan."

"Aiyee, what can it mean, Batu?" Burong asked.

The flickering light from the fire lapped against Batu's face. The night seemed particularly dark and he inched closer to the warmth and light of the fire. He contemplated his brother's question. *What did it mean?* There had been so many strange omens these past few seasons. So many mysterious signs and events that he could not understand.

Batu glanced at each of the anxious faces of his clan before he spoke of the things he knew.

"It is known that a man's shadow is a reflection of a man's spirit. The white man must have a very large spirit. It will be a difficult thing to bury his shadow when he dies."

The Punan silently nodded their agreement and stared contemplatively into the flickering flames of the fire, each seeking his own meaning for why a white man, a man with a long shadow and hair the color of the orang-hutan had come to this land.

"In the morning, we will leave this place," Batu said.

The Punan muttered agreement. It was much better to return to the recesses of the thick jungle where they understood their world and were not forced to contemplate the coming of the white man with the long shadow.

# CHAPTER EIGHT

## I

## Kampong Batang

Like a totem, Rentab stood mute and rigid as he listened to an account of the Kayan attack which decimated Kampong Batang. He stared, unbelieving, at the pile of ashes, all that now remained of his once proud village, but managed to contain the conflicting emotions of rage and sorrow that battled within him.

"And the other villages?"

"Burned, all of them...Lintang, Nadai and Besok too."

Sadly, Rentab shook his head and asked the question he had avoided. "My wife? Children?"

The survivors simply lowered their heads and remained quiet. Their silence answered his question.

Rentab felt the unfamiliar sting of tears well up in his eyes, but before they could flow, he pushed himself through the crowd and ran to the river where he found a quiet spot beneath a *durian* tree and secluded himself with his grief.

He thought of his boy whose head had been taken years earlier and he thought of his wife and daughter and Rentab cried for a long while before he thought of other things.

Eventually, Rentab pushed his grief aside and reflected upon Chopak's reading of the bones before the attack at Siniawan. He had not led his warriors to a great victory that day, nor had he become a *Pengulu* as he supposed he would. But the spirits had given him a choice and he admitted to himself that he had chosen the path of self aggrandizement. Silently, Rentab cursed himself for making the choice he did and for the first time in his life, began to understand the burden of leadership. A wise *Tua Kampong* must be more interested in the welfare of his village, protecting it and helping it prosper and less interested in the glory he thought he could achieve through raids and the taking of many heads. As a leader, Rentab recognized that he had failed and the price for failure had been devastating.

"*Tua Kampong*, my heart grieves with your heart. I am saddened that this terrible thing has happened to Batang." The voice was Chopak's. He, like other Iban who had avoided death or capture at Siniawan, had made his way overland to reach Batang several days before Rentab arrived. He touched the old warrior's withered shoulder and sat down next to him.

For a while, neither man said anything. Then Chopak broke the silence by asking, "What shall we do now?"

Rentab thought about the question for a moment. A part of him wanted to avenge the loss of his family and village. Like a migration of biting red ants crawling beneath his skin, his grief turned to anger and rage bit at his insides. He clenched his jaw and the folds of muscles along his neck and face showed the strain of containing his wrath.

But another part of him began to understand what leadership demanded and what must be done. "We will rebuild our village," he finally said. "We will gather our people and tend the rice paddy fields and fish and hunt until we are strong once again."

"There will be no reprisals against the Kayan?"

"No reprisals," Rentab said, simply. "I have given my word to the white Rajah that we will live in peace."

"White Rajah? I don't understand, *Tua Kampong.*"

"I too, do not understand these things," Rentab said. He explained to Chopak how the white man had interceded and prevented the execution of the captives at Siniawan. "The white man said he would speak to the Rajah Hasim to spare our lives if I would promise to live in peace. I gave him my word. Later, all of the captives were released as the white man promised. But I was taken to a great ship with many guns which sailed with the Rajah Hasim to Brunei. On the voyage, the white man, through his companion, a large Sulu Malay, asked me many questions about the Iban and how we lived. These questions puzzled me," Rentab said, speaking softly. "But I answered the white man's questions truthfully."

Rentab plucked a blade of grass and rolled it between his fingers a moment and then said, "It was on the ship that I learned that the Rajah Hasim would soon be Sultan and the white man was given the Raj of Sarawak. When we neared the Rajang River, the white man came to me and said he would release me at the Rajang to return to my village if I promised not to follow *Awang* Api again." Rentab tossed away the blade of grass and lowered his head almost shamefully and added, "And he made me promise that I would not hunt heads again. Perhaps it was a promise I should not have made."

"Perhaps it is a good thing," Chopak suggested.

Rentab shook his head doubtfully. "How can it be a good thing? How can there be peace when our enemies, the Kayan, seek to destroy us?"

"This white man, the one who has become Rajah of Sarawak, do you trust him, *Tua Kampong?*"

Rentab reflected for a moment. "Yes, I trust him. He has a long shadow, a great spirit."

"Then go to him in Kuching. Tell him of your desire to keep your promise of peace and of our fear of the Kayan. Ask for his help to protect us from our enemies."

"He will do this for us?"

Chopak shrugged. "Maybe this white Rajah will be different from the others. Maybe he truly wants peace in Sarawak."

Rentab sighed, he suddenly felt very old and tired. He had known nothing but war his entire life. *Is peace a possibility?* he wondered. "Soon I will be an old man and my bones are no longer as strong as they once were. Peace may be a good thing."

Chopak seemed moved by Rentab's transformation. He touched him lightly on the hands and said, "Yes, I think you are very wise, *Tua Kampong*. There has been too much death and destruction. Peace *will* be a good thing."

Rentab stood up. His tears had dried and his face suddenly seemed filled with purpose and resolve. "Yes, peace. But before I go to Kuching and discuss this matter with the white Rajah, we will rebuild our longhouse. Come, Chopak, there is much that needs to be done."

## II

*HMS Skimalong*
Kuching, Sarawak

"*Selamat Hidup! Selamat Hidup!* Long Live Rajah James! A Long Life!
A Long Reign!"

The chant was deafening. The people of Kuching pressed near the wharf to get their first glimpse of the new ruler of Sarawak. Word from Brunei about the white man's appointment as Rajah of Sarawak reached the ears of the people of Kuching days before the return of the *Skimalong* from Brunei where James had waited until the ceremony establishing Hasim as Sultan was completed.

"Impressive welcome, James," Captain Irons said over the noise of the cheering crowd. "How does it feel to be a king?"

"I'm really not sure." James had not expected the tumultuous welcome and he was uncertain how to reply to Timothy's question. *King!* The word reverberated in James' head, conveying both power and responsibility. But the word had a sobering effect on him as well. Until this very moment, James considered his good fortune as nothing more than the culmination of his dream, a proxy allowing him the opportunity to exploit a fortune from this savage land and return to England as a wealthy man.

But now, as he stood atop the *Skimalong's* forecastle deck and viewed the ecstatic faces of the crowd, he realized that he was no longer a simple adventurer, he was a king. Instead of gaining a simple right to trade, he had been given the burden of rule.

James replaced his surprise with an expression of staid anticipation. He drew himself up tall and proud and prepared himself to face his newly acquired subjects and the task that Fate had bestowed upon him.

James turned to Captain Irons when he heard him shout an order to lower a dinghy to transfer James and his small party to shore. "Will you be coming ashore, Captain Irons?"

"I think not. It's time I should be returning to Singapore. The Governor-General will be anticipating my report."

James was clearly disappointed, but he said, "I understand, Captain."

James started to extend his hand to Captain Irons, but withdrew it quickly. "Oh, one thing, Captain." James extracted a packet from his coat pocket. "I wrote these on the way from Brunei. I wonder if you would be so kind as to post them for me when you get back to Singapore."

"Of course, Mister Brooke."

James handed Timothy three letters, each carefully wrapped in oilskin. One, the thickest, was addressed to his mother, another to George Barton and the third to Elizabeth Wethington.

James handed Timothy a larger, sealed packet. "This is to be delivered to Governor McDonald," James said. "It contains a copy of the Sultan's concession to me as well as a request of the British Parliament to establish Sarawak as a British Protectorate. The Governor-General will know what to do with them."

Timothy took the envelopes and tucked them safely away in the pocket of his own coat. "I'll see to it that they are safely posted, Mister Brooke."

"Thank you, Captain. One other thing, if you will." James fumbled in his pockets a moment before extracting another sealed envelope. "This letter is to be hand delivered to Henry Steele. You can probably find him somewhere near the shipyard in Singapore. It is to inform him that Si Tundok and I will not be returning to Singapore as originally planned and to tell him to hire a crew and bring the *Jolly Bachelor* to Kuching as soon as possible." James scanned the *Skimalong* with a toss of his arm and said, "Now that I realize that the *Skimalong's* guns won't be around any longer, I'm beginning to feel somewhat naked."

Timothy accepted the letter and chuckled. "A few minutes ago, I asked you how it felt to be a king. You didn't really answer me until now."

James smiled and offered his hand. "I truly appreciate what you've done here, Captain Irons. I've made a point to mention it in my dispatch to Governor McDonald."

Timothy took James' hand and shook it vigorously. "It's been my pleasure, Mister Brooke. It isn't everyday that I have a chance to watch a mere mortal become a king." He smiled broadly, but he knew he would miss the company of this man whom he had come to admire. "Do take care, Mister Brooke and I am hopeful we will see each other again."

"I will look forward to it, Captain Irons."

James crossed the ship's deck and crawled down a rope ladder to board the dinghy where Si Tundok and the *Datu* Temanggong awaited.

"Good sailing!" James called to the captain who was peering over the ship's rail. Both Si Tundok and the *Datu* Temanggong waved their farewells too as the bluejackets pushed the dinghy away from the *Skimalong's* monstrous hull.

"Good luck, Rajah Brooke!" Captain Iron's called. "Do try to keep your head about you!"

James waved a final time, but suddenly he felt very much alone.

III

The Sarawak River
South of Kuching

James had awakened early the morning following his formal induction as Sarawak's newest Rajah. It was then that he informed Si Tundok and the *Datu* Temanggong of his desire to visit native villages along the Sarawak River. His questions to the Iban leader, Rentab, on the trip to Brunei had provided James with some fascinating answers and he was anxious to view a longhouse and see first hand how his native subjects lived.

Dutifully, the *Datu* Temanggong had gathered enough warriors to man three large *praus* and had stocked them with enough provisions for several days of travel. Now, as the *praus* skimmed the quiet early morning water nearing their first destination, James recalled the culminating events of the previous afternoon and pondered his new role as Rajah of Sarawak.

After James, Si Tundok and the *Datu* Temanggong were put ashore by the *Skimalong's* dinghy, they waited until the bluejackets returned to the ship and the man-of-war slowly eased itself down the river and disappeared. After an effusive greeting with a contingent of Kuching's Malay nobility who pledged their support, James was led to the steps of the palace which had been finely decorated with flowers and palm branches. A simple ceremony ensued and James was finally introduced to the citizenry as the new Rajah of Sarawak.

Following the pronouncement of his accession, James faced the crowd of expectant faces. He held his hand in the air, commanding silence. The crowd hushed and all eyes focused upon him. Speaking in a loud voice and using the Malay that Si Tundok had taught him, James announced, "People of Kuching...People of Sarawak. It is with the greatest sense of responsibility that I assume the Raj of Sarawak. May God grant henceforth, that this land and all her people be ruled with fairness and justice. Long live Sarawak!"

"Long live Rajah James! Long live Sarawak!" the crowd chanted. Most of the crowd was surprised that James addressed them in their language. For those in the crowd who were old enough to remember the reigns of the previous Rajah, including the short rule of Hasim, none could ever recall of a Rajah speaking of fairness and justice. Rajahs came and went, but the oppression and injustice remained. It was a system never questioned, but the words of this foreigner, this white Rajah, as brief as they were, kindled a sense that change was definitely coming to their land. Whether the change would be for the better, only time would tell.

James remained deep in thought as he pondered the awesome responsibility he had assumed and the commitment he had made when the *Datu* Temanggong pulled him from his reverie. "That place is Sin Bok, Rajah James," the *Datu* said, pointing to a neat village on the west bank of the river. "Do you wish to visit it?"

"Is it a native village?" James asked, noting that the structures were unlike the longhouses which had been described to him.

"No, Chinese."

"Perhaps we will stop on the return trip. For now I only want to visit...what did you call that village, *Datu*?"

"Kampong Bau. The Bidayuh village. It is the closest to Kuching other than Sin Bok."

"Yes, that's it. Kampong Bau. They live in a longhouse like the Iban, don't they?"

"Yes, Rajah James, but the Bidayuh are very different than the Iban and other tribes in Sarawak."

"How so?"

"You will see for yourself when we arrive. They are very shy, peaceful. But they are also very poor."

James felt fortunate to have the old Malay war chief with him. He was certain that Hasim would keep the *Datu* with him in Brunei, but evidently the *Datu* was able to convince Hasim otherwise. In the halting Malay that James was rapidly learning and with the help of Si Tundok, he flooded the *Datu* with questions. James was fascinated by the thick forest which covered the river banks, making it impossible to see what lay beyond. *If ever there was a virgin land, this is it,* he thought. That people could exist in such a place seemed quite remarkable to James.

"It's like a dream," James said to Si Tundok. James' expression had a far and distant look to it as he watched the endless jungle skim by. "So peaceful and pristine. Imagine what a unique opportunity this may be. I may be the first white man to ever lay eyes on such a world." It reminded James of his boyhood trips, sailing the River Wensum and imagining far away places.

Si Tundok seemed unimpressed. "The forest is like a cobra. It never shows how dangerous it is until it raises up and shows you its hood. By then, it's too late."

"I take it you're not impressed with Sarawak?"

Si Tundok shrugged. "It is a place like any other."

"Well, I plan to make it a great place," James said with enthusiasm. "First, I need to visit the people, learn things about them and about the territory itself. We'll need a census, make maps, organize a government, establish laws and a court...so much to do..." James said, his voice trailing off under the weight and enormity of it all.

"There is Kampong Bau," the *Datu* shouted.

The *praus* slid easily onto a mud-packed beach alongside several other empty canoes. The mud was black and sticky and smelled like raw sewage. When the party emptied the praus and made their way through the mud to dry land, James, fascinated by the site of the Bidayuh longhouse, kept his eyes glued to it and ignored the *Datu* Temanggong's curses from being sucked into the filthy slime.

The longhouse was built from similar materials as the individual houses James had seen in Kuching except that Kampong Bau was a single, gigantic house with a bamboo deck in front of a raised platform which served as a walkway between the individual rooms or *bileks,* as they were called. Although the posts which supported the enormous structure above the ground appeared to be of hardwood, the walls were constructed primarily of woven rattan and split-bamboo. The roof was made of dried thatch.

As the Rajah's party climbed the sloping hill leading to the longhouse, James was taken with the fact that there were few villagers in site, far fewer than he would expect to occupy such an enormous structure. And of those who cautiously approached them, none appeared overly exuberant by his arrival.

"That one is Endap, spokesman for the village," the *Datu* said, pointing to a wasted little man wearing nothing but a *chawat* made of beaten bark. As the man approached, he remained quiet and his eyes lowered in obeisance.

The *Datu* Temanggong introduced James as the new Rajah of Sarawak. The announcement seemed to surprise the Bidayuh headman, but he said nothing.

"As you can see, Rajah James, this village, like most of the Bidayuh villages in Sarawak is of little consequence." The *Datu* waved his arm about the village and said, "These people are very poor. The forest is barely able to sustain them and they have little of value."

James could see that the beleaguered village appeared to be hanging on by a mere thread of existence. Of the few curious villagers who huddled near Endap, James could tell from their pale and lifeless bodies, that they were probably suffering from malnutrition. Even the children seemed solemn and inanimate and their distended abdomens indicated severe malnutrition, parasitic worms or possibly other afflictions.

"Why?" James asked.

The *Datu* Temanggong seemed puzzled by the question.

"Why do these people seem to have so little while the Malay I've seen in Kuching and Brunei have so much?"

Perhaps it is because the Bidayuh are so lazy?" the *Datu* proffered.

Si Tundok interjected. "It is because of the *serah*, James."

"The *serah*? What's that?"

"It is the duty the natives are forced to pay to the Malay princes in goods and services. The tax keeps the natives poor. I have seen this system before, in the Celebes and in Marudu."

James made a mental note to learn more of this system of taxation, but for now, he wanted to see more of the village. "What is that smell?" James asked, wrinkling his nose.

"The people toss their garbage and relieve themselves through the floor of the longhouse. Usually, the pigs and chickens will take care of the waste, but this village does not have enough animals so the waste accumulates and decays beneath the longhouse," Si Tundok explained.

"Endap?" James asked, "would you show me your longhouse? I would like to see the inside of it."

Endap seemed surprised by the request. The Malay princes simply did what they wanted. *Why did this white man feel it necessary to ask?* he wondered. Perhaps the white Rajah wants to see if there was anything of value, anything he could take in *serah*, he surmised.

"Yes, Rajah," Endap said and led the small party to the longhouse.

"Amazing," James said after they climbed the steps and stood along the *ruii*, the long deck which led to each of the *bileks*. "Absolutely fascinating."

The *Datu* glanced at James peculiarly. He didn't understand what it was that James found so interesting in a crumbling mass of dried bamboo and thatch.

James walked slowly along the *ruii*, stopping often to ask questions about something which caught his attention. Before long, Endap, still unsure of what a white Rajah meant to the future of his village, eased into a comfortable, if not altogether spontaneous dialogue with James.

"What is the meaning of that?" James motioned to an old Bidayuh woman who was sitting alone near the entrance to one of the *bileks*. Her only covering was a black sarong which covered her from her waist to her knees. Below her knees were a number of brass rings which circled the old lady's legs from her calves to her ankles.

"It is our custom, Rajah James," Endap explained. "When the women are but small girls, they place the brass rings on their legs. It makes them beautiful, do you not think so, Rajah?"

Before James could express an opinion, the *Datu* Temanggong spoke up. "It is an example of how ignorant these people are. The Bidayuh are the only tribe in Sarawak who practice such a thing. Because of the rings, the girls' legs cannot form properly as they grow. Instead of being beautiful, the Bidayuh women are nothing but cripples."

"Don't be too quick to judge, *Datu*," James said. "Even where I come from, our fine English ladies have certain beauty practices I fail to understand."

Endap seemed to appreciate the comment.

James stepped from the *ruii* and peaked into one of the *bileks*, a family's private quarters. The interior was small and simple. Several woven blankets were rolled up against one wall. There was little ornamentation or decoration on any of the walls. To the rear of the room was a cooking area cluttered with a few iron utensils and clay pots. A stack of dried firewood sat next to a small raised brick fireplace. The only light which penetrated the smoky interior came from a single window at the back of the room and shafts of dusty light that filtered through the cracks in the walls and the roof. A few worn woven baskets hung suspended from the room's rafters.

Other objects hanging from the rafters also caught James' eye. He stepped inside, stooping to enter the short doorway to get a closer look. There, suspended between several baskets by rattan netting, was a row of six skulls. Each was covered in a layer of dust and missing the lower mandible and they appeared to have been charred and quite old.

"Look at this, Si Tundok," James said. He recalled the headless corpses of *Datu's* fallen warriors at Siniawan and had learned that most of the indigenous tribes were headhunters, but he had no idea as to how the skulls were treated after they were taken.

"Headhunters," Si Tundok grunted in disgust.

"Fascinating," James breathed. "Endap, what is the meaning of these skulls?" James knew that if he were ever to bring peace and stability to Sarawak, he would have to find a way to eliminate the perpetual raids between tribes and the grotesque practice of hunting human heads that fostered the raids.

The Bidayuh spokesman seemed genuinely embarrassed by the question. "Long ago my people were very primitive, like the Iban. Our ancestors hunted the heads of their enemies to prove their manhood. We no longer do such things, Rajah." As if to emphasize the point, Endap quickly added, "As you can see, the heads are very old."

James clasped the little man on the shoulder. "It is good that your people no longer hunt heads," he said.

Endap seemed pleased with the Rajah's comment. "If it would please the white Rajah, we will bury the skulls."

"It would please me greatly," James said, withdrawing from the room. "Not as primitive as they seem at first glance, are they?" James said to Si Tundok in English when they reached the *ruii*.

James spent another hour surveying the longhouse and receiving answers to his questions then he took Endap aside and talked to him in private for a long while. He learned details of how the Malay demand for *serah* had been most responsible for the demise of the Bidayuh village. That and the fact that the Bidayuh were taken advantage of by the Chinese merchants at Sin Bok. Endap and the Bidayuh had paid a heavy price for their peaceful ways, James determined.

When James returned to the praus where the *Datu* and Si Tundok awaited him, he was not in a particularly pleasant mood. "*Datu*," James said, climbing aboard the craft. "I want to visit more of the villages along the Sarawak River."

"Yes, Rajah James, but they are much the same...."

"I suspect as much," James said, raising his palm and cutting the old warrior off in mid-sentence. "Poor and ignorant, isn't that what you said earlier? Well, I think I know the reason for it and I damned bloody well am going to do something about it," he fumed.

IV

Kuching, Sarawak

It was a joyous day for James and Si Tundok when Henry sailed the *Jolly Bachelor* into Kuching's river harbor. James and Si Tundok didn't wait for Henry to disembark. Instead, they had a *prau* row them to the refurbished ship and after an enthusiastic reunion between the three friends, Henry introduced them to ship's captain.

"James, Si Tundok, this is Captain Alfred Periweg," Henry said effusively. "Best damned captain that ever sailed the South China Sea!"

"Henry is much too generous with his praise, gentlemen," the captain said. "I may not be the best, but I am damned sure I'm the oldest."

James shook the captain's callused hand. The captain's grip was firm and strong even though James guessed that the man was pushing sixty years of age. Other than his age, Captain Periweg looked every bit the part of a ship's captain. He was attired in an ancient blue jacket and trousers which showed traces of stitch marks where brass buttons and epaulets had once been attached. A broad brimmed cock-and-pinch hat sat square on the man's round face which was mostly covered by a thick growth of white mutton-chop whiskers, neatly trimmed, except for his lower jaw which was clean shaven. His close-set eyes were held in a narrow squint above a layered mass of wrinkles, but his eyes were clear and intelligent looking.

"We're grateful you could join us, Captain," James said as the captain shook hands with Si Tundok. "How did the *Jolly Bachelor* handle herself on the voyage over?"

"Like me, she's an old one. Protests every change in wind direction and water current with a creak and groan, but she sails straight and true. Your man Henry here did a fine job getting her re-fitted."

"Took most of the money you gave me," Henry replied somewhat sheepishly. "How about a look around, see how your money was spent?"

"Of course. Will you join us, Captain?"

Captain Periweg shook his head. "Please excuse me, Mister Brooke, but there are a number of things I should attend to. Perhaps I will join you later if that's all right?"

"Quite all right, Captain," James replied. He turned to Henry and said, "Let's have the grand tour Henry, see what my money bought."

As the three of them walked along the main deck away from Captain Periweg, James asked, "Where did you find the captain, Henry?"

"Took some doing. He's been retired for several years, but talk has it in Singapore that he was the best man available. I believe it too, seeing how he maneuvered the ship through the shallows of this river."

"They are tricky," James affirmed.

"What do you think of him, James?"

"You did all right, Henry," James replied. "I like him."

Henry seemed pleased. "I only hired on a skeleton crew, just enough to get us here. I figured we could find some hands here if we needed them." Henry stopped in mid-stride and took James' arm. "Now fill me in on this Rajah business Captain Irons was telling me about."

"Later, Henry," James said. "Right now, I want to see the ship."

Henry nodded and pointed to the ship's cargo holds. "I filled up the holds with supplies and goods, everything I thought we might need. Hope I didn't forget anything."

James clasped Henry's shoulders. "You couldn't have done a better job, Henry. And you couldn't have come at a better time. You don't know how glad Si Tundok and I are to see the ship's guns."

Henry frowned. "Trouble?" he asked.

"We'll tell you all about it later. Right now, let's take a closer look at the *Jolly Bachelor*."

James was impressed with the transformation. Except for its lines, the *Jolly Bachelor* in no way resembled the decrepit and barnacle eaten *Lisbon*, the ship it once was. New railings and decking had been installed along with crisp, new sails and the ship had been scrubbed, oiled and painted. Fourteen eighteen-pound guns had been mounted, seven on each side of the main deck as well as an additional dozen eight pounders, four starboard and port and two each on the fore and aft decks. The *Jolly Bachelor* was smaller than James remembered, only 120 feet from stern to beam, but Henry claimed she could hold 550 tons of cargo.

When they completed the tour of the ship, Henry asked, "Well, what do you think of her?"

"You did a grand job, Henry," James replied with a huge smile.

Si Tundok confirmed the appraisal with a grunt and nod.

"Well, Henry," James said with an affectionate pat on his friend's small back, "you're probably ready to stretch your legs on land for a change. How would you like a tour of my capital city and the palace?"

Henry's first impression of Kuching from the deck of the *Jolly Bachelor* did not excite him. But the mention of a palace did. "Palace? You have a *palace*, James?"

"Every king has a palace," James laughed. "But don't get your hopes up. It isn't exactly Buckingham, and we won't be living like King George, either."

## V

### Rajah's Palace
### Kuching, Sarawak

After his inspection of the *Jolly Bachelor*, James, along with Si Tundok, gave Henry and Captain Periweg a walking tour of Kuching. Neither Henry nor the captain seemed particularly impressed with what they saw. When James suggested they return to his palace, Captain Periweg asked to be excused, preferring to return to the ship to unload the cargo and supervise a few needed repairs. James surmised that the captain, who spoke with reverence about all things connected with ships and water and as irreverently about anything associated with land, was more anxious to return to the comfort and security of the *Jolly Bachelor*, than he was interested in learning more about James' Raj. James excused the captain, again telling him how grateful he was to have the captain in his employ and he, Henry and Si Tundok walked to the palace.

After showing the unpretentious palace to Henry and answering Henry's questions concerning the circumstances which led to James becoming the Rajah of Sarawak, the three men settled comfortably around a table in the palaces *dapor*, a relatively large kitchen and eating area secluded behind the throne room. James set a bowl of fresh fruit on the table and the three men ate and talked.

"On board the *Jolly Bachelor*, you mentioned something about trouble. What's going on?" Henry asked as he peeled a *longan* and popped it into his mouth.

"A few days ago, we received word from Brunei that *Awang* Api has been seen with the Kayan. He's evidently incited them to raid along the Barum River near Brunei."

"Whose *Awang* Api?" Henry asked.

"The Sultan's brother, the one I told you we almost captured at Siniawan."

Henry nodded that he remembered and plucked another handful of the sweet fruit from the bowl.

"It is clearly apparent that Api intends to take Brunei by force, dispose of Hasim and make himself Sultan."

"What does that have to do with us?"

"If Api becomes Sultan, I'll lose my concession."

"And Sarawak?"

"And Sarawak," James affirmed. "From what we've learned about Api, he's ambitious and brutal. Apparently he won't stop until he gets what he wants or—"

"Or you stop him," Henry offered.

"That's right. I had hoped his banishment would solve the problem, but apparently I was wrong."

"What's wrong with the Sultan? He must have an army of some sorts. Why doesn't he try to stop his brother, go after him?"

Si Tundok and James exchanged glances. "The Sultan is a coward," Si Tundok said simply.

James confirmed Si Tundok's assessment of Hasim with a nod of head, but went on to say, "Hasim did send warriors to stop the Kayan, but they were annihilated."

"Forgive me for asking, James," Henry said, "but if the Sultan can't stop his brother and the Kayan, how do you propose to do it?"

"Two days ago, I sent the *Datu* Temanggong, the Malay war chief I told you about earlier, to assess the situation. I gave him instructions to send word to the Kayan chieftain, a fellow by the name of Jau, to cease his raiding activities and to dissociate himself from Api."

Henry blurted out a laugh and then started choking on a piece of fruit. He coughed and spit out the fruit. With his face flushed red, he shook his head and struggled to say, "I'm sorry, James, but you don't really believe that this Kayan, Jau, will really stop his raids just because *you* tell him to, do you?"

"Probably not," James replied truthfully.

"Then you will be forced to go in after him yourself, is that it?"

"That's what it may be leading up to."

Si Tundok noted the look of incredulity on Henry's face. "The Kayan live in a remote region of the jungle, at the headwaters of the Barum river. The Sultan's warriors were defeated because they were unfamiliar with the terrain."

"And the two of you are familiar with the terrain?" Henry asked cynically.

"No," James replied. "But the Iban are."

"The Iban? Weren't they the savages you defeated at...what was the name of that place?"

"Siniawan."

"Yeah, that's it." Henry was still puzzled. "I don't understand," he said, glancing from Si Tundok and back to James for an answer.

"We captured the leader of the Iban at Siniawan, a fellow by the name of Rentab. I had an opportunity to conduct several lengthy discussions with him aboard the *Skimalong*. In return for his release, he promised to give up raiding and headhunting. As far as I know, he has kept his word."

Henry still looked perplexed.

James continued. "Knowing that it was unlikely that either Api or the Kayan, Jau, could be dissuaded, I empowered the *Datu* Temanggong with the authority to make Rentab a *Pengulu,* a title which gives him leadership over all the Rajang and Barum Iban tribes. In return, he is to provide a force of warriors in the event it becomes necessary for me to go after Api and the Kayan."

"The Iban and Kayan are natural enemies," Si Tundok interjected. "As we saw at Siniawan, the Iban are fierce warriors and they know the terrain too."

Henry shook his head dubiously.

"What is it, Henry?" James asked.

Henry leaned forward, his elbows on the table and looked directly at his two friends. "In Singapore, when Captain Irons told me that you were granted a trade concession, I danced a jig. When he told me you were made Rajah of this whole bloody land, I could hardly believe my ears. I said, 'Henry, my boy, this is it, the opportunity of a lifetime, a chance to get rich trading with savages,' just like you said, James. But now that I'm here, I'm finding out you want to fight the people we're supposed to be trading with. It doesn't make bloody sense to me."

"Things got complicated in a hurry," James admitted.

"Why not make things simpler, James?" Henry said, peering directly into James' eyes.

"What do you mean?"

"Why not get on with what we came here to do in the first place? We could fill up the holds of the *Jolly Bachelor* and be out of here *before* the Sultan is overthrown. By the time his brother takes over the country we will have sold our cargo and begun enjoying the good life in some civilized part of the world far from here."

"It's not that simple anymore, Henry," James replied.

"Not that simple? I don't understand what you're trying to say, James." Henry leaned closer to the table and cocked his head. "If you're telling me that you're taking this king thing seriously, I'll tell you that you're a bloody fool." Henry wet his lips and his eyes darted from James to Si Tundok and then back to James. "We have the perfect situation. Why ruin it by taking a chance of getting ourselves killed? As the Rajah, you control the country. We can go any place and do anything we like. What could be better for us? We could strip this patch of jungle clean before anyone is the wiser for it."

James showed his disappointment with a deep sigh. He had hoped for better from Henry, but he could also understand, given Henry's background and the presumption that a fortune awaited them once James extracted a concession in Sarawak. "I apologize if I have misled you, Henry," James

219

explained. "But things have changed since we made our plans in Singapore. As a Rajah, I have certain obligations to the people of Sarawak. I don't intend to betray that responsibility by bilking them of their goods, nor do I intend to allow a man like Api become the master of these people. I've already seen what his kind has done to the natives of Sarawak."

"So this king thing, it really has gone to your head," Henry said. Exasperated, he leaned back in his chair and tossed up his hands. "I can't believe you're serious, James. From what I've seen and heard, these people don't give a bloody damned about your obligations to them. They've been living the same way for hundreds of years. They *expect* to be bilked for God's sake! It's their way of life."

When James remained silent, Henry looked to Si Tundok for support of his argument. "You're a Malay, Si Tundok. You know how these people live. Tell James what they really expect from their leaders."

"You are right, Henry," Si Tundok said. "They know of no other way..."

"See, James," Henry interrupted. "What did I tell you?" Henry folded his arms across his chest and beamed as if the point had been sufficiently made to win the argument and convince James to do as he suggested.

James managed to keep an even tone of voice when he said, "Just because these people have lived at the mercy of the Malay princes for untold years, doesn't mean that they can't accept a more civilized—"

"Civilized?" Henry blurted angrily. "We are not bloody missionaries, James! Si Tundok and I didn't come here to waste our time trying to civilize a bunch of bloody savages. We came here to trade, make our fortunes, just like you said in Singapore, James." Quickly turning his head to Si Tundok, Henry added, "Didn't we, Si Tundok?"

Si Tundok locked his piercing gray eyes onto Henry. "That's why I came, Henry," he conceded. "But that's not why I have chosen to stay."

Henry cast Si Tundok a look of puzzlement. "What do you mean, Si Tundok?"

"James and I visited many of the villages along the Sarawak River. We saw what Api and some of the Malay princes have done to the natives. They live in poverty and fear. They live that way because they know of no other way. James can give them a better life, but first Api must be destroyed."

"You're telling me that you're willing to give up the chance to make a fortune because you think you can help make things better for these...these... savages?" Henry asked incredulously. "Is that what you're telling me, Si Tundok?"

"I never thought much about making a fortune, Henry...even when it was discussed in Singapore. I came with James because he is my friend and I owe him my life, that is the reason I am here now and that is why I choose to stay."

Si Tundok's words hit Henry like a volley of cannon balls. In his exuberance to become a rich man he had forgotten that he was still alive because of James. He too, like Si Tundok, felt the same obligation to James, but he allowed his greed to interfere. Suddenly, Henry felt very ashamed.

Si Tundok remained stoically silent, waiting for Henry to respond. He had never felt as sure about anything in his life as he felt about James Brooke. James' bravery had been proven, but there was even more to this white man that Si Tundok had recently discovered. There was a compassion and sincerity in James that Si Tundok had never before encountered in one of James' kind. He was convinced that James was doing the right thing, and he owed it to the man who had saved his life to help him accomplish his dream, a dream Si Tundok now wanted to share.

Henry glanced uncomfortably between James and Si Tundok. Nervously, he ran his fingers through his thinning hair and managed an embarrassed grin. "Sweet Jesus," he muttered. "What a bloody fool I've been."

"Does that mean you're willing to give up trading for a while, Henry? Stay here with Si Tundok and me?"

"I guess that's what it means," Henry sighed. "But I'll be damned if I'll ever figure out how you gentlemen of breeding ever come up with the crazy notions you do."

# VI

## Sin Bok, Sarawak

News of the banished prince's arrival reached Loi Pek only moments before Api disembarked a *prau* manned by six heavily armed Kayan warriors and made his way towards Loi Pek's shop with long, purposeful strides.

Loi Pek called to the slave girl who was busy removing bottles of soy and oyster sauce from wooden crates and stocking the shelves of Loi Pek's outer storefront. "Kameja, bring tea and rice cakes. We have an unexpected visitor." The tone of Loi Pek's voice was smooth and even despite the anxiety he felt because of *Awang* Api's impromptu visit.

As quickly as his old legs could carry him, Loi Pek entered his inner office and pulled the drape separating the two rooms of his shop tightly closed behind him. With one sweeping glance, he checked to make certain that no traces of his day's activity remained in the room for Api to discover. His gold dust was safely sealed beneath the floor under the vase and as Loi Pek sniffed the warm and humid air within the room, he concluded to his satisfaction that there were no lingering signs of the opium he had been smoking earlier. Quickly, he pulled out a chair and placed it at the table in the center of the room so that it faced the draped entry to his inner office. He sat down and began to toy with an abacus, pretending to work on his store's accounts, when he heard the outer door open.

Api stood arrogantly in the doorway before he spotted Kameja stoking a raised hearth with slender sticks of dried wood. "Loi Pek? Where is the old Chinaman, girl?" he demanded haughtily.

Kameja motioned to the inner office without daring to look at her former master and tormentor.

Api scowled and strutted past her. Without announcing his presence, he ripped open the curtain to Loi Pek's inner office and stepped inside.

"Ahhh, *Awang* Api, such a pleasant surprise." Loi Pek rose slowly from his chair and opened his arms in greeting and motioned for Api to take a seat at the table. "Girl, bring refreshments for our important guest," he called to the front of the shop.

Loi Pek pasted a smile on his drawn face and sat down, his long fingers clasped casually in front of him. "And to what do I owe this unexpected pleasure of your visit, *Awang* Api?"

"There is no pleasure in my visit, Loi Pek," Api said sharply. "Simply necessity."

"Necessity?"

Api leaned into the table, his eyes burning like embers. "Let us not play foolish games with one another, old man. I have neither the time not the patience for such folly."

Loi Pek cocked his head in a way to suggest his puzzlement.

"You are aware of what happened at Siniawan, are you, not, old man?"

It was useless for Loi Pek to play the fool. After all, it was the Chinese musketeers whom he had provided to the Rajah that had helped defeat Api and his renegades. Loi Pek nodded uncomfortably. "I have heard," he confirmed.

With sarcasm, Api said, "Of course you would know. Your musketeers would have told you all the details by now, I'm sure."

Loi Pek shifted uncomfortably. "My men were our *serah* to the Rajah Hasim, nothing more. I had no knowledge that you planned to attack Siniawan."

"Without your musketeers and the cannon, I would have easily taken Siniawan," Api countered, his bitterness evident on each word he spoke. "I would have killed the white intruders and marched upon Kuching and disposed of my incompetent brother. Had that happened, I would be Sultan today."

"Forgive me for saying so, *Awang* Api, but neither of us can change what has happened. The past must be forgotten and we must look to the future." Loi Pek was aware he was treading upon dangerous ground with the volatile prince, but the subject of their future relationship had to be broached. "Your defeat at Siniawan has caused major changes in Sarawak which have implications with regard to our continuing relationship."

Api leaned back in his chair and sneered. "So you have heard, have you, old man?" Api's eyes narrowed sinisterly at the old Chinaman. "You know that my cowardly brother has been made Sultan and a white man now sits on the throne in Kuching?"

"I know all these things," Loi Pek said slowly. He also knew that Api had been banished and his power broken. But Loi Pek also understood the raging fire of ambition which burned within Api and he believed that such fires were dangerous. It would pay to be cautious.

Api's mouth turned up at the corner and he glowered at Loi Pek. "You believe I'm finished, don't you Loi Pek?"

"Believe it or not, one must be practical."

"Then let me give you something practical to think about, Loi Pek. Hasim's banishment of me means nothing to me. Nothing!"

"Perhaps," Loi Pek said evenly. "But you have lost the support of the Iban. I have been told that they have promised the white Rajah that they will no longer follow you."

Api's eyes narrowed and his jaw tightened. "Believe me when I say that I will drive the white devils from Sarawak, Loi Pek. Nothing will stop me from becoming Sultan."

"And how do you intend to accomplish this task? You no longer have the power to—"

Api's eyes blazed with anger. He reached across the table and grabbed Loi Pek's wrist and twisted it until the old Chinaman gasped from the pain. "Don't think I haven't the power, Loi Pek. When I want something, I reach out and take it!" He held Loi Pek's withered wrist for a long moment to emphasize the point. When he released it, he said, "You understand me, don't you, Loi Pek? I am not a man who is easily defeated."

Loi Pek rubbed at his wrist. "What has any of this to do with me?"

Api leaned back in his chair with one arm draped nonchalantly over the back of it. He cracked a wicked grin and said, "Oh, it has everything to do with you, my friend. I am certain that you would prefer our relationship continue as it has in the past rather than lose your precious mines to the foreign devil."

"What do you mean?" The mention of the mines broke Loi Pek's placid mask.

"Do you think the white Rajah will allow you to keep your mines, be content with only a nominal part of your diggings as I have been? You know the greed of these foreigners, don't you, Loi Pek? He will take the mines from you, old man. All of it."

There was truth in what Api told him, Loi Pek thought. He knew of how the white devils were exploiting his native China even now as the two of them talked. What would prevent the white man from taking his mines now that he had the power of a Rajah?

Seeing Loi Pek's discomfort at the thought of losing his precious mines, Api leaned forward and said, "But I have a plan that will save your mines, my friend, but you must help."

"What must I do?"

"I intend to take Kuching and dispose of this white interloper."

"How do you...?"

Api waved off Loi Pek's question with a toss of his wrist. "I have made an arrangement with certain, uh, friends in Marudu Bay and others," he said.

"Pirates?"

"Opportunists," Api corrected. "They have agreed to help me take Kuching and in return I will grant them certain favors after I have been made Sultan."

"But the Sultan is in Brunei. How does an attack on Kuching...?"

Api chuckled, pleased that Loi Pek's information about his demise was incomplete. "Apparently you haven't heard everything, Loi Pek. You, like many others, have assumed that my power in Sarawak has been broken. Far from it, my friend. I may have lost control over the Iban, but I have gained a certain advantage with the Kayan tribes along the Barum River. They will take care of Brunei for me." Api grinned, certain that he was telling the old Chinaman something he didn't know. "Already the Kayan have defeated a force of Malay warriors sent by my cowardly brother to stop the Kayan raids. Soon the Kayan and their allies will overwhelm Brunei. And I will take Kuching. It's only a matter of time before I become Sultan, Loi Pek. Count on it."

Kameja entered the room carrying a tray filled with a steaming pot of tea and a plate of freshly fried rice cakes. Silently, she set the refreshments on the table and poured each of the men a cup of tea. She could feel Api's eyes fondle her body as she served them, but she kept her hands steady and kept her eyes averted from him.

"Leave us, girl," Loi Pek ordered when she finished pouring the tea.

Api watched Kameja as she withdrew from the room and wished he hadn't given her to Loi Pek when he did. He knew he could culminate his desires with her now. "My gift has proven satisfactory, Loi Pek?" Api asked with a lascivious grin.

"As slaves go, she has been adequate."

Api stared at the rice cakes and tea. He thought of asking Loi Pek to provide him with some of his Chinese wine, but he reached for the tea instead.

"What do you think of my prospects now, Loi Pek?" Api said to continue the previous discussion.

Loi Pek made a noncommittal shrug with his shoulders. "I fail to see what it has to do with me," he said.

Api smiled wickedly. "Oh, it has *everything* to do with you, my friend."

"What do you mean?"

"When I am prepared to attack Kuching, I expect you to provide me with the same musketeers which were used against me at Siniawan."

Loi Pek almost choked on his tea. He had always dealt in subtleties, discreet manipulations. Now Api was suggesting open rebellion and he would be complicit if he provided the musketeers as Api demanded. Rebellion was much to bold for Loi Pek's liking. And dangerous.

"In fact, Loi Pek, I will expect you to provide me with as many men as I find necessary." Api smiled. He enjoyed the Chinaman's discomfort.

"It is too dangerous. If you fail—"

"I won't fail, old man. Just remember what you will lose if I don't dispose of this white Rajah. You haven't forgotten, have you?...your precious mines, remember, old friend?"

The thought of losing control of his mines, the source of his wealth and influence, was the worst thing that could happen to Loi Pek and he believed Api when he said that the white Rajah would take control of the mines once he learned of their existence. Still, he was reluctant to commit himself to Api's dangerous plan.

"I must have guarantees," Loi Pek said.

"Guarantees? You wish guarantees, do you, old man?" Api laughed evilly before turning dour. When he next spoke, the words crawled like menacing spiders from between his teeth. "I will give you guarantees, Loi Pek. If you do not do as I ask, I *guarantee* that I will have my Marudu friends torch Sin Bok as well as Kuching. They will line the street of your precious *kongsi* with Chinese heads, including your own. *That* is my guarantee, old man!" Api leaned back in his chair and said almost casually. "Fail me in this, and I will most certainly destroy you, Loi Pek."

Loi Pek tried to return the cup of tea from his hand to the table, but Api's threat had unnerved him and the hot liquid spilled on his wrist. He wiped his hand and tossed a disconcerted glance toward Api. "I will do as you say, *Awang* Api," he sighed in defeat.

Api smiled broadly, exposing his broad band of white teeth. "I knew you would see it my way, old friend."

Even as Api raised his tea cup in a mock toast to their agreement, Loi Pek was thinking of a way in which he might extricate himself from the uprising, just in case Api's plan failed.

# CHAPTER NINE

## I

Anglican Mission
Towchi, China

Arthur Claygate removed a soiled bandage from the little girl's arm and inspected her wound. Apprehensively, the six-year-old Chinese girl's dark brown eyes followed his fingers as he gently touched the sutures he had sewn into her forearm several days earlier to close a four inch gash she sustained after falling on the blade of her father's plow. A scab had formed along the wound and Arthur could see no redness or swelling to indicate complications with the wound.

"Your arm has healed nicely," Arthur said with a wink in his halting Hakka. "I'm going to put another clean bandage on it. Try to keep this one out of the mud," he said with a smile. "Then come and see me again in three days." Arthur held three fingers in front of the girl's eyes and repeated his instructions until she nodded that she understood.

Arthur pretended to busy himself with the contents of his medical bag and watched the girl from the corner of his eye. She folded her tiny arms in front of her, refusing to move. "What is it, Tsu Tse? Have I forgotten something?"

"Medicine," she said flatly.

"Oh yes, how silly of me." Arthur reached into his shirt pocket and pulled out a stick of sugar candy and held it front of the girl's eager eyes. "Do you promise to eat all of this medicine until it's all gone?"

She shook her head vigorously, then plucked the candy from his hand and put it in her mouth. Arthur mussed her hair and laughed heartily as the girl hopped down from the stool she was sitting on and ran out the door. He watched as she dashed across the dusty road by the mission clinic and disappeared beyond a cluster of shops facing the clinic on the opposite side of the road. Arthur chuckled to himself. He enjoyed playing the game of 'medicine' with the village children, but he suspected that many of their minor scrapes and abrasions were self-inflicted in order to deprive him of his candy supply.

He walked to a wash basin along the far wall of the clinic and began to lather and wash his hands. He took a towel from a hook near the building's one window and dried his hands. As he rubbed the towel over his hands and fingers, his eyes strayed out the window. He caught sight of his wife, Margaret, leading three children over a rise beyond the small village.

Arthur tossed the towel to the hook, missed it and watched it fall to the floor. He didn't bother to pick it up. Instead, he plopped down on a cot, deciding it was time for his afternoon nap. Before he fell asleep, his mind wandered to thoughts of Margaret and the three orphan children she led every afternoon at this time to a quiet grove of acacia trees beyond the village to instruct them in the virtues of Christianity and teach them smatterings of English. Arthur was proud of his wife, but he felt sorry for her too.

Other than the success of his clinic, their missionary efforts had not gone well. The villagers, while friendly, adamantly refused to listen to Margaret's pleas to attend her services and hear the Word of the One True God. But Margaret refused to give up on them. She managed to gather three of the villages' orphaned children and optimistically announced to Arthur that she would reach the soul of the village through God's children. Her altruism and indefatigable enthusiasm for their mission was a constant source of amazement to Arthur. And love. He even found himself praying to God with other than feigned sincerity for Him to grant his wife success as a reward for her efforts in His name. As Arthur drifted into sleep thinking of his wife, he was unaware that someone else was also thinking of her.

Geoff, sitting on a block of wood at the back of a Chinese shop across from the mission clinic, drew his knife and absently cut away at his dirt-encrusted fingernails while he slipped into angry thoughts about how much he detested the Chinese and the Orient. Through his contact with a nefarious Irishman, Geoff had done his part in diverting a portion of opium bound for Hong Kong to the shop at Towchi where Chin was inside making arrangements with his Heaven and Earth brethren to transport the cargo to Borneo aboard one of their junks.

"Damned slant-eyed bastards," he muttered to himself. Again, he had been excluded from the negotiations with Chin's Heaven and Earth brothers and it angered him. "Can't understand their bloody gibberish anyway," he murmured to console himself for his exclusion. "Soon as this deal is finished, I'm heading back to England. Be around folks who speak a proper language and be done with these bloody heathens!" He cut away a length of fingernail and flipped it to the ground.

Geoff raised his head to the sound of children laughing. Beyond a stone hedge that separated the rear of the shop where he sat from a bamboo thicket and a stand of acacia trees, he saw a woman leading three Chinese children hand-in-hand to the top of a small knoll. He watched as they settled into the shade of the acacia trees. The woman appeared to be a European. Geoff rubbed at the stubble of his beard and grated his yellow teeth together. It had been a long time since he had seen a white woman. Curious, Geoff decided to take a closer look. He replaced his knife in its scabbard, eased himself up from the block of wood and moved slowly toward the stone hedge. Using the stone fence for cover, Geoff slithered along its meandering path until he reached the bamboo thicket. He could clearly hear the woman's voice now and she was speaking English as well as Chinese.

Carefully, he eased himself over the stone fence and moved silently through the thicket of bamboo and grass. Arriving undetected at its edge, he parted his cover enough to allow a direct view of the woman and the three children sitting beneath the acacia trees. He heard the woman give a short prayer of thanksgiving and then watched her dole out bowls of rice and vegetables from a tin canister she had carried with her. As the children ate, the woman spoke short, simple phrases of English to which the children responded, mimicking her as best they could.

With growing impatience, Geoff licked at the beads of sweat that broke out on his upper lip while the woman droned on, telling the children about Jonah and the whale. When she finally finished the story and the children completed their sparse meal, the children returned their bowls to her, bowed politely and, after receiving a final blessing from the woman, scattered amid a flurry of giggles down the knoll and towards the village.

With her back towards him, the woman kneeled down to place the empty bowls into the tin canister and began to gather up her belongings, an umbrella and a well-worn bible.

With the stealth of a cat, Geoff emerged from the thicket and circled around the clump of acacia trees below Margaret, cutting her off from the village.

"Good day, my lady," Geoff said, his yellow teeth flashing a smile.

"Oh dear!" Startled by the sudden appearance of the stranger, Margaret dropped the tin canister and automatically brought the fingertips of her empty hand to her lips. "You...you frightened me, sir."

"My apologies, my lady," Geoff said. He feigned a mock bow, pretending to doff a cap which he did not wear. "Simply came along to aid a lady. Nothing to get all upset with, now is there?" Geoff bent over to retrieve the fallen canister.

Margaret snatched it from him and with the canister and her umbrella in one hand and her bible pressed firmly to her chest with the other, she raised her chin authoritatively and said, "It is totally unnecessary, sir. I am perfectly capable of carrying my own things. Good day to you—"

As Margaret started to move by him, Geoff's hand reached out like a striking snake and grabbed her by the arm and twisted her around towards him. "No need to be rude, my lady," Geoff said, his Neanderthal eyes suddenly squinting evilly. "It's not nice to put off the help of a gentleman such as me. Not nice at all."

"Please let go of my arm," Margaret pleaded, her voice shrill. "You are hurting me!"

Geoff relaxed his grip on Margaret's arm, but he didn't let go. A sinister chuckle arose from deep within his throat. He was enjoying tormenting this pencil-thin woman. It excited him.

Margaret's frightened eyes flitted down the knoll toward the village. She prayed that someone, anyone, would appear to extricate her from her fearful situation. There was no one. "Please...please, let me go..." she began to plead.

Geoff raised his bushy brows. His yellow-fanged smirk dropped into a spurious frown. He extended a single finger in front of Margaret's face and wiggled it. "Naughty lady," he mocked, "not to accept a gentleman's kind offering." Geoff clicked his tongue and shook his head mischievously from side to side. "Could be you're not a lady at all. Could be I done made me a mistake about that? Could be old Geoff's found himself a real *naughty* lady, could be, huh?"

Panic gripped Margaret. With fear guiding her, she jerked her arm from Geoff's grip, dropped her belongings and bolted for the village screaming.

But she was too late. Geoff caught her around the head and mouth after only a few steps and stifled her cry for help. His other arm encircled her small waist and he lifted her easily from the ground. Margaret tried to kick him, but it was futile, so tightly did he have her in his grasp. He carried her deeper into the stand of acacia trees then slammed her into the trunk of one of them and pinned her against it with her feet raised above the ground.

Margaret's head hit the tree trunk with a hollow thud and she wilted in Geoff's grasp. Her brain swam in confusion, but it still tried to relay its final instructions to her mouth and throat. Margaret bit the assailant's hand and as he retracted it from her mouth in pain, she tried to scream.

But a blow from Geoff's fist silenced her and she slumped, unconscious against the tree. Geoff let her sink to the ground. Breathing heavily from the excitement, Geoff glanced around to make certain he had not been seen. There was nothing, not even the sound of a bird or the rustle of a breeze.

Margaret moaned and turned on the ground, struggling to regain her senses. Slowly she raised a hand to the back of her head and touched at the throb of pain ripping through her skull. Her eyes flickered, but she couldn't open them completely.

Geoff dropped to his knees and straddled Margaret's lower body. He was only a blurry shadow, but Margaret muttered something incoherently and tried to push the shadow away from her.

"Ahh...the naughty lady is trying to fight off old Geoff, is she? Doesn't think old Geoff is good enough for her, does she?" Geoff pulled his hand back and struck Margaret a violent blow to the side of the face. Margaret's eyes slammed shut and she fell limp. A trickle of blood oozed from the corner of her mouth.

"Well, old Geoff here's going to show the naughty lady a thing or two, yes sir. But first, he's going to see just what it is the naughty lady's been hiding from him."

Geoff reached out and grabbed Margaret's high-collared dress with both of his hands and ripped it open, slips and all, and revealed her small, almost pubescent breasts.

"Ahh..." He breathed heavily, taking in the sight of her exposed torso. "Just look at what the naughty lady's been hiding from me all this time." His fingers and crooked thumb fell upon her breasts and he squeezed and massaged them with his callused hands. Hungrily he fondled Margaret's small breasts for several long moments and dug his fingers into them and twisted them as if to wrench them from her body. Sweat dripped from his forehead and upper lip and fell with tiny defiling splashes against Margaret's bare chest.

"Now, naughty lady, old Geoff's going to see what else you've been hiding," he wheezed, barely able to contain the raw animal desire surging through his groin. His fingers trembled with anticipation as he crudely and frantically ripped away the remainder of Margaret's clothing and flung them aside.

He groaned with pleasure at the sight of her brown pubes and placed both of his rough hands between her legs. With his thumbs, he spread her open until her pink, inner flesh was revealed to him. Crudely, he forced two fingers of his hand into her and pumped them along the walls of her vagina while his free hand tore at his own breeches until his blood-engorged penis was exposed.

"Going to grease you up real good," he puffed while he used both of his hands and fingers to violate her further. "Then old Geoff is going to teach you some manners on how to treat a gentlemen...going to make a *real* lady out of you."

Unable to contain himself any longer, Geoff spread Margaret's legs wide apart and fell onto her. Margaret gasped through her unconsciousness and screamed silently within as Geoff forced himself into her. She tossed her head from side to side murmuring, "No...no...please God...no."

Geoff countered with a swift slap to her face and then he lurched and thrust and pushed himself in and out of her until he exploded in a great shaking spasm. He continued his ravenous attack a second time, finally shuddering, spent, and collapsed on top of her.

His passion abated, Geoff slowly pushed himself to his knees and fastened his breeches. He stood up and stared at Margaret's bruised and battered face with disgust. She was ugly, he decided.

Margaret whimpered incoherently. "Begging old Geoff for more of the same, are you now? Isn't nice to beg." Geoff's tormenting voice transformed and with it, his grin changed to a tight-jawed scowl. "Maybe the naughty lady needs to be taught some manners." He brought back his foot and kicked Margaret in the side of the head. Again and again he kicked at her until his boot was coated with her blood and she lay unmoving at his feet. Then, whistling a sea ditty, Geoff casually strolled back to the shop, leaving Margaret's ravished body in the acacia grove, knowing she was dead.

# II

## Wethington Villa
## The South of France

From her perch on the verandah of the country villa owned by Elizabeth's deceased father, Mollie watched pensively as Elizabeth strolled among the greenery of the estate's newly emerging spring garden. Concern for her mistress' welfare showed on her furrowed brow and watchful eyes, but she felt somewhat gratified to know that she had witnessed some improvement in Elizabeth's health over the past several weeks.

Physically, Elizabeth seemed stronger. Her once pallid cheeks were beginning to exhibit signs of color and she was starting to fill out her dresses which had hung limp around her small frame from the weight she had lost. But sadly, Mollie wondered if her mistress would ever truly recover from her melancholy and return to be the same buoyant and vivacious young woman she had once been. Mollie sighed to herself and tried to expunge the lingering memory of that fateful morning in July of the previous year when she found Elizabeth lying on the floor next to her bed, unconscious and bleeding, but she couldn't.

*Mollie, carrying a pitcher of heated water for Elizabeth's morning toilet, entered Elizabeth's room to awaken her when she spotted her charge lying on the floor in a pool of blood. She dropped the pitcher to the floor and rushed to Elizabeth's side. "Oh, dear Lord in Heaven! What has happened to you, my lady!"*

*Reaching Elizabeth, Mollie dropped to her knees. "Oh my God...my lady...sweet Jesus, no...!" Mollie placed her plump hands to Elizabeth's pale face and determined that Elizabeth was still alive. With some difficulty, Mollie calmed herself enough to make a quick examination of her charge. Elizabeth's muslin nightgown was pulled above her waist. Below, she was naked and a thick stream of clotted blood ran from between her legs and gathered in a crimson pool beneath her hips and buttocks.*

*"Oh, God in Heaven, what have you done to yourself, my lady?" Mollie's trembling hands reached down and carefully extracted a riding crop from Elizabeth's vagina. Mollie saw that the leather wrapping of the instrument had been removed, exposing its bare metal handle which was grotesquely coated with clumps of Elizabeth's blood. With a supreme effort to maintain her self-control, Mollie removed her shawl and wiped at a trickle of blood which began to flow when she removed the riding crop. Mollie frantically*

233

*wiped at the blood trying to stem its flow while fighting against her growing nausea and panic. "Please, God... no!...Don't let this innocent one die...please...no...don't let her die," she repeated over and over again. But even as Mollie prayed for Elizabeth's life, she knew by what she had seen, that Elizabeth was not so innocent. Elizabeth's attempt to abort herself was evidence of that.*

*Shortly, Mollie's attempt to halt the flow of blood proved successful and she managed to lift Elizabeth and place her gently onto the bed. It was only after Mollie sensed that her charge was breathing normally and resting comfortably did she realize that she hadn't screamed for help. At that moment, she considered summoning assistance but quickly decided against it. Had she done so, her charge would be forever tarnished and the incident would most likely lead to scandal and the ruination of Lord Gray's political career. Instead, Mollie hastily retrieved another pitcher of warm water and fresh towels. She removed Elizabeth's red stained nightgown and bathed her with wet towels and placed a fresh gown on her before covering the girl with soft blankets. With Elizabeth resting peacefully, Mollie quickly cleaned the pool of blood from the floor, picked up the broken shards from the smashed water pitcher and mopped up the water that spilled to the floor. Satisfied that all traces of the incident had been removed, Mollie sat by Elizabeth's side on the bed and dabbed a wet towel on Elizabeth's forehead and prayed.*

*These were anxious moments for Mollie. Again she debated whether she was doing the right thing, but finally Elizabeth began to stir and slowly she regained consciousness.*

*"Thank God in Heaven," Mollie whispered and softly stroked Elizabeth's face. Tears gushed from Mollie's eyes and strayed along her cheeks. "Thank God in Heaven," she repeated.*

*Elizabeth sighed and slowly turned her head toward Mollie. She opened her eyes and her lips moved, trying to form words, but her words had no sound.*

*Tenderly, Mollie touched Elizabeth's lips. "Shush now, child, don't try to talk. Everything will be just fine."*

*Straining against her weakened condition, Elizabeth labored to speak. "No...one...must...know...ever," she whispered.*

*Mollie tried once again to silence Elizabeth with a touch to her lips. "Shhh, rest child." She said.*

*Elizabeth shook her head almost imperceptibly and whispered, "Promise me...you must...promise me..."*

*"I promise, my lady. No one shall ever know," Mollie assured her.*

*Elizabeth sighed deeply and her lips curled into the beginnings of a smile, then she closed her eyes.*

*"Rest, child. Don't worry, your secret is safe with me."* Gently, Mollie stroked Elizabeth's forehead until the girl drifted into a deep slumber.

Anxious days followed. Mollie attended to Elizabeth's recovery night and day and successfully passed off her mistress' condition as a consequence of her emerging womanhood which the Grays seemed willing enough to accept. Lord Gray suggested that a physician be called, but Mollie assured him that Elizabeth would be fine under her own care and convinced them that the problem would soon pass. It was a daring act of deception on Mollie's part, but she was determined to keep Elizabeth's self abuse a secret, regardless of the risk involved.

Although Elizabeth's physical condition improved, her melancholy deepened. Finally, at Mollie's insistence, the Grays permitted Mollie and Elizabeth to leave England and travel to the South of France to reside at a villa owned in Elizabeth's trust. It was agreed by everyone that an escape to a warmer climate would be of benefit to Elizabeth's recovery.

"Elizabeth!" Mollie called from the porch. "I think you have been outside long enough. It is time to come inside and rest a bit. I'll make you a fresh pot of tea."

With a saddened heart, Mollie watched as Elizabeth responded almost catatonically to the sound of Mollie's voice calling to her. Mechanically, Elizabeth turned on the garden path and followed it slowly back to the villa. When she reached the edge of the garden, she bent down and plucked a purple crocus from the ground. Dreamily, she examined the small flower for a long moment before she brushed it lightly against the nose of the baby she held bundled closely to her breasts. The baby cooed and giggled as it's nose was tickled, but Elizabeth didn't smile.

As Mollie watched Elizabeth return to the villa, she couldn't help but wonder whose seed had been responsible for her mistress' unhappiness. Young Phillip Ansley, perhaps? Or maybe the Brookes' son, James? Perhaps another? Silently, Mollie reprimanded herself again for wishing that Elizabeth's attempt to abort herself would have been successful.

# CHAPTER TEN

## I

Rajah's Palace
Kuching, Sarawak

Several weeks passed before the *Datu* Temanggong returned to Kuching from Kampong Batang. Anxiously, James listened to the Malay war chief as he explained what had transpired. The news was not good.

"As you ordered, Rajah James, I conferred the title of *Pengulu* upon the Iban, Rentab and instructed him to send an envoy to the Kayan leader, Jau. *Pengulu* Rentab complied with your order and sent a peace mission to Long Selah'at to inform Jau that he must stop his raids and dissociate himself from the banished rebel, *Awang* Api." The *Datu* seemed hesitant to complete his report. Like most subordinates, he was reluctant to be the bearer of bad news.

"Well?" James asked. "What happened? What did the Kayan leader say?"

The *Dutu* shifted his feet uncomfortably. "The headless corpses of *Pengulu* Rentab's peace mission to Long Selah'at were found floating in the Barum River several days later."

"Killed by the Kayan?"

The *Datu* nodded.

"Damn!" James slammed his fist in the palm of his hand.

Quickly, the *Datu* Temanggong relayed the remainder of his report. "When the news reached Kampong Batang, it was all I could do to contain the *Pengulu* Rentab. He wanted to lead an expedition against Long Selah'at, but I convinced him to gather his warriors and wait for your instructions." The *Datu* peered anxiously at James and added, "It is what the Rajah wished me to do, is it not?"

"Yes, yes," James confirmed. "You have acted properly, *Datu*, thank you."

Relieved, the *Datu* Temanggong asked, "What does the Rajah wish for me to do now?"

"Jau has given me no alternative. He must be stopped before he and Api seize Brunei. I have no choice but to lead an expedition against the Kayan and their allies." James pondered the situation for a moment and then said, "Gather as many warriors as you can, *Datu*. I'll inform Captain Periweg to make ready the *Jolly Bachelor*. We set sail in the morning."

## II

Kampong Batang
Sarawak, Borneo

The *Jolly Bachelor* reached the sandy delta of the Rejang River in two days' time, slowed by the *Datu* Temanggong's force of nearly two hundred Malay warriors following close behind the brigantine in two dozen war *praus*.

James instructed Captain Periweg to remain anchored offshore and await the expedition's return. Si Tundok remained in Kuching to watch over things, but Henry, feeling a renewed enthusiasm for adventure, persuaded James to allow him to accompany the expedition to Kampong Batang.

Initially, James intended to remove two of the *Jolly Bachelor's* cannons and haul them up-river, but after seeing the difficult passage that faced them, he thought better of it. Instead, he and Henry armed themselves with musket pistols and sabers and joined the *Datu* Temanggong in his lead canoe and began the difficult journey up the Rajang to meet the *Pengulu* Rentab at his longhouse at Batang.

A swiftly flowing river, barriers of enormous boulders blocking their way in many places, and numerous twists and turns made the passage up-river extraordinarily difficult. Finally, near sundown on the second day, James and the Malay force approached Kampong Batang to be greeted by a cacophony of gongs breaking the silence of the jungle surrounding them.

"What in the bloody hell is that?" Henry glanced suspiciously to the dark jungle wall on either side of them.

"It is a welcome from the Iban," the *Datu* explained. There will be a *gawai*, a party in honor of the Rajah's arrival." The wizened old war chief cracked a broad, lascivious grin. "There will be much drinking and dancing. Perhaps the Rajah and *Tuan* Henry will *niap* this evening as well."

Henry had never learned a language other than English, but he was rapidly picking up the simple Malay language. Still, he didn't understand all that was said and asked James for a further explanation.

"I guess we'll find out what it means after we arrive, Henry," James said. "But the *Datu* referred to you as '*Tuan*' which means, 'lord,' Henry. Not a bad promotion for a Welshman who was only a private in the King's Army a short year ago, eh?"

Henry brightened and said, "Hey, that's not bad, not bad at all. I'm beginning to like this place better and better."

Upon landing at Kampong Batang the Rajah's party was welcomed by an impressive array of Iban warriors, nearly two hundred of them whom Rentab had gathered from the surrounding villages with his newly acquired authority as *Pengulu*. No sooner had James stepped from the canoe than Rentab's rough hands enveloped his own and shook them enthusiastically. Rentab smiled broadly through his black, beetle-nut stained teeth and led James and his entourage through the mass of gleeful spectators toward the newly constructed longhouse of Batang.

At the base of a log-hewn stairway which led to the *ruii*, James stopped to look up, his attention drawn to the sight of Iban women crowding near the entrance to the longhouse. They wore their straight black hair drawn tightly back and rolled into neat buns at the nape of their necks. Their brown, oval faces smiled exuberantly. Their chests were bare and they wore black sarongs covering them from the waist to their ankles. Many of the women wore necklaces of silver and bracelets of gold, silver and brass and a few had diadems of freshly cut flowers or beautifully crafted silver rimming the tops of their heads. The women giggled and motioned for James and the rest of them to climb the stairway. Somewhere behind the women, drums and gongs hammered out a rapid, discordant rhythm while a melodic sound of chanting rose above the beat of the drums and the clanging of the gongs.

"*Jaga-jaga*, Rajah, be careful," Rentab advised as he held James' elbow. "The steps are slippery."

With curious anticipation, James maneuvered the log stairway and stepped onto a bamboo floor nearly fifteen feet above the ground. The platform was roofed and ran parallel to a long line of individual rooms to James' left. To his right was a second platform, uncovered and obviously a general work area that was littered with baskets, tools and bundles of rice.

The Iban women formed a single long line approximately a quarter of the length from the entrance of the longhouse to its far end and held out glasses filled with a white, milky substances. The woman first in line and closest to James was an older woman with pancake breasts and a wrinkled face. She pushed a glass to him and smiled, revealing the black stubs of her meager teeth.

"It is the Iban custom," the *Datu* Temanggong said, moving in behind James and Henry. "Each of these women represents a *bilek*, a room in the longhouse. They offer you *tuak*, a sweet rice wine to show their hospitality. You must drink from each of their glasses, Rajah, or take the glass and then offer it back to the woman who gives it to you and she will drink it for you."

James allowed the old woman to place the glass to his lips. She reached up, held his head and poured the contents of the glass into his mouth. Surprisingly, James found the thick liquor to be pleasant and he easily downed several successive glasses. Henry and the *Datu* Temanggong followed James down the row of Iban women. Henry also enjoyed the sweet taste of the liquor, but the *Datu*, because he was a Moslem as were all of the Malay warriors, didn't consume alcohol for religious reasons, and proffered it back to the woman who offered it.

"Hey, this is some kind of party, all right," Henry laughed. "Liquor, naked women, music...and I thought we only came here to fight."

"Enjoy it while you can, Henry," James chuckled. "The fighting will happen soon enough."

By the time James reached the middle of the line, he felt his head reeling from the numbing effects of the alcohol and he began passing the glass back to the women, hoping he could reach the end of the line without falling down.

But Henry found it difficult to resist the pleasant wine and continued to down each glass as it was handed to him. "If Si Tundok saw us now, James, he would never allow you to leave him behind again."

When James, Henry and the *Datu* Temanggong reached the end of the gauntlet, Rentab seated them on the floor of the *ruii*, in a semi-circle with himself sitting to James' right and Henry to James' left next to the *Datu* Temanggong. Children and women continued to chant and beat on the drums and gongs until well after the men were seated then the women brought platters of food and bowls of rice and additional quantities of *tuak* and placed it on the floor in front of the men.

"We eat now, Rajah James," Rentab said, offering the food with a sweep of his hand. The music and singing stopped and as many Iban who could, squeezed themselves around the leaders and watched Rentab and his guests eat the elaborately prepared meal. Most of them had never seen a Rajah before and few of them had ever seen a white man. They poked and giggled with one another and listened to each other's explanations as to the color of the white men's hair and the pallid pigmentation of their skin.

Other than the bowls of rice, James and Henry were unfamiliar with the contents of any of the dishes displayed before them and had to ask Rentab what each of them contained before they sampled them. The aroma of the food was pleasantly fierce, signaling the variety of spices and hot peppers used in the preparation of it. Fruit bats, pork, snakes and chicken comprised the main ingredients of the meat dishes and each was either roasted or drowned in a pleasant curry sauce. Even the rice was different from the Indian rice that James and Henry were accustomed to. The Iban hill *padi*, was of a larger grain with a hue of purple running through each of the grains and its taste was sweeter, more flavorful than any rice they had eaten before. Henry and James agreed that the roasted pork, its soft white flesh coated in a sweetened sauce was the most delicious of all the foods. The *Datu*

Temanggong, again to maintain religious propriety, refrained from sampling the pork, but agreed on the basis of the aroma that the dish must be extraordinarily delicious.

By the end of the feast, the strong spices had taken their toll on the European's unaccustomed palates and they were brought tea and bowls of fresh fruit, *rambutan* and *jumbo biji* to quench the fire in their mouths. No sooner had the men indicated their fill than the gongs sounded once again and a slow, haunting rhythm of sound filled the longhouse. Immediately the crowd separated and several Iban warriors brandishing their *parangs* and wooden war shields entered the vacated space and began to perform a slow, methodical dance punctuated with delicate, bird-like movements of their hands and feet. Gracefully, the warriors wove in and out among one another in an expression of mock combat to the slow and gentle beat of the gongs as they danced their *nanjat*. Even Rentab, gleefully feeling the effects of the *tuak* and the excitement of showing off his important guests to his kinsmen, joined the dance. But unlike the younger warriors, his movements were less fluid and not as graceful.

Several times during the course of the celebration, the Iban would migrate, with their guests in tow, to the river's edge to bathe. More than simply a respite to cleanse themselves, the ritual was intended to revitalize and freshen the celebrants so that, upon returning to the longhouse, the refreshed party could continue with the same vigor as before. It was at the river that the *Datu* Temanggong cautioned James that the Iban celebrations often lasted for several days. Henry thought it was a great idea, but James preferred to lead a sober and well-rested war party to Long Selah'at and indicated his wishes to Rentab.

"We must end the celebration, *Pengulu* Rentab. We have much yet to discuss and I wish to get an early start for Long Selah'at in the morning."

The Iban leader showed his disappointment. He had intended for the *gawai* to last a minimum of three days. If James had been a lesser lord and not a Rajah, he would have made an attempt to persuade James to continue the revelry, but instead he said, "As you wish, Rajah James. Come, we will return to the *ruii* where we can talk and then I will take you to a *bilek*, a room where you, *Tuan* Henry and the *Datu* Temanggong can sleep."

Upon returning to the longhouse, the four of them gathered on the *ruii* away from the merriment and began formulating their plan to take Long Selah'at. After reiterating that it was his intention to punish Jau for his raids and the slaughter of Rentab's envoy to Long Selah'at James asked, "Rentab, you are familiar with Jau's village?"

"Yes, Rajah, I have been there many times when I was younger." Rentab didn't add that he had been seeking heads at the time.

"In your opinion, *Pengulu*, what is the best approach to Long Selah'at from here?"

"We should follow the Rajang River until we reach the Belaga River. Then, we can go upriver on the Belaga until we reach its headwaters. From there we must go overland to reach the Baram River at Long Akar. We can reach Jau's village from the Barum River."

"How long will the trip take," James asked.

"For a war party this size? Two, maybe three days," Rentab replied. "The rivers are low this time of the year so passage is more difficult."

"Can't we just march overland?" Henry asked.

Rentab shook his head emphatically. "Too difficult. The forest is much too thick. The only place to cut overland is between the Belaga and Barum rivers. There are paths through the jungle there. It is the only place where we can carry the canoes through the jungle."

James thought a moment and then he said, "*Datu*, Henry, what do you think?"

"It is a good plan, Rajah James," the *Datu* Temanggong replied.

"Got to trust the bloke who's been there," Henry concurred in English while he nodded in Rentab's direction.

"Very well, it's settled. But there is one more thing," James said, shifting his gaze to Rentab. "*Pengulu* Rentab, as we have discussed previously, no heads are to be taken by your warriors."

Rentab almost objected. He was anxious to take his revenge on Jau and the Kayan for what they did to his family, his envoy and the torching of Batang and the other Iban villages, but he held his tongue. He was *Pengulu* now, and his wisdom seemed to be growing along with his elevated status. And he remembered his promise to the white Rajah. "No heads," he replied.

"Good! We'll leave for Long Selah'at first thing in the morning," James said, pushing himself to his feet and signaling that the meeting was over. "Now, where are those sleeping quarters you mentioned, *Pengulu* Rentab?"

Rentab led James, Henry and the *Datu* to a vacant *bilek* near the entrance of the longhouse. On his orders, two girls brought oil lamps which lit the room's dark interior, revealing a melange of neatly arranged paraphernalia which indicated that someone had given up their own sleeping quarters so that the Rajah and his two lieutenants would be comfortable. The two girls rolled out three rattan mats from along one wall and loosened three mosquito nets from the rafters which tumbled down to form a protective canopy over each of the mats. Before withdrawing, the two girls placed a hand loomed blanket inside each of the mosquito nets and set each of the two oil lamps between the three beds.

"Sleep well, Rajah," Rentab said. "My warriors will be ready to take you to Long Selah'at in the morning."

James thanked Rentab for his hospitality and made a short statement about the importance of their mission to the Kayan territory before Rentab politely closed the door of the *bilek* and the three men crawled into their mosquito nets with James taking the one closest to the door, Henry next to him and the *Datu* Temanggong at the end.

James drew his knees to his chest, enabling him to fit inside the walls of the mosquito netting which had been woven for the much shorter Iban. He then lay on his side with his hands folded under his head forming a pillow. He was surprised to find that the thin rattan mat provided more comfort than he imagined it would. He stared through the mesh of the netting and watched the dancing shadows that played upon the walls from the flickering light of the oil lamp. The playful shadows seemed to mesmerize him and his thoughts drifted to these people, the Iban...his people. At Siniawan they had proven themselves to be brave and courageous opponents and now they were warm and friendly allies. Perhaps it would be the same with all the tribes in Sarawak, he thought as he closed his eyes and fell into a deep slumber.

Henry didn't fall asleep for a long while. He lay on his back with his arms folded under his head and thought of his decision to remain in Sarawak with James and Si Tundok. *It had been a good decision,* he decided. He had the company of the two people he admired most in his life and he had developed a fondness for the *Datu* Temanggong and the Malay warriors during the *Jolly Bachelor's* short voyage to the Rajang. And he was absolutely fascinated by the Iban. So ferocious they appeared when he first caught sight of them with their short, muscular bodies decorated with mystical purple tattoos and their black teeth and alert eyes. But tonight they had proven themselves to be a hospitable and friendly people also, qualities that Henry seldom encountered in the people he had met in his life of wandering. Long after the village fell silent and with only the isolated grunts of the pigs rutting in the garbage beneath the longhouse, did Henry finally blow out the oil lamp and roll over and fall asleep.

None of the three men heard the door of the *bilek* ease open in the middle of the night or heard the soft shuffle of footsteps approach the mosquito nets. A dark form lowered itself in a squatting position near the foot of Henry's mosquito net.

"Ayyyiee...orang...puteh...datai..." the chant began.

"What the bloody hell-?" Henry bolted to a sitting position and stared at the shadow falling against his mosquito net.

James and the *Datu* Temanggong both awakened with the same start, but the old Malay simply rolled his eyes and lay back down on his mat.

The chant continued.

"James? What the hell is going on?"

"I don't know Henry." James lifted a corner of his netting and peered at the gossamer-like figure weaving in cadence to the sound of its chant. Slim shafts of moonlight penetrated the cracks in the thatched walls of the *bilek* and revealed the outline of a woman who James recognized as Dawas, one of Rentab's sisters. She was seated calmly with her hands crossed in her lap, chanting her melodious Iban tune without regard to the conversation between the two men.

Wearily, the *Datu* Temanggong explained. "It is *niap*, an Iban custom. The woman is courting you, *Tuan* Henry."

"Courting me? I don't understand."

Knowing that he wouldn't get back to sleep until he explained, the *Datu* sighed and said, "When Iban men come of age, they enter the *bilek* of an Iban girl who has reached puberty and chant a love song to them. If the girl likes the boy's proposal, she allows the boy into her mosquito net to let him lie with her. They then make love." Feeling the explanation was adequate, the *Datu* turned over and closed his eyes.

"But what am *I* supposed to do?" Henry pleaded.

The *Datu* sighed in frustration. He yawned and said, "If you want to make love to her, open your net and let her inside. If you don't, go back to sleep."

"James?" Henry called in a pathetically pleading voice. "What shall I do?"

James chuckled and laid back down. "Well, Henry, I guess that's up to you. Evidently she's of the opinion that you are the best choice from among the three of us. It's your decision to make. As for me, I'm going back to sleep."

# III

March 28, 1826
Kampong Batang

The morning following the *gawai*, the longhouse awakened as a single entity: the women and children mechanically performing the laborious tasks of gathering firewood and preparing rice gruel for the morning meal and the men gathering their war shields and sharpening their *parangs* and spears.

The women stuffed stalks of freshly cut bamboo with a mixture of rice, fish, vegetables and water and laid them across a fire after sealing the open ends of the stalks with banana leaves. After the mixture was properly steamed, it would be removed from the bamboo, separated into small bundles and wrapped in banana leaves. Then, tied with rattan cords, the bundles of food would be distributed among the warriors as their only provisions for the expedition against the Kayan.

Henry was the last to awaken. He tried to massage away the throb in his head and wished he had used better judgment on his consumption of *tuak* the previous evening. With some effort he managed to overcome the vestiges of the celebration, but he moved slowly, averted his eyes and avoided conversation for fear that the pounding in his head would return. Henry had questions to ask of the *Datu*, but he waited until his head cleared and the warriors were all loaded into the armada of war *praus* and had begun the first stage of the journey up river before he asked sheepishly of the *Datu* Temanggong, "About this *niap* custom? You said it was the boys who did the chanting and the girls who either accepted or rejected the boys, right?"

"That is true."

"Then why was it that Rentab's sister *niaped* me?"

"Because she was unclean," the *Datu* answered simply.

"What? Unclean!" Henry's mouth fell open in shock.

James, seated in the bow of the *prau* near the two men overheard the conversation and was just as surprised by the *Datu's* answer as was Henry. He reflected upon the sailors and vagabonds he had seen crowding the slums of port cities all over the Orient who suffered from the 'unclean disease'. It was not a fate he would wish upon anyone, particularly Henry.

"Oh, my God!" Henry suddenly felt dirty. His hand unconsciously rubbed his forearms in search of crusty scabs and he imagined his face and body teeming with pus-infected sores as a result of his previous evening's escapade.

"Oh, not unclean as you think of it, *Tuan* Henry," the *Datu* hastened to add when he noted Henry's discomfort. "The woman is taboo, that is all."

"Taboo?" The question came from both James and Henry at the same time.

"Yes," explained the *Datu*. "The Iban believe that when evil spirits cause a man to die from an accident they capture his spirit. The dead man's spirit, his *hantu*, will then roam the forest and do mischievous things like the evil spirits which have captured him. That is why the widows of those who die in such a manner are isolated from the community as was Rentab's sister. It is considered taboo for anyone to marry the widow for fear that the husband's *hantu* will return and bring misfortune to the new husband and the village."

"Better to be haunted than to get a disease, don't you agree, Henry?" James chuckled.

The *Datu* explained further. "Surely a woman who has been denied the pleasure of a man has needs that must be satisfied. That is why the Iban allow the widows of their men to *niap*. It is a very interesting custom, do you not think so, *Tuan* Henry?"

Henry nodded that it was, indeed an interesting custom, and was relieved to know that he hadn't been infected with some hideous social disease. But he had more questions for the *Datu* about this strange custom of *niap*. "Does a girl accept more than one suitor to her mosquito net when she comes of age? What if she becomes pregnant, what then?" Henry glanced sheepishly from James to the *Datu*, knowing that they must have heard the noise of his coupling the previous evening and asked, "And what about her parents, don't they hear what's going on?"

"Of course the girl can accept as many suitors as she pleases. When she becomes pregnant, she simply announces it to her father and tells him of her choice for a husband from among those who have slept with her. Her father then arranges the wedding with the parents of the boy she has chosen. If the boy elects not to marry the girl, which seldom happens, then his parents must pay a fine to the girl's family, usually some chickens or maybe a pig. Since the parents know who has lain with their daughter, it is always a simple matter to find a willing husband."

"Bloody amazing," Henry gasped, knowing that he had much to learn from this strange land and the people who inhabited it.

James pondered the fascinating Iban custom as the war canoe skimmed easily along an unusually calm stretch of river. He, too, considered how much he needed to learn about this primitive land and its people; his land, his people.

# IV

## Kampong Long Selah'at
## Sarawak, Borneo

"Iban! Iban!" A Kayan warrior sprinted through the village, sounding the alarm. Conditioned as a consequence of their often violent way of life, the Kayan men ran to their *bileks* and gathered their weapons and war shields while the women hurried to gather their children and a few precious belongings and flee to the safety of the surrounding jungle without waiting to learn the details of the alarm.

Jau, his head adorned with a war bonnet-a monkey-skin cap imbedded with tufts of leopard skin and colorful hornbill feathers-and carrying his *parang* and a brightly painted war shield rushed to the panting messenger. "Where? How many?"

Sweat dripped from the messenger's hairless face, his arms, chest and legs were torn and scratched and his torso heaved from the effort of his cross-country sprint. "They were moving up the Barum below Long Akar when I spotted them *Tua*," he wheezed.

"How many?" Jau demanded.

"Hundreds, Malay too!"

Jau squeezed his teeth together. *Iban* and *Malay...and in such large numbers!* The Malay Prince, *Awang* Api had led Jau to believe that the Sultan would not send his warriors against Long Selah'at following Hasim's earlier defeat at the hands of the Kayan. Jau wanted to know what event prompted the expedition against Long Selah'at, but Api had left Long Selah'at for Marudu Bay and there was no time now for Jau to contemplate Api's miscalculation. "We must meet them at the river," Jau shouted to his gathering warriors. "They will be forced to carry their *praus* through the rapids above Long Akar. That is where we will attack them!"

Jau turned to the warrior who had brought the news. "Quickly, go to our brothers, the Kenyah and Kedayan. Tell them that I command that they send their warriors to meet us at the rapids at Long Akar!"

The warrior hesitated and shuffled his feet nervously.

"What is it? Why do you remain?" Jau demanded.

"I saw another thing, *Tua*," he said, his voice faltering.

"What is it? Quickly, we must hurry if we are to reach Long Akar in time."

"There were two strange men riding in a Malay war *prau*. They have white skin and hair the color of the orangutan," the warrior said. "One of them has a shadow longer than any I have ever seen!" the warrior exclaimed, his voice trembling in awe. "What can it mean, *Tua* Jau?"

Jau bit at his lip. He had heard of the men with the white skin from the Punan, Batu, but he had passed it off as just another interesting tale of the superstitious children of the jungle. But the Malay prince, *Awang* Api had told him about foreign devils who had also come to Sarawak. *Could they be the same,* he wondered?

Jau boldly raised his *parang* over his head. "These white skinned things are nothing but animals captured by the Malay. They mean nothing!" he shouted to his warriors.

Jau's warriors appeared hesitant to accept his interpretation of the sighting of the strange white skinned men. Jau had to act quickly to dispel any trepidation his warriors may have if he was to defeat the enemy. Jau scowled and banged his *parang* against his war shield and shouted, "I, Jau, killer of my enemies and leader of all the tribes of the Barum do not fear these white animals! I, Jau, will take the heads of these white animals with my *parang*! Together we will achieve a great victory today!"

Inspired by their leader's bold words, Jau's warriors began to pound their spears and *parangs* against their war shields and chant, "Death to the Iban! Death to the Malay! Death to the white animals!"

# V

## Long Akar

"Rapids!"

Rentab recognized the crushing sound of the cataract before the warning reached his ears. "We must stop here, Rajah James," he said. "The rapids are impassable. We must carry the *praus* through them before we can go on."

James surveyed the narrow path of the river ahead of them. Water raged through the channel, crashing against the granite boulders which littered its runway. Although the water was not deep, its force prohibited the *praus* from passing further upstream. "How is the river above the rapids?" James asked. "Is it passable?"

"Yes, Rajah, it is passable once we get through this stretch of rapids."

"How far must we portage the *praus*?"

"Not far, Rajah. Just to the bend in the river," Rentab said, pointing to a spot above the rapids where a wall of jungle pressed against the banks of the river.

James glanced at the jungle squeezing in on both sides of the rapids. It was a perfect spot for an ambush. His warriors would have to place their shields and weapons inside the boats while they labored to pull the canoes through the rapids and would temporarily be unarmed. But, the alternative, carrying the canoes through the severe stand of jungle would be impossible. Although it made him uneasy, James had no choice but to order his force to drag the canoes through the rapids.

"All right," James said, decisively. "We'll move through the rapids in two groups. Henry, you and Rentab will lead the Iban through first. Move your warriors through as quickly as possible. Once you reach the calm water above the rapids, form a defensive position along the south side of the river and wait there until the *Datu* and I bring the Malay force through."

Henry and Rentab vaulted out of the *praus* and into the tepid water. The river was only waist deep with a clear and sandy bottom. Quickly, they waded upstream and conveyed James' orders to the Iban warriors. Within moments, the Iban had stowed their weapons and war shields and began dragging the *praus* through the current as James had commanded.

"*Datu*," James said, "we will hold your men here until the Iban have worked their way through the rapids then we will follow."

"Yes, Rajah James." The *Datu* Temanggong relayed James' orders to his warriors then turned to watch the progress of the Iban through the rapids.

249

Nervously, James' eyes flitted between Henry and the Iban and the dark walls of jungle on either side of them. Suddenly, the green barrier on the north side of the river seemed to rustle and move. Before James could shout a warning, a rain of spears filled the air and fell upon Henry and the defenseless Iban.

A dozen Iban warriors dropped into the river from the first salvo of Kayan spears before Henry realized what was happening. Above the noise of the rapids, he heard the Kayan war cries although they remained hidden in the dense foliage of the jungle. He drew his musket pistol and fired blindly into the jungle on the north side of the river bank although he didn't know from which side the attack had come. A second volley of spears vaulted through the sky as if in response to his gunfire. Henry staggered and barely managed to duck a plummeting spear point. An Iban warrior next to him fell face down in the water, clutching the wooden shaft of a Kayan spear imbedded in his chest.

"Henry!" James shouted. "Forget the canoes! Get to the forest on the south side of the river!" James frantically tried to wave Henry and the Iban to the side of the river opposite from the Kayan attack, but through the noise of the rapids and the din of the Kayan war cries, he wasn't sure Henry had heard him. Cut off by the rapids in front of them and the impenetrable forest on either side of them, James realized there was nothing the *Datu's* warriors could do to help Henry or the Iban. His main concern now was to save the vulnerable Malay force.

"*Datu*, order a retreat down river!" James tossed a backward glance above the rapids. In the melee, he couldn't separate friend from foe and he didn't catch sight of Henry.

Within seconds of the *Datu* Temanggong conveying James' command, the Malay war canoes, aided by the river's current, had disengaged and were speeding rapidly down river. James' command came just in time. A hail of spears filled the clear sky above the trailing Malay canoes, but because of their quick response to the order for retreat, the Kayan spears fell harmlessly in the water behind them.

James pulled a musket pistol from his girdle and cast another backward glance above the rapids as the *Datu's* war praus picked up momentum. He thought he caught a glimpse of Henry scrambling toward the south bank, but he couldn't be sure. To split his forces had been a tactical mistake and James knew it. But there had been no other alternative at the time. He couldn't expose the *Datu's* warriors to the same deadly rain of spears that cut the Iban forces to pieces so James' only thought now was to disengage his Malay force intact and then figure out a way to circle back and rescue Henry. He only hoped Henry and Rentab's Iban could survive until then.

Henry didn't hear what James was yelling to him, but he understood by James' arm motions that James was exhorting him to retreat to the south bank of the river. "Rentab!" Henry shouted. "This way! Follow Me!" Henry pulled his second musket pistol from his belt and fired into the forest. "This way!" he screamed.

The Iban were in disarray, floundering in the waist deep river in utter confusion. Another volley of Kayan spears filled the air and fell upon the hapless Iban warriors. Rentab didn't see Henry, but he heard his command and the bark of Henry's musket pistol. Hastily he rallied the surviving Iban and herded them towards Henry.

Henry spotted Rentab in the midst of the escaping Iban warriors. "Rentab! To me!" he shouted.

Rentab's men frantically splashed their way towards Henry who was leading them to the south bank of the river. However, before they could reach the relative safety of the forest, another volley of Kayan spears rained more death upon their shrinking band. Ignoring the screams of his fallen warriors, Rentab exhorted the survivors onward. A warrior next to him caught a glancing blow in the leg with a spear point and went down. Rentab grabbed the warrior's arm and dragged him to the shore and into the forest where he lay the man down and then fell exhausted near Henry. Soon, they were joined by others who had survived the initial Kayan attack.

Jau, frenzied by the success of his ambush of the Iban, charged from the cover of the jungle. "Pursue the Iban dogs before they escape!"

Like raging demons, Jau's warriors leaped from their hiding places in the forest and raced to follow their leader into the river. With their long *chawats* streaming behind them, the Kayan warriors whooped and hollered as they plunged into the river in pursuit of the retreating Iban. But intoxicated as they were by their victory and of the sight of so many Iban warriors floating in the river, the Kayan warriors couldn't resist stopping and decapitating each dead and wounded Iban they came across.

Jau pushed his muscular thighs against the current of the river and retrieved a spear from the body of an Iban corpse. From the corner of his eye he saw the white animal scramble up the far bank and disappear into the forest. "To me!" he shouted to his warriors. "Leave the dead. There will be time to take the heads later! We have fresh Iban dogs to kill!" Before Jau continued his charge across the river, he glanced downstream, beyond the rapids now running red with Iban blood. To his satisfaction, he saw the Malay *praus* retreating down river beneath a barrage of Kenyah and Kedayan spears. Now that his brothers had joined the battle, his victory was assured and he could already hear the songs his people would sing glorifying his great deed.

"The white dog is mine!" Jau screamed and made for the far side of the river.

Just as James thought his Malay force had successfully avoided the Kayan attack, the forest wall on the north side of the river seemed to explode. The late-arriving Kenyah and Kedayan warriors burst forth from the jungle and sprinted into the shallows of the river, screaming their ferocious war cries and hurling their deadly spears at the retreating Malay. This time they found the range.

Malay warriors in the trailing *praus* caught the brunt of the sudden attack. Malay warriors screamed as the enemy spears pierced their naked bodies. Some slumped forward, dying in the canoes where they sat while many of their companions were knocked out of the boats altogether by the force of the spears. Those who survived, paddled for their lives as the enemy swarmed to cut them off from the lead canoes.

"*Datu!*" James yelled. "Keep moving! Stay in the current! Don't slow down!" James fired his musket pistol and dropped a bold Kedayan warrior who was about to reach his boat. For whatever reason, James realized that the enemy had not set up a proper ambush and the Malay war canoes, aided by the current, were rapidly leaving their attackers behind. The enemy tried to press the attack, but the water and the thick jungle slowed them and they could do nothing but whoop and jeer at the retreating Malay.

When they rounded a bend in the river, James surveyed the southern shoreline and ordered the Malay force to head for a gravel sandbar which jutted into the river several kilometers below the rapids. Confused, exhausted and frightened, the Malay warriors dragged their boats to the shore and collapsed beside them, knowing they were fortunate to be alive. James pushed his way through the weary warriors until he found the *Datu* Temanggong who was aiding a Malay warrior with a Kenyah lance embedded in his shoulder.

"*Datu*, designate a few of your men to haul the wounded down river to the *Jolly Bachelor*. The rest of us will make our way through the jungle along this side of the river until we can join up with Henry and the Iban."

The *Datu* Temanggong shook his head reluctantly and continued to treat the wounded warrior.

"What is it, *Datu*?"

"The jungle is no good, Rajah James." The *Datu* Temanggong turned the treatment of the warrior over to others and stood up, facing James. "The forest is too thick here and passage will be difficult. Also, the Kayan will likely be waiting to ambush us again."

"Maybe not," James said. "Let's hope they think we're in full retreat. They won't expect us to move upriver by land."

When his war chief continued to appear less than convinced, James added, "In either case, we have no choice. I don't intend to let Henry and the Iban be sacrificed because we turned tail and ran."

The *Datu* saw the resolve harden on James' face. He had trusted the white Rajah's judgment before, at Siniawan and he would trust him this time also he decided. "Yes, Rajah James. We will do as you wish." The old war chief puffed his tired chest and relayed the Rajah's orders to his men. Quickly they obeyed. Three *praus* carrying the dead and wounded pushed off from the sandbar and headed downstream while the remainder of the Malay force followed James and the *Datu* Temanggong into the forest to begin the laborious march through the jungle in an attempt to link up with Henry and the surviving Iban.

Disoriented and confused, the Iban survivors gathered near Rentab and Henry. They tossed furtive glances toward the river, knowing the Kayan were in pursuit.

Henry breathed heavily and wiped the sweat from his forehead. He noted the trail of bent grass and broken underbrush and knew it was only a matter of minutes before the Kayan picked up their trail and were upon them. If they stayed where they were, the Kayan would overwhelm them and if they scattered through the forest, surely the Kayan would pick them off one by one. What could he do to save himself and the defeated band of Iban? What would James do?

"We will fight the Kayan here!" Rentab exclaimed and boldly rose to face the path from which he came.

"No good," Henry said, considering the depleted Iban force. "We wouldn't stand a bloody chance in hell. There are too many of them."

"Iban do not run away like the Malay!" Rentab scowled and his voice conveyed his bitterness at the Malay defection.

"They had no choice, *Pengulu*," Henry explained in his halting Malay. "It would have been suicide for them to try to reach us through the rapids."

Rentab remained obstinate and unconvinced. He tensed his lean muscles and raised his *parang*. "We will fight here!" he repeated.

The Iban listened to the debate between their *Pengulu* and the white lord with mounting anxiety. Already they could hear the Kayan crashing through the forest toward them. Henry heard them too. He had to do something and quickly. But what? He stepped forward and faced the Iban chieftain. He decided he would rather take his chance being killed by Rentab than being slaughtered by the Kayan.

"No, *Pengulu*! We will *not* fight here!" I know the Rajah, he will not leave us here to die. But we must save ourselves now or there won't be any of us left for the Rajah to rescue."

Rentab's face was set in concrete. This white man annoyed him, confused him with his talk of the cowardly Malays coming to their rescue. He squeezed the handle of his *parang* and sneered at Henry.

Henry grabbed Rentab's wrist, prompting the Iban warriors to press nearer the two men, their anxious eyes watching Rentab for his command to cut the white man down. Henry knew it was his last chance. In the next few seconds, he would either convince the *Pengulu* to do as he said or he would feel the cold steel of Iban *parangs* hacking his body to bits.

"You owe the Rajah James your life, Rentab. He would not want his *Pengulu* to throw away his life unnecessarily, a life that does not belong to you, Rentab."

For a moment Rentab glared defiantly at Henry. He could easily order the white man cut down, he thought. But he also understood Henry's words. The brave white man who led the charge against his warriors at Siniawan and who was now Rajah of Sarawak was not a coward, Rentab admitted to himself. He *would* lead the Malays back to save them. Rentab's face softened and he eased the grip on his *parang*. "What would you have me do, *Tuan* Henry?"

Henry breathed a sigh of relief. Hastily he told Rentab of his plan. "Send six of your warriors in that direction," Henry said, pointing to the expanse of jungle which paralleled the river downstream of where they stood. "Have them slash the forest and make as much noise as possible. They must make it appear that we have all headed in that direction."

Rentab gave the order immediately, without waiting to hear the remainder of Henry's plan.

"The rest of us will hide here," Henry said. "Have your men scatter and melt into the forest without leaving signs of their hiding." Henry didn't wait for Rentab to convey the message. With a long, purposeful stride, he stepped over a patch of underbrush and delicately parted a barrier of thick vines and closed it behind him. Within seconds, Rentab's surviving band of warriors melted into the jungle in similar fashion and silently awaited the arrival of the Kayan.

As the *Datu* Temanggong had predicted, progress through the thick jungle was slow and difficult. Two dozen Malay warriors slashed a pathway through the forest ahead of the main body of James' force. Still, creeping vines grabbed at their legs and the marshy ground pulled at their feet, slowing the Malay advance to a mere crawl. For over an hour, James' Malay hacked and chopped, pushed and shoved and, at times, even crawled and waded through the impassable jungle. The high jungle canopy blocked out the waning afternoon sun, but it also trapped the sun's heat and pressed it to the forest floor, creating a natural oven of heat and humidity. Sweat poured from James' lean face and body. His shirt and breeches were caked in mud and grime and soaked in sweat and his clothing clung tightly to his skin and began to rub his inner thighs raw with each agonizing step he took. As anxious as James was to reach Henry and the Iban, he began to realize that his efforts to reach Henry and the Iban were hopeless.

Breathlessly, James called a halt to the advance and asked, "*Datu*, how long before nightfall?"

The old war chief wiped the sweat from his eyes and lifted his tired head to the canopy above him. "Perhaps an hour," Rajah James. "No more."

James weighed his options. Finally he said, "At the rate we are moving, we will never reach Henry before nightfall. We will wait here, rest up. When it gets dark, we will follow the bank of the river. It should be easier going and if it is dark enough, we won't be seen. What do you think, *Datu*?"

The *Datu* Temanggong slumped wearily to the forest floor. "It would be easier following the river, Rajah James..." His voice trailed off, leaving something unsaid.

"What is it?" James asked, noting the look of doubt on the war chief's face.

"Even if we make it above the rapids, there is little hope that *Tuan* Henry and the Iban will be alive."

James hung his head. "I know," he said softly. "But we have got to try. Even if the Kayan have wiped them out, I must know that we tried." James collapsed to his knees next to the *Datu*. The thought of Henry's probable death weighed heavily on him. He thought of all of the decisions he had made before and during the Kayan attack and questioned each of them. *He* should have recognized the possibility of ambush sooner and *he* should have led the Iban through the rapids and *he* should have ordered the Malay forward to support Henry instead of retreating and *he* should have heeded the *Datu* Temanggong's warning on how difficult their advance through the forest would be. But even as James silently reprimanded himself for the faulty decisions he had made, his training as a British Army officer came back to him and he knew he couldn't dwell on what should have been done then but only on what must be done now.

"If Henry and the Iban have all been killed, *Datu*," James said with a look of determination on his lean face, "I promise that we will take Long Selah'at and teach that rogue Jau a lesson he won't soon forget."

The *Datu* Temanggong doubted James' words, but not his resolve. He supposed, however, that based upon his previous experiences with this white

Rajah, all things truly were possible. The *Datu* slowly pushed himself to his feet. "I will have the men cut a pathway to the river so that we will be ready to leave when it is dark."

*Please, God, don't let them spot us,* Henry silently prayed when he heard the Kayan enter the small clearing where he and the Iban had stood only moments earlier.

"There!" Jau shouted when he noticed the large break in the forest where the six Iban warriors had forced their way through the jungle. "The Iban dogs are fleeing downriver through the forest!" Using his war shield as a battering ram against the vegetation, Jau led his warriors to the break in the forest wall and they crashed through the jungle and followed the path of Iban retreat.

When the jungle returned to silence, Henry allowed himself to open his eyes and gasp for a gulp of air. In his fear of being discovered, he had forgotten to breathe. His heart thumped against his ribs and with a trembling hand he wiped away the sweat streaming into his eyes. It was a narrow escape, but only a temporary one, and Henry knew it. Cautiously, Henry stepped from his hiding place. His shaking knees nearly buckled under him and he almost collapsed, but the thought of the Kayan's likely return steadied him and he began to think of what he now had to do to save himself and the small band of Iban survivors.

As a single silent entity, the Iban emerged from their hiding places. Rentab approached Henry. He was glad that he had followed the white man's advice. He knew that the white Rajah had a strong spirit, his long shadow attested to that. But this other white lord-who was not much taller than Rentab himself-must also be blessed with a strong spirit. Rentab's admiration for the white men was beginning to soar and he found that he was developing a particular fondness for the one who was with him now.

"We have deceived the Kayan," Rentab whispered. "Shall we pursue them now?"

"No," Henry answered in a hushed voice. He scanned the faces of his diminished force and the darkening canopy above them and prodded his mind for an idea of what to do next. "Rentab, how much time before dark?"

Rentab glanced upward. "Only an hour, no more, *Tuan.*"

Henry had an idea. A little crazy, he had to admit, but it was better than waiting where they were in the hopes they might be rescued before the Kayan returned. "Rentab, do you know how to find Long Selah'at from here?"

"Yes, but—"

"How far is it?"

"Not far, *Tuan,* but—"

"Can we get there before nightfall?"

Rentab nodded that they could. "What do you intend, *Tuan* Henry?" Rentab asked quizzically.

"Won't the Kayan village be undefended?

"Most probably," Rentab concurred.

"And we still have enough warriors to take Long Selah'at, don't we?"

Rentab's face slowly brightened as he understood what Henry was suggesting. It was a good plan, a daring plan and one the Kayan would not expect. And it would remove the sting of the day's defeat and salvage a victory as well as exact revenge for the burning of the Iban villages by the Kayan months earlier. "The Kayan will not expect us," Rentab said with growing enthusiasm. "If we hurry, we can reach Long Selah'at before nightfall."

"Good! No matter what happens afterwards, we will have accomplished something of what we intended to do in the first place—burn their bloody village to the ground!"

Rentab beamed through his blackened teeth. "It can be done, *Tuan!*"

Henry clasped Rentab's shoulders. "Then let's be on our way. Give the order to move out, *Pengulu.*"

Moments later, Henry's band had backtracked to the river. After safely determining that there were no enemy warriors in the vicinity, Rentab and Henry led the Iban into the shallows along the near bank of the river and waded stealthily upstream toward Long Selah'at.

Anxious to know the fate of Henry and the Iban and disregarding the increased danger of being spotted by the enemy, James ordered the Malay into the river a full half-hour before sunset to begin their trek upriver in search of survivors of the Kayan attack. Corpses, most headless and many already bloated in the warm water and torrid heat floated silently by them and in the waning light, James scanned the carnage hoping he wouldn't spot Henry's body among them. There were no signs of the enemy and James suspected that they had taken their trophies and returned to their villages to celebrate their victory. Grim and determined, he pressed the Malay force forward.

Wading knee deep in the river near the south bank, James glanced over his shoulder to check the progress of the serpentine line of Malay warriors following close behind him. Nearest him, the *Datu* Temanggong quietly exhorted his warriors forward despite his own weariness. Not once had the old warrior complained or questioned James' orders and James felt fortunate to have him.

The Malay force had just rounded a long bend in the river below the rapids when they were paralyzed by a singular scream echoing from the jungle to their right. Instinctively, the Malay stopped and lowered themselves closer to the water while their eyes turned and peered into the blackness of the forest in search of the source of the cry of death they had become so familiar with.

"*Datu*, have your warriors take cover," James whispered. "Stay here. I'm going to check it out." James pulled himself from the water and eased himself onto his stomach and crawled through the underbrush toward the sound of the scream.

Another scream ripped through the silence. James continued to inch himself forward. He heard a commotion and feared he had found Henry and the Iban too late.

Cautiously, James pulled himself to his knees behind the cover of a sago palm. He saw nothing. Crouching, he darted from bush to bush and tree to tree, following the source of the sounds in front of him. He saw movement.

James dropped to his stomach and drug himself forward with his arms and elbows until he came to a moss-eaten breadfruit tree which had toppled over and was in the final stages of decay. He placed his hands on the rotting bark and carefully eased his head above the fallen log. Fifteen meters in front of him, in a rare clearing of lalang grass, James spotted the source of the screams.

"Finish them!" Jau ordered. "We must catch up to the others or they will escape in the darkness!" Jau believed that the six Iban they had caught up to were merely stragglers and that the main body of the defeated Iban were still fleeing downriver and he intended to kill as many of them as he could find before nightfall.

Four Iban warriors were already dead and decapitated. Several Kayan were stripping them of their bracelets and necklaces while those who watched taunted the spirits of the headless corpses by prodding the limp bodies with their spears and *parangs*.

James watched with revulsion as the Kayan forced the remaining two captives to their knees. Kayan warriors pulled the Iban's hair, stretching their necks from their tightly held shoulders while other Kayan brought their *parangs* down on the necks of their helpless victims and severed their heads from their bodies. The Iban heads tumbled to the ground like ripe fruit as cheers of glee from the Kayan mocked their headless foes. They laughed in delight as the Iban's decapitated corpses jerked awkwardly like stringless marionettes and spewed their life's blood to the jungle floor.

James swallowed a bitter bile which had reached his throat. He wasn't sure he could have held the contents of his stomach if one of the captives would have been Henry. With repugnance, James waited until the Kayan had finished their short celebration and began to follow Jau into the darkening jungle before he turned and scrambled back to the river.

"Kayan!" James gasped to the waiting *Datu*. "They caught up with some of the Iban...killed them. My guess is that Henry and the Iban are trying to make their way downriver through the jungle where they expect us to be waiting with the boats."

"We go back then?" the *Datu* asked.

"No, we outnumber the Kayan. I think we can surprise them, but we need to hurry. There's not much daylight left."

James quickly scanned down the long line of Malay warriors pressed near the forest. "*Datu*, take half of the men and go back downstream. I'll take the other half with me through the forest and follow behind the Kayan. My men will attack as soon as we catch up to them. When you hear me fire my musket, that will be your signal to leave the river and attack from the flank." James clasped the old warrior on the shoulder and said, "Good luck," in English.

"Go now, hurry! We don't have much light left."

The *Datu* Temanggong didn't comprehend James' English words, but he did understand the intent. Quickly, the *Datu* divided his warriors and conveyed the plan of action. James gathered his contingent at the bank of the river. He withdrew his musket pistol from his belt and raised his saber to his throat, making it clear to the Malay warriors what he expected from them when they encountered Jau's warriors.

Rentab easily found the footpath which led from a feeder stream from the Barum River. Moving at a fast pace, he led Henry and the Iban warriors through a wide stand of *lalang* grass to a stony *bukit*, a hill overlooking the longhouse of Long Selah'at. It was the same path Jau had followed when he had returned from his raid on Rentab's longhouse and one familiar to Rentab as well.

As a young man, Rentab found sport in proving his bravery by hiding near the footpath, observing his Kayan enemy fish the feeder streams of the Barum River and harvest sago and tubers from the flat expanse of *lalang* grassland, all the while hoping that an innocent Kayan child would wander near him so that he could claim his first head. But none ever did.

"The longhouse appears empty," Henry said, catching his first glimpse of the Kayan village which was similar in appearance to Rentab's own village. Darkness was descending rapidly on the village, merging its black tentacles with the long shadows of the longhouse and the jungle surrounding it.

"Yes," Rentab confirmed. "The Kayan warriors have not yet returned from Long Akar and the women and children are still in hiding. "We should attack now, *Tuan*."

Henry grabbed Rentab's arm. "Wait. How can we be sure it's not a trap?"

"No trap, *Tuan*. If the Kayan had returned they would be celebrating their victory. The village is dark and quiet. No fires...no sound of gongs."

"All right, let's go!" Henry said.

Rentab's warriors needed no prompting. They sensed that the village was undefended and they were anxious to avenge the deaths of their friends and relatives who had died from Kayan spears at the rapids of Long Akar. Rentab shouted out a bone-chilling war cry and initiated the attack upon the village. Henry gripped his broadsword in one hand and his freshly loaded musket pistol in the other and chased after the charging Iban. Henry whooped in a feeble attempt to mimic the Iban war cry, but there was no one in Long Selah'at to hear.

As Rentab suspected, the village was empty. Moments after they reached the Kayan longhouse, the Iban tendered a fire in the leading *bilek* and made torches from bamboo batons stripped from the longhouse wall. They didn't bother to pillage the longhouse or search for valuables. Within a few short minutes, the longhouse of Long Selah'at was a hundred meter pillar of flame and smoke and Henry and the Iban were retracing their tracks back to the Barum River.

James and his contingent of Malay caught up with the Kayan near the sandbar where they had left the canoes earlier. A young Kayan warrior, his ears pierced and stretched by the weight of brass rings, was the first to fall. A lead ball from James' musket pistol split his flesh in the center of his spine. On cue, the *Datu* Temanggong led his Malay force from the river to the sound of James' musket fire and caught the enemy in a human vise between James' force and his own just as James planned they would.

The Kayan were as much overwhelmed by the surprise and swiftness of the Malay attack as they were by the confusion spreading through their ranks. The Malay were everywhere; nipping, attacking and killing like wild dogs. Panic gripped the surrounded Kayan and it became impossible for Jau to keep his warriors grouped together and they soon became easy targets for the Malay and their superior numbers.

Eventually, Jau managed to rally two dozen warriors to his side. Together they chopped and hacked their way through a line of charging Malay warriors and escaped the mounting slaughter by leaping into the water and melting into the forest along the opposite bank of the river.

James, his mind still reeling with the fresh image of the execution of the Iban captives and the headless Iban corpses floating on the river and Henry's probable death, fought like a man possessed. His white skin raged luminous against the growing darkness as he slashed and parried his deadly saber. Never did James stop to prime and pack his musket pistol. After his initial firing, he used the pistol as a club, swinging it alongside his bloodied saber like dual grim reapers. Before they died or scattered from James' deadly assault, the terrified Kayan yelled, "*hantu!*" believing that the man with the luminescent skin was surely a demon released from the spirit world to exact a swift and terrible vengeance upon them.

Within fifteen minutes, the battle was over. The surprise attack and the Malay's superior numbers had totally crushed the Kayan. Few escaped. Dead bodies littered the jungle floor and the sandbar of the river. Only the agonizing cries of the wounded permeated the now darkened forest.

"Enough!" James shouted as he pulled a Malay warrior away from spearing a downed Kayan. "Leave them! No more killing!" In the encroaching darkness James called for the *Datu* Temanggong.

"Here, Rajah James." The Datu separated the tallest shadow from among the Malay and walked to it. Proudly he raised his crimson coated *parang* and shook it jubilantly. "A victory, Rajah James!"

James was silent. He held his pistol and sword at his side, too weary to sheath them. Slowly he scanned the carnage. The cries of the wounded and dying reached his ears and the metallic scent of blood stung his nostrils. Sadly, he shook his head. "Not a victory, *Datu*," he said. "A slaughter." His land, his people and he had massacred them. *There must be a better way. There had to be. God grant that I find it because I could never go through with this again*, he thought to himself.

The *Datu* Temanggong interrupted James' reverie with the obvious. "Rajah, *Tuan* Henry and the Iban are not here as we suspected they might be," he said. "What would you have me do?"

James thought about it for a moment then replied, "Send a dozen warriors upriver to scout for them...or their bodies. Then have the others gather up the dead and make a pyre. We'll burn the dead and tend to the wounded."

Two hours later, the Malay scouts returned, leading Rentab's surviving Iban toward the light of the pyre and a scattering of campfires on the sandbar. Henry cradled Rentab's limp body over his shoulders and staggered toward one of the campfires. Nearing it, he collapsed to his knees and gently rolled Rentab's body to the sand.

"Henry!" James rushed to the side of his friend. "My God, I thought you were dead. I was sure the Kayan had killed you."

"They almost did...twice," Henry said with a weary grin.

James ordered the Malay to fetch food and water for Henry and the Iban stragglers then turned his attention to Rentab. "Is he dead?"

"No, but he caught a Kayan spear in the thigh. I think he'll be all right."

On James' orders, several Malay moved Rentab's unconscious body nearer the fire and replaced the blood soaked bandage on Rentab's thigh. James saw that Henry had initially used his own shirt to wrap Rentab's wound. "What happened, Henry? I worried that you didn't make it out of the rapids."

Henry waited until Rentab's bandage had been changed and that the *Pengulu* was properly being administered to before he answered. "About half of us managed to escape into the jungle..."

Henry related the whole story; how they had deceived the Kayan to take the false path through the jungle, of their attack and destruction of Long Selah'at, and of their subsequent return downriver where they anticipated James would be waiting. Then he told of their chance encounter with Jau and his fleeing warriors.

"...we were on the far bank of the river, above the rapids when we walked into the Kayan. They were as surprised as we were. It was too bloody dark to see much, but they hurled their spears at us before they disappeared into the jungle. One of the spears caught Rentab in the leg and pinned him to a tree."

Henry shook his head and whistled softly. "Bravest damned thing I ever did see, James." Henry pushed the hair from his eyes and looked fondly over at the heavily breathing Iban chieftain. "Bloody fool just stood there, pinned to that tree, waving his *parang* and cursing and shouting like the devil himself at the Kayan—challenging them to come out of hiding and fight. Never saw anything like it. He didn't even pass out until after I pulled the spear from his leg."

Henry tilted his head up to James and added, "He's one hell of a bloke, James. And these are some fine people. Even with all that's happened, I'm glad I decided to stay on."

James mussed Henry's thin blonde hair and said, "I'm glad you did too, Henry."

"What about you?" Henry asked. He looked at the pyre of burning corpses. "I knew you wouldn't be able to help us during the ambush. But what's this all about?" he asked, sweeping his hand toward the pyre.

James told his story. When he finished he said, solemnly, "A lot of people died today, Henry. Good people, brave people. I only pray to God it was necessary in order to set things right in Sarawak."

"What about that Malay prince, Api? Did you get him?"

James shook his head. "Never saw him. We interrogated some of the wounded Kayan. They told us that Api had left days ago for Marudu Bay—probably trying to find someone else to do his dirty work for him."

Henry sensed the pain James felt for the loss of life and his disappointment at not apprehending the Malay prince. He reached out and touched James' arm. "It was the only way, James. If it's your intention to stop the raids and the headhunting and begin to civilize these people, then everything that happened today was necessary." Then Henry shook his head and added, "But I wouldn't want to go through this again. Let's hope to God that once is enough."

# VI

Night
April 4, 1826
The Jungle
Near Long Selah'at

"What does it mean, Batu?"

Batu sat on his haunches across from the clan's evening campfire and contemplated his brother's question. He pulled at the silky skin of a fruit bat he had shot earlier in the evening with a dart from his blowpipe. Eventually he was able to separate the skin from the bat's oily flesh. He wrapped the carcass of the flying mammal in a banana leaf and set it at the edge of the fire, tucking a few coals from the fire around it.

When he finished, he peered across the flames and gazed at the solemn faces of his tiny clan. Their peripheral world had changed and it frightened them. Over the past two years, they had witnessed the burning of Brunei and Long Selah'at and many Iban villages-and the coming of the white man with the long shadow; all of these things were mysterious events and they hoped for an explanation that would calm and comfort them. Anxiously, they searched Batu's face for meaning.

Batu pondered the question long and hard. He gazed beyond the heads of his band and could still see the dying glow of Long Selah'at against the moonless sky miles below their camp. Could it be the end of the world? Vaguely, he tried to recall the stories told around the fires of his parents' clan when they were still alive.

"Perhaps it is the coming of the end of the world," he said softly, knowing that he had no other explanation to comfort his clan. "The old ones spoke of such things long ago."

Batu's brother spoke up. "I remember the old one's who spoke of such things," he said, his voice quivering. "They told of many strange things which would happen before the end of the world."

Batu's young wife looked anxiously at him. She pulled the sleeping head of her child closer to her breast as if to protect it from what was being said. "Did the old ones speak of the white men with big spirits?" she asked.

Batu nodded solemnly. "They spoke often of those with long shadows."

# CHAPTER ELEVEN

## I

April 3, 1826
Kuching, Sarawak

Si Tundok anxiously scanned the haggard faces of the Malay warriors filing down the dock after disembarking from their war *praus* and then waited dockside until James arrived in a pinnace from the *Jolly Bachelor*.

"Where's Henry?" he asked.

"He's all right, but he stayed behind," James replied wearily. "I'll explain later."

James, as tired as he was, chose to remain at the dock until all the Malay filed past to meet with their families crowded near the wharf. Singularly or in groups, James thanked each of the warriors for their contribution to the success of their expedition against Jau and the Kayan and extended his condolences to the families of those who had fallen at Long Akar.

When the last of the expedition had finally departed, the *Datu* Temanggong tentatively approached James. The old war chief was cognizant of the self-imposed torment James was dealing with since the battle of Long Akar. The horrible toll in human life had greatly disturbed the white Rajah and James' sadness revealed more of the new Rajah's character than the *Datu* previously knew. The white man was not only a brave man, but he was a compassionate man as well. This new Rajah was equally saddened at the loss of the enemy as he was at the loss of the Iban and Malay warriors. It was a trait the *Datu* Temanggong had not seen in any of the previous rulers of Sarawak he had served.

"Forgive me, Rajah James..."

"What is it, *Datu*?"

"You must not feel sad about this thing, Rajah James. It was necessary. It was the only way to stop the raids. You did the right thing, Rajah."

"I only hope you are right, *Datu*," James said with some uncertainty.

The *Datu* confirmed his statement with a nod and then asked, "Is there anything the Rajah wishes of me before I go to my *rumah*?"

"Just see to it that the wounded are properly attended to and do what you can to comfort the families of the men we lost at Long Akar, *Datu*. Then get some rest. We will talk in the morning."

265

"As you wish, Rajah James." The *Datu* Temanggong bowed courteously and departed, leaving James and Si Tundok alone on the pier. James leaned against a pylon and watched the *Datu* walk away.

"You are fortunate that Hasim released the *Datu* Temanggong to serve you, James," Si Tundok said.

James nodded and pushed himself away from the pylon. "The *Datu* and his warriors performed splendidly at Long Akar. Without him, we surely would have failed." Wearily, James began to walk towards the palace with Si Tundok at his side. "And I am fortunate to have you and Henry," he added. "I don't mind telling you, Si Tundok, but the responsibility of Sarawak is becoming more than I ever imagined it would be."

Si Tundok noticed that James' shoulders were slumped as if the weight of an anvil had been sewn to his back. His face was drawn and his eyes were swollen from lack of sleep. James hadn't shaved since the expedition set sail, and the red-blonde stubble of his beard against his dirty, sweat-streaked face made him look old and sickly. "You need to eat and rest, James," he said. "In the morning, you will feel better."

James nodded ascent without comment.

As they trudged along the path leading to the palace, Si Tundok asked, "And Henry? You say he is all right?"

"Yes, Henry's fine. The *Pengulu* Rentab was wounded in the battle and Henry wanted to stay and look after him for a while. Henry developed quite a fondness for the *Pengulu* during the course of the expedition. And then Henry came up with an idea to set up an outpost along the Bintulu River so that we could station a few men there and keep an eye on things for a while."

"Sounds like a good idea."

"Yes, I believe it is. Then we had to spend some time tracking down the Kayan leader, Jau, and make him understand that his raids in Sarawak and Brunei will not be tolerated."

"He accepted this?"

James nodded. "He had no choice. He lost a substantial number of his warriors in the battle and Henry and the *Pengulu* Rentab torched Long Selah'at. He was a broken man when we finally found him. Of course he's still the accepted leader of the tribes along the Barum River so I suppose he could give us trouble if he wanted to."

"Will he?"

"I don't think so. He seemed to be angry with *Awang* Api for misleading him and once Henry has the outpost built, we will be able to monitor the Barum River tribes more easily."

James shook his head and clicked his tongue with a look of puzzlement on his face. "For some reason, Jau seemed to be in awe of me. I don't know how to explain it, but he kept referring to my white skin and long shadows. I don't know what it all meant, but judging from the way he said it and from what I observed, I'm reasonably certain Jau will keep his word."

Si Tundok explained the native's concept of associating the strength of a man's spirit with the size of the shadow he cast.

"Interesting concept," James said.

"Because of their belief and from what you said, James, I, too, believe Jau will keep his word."

"I surely do hope so," James sighed.

Si Tundok was about to tell James of things he had learned while James was away, but they had reached the steps leading to the palace and he decided to wait until after James had a chance to refresh himself.

Wearily, James struggled up the steps to the palace and entered the throne room. The room was dark, but beyond the partition which separated the large outer room from the other rooms in the palace, a bright light streamed from several oil lamps and danced against the throne room floor. James saw a shadow cross the flow of light. Someone was moving inside. James reached for the hilt of his sword.

"No need to worry, James," Si Tundok said. "It is only a woman."

"A woman?"

Si Tundok led James down the corridor beyond the throne room and they entered the palace's private dining room and food preparation area, complete with table, chairs and a raised clay cooking stove. Vegetables, cleaned and chopped were stacked in neat piles along the top of a small work table to the side of the clay oven.

Kameja stopped her work and turned to face James and Si Tundok. She quickly pulled the top of her sarong over her small breasts and tucked the fold of the garment under her arm and proffered a low, self-conscious bow.

"Who is she? What is she doing here?" James asked in English.

"She was given to you."

"What? Given to me? Why? Who...?"

"Loi Pek, *Kapitan* of the Chinese community of Sin Bok brought her here a few days ago as an offering of his allegiance to you. He also left some other things as well; some porcelain vases, silk...and a few other gifts."

"She's a slave?"

Si Tundok affirmed that she was.

James was flabbergasted. "But I cannot have a slave. It is a disgusting custom. Tell her that she is free to go." James unfastened his leather girdle containing his musket pistols and saber and laid it on the table, glad to be rid of the weight of it.

"I already told her that, James. But she says she has no place to go. She has been a slave all of her life. She knows nothing else."

James stepped around the table and spoke directly to Kameja in Malay. "What is your name, girl?" he asked.

"Kameja, Rajah James," she replied softly. Slowly she raised her head and allowed her eyes to access her new master. James was the first white man she had seen since the man, the one they called Geoff, had come to visit with Loi Pek. She expected all white men to look the same and it surprised her that they were not. The Rajah was tall, the tallest human being she had ever seen. And although he looked gaunt and fatigued, there was a kindness in his swollen blue eyes. Having had so many masters in the past, Kameja had learned to appraise them quickly and, from experience, knew that her first impressions were generally correct. Her instincts now told her that this was a good man, a kind man. She silently thanked the spirits for being given to him.

"Kameja..." James repeated and then tried to explain, "...Kameja, understand that you do not belong to me. A human being cannot belong to another human being. It is not right. You are free, free to return to your own people."

Kameja looked perplexed for a moment and then tears began to flow over the edges of her smooth cheeks.

It was James' turn to be confused. "What is the matter? There is no need to cry..." James turned to Si Tundok. "Why is she crying?" he asked in English.

Si Tundok shrugged. "She has nowhere else to go. She doesn't even remember where she came from." Si Tundok plucked a diced fern tip from the table and popped it into his mouth. "She's been a lot of help around here since you've been gone, James. I've been eating very well for a change." He cracked a rare smile.

James remained adamant. "I will not condone slavery in Sarawak! It degrades the entire human race!"

He turned to face Kameja once again and his voice softened. He reached out a hand and wiped the tears from her cheeks. "Please don't cry," he said softly. "But you must understand you are no longer a slave. I am releasing you from your bondage. You are free to choose a life for yourself."

Kameja stopped sobbing and gazed directly at James with her bright, almond eyes. "Then I choose to remain here with you, Rajah James."

James sighed and shook his head in frustration. "Si Tundok, *you* explain it to her."

"She is free, is she not, James?"

"Yes, of course."

"And she has chosen to stay here, with you."

"But she can't!"

"James, you yourself gave her the freedom to make her own choice. She has made it."

"But—"

"Perhaps you could hire her as an *amah*, a maid. She could cook and clean for you and yet she would still be free to do what she wants to do, leave when she feels up to it," Si Tundok suggested as a compromise.

James considered Si Tundok's proposal and evaluated the girl once more. "All right," he said finally. "She can stay in the palace tonight and we will find her permanent living quarters later."

Si Tundok happily translated James' English pronouncement for Kameja.

"*Terima kasi banjak*, many thanks, Rajah James." Kameja bowed profusely and her full lips erupted into a broad smile of gratitude. It was her first genuine smile in many years and it felt good. Dutifully, she stepped around James and removed his leather girdle and weapons from the table. "You will clean yourself, Rajah and I will finish cooking the food for you." She carried James' weapons to his bedroom and hung them on a hook near his rattan cot.

James appeared a bit sheepish and somewhat confounded by the attentions of the girl. He cleared his throat. "Well, now, that's settled. I believe I'll clean up and then we will eat and talk."

Si Tundok chuckled to himself and pilfered another piece of vegetable from the table.

James stepped across the hall and entered a small washroom. He was both surprised and pleased to see that a fresh pair of breeches and a perfumed shirt had been laid out next to a large wash basin. The basin had recently been filled with clean water from large vases set below the eves of the palace to catch rainwater as it streamed from the palace roof. Soap, razor and powder were neatly stacked on a folded towel near the basin and a hand mirror was propped against the side of a small tub. *Perhaps having an amah was not such a bad idea after all*, James thought as he stripped and lowered himself into the tub and began to pour the cool rainwater from the basin over himself.

Later, after James and Si Tundok had devoured the tasty meal prepared by Kameja, the two of them remained at the table and sipped Chinese brandy while Kameja removed the dishes.

James answered all of Si Tundok's questions about the expedition against the Kayan. When he depleted the topic, he said, "Hopefully, the word will spread to all the villages in Sarawak that raiding and headhunting will no longer be tolerated. Once Sarawak is stabilized internally, then we will be able to promote trading activity."

"There have been reports of pirate activity along the coast, James. What do you intend to do about it?"

James shook his head. "There is not much we can do right now. We'll continue to patrol the coast with the *Jolly Bachelor*, but one ship will not be a total deterrent, I'm afraid. But I have appealed to His Majesty's government to consider Sarawak as a British Protectorate. If my application is granted, any pirates who dared raid along the coast of Sarawak would risk being blown out of the water by British ships. I'm hopeful we will hear something soon in that regard."

James sipped from his glass and sighed. "When I accepted Sarawak from Hasim, Si Tundok, I will have to admit that I didn't realize that the price would be paid in so many lives. But, thankfully, there appears to be an end in sight. If we can resume the trade activity and stimulate the economy of Sarawak, then I can begin to think about the other things this country needs- education, a judiciary system, clinics, practical things such as those."

"Haven't you forgotten one other thing, James?"

"What's that?"

"Api."

Kameja had just approached the table to refill the men's glasses. Although they spoke in English, she heard the Malay princes' name mentioned and she gasped, spilling a portion of the brandy on the table.

"Kameja, is something wrong?" James asked in Malay.

"Forgive me, Rajah James," she said, dabbing at the spilled brandy. "But I heard you speak the name of the evil one, *Awang* Api."

Si Tundok and James exchanged glances. "You know him?" James asked.

"*Awang* Api was once my master. He is a very cruel man. He gave me to the Chinaman, Loi Pek. He often returns to Sin Bok to discuss things with Loi Pek."

"Do you know what they discuss?"

Kameja nodded that she did. "They talk of many things, but I only know some of it. *Awang* Api wishes to become Sultan of Brunei. Several weeks ago, he came to Sin Bok to discuss his plans with Loi Pek. I didn't hear most of their conversation, but *Awang* Api does not like you, Rajah James. He wishes to do you harm. You must be very careful. Api is a very dangerous man."

James recalled his brief encounter with Api at the battle at Siniawan and the hate that he had seen in the Malay prince's eyes. There was no doubt that Kameja's warning was true.

"Are there other things?" Si Tundok asked of the girl.

Kameja told them all of what she knew; about Api and about Loi Pek's gold mines. When she finished, James said to Si Tundok, "Perhaps we should plan a visit to Sin Bok and talk to Loi Pek about his dealings with Api."

Si Tundok nodded. "And about his gold mines. They belong to you by right of the Sultan Hasim's concession to you, James."

Finally, deep into the night, James and Si Tundok broke off their discussion and retired to their bedrooms. Kameja had withdrawn hours earlier to the room the *Datu* Temanggong used on occasion. Moonbeams permeated James' room through a single window and James felt his delayed weariness settle over him as soon as he caught sight of the rattan cot nestled beneath the open window. He removed his shirt and tossed it to the floor. Sitting on the side of his bed, James pulled off his boots and let them drop to the floor and laid back on the bed without removing his trousers, his forearm resting across his forehead and watched the waning moon-shadows streaming through the window.

As if the moonbeams infused his thoughts with melancholy, James reminisced of England, his father and mother and of Elizabeth. Without unfastening the string which held his mosquito net in place above the cot, James sank like the moon itself into a dark recess in some far off corner of his mind.

He dreamed of Elizabeth, but her face appeared blurred and her image wavered when he called for her to come to him. When the beckoned specter of Elizabeth approached him, her face faded and shimmered until it reconstructed itself with brown skin and almond eyes. And when he reached out to touch her, the apparition totally metamorphosed. Standing before him in his dream was Kameja. She was frightened and tears streamed down her face. He embraced the ghostly apparition and held her tightly to him and asked her for the source of her fear. She told him to look beyond her and he did and in his dream, he saw an army of brown-skinned phantoms carrying blood-soaked *parangs* and spears and war shields splattered with gore and they were marching slowly toward him. He felt his fear and cried out loud, "What do you want? What do you want from me?" But the amorphous images didn't reply. They couldn't. They were all headless.

James awakened with a start. His eyes shot open and he pressed his back against the wall and drew his arms and legs into his chest like a fetus. He squeezed his eyes shut, trying to drive away the headless phantoms from his mind. His hands trembled and his face and chest exuded rivulets of sweat. He slapped his hands to his face and massaged his temples. "God help me!" he cried. "What have I done?"

When he next opened his eyes, one brown-skinned figure did not evaporate along with the others. Tentatively, Kameja reached out and touched

James softly on the shoulder. "Rajah James, you cried out in your sleep. Are you ill?"

"No...no, I'm all right," James murmured. He stared at Kameja, her lovely, round face absorbing a single shaft of moonlight and reflecting her anxiety and concern for him. "It was only a dream, nothing more. A bad dream." James straightened his legs and moved to the side of the bed. He could still feel his hands tremble.

"I can get you something, Rajah," Kameja offered. "Some tea or brandy?"

James took a deep breath and shook his head. "That won't be necessary, thank you, anyway. I'm quite all right now."

Nightmares were not unfamiliar to Kameja. Hers were always the same; arms pulling her away from her mother's breast while her father lay dead on the ground and her brothers and sisters wailing in fear. Even now, years following her abduction, she dreamt the same dream although the faces of her family had dimmed with the passage of time. That was her nightmare, and she assumed it was James' too.

"The bad dreams come when we think of our homes, our family," Kameja said softly. "Were you dreaming of your home and family, Rajah James?"

"I guess I was, in a way," James replied. "But this is my home now."

Kameja nodded as if she understood. "As it is now my home, Rajah James."

## II

### April 26, 1826
### Singapore

Arthur Claygate peered over the top of a copy of the *Straits Times* and observed his wife. Margaret sat completely rigid, her back turned to him and stared out the window of the two room flat Arthur had rented for them while they waited to make connections with a ship which would take them to England in a few days.

Like a marble sentinel, Margaret sat in a hard backed chair close to an open window and stared pensively with vacuous eyes at the street below. She didn't respond to the soliciting cries of the street merchants hawking their wares, nor did her eyes follow the bustle of activity on the crowded street below and she didn't blink against the afternoon sunlight splashing against her face. She remained her same inert and rigid self as she had since Arthur found her raped and beaten a month earlier.

Arthur's heart lamented as he watched her. Physically, Margaret had improved and for that he was grateful. But she refused to communicate with him, only accepting his gentle attentions to her care and grooming with catatonic resignation. Arthur feared that his wife was on the edge of a dark abyss from which she may never escape, but none of his ministrations helped release her from her depression.

Arthur started to say something to her, thought better of the idea and opened up the newspaper and began to read.

"My God!" he blurted after a few minutes into his reading.

Margaret blinked and she tilted her head slightly to the sound of Arthur's startled voice.

Arthur shot up from the skirted lounge chair. Aloud, he verbalized the substance of the article that had surprised him. "This article in the *Times* is about James...James Brooke, the young man I introduced you to aboard the *Castle Huntley* on the voyage over, Margaret. Apparently, he's been in a battle of some sort or another—in Borneo of all places...says here he was responsible for the slaughter of over two hundred natives..."

"James? James Brooke? Oh, yes, I remember him, Arthur. A very nice man as I recall," she said in a hushed tone.

"Margaret?" Arthur swung his head toward his wife. *Had she spoken?*

"What was that you said?" he asked softly, slowly approaching her. He bent down, listening and wondering if he had been mistaken.

273

"What else does the newspaper say about Lieutenant Brooke?" Margaret asked in a normal tone of voice.

*She had spoken!* Joy swept through him, erasing the many doubts he had of his wife's recovery. He almost grabbed her in his excitement, but stopped himself. *Too soon*, he thought. His eyes scurried back to the newspaper and he related the substance of the article to her, anxiously glancing from the newspaper to her to see if she continued to show any visible signs that she was reacting to what he was conveying to her.

"It seems James was appointed Rajah of Sarawak by the Sultan of Brunei...seems to be some question of the legality of the whole thing...and then a bit about his military actions in Borneo..."

When Arthur finished conveying the essence of the article to his wife, he looked up from the paper and added, "Seems that James has somehow found the key to the fortune he sought, but when he opened the door, he got himself a whole peck of trouble."

"I don't want to return to England, Arthur." Margaret turned in her chair and looked directly at her husband.

Arthur's mouth dropped open in surprise. His wife was looking at him in the same manner in which he was accustomed before the assault had whisked her mind away from him. He rushed to her and fell to his knees at her side and clutched her delicate fingers in his hands. "What did you say, dear?" It didn't matter to him what she had spoken, only that she did.

A remorseful smile formed on Margaret's lips. "Arthur, is there any way you can still love me...with all that's happened, I mean?"

Arthur laid his head onto her lap and embraced her skeletal waist. Tears of joy formed in the corners of his eyes. "Oh sweet God in Heaven...Margaret...Margaret...I'll always love you no matter what has happened in the past or whatever God wills to happen in the future."

Margaret held Arthur's head in her lap and wept, the warm tears purging her guilt. "I want to tell you everything, Arthur...everything that happened."

# III

April 26, 1826
Wethington Villa
The South of France

Mollie tipped the carriage driver handsomely for delivering the letter. She turned it over in her hand and saw that it was stamped in Singapore and had been sent to England before finding its way to the Wethington villa in France. It was from Lieutenant Brooke, she surmised.

When she entered the villa, Mollie walked to a marble topped desk lining one wall near the entry and opened the desk's singular drawer. "Now where is it?" she mumbled to herself as she rummaged through a pile of stationery and quill pens. Unable to locate the letter opener, she turned abruptly and walked to the kitchen. She returned to the hallway carrying a thin bladed kitchen knife in one hand and the letter in the other and marched up the stairway to where her mistress, Elizabeth Wethington, was preparing to take her morning bath.

"A letter for you, Miss Elizabeth, from Lieutenant Brooke, I believe," she announced with as much flair and joy in her voice as she could muster when she entered Elizabeth's bedroom. "I apologize, mistress, but I couldn't locate the letter opener. You will need to use this." Mollie placed the letter and the knife at the corner of Elizabeth's dresser then busied herself with making the bed.

Elizabeth sat at her mirrored dresser and stared vacantly into the glass and made no attempt to acknowledge Mollie's presence or reach for the letter. A child's cry of discomfort emanated from an adjacent room.

"Soiled diapers again, I suspect," Mollie said with a sigh. "I'll take care of him, Miss Elizabeth." Before exiting the room, Mollie stopped and gazed compassionately at Elizabeth's wan reflection in the mirror and placed her plump hand affectionately on Elizabeth's shoulder. "Please, Miss Elizabeth," she pleaded. "Open the letter. Perhaps the news will do you some good."

When Elizabeth didn't respond, Mollie frowned and not knowing what else she could do, affectionately patted Elizabeth's shoulder and walked from the room to attend the child.

"There, there, my precious one," Mollie cooed as she lifted Elizabeth's baby from its bassinet and placed him gently on a soft rug to change his soiled undergarment.

When she finished, Mollie bundled the baby in her arms, carried him to a rocking chair squeezed into the corner of the tiny room, sat down and rhythmically rocked and hummed softly to the child until the baby stopped sobbing. She felt the baby's tiny heartbeat against her breast and knew that the child had fallen asleep. Mollie continued to rock. *Such a beautiful baby*, she thought. *How could Elizabeth refuse to care for it?* she wondered.

Mollie silently answered her own question by attributing it to Elizabeth's illness. Mollie had witnessed the fog of depression which had enveloped her mistress even before the birth of the child. A bastard, that's what Elizabeth had called it in a final fit of rage before she withdrew into her own world and her own thoughts—a silent world in which she had yet to emerge. Mollie sighed deeply. *What ever would become of a child that wasn't wanted? What would become of Elizabeth? How long could Elizabeth live with the secret of her indiscretion before the guilt of her mistake ravaged her completely?*

Mollie didn't have the answers to the questions she posed to herself. Perhaps the letter from Lieutenant Brooke would help, she thought with just a glimmer of hope. She recalled how Elizabeth had told her of James' proposal of marriage and how she intended to accept once she convinced him to give up his ideas about returning to the Orient. But the young lieutenant did not bend to Elizabeth's will and it was only after he returned to the Far East that Elizabeth admitted to Mollie how much she was in love with him and confided that she was carrying a child. How sad it was, Mollie thought. Futures so filled with promise then seemed utterly devastated now. Mollie held the tiny baby tighter to her breasts and continued to rock and hum a lullaby.

Elizabeth glanced pensively at the letter lying on the dresser, but didn't bother to open it. She knew what it contained. It was the same as the others, a plea from James for her to change her mind, join him in the Far East and marry him. How much she wished she could forget everything that happened and sail to him. How very much she wanted to wrap herself in his arms and tell him how wrong she had been, that she loved him and that she would do anything to keep him close to her forever. But she couldn't.

She intended to deceive him into thinking that the child she carried in her womb was his. But when he told her that he would honor his promise to his father and return to the Orient and asked her to consider marrying him and accompanying him to the Far East, she had reacted petulantly, having convinced herself that James would relent and remain in England with her. But he didn't and she soon understood how very wrong she had been to think she could live a life based upon a lie.

*And now it was too late*, she thought. *Who would accept a bastard child that she herself did not want? Who would marry a woman who had such a child out of wedlock? Who could ever see her as anything more than the harlot she was? Who could ever forgive her for her indiscretion?*

Tears strolled lazily down Elizabeth's drawn cheeks, but she made no attempt to wipe them away. She answered her own questions and the answer to each was always the same. *Nobody.*

Elizabeth picked up the knife from the top of the unopened letter and slowly came to her feet. She dropped the robe she was wearing from her shoulders and let it fall to the floor. Naked, she turned and walked to the side of the bath Mollie had drawn for her. She stepped into the cast iron tub and lowered herself slowly into it. She held the knife tightly in her hand. *Who would ever care?*

Again, her answer was the same. *Nobody.*

# CHAPTER TWELVE

## I

June 14, 1826
*HMS Skimalong*
South China Sea

"Ship off the port beam, Captain!" The *Skimalong's* lookout in the mainmast crow's nest pointed toward the landward horizon.

Captain Irons, standing amidships, sauntered to the ship's railing and peered toward shore. He raised his hand to shade his eyes from the glare of the sun, but the reflection from the water's surface made it difficult to see more than a dark speck on the water off in the far distance. "Can you make her out, Cockaran?"

"Looks like a Chinese junk to me, Captain."

Captain Irons turned to his second officer, the same spirited young man who ably directed cannon fire for James at the battle of Siniawan. "Bring her about, Mister Harris. We had best check her out."

"Aye, Captain!" Harris took several quick steps aft before forming his hands into a bullhorn. He relayed Timothy's order to the ship's pilot to bring the *Skimalong* to a course to intercept the suspicious ship.

No sooner had the *Skimalong* altered its course, tacking into the wind, than the lookout yelled, "She's turning about, Captain! She's spotted us and she's running!"

"Maintain our present course, Mister Harris," Timothy said calmly. "Let's stay on her heels if we can."

"Aye, Captain. Keep her steady to the wind!" he called.

Harris stepped next to Captain Irons. He lowered his cock-and-pinch cap over his forehead and squinted into the glare of the coastal sea. "Is she a pirate do you think, sir?"

Timothy read the eagerness expressed in Harris' question. Since returning from Siniawan with James Brooke, Timothy's second officer was infused with confidence and a desire to engage the enemy again. Victory in battle did that to men sometimes, Timothy reasoned. For months now, the *Skimalong* had been patrolling the South China Sea and had yet to engage a pirate vessel and Timothy had little hope that this particular encounter would be any different.

"Could be, but don't get your hopes up that we will catch her, Mister Harris. If she's a junk, she will easily outrun us."

"She's moving away, Captain," came the confirmation from the crow's nest.

"Damn!" Harris exclaimed.

Timothy was also disappointed. Smuggling from China and pirate activity along the southern region of the South China Sea had increased, and Captain Irons was frustrated that the *Skimalong* had not yet played a role in suppressing it as he was directed to do. "Keep her on course, Mister Harris. The junk is probably bound for Marudu Bay. We'll tail her that far. It won't hurt to let her know we're onto her."

"Aye Captain." Harris conveyed the order to the ship's pilot then said, "At least we forced her off course, Captain."

"That we did, Mister Harris." If only he had the authority to enter Marudu Bay, the *Skimalong's* guns would make short work of the pirate stronghold, Timothy thought. But that part of North Borneo along with the Philippines and the Celebes Islands was under Spanish suzerainty and, by treaty, it was off limits to British incursion.

*Just as well*, Timothy thought. Although his standing orders were to intercept and engage all ships suspected of smuggling or piracy, he had more pleasant duties to attend to and he was looking forward to the second leg of the *Skimalong's* journey. The first leg of the trip had taken them from Singapore to Brunei where Timothy conveyed documents and gifts to Sultan Hasim, granting recognition of Hasim's government by His Majesty, King George IV of England. That task completed, Timothy was instructed to pay a call upon the Rajah of Sarawak and present James with documents from the Governor-General which would be of major interest to the new Rajah. In addition, Timothy had correspondence from England for James and passengers bound for Kuching. Although he was disappointed that the *Skimalong* was not able to engage the fleeing junk, Timothy was looking forward to seeing his friend, James Brooke, once again.

# II

June 15, 1826
Marudu Bay
North Borneo

"What did they say, Chin?"

"They say they will not leave Marudu Bay, not with the English man-of-war in the area."

"Damn! Did you offer them more money?"

Chin nodded that he did. "But they still won't go." Chin rubbed at an irritation above the scar on his useless eye and reached for a bottle of rice wine sitting on the table. Geoff had already consumed half of it while Chin negotiated with the Chinese smugglers who had brought the two of them from China with their cargo of opium destined for Loi Pek. But before they could reach Sarawak, the Chinese junk was intercepted by a British warship and forced to anchor in the safe harbor at Marudu Bay.

"Damn their bloody hides!" Geoff pounded his fist against the dirty table and looked beyond the open market of the pirate stronghold to the harbor. "What the hell do we do now, Chin? We've got to get that shipment of opium into Sarawak. It can't wait."

Chin took a deep pull directly from the bottle of wine and belched. "There are others who may be willing to make the run," he said, seemingly unruffled by the delay.

"Others? Who?"

Chin half-turned in his chair and tossed his head toward the harbor. "I've been asking around. Do you see those two standing next to the triremes?"

"Yeah, I see them." Geoff noticed that the two men appeared to be talking with a flurry of animated gestures. The shorter, older man was doing most of the listening while the taller man, a Malay wearing a gold and red sarong, seemed to be doing most of the talking. "Who are those blokes?" Geoff asked.

"The short one's a Sulu pirate leader. His name is Lutu. The triremes belong to him. I've been told he is on his way to Sarawak."

"I don't know, Chin. Could be risky hitchin' a lift with a pirate."

Chin chuckled. "They are all pirates here," he said. "Unless you want to wait around for the junk to leave, it's our only way out of here."

"What's to keep this Lutu fellow from slitting our throats and taking the opium for himself once he knows what we've got with us?" Geoff asked.

Chin wrinkled his lip into a sneer. "The Malay he's talking with," answered Chin. "He's the brother of the Sultan of Brunei. The Chinese say he can be trusted...for a price."

"How much?"

Chin shrugged. "Probably half the value of the cargo." Noisily he chugged from the bottle of rice wine, draining most of it.

"Half! That's bloody ridiculous!" Chin's callous disregard for money often amazed Geoff. Sometimes it seemed to him that Chin was more interested in killing than getting rich.

"No choice," Chin said simply. "The opium does us no good sitting here." Chin rolled his one good eye suspiciously from side to side and whispered, "And it won't be long before the word gets out about what we've got."

Chin made a good point. Geoff cast a wary eye to the crowd of brigands and cutthroats combing the market and dockside shore. Any one of them, if they had the opportunity, would jump at the chance to bash his and Chin's brains in to get at the opium. Marudu Bay, the strongest pirate stronghold from the Celebes to Jakarta, was safe from European ships, but it was not safe from its own kind. "All right, Chin. We'll give him half. But I want to get out of here as soon as possible, understand? This place makes me nervous."

Chin nodded that he understood and sucked down the last of the wine. "I'll go talk to the Malay."

# III

June 16, 1826
Outpost
Bintulu River, Sarawak

Chopak shook Henry awake.

"Wha...what is it?" Henry bolted up and looked around the temporary shelter where he slept. It was too dark to see, but he recognized the high pitched voice of the *seperti perempuan*, one of the dozen Iban *Pengulu* Rentab had assigned to assist in the construction of the Rajah's small fort along the bank of the lower Bintulu River.

"*Tuan* Henry, you must come. There is a fire near the coast. I think the Malay village of Bintulu is burning."

Henry pulled a sarong around his waist and followed Chopak into the night and onto one of the fort's finished ramparts.

Chopak pointed to the coast. "See there, *Tuan* Henry? You can see the glow of the fire against the sky."

Henry wiped the grit of sleep from his eyes and peered northward. "Kayan?"

Chopak shook his head emphatically. "No, *Tuan*. Since Long Akar our people and the Kayan have respected the Rajah's wishes. No more raids."

"An accident, maybe?"

"No accident. The Malay villages have separate *rumahs*. One house may burn by accident, but not the entire village."

"So what caused the fire then, Chopak?"

"Maybe pirates-"

"Pirates? Damn! If it's not one thing it's another in this bloody country," Henry exclaimed. Henry's outpost was far from being complete and Henry only had a dozen Iban with him. If the pirates were on their way up the river, he wouldn't have much of a chance to stop them.

As if he read Henry's thoughts, Chopak said, "Not to worry, *Tuan*. The pirates will not travel up the Bintulu River. This is Iban territory. They will stay near the coast."

"Chopak, gather up three or four of the men. We'll take a *prau* downriver and check it out. I'll get my weapons."

Henry turned on his bare heels and returned to his shelter. He quickly changed to his breeches and shirt and hurriedly rummaged through the darkness for his musket pistol and sword. *James was right again*, he thought.

If the pirates from Marudu Bay continued to prowl the coastal waters of Sarawak unimpeded, trade would never flourish. Henry knew there would be little he could do for the village of Bintulu, but he decided he would survey the situation and then return to Kuching to report his findings to James.

# IV

June 16, 1826
Kampong Bintulu
Sarawak, Borneo

Geoff watched from the muddy beach as the Malay village of Bintulu burned to the ground. He leaned against a trireme's bow with his feet resting in the cool surf and listened to the shouts of mayhem as Lutu's men pillaged the village. He also heard the helpless cries of the villagers as they were butchered and raped by Lutu's band of cutthroats. He watched the shadows of scurrying men silhouetted against the flames as they pursued fleeing villagers and raced each other to abscond with whatever valuables they could find.

Geoff sulked angrily and kicked at the yielding surf with his feet. Not that he cared a damn for the pitiful screams of the dying villagers or felt any remorse for the destruction of their village, but he was annoyed that Chin had not been able to persuade the pirate leader, Lutu or the Malay prince, Api, to maintain a course directly to the Sarawak River and not waste time razing a coastal village.

"Don't worry," Lutu told Chin and Geoff after deciding to raid Bintulu. "It won't take long to raid the village and then we will be on our way." Lutu had scowled at them and spat a stream of beetle-nut juice to the deck of the trireme. He didn't bother to wipe his lips and his bright red saliva dripped from the corner of his mouth as if he had just consumed raw flesh. Through Chin, Geoff had tried to object to the tall Malay prince, but their protest was dismissed with a cold glare and an emphatic shake of the head.

"Chin, can't you talk them out of it?" Geoff had pleaded. "We're paying to get to Sin Bok and dammit to hell, that's where I want to go!"

The one-eyed Chinaman pulled him to one side and said, "Best keep your mouth shut. Too much talk about the delay may get you your throat cut." Chin tossed Geoff a wicked grin and slapped him on the shoulder. "Besides, Geoff, the raid might be fun." The half-breed Chinaman turned from him and joined Lutu's men making preparations for the raid on Bintulu.

"Stupid bastard," Geoff had mumbled to Chin's back. "We have a fortune in opium at risk and he wants to go raiding with these bloody brigands," he mumbled.

But that was earlier. Now Geoff noticed some of Lutu's men returning to the triremes. Unconsciously, he rubbed at his crippled thumb, hoping that one day it would return to normal, but it remained as lifeless and stiff since being mangled by the big Malay half-breed in Madras. *Good, they're finished. Now we can get on to Sin Bok.*

Geoff straightened when the men approached and stepped away from the trireme to allow three dark skinned pirates of unknown Oriental origin to board the ship. They were in a celebratory mood and each of them had their arms loaded with paraphernalia scavenged from the village. One of the three balanced a bloody *parang* between his armload of stolen goods and his chin. One of his hands clutched the long hair of a severed head.

"Bloody savages," Geoff muttered under his breath. He turned and walked a few paces up the foul-smelling beach and sighted Chin returning from the flaming ruins.

"Have a good time?" Geoff asked sarcastically.

Chin smiled smugly. "These Malay women can be very cooperative when they want to save their necks." Chin belched out a wicked laugh and added, "They were so cooperative I almost didn't want to cut their begging throats when I finished with them."

Chin, holding the crimson blade of his knife to his neck, drew it across his throat in mock execution and laughed. "Here, I brought a souvenir for you." Chin tossed something and Geoff plucked it out of the air. It was soft and wet. Chin turned, bellowed out a throaty laugh and boarded the trireme.

Geoff peered at the object in his hand. "Christ Almighty!" he exclaimed in disgust and then tossed the severed breast into the water.

# V

## Kuching, Sarawak

Kameja lowered a *bakul*, a basket filled with rice balls stuffed with salted fish and wrapped in banana leaves and an assortment of fresh fruit to the men in the *prau* while James repeated his instructions to Si Tundok and the *Datu* Temanggong.

"Let the *Kapitan* of Sin Bok know that I am aware of his mining activities and that I don't intend to interfere as long as he is willing to purchase a concession from me." Knowledge of Loi Pek's gold mines couldn't have come at a better time for James. He had spent most of his fortune refitting the *Jolly Bachelor* and purchasing supplies for his new Raj. What little he had left would soon disappear when it came time to pay the crew of the *Jolly Bachelor* and replenish needed stores. A sale of a concession to the *Kapitan* of Sin Bok would be a big boost to James' financial situation and hold him over until he could start exporting goods from Sarawak. Then, he hoped that he could begin to implement a few public works projects which he had been mulling over in the back of his mind.

The *Datu* Temanggong nodded that he understood. "And, as you have instructed, Rajah, we will force him to release any slaves he may have."

"Don't force him," James cautioned. At the *Datu's* suggestion, only three warriors accompanied Si Tundok and the *Datu* Temanggong. It was the *Datu's* contention that dealing with Loi Pek would not require a massive show of force, but although James was skeptical, he deferred to the *Datu's* judgment. "We don't want a confrontation with him. I just want you to make it clear that it is my wish that slavery be abolished in Sarawak. Leave him with the thought that I intend to check up on him from time to time."

Both Si Tundok and the *Datu* Temanggong nodded that they understood James' orders. "Don't worry, Rajah James," the *Datu* said. "We will return tomorrow with Loi Pek's agreement to the concession." He gave the command and together, his small force pushed the *prau* away from the dock and began rowing upstream.

"If it looks as if he is going to give you any trouble, return to Kuching and we will deal with him later," James called as the *prau* pulled away. James did not know why he said it, but he had a growing feeling of apprehension about the trip to Sin Bok. Maybe his sense of anxiety was a result of the occasional nightmares plaguing him recently, he rationalized to himself.

"Good luck!" he shouted after them in English and saw Si Tundok wave a parting farewell with his massive arm. James wished he had changed his mind and gone with them, but he decided it was best to remain in Kuching since he was expecting word from Singapore any day now about his request to the British government to consider Sarawak as a British Protectorate.

James and Kameja stood at the dock and waited until the *prau* had disappeared around a bend in the river. The disquieted feeling remained in the pit of James' stomach and it manifested itself with furrows of worry on his brow.

Sensing James' discomfort, Kameja said, "Do not worry, Rajah James. Your friends will find no trouble at Sin Bok. They will return unharmed."

"I am certain you are right, Kameja," James said, but the disquieting feeling remained.

As the two of them began to return to the palace, gongs sounded along the lower river. Kameja turned and was first to spot the subject of the clamor. "Look, Rajah James, a ship!"

"It's the *Skimalong!*" James said with excitement.

The two of them raced back to the dock and watched the man-of-war sail smoothly to the deepest part of the harbor and drop anchor near the *Jolly Bachelor*. In his excitement at the arrival of Captain Irons' ship, James had already forgotten any misgivings he had about Si Tundok and the *Datu Temanggong's* trip to Sin Bok. Both of them waved enthusiastically. Shortly, they watched a dinghy being lowered to the water's surface followed by three people descending a hemp gangway assisted by six bluejackets. James easily recognized Captain Irons by his uniform and his smooth, athletic descent to the small boat. He didn't immediately place the second person being helped into the dinghy, but the third to board was a woman.

*Elizabeth!* James raced to the edge of the dock and strained his eyes to see her. His shoulders slumped perceptually when he realized it wasn't Elizabeth at all, but someone he only vaguely recognized.

With the regular rhythm of a heartbeat, the bluejackets rowed the boat toward the dock. By now James recognized its occupants and they recognized him and they began waving to one another.

"Arthur! Margaret! What a pleasant surprise!" James' broad smile extended almost as far as his ears and he had already forgotten about Elizabeth when he extended a hand to assist his friends from the boat.

He shook hands with Captain Irons, the first to reach him. "So good to see you again, Captain," James said effusively.

"Likewise, Mister Brooke. As you can see, I have brought along a couple of your old friends."

When Arthur stepped onto the dock, James embraced him unselfconsciously and welcomed Margaret with a gentlemanly bow and a kiss on her hand. James noted that Arthur's wife appeared thinner and more drawn than he remembered her to be. He wondered if she had been ill.

Arthur stepped back and spread his arms open wide in front of his barrel chest. He pretended to evaluate James from head to toe for a moment, then bellowed, "So this is what a white Rajah looks like." He clicked his tongue. "My, my what a disappointment. No jewels, no dark-skinned girls fanning him with ostrich feathers and no golden chariots to whisk his friends away to his marble palace, I suspect!"

When they all finished laughing at Author's comments, James retorted, "No jewels and no gold yet, Arthur, but I do have a palace, believe it or not. Of course it's not exactly made of ivory or marble—that one is still in the planning stage."

James, elated by the surprise arrival of his friends, could not stop talking. First he ordered Kameja to return to the palace and prepare refreshments for his guests and then he began to flood each of them with a host of questions.

Arthur finally threw his hands into the air in mock surrender. "Enough, James!" he bellowed. "Give us a chance to work the salt out of our system first. Our legs haven't touched dry land in days."

"How unthoughtful of me. Of course you must be tired. Let's gather your things and I will take you to the palace. We can talk there. I've got so much to ask each of you."

Arthur feigned chagrin. "No litter bearers? No carriages to take us to the palace?"

"The only means of transportation around here are your own two feet no matter how much salt you have in them," James quipped.

Minutes later, the small group arrived at the palace. After a few good-humored remarks by Arthur which jokingly disparaged James' wooden palace, the guests were seated around the table behind the throne room. Kameja, in her normal efficiency, had a bounty of food waiting for them; rice cakes, *rambutan*, and *lychee* nuts graced the center of the table. She brought them freshly brewed tea and James asked her to sit with them after he had introduced her to his friends.

That final accommodating gesture of James' confirmed Margaret's suspicions that the pretty almond-eyed girl might be more than just an ordinary servant to James.

"Now tell me, Captain Irons," James said, leaning forward on the table, "what news from Singapore? Has Governor McDonald heard from Parliament yet about my request for a Protectorate for Sarawak?"

289

Timothy stopped peeling the hairy skin from a plumb *rambutan* and reached to the floor and opened a leather brief. He extracted a number of sealed parcels and handed two of them across the table to James. "Here is the dispatch from the Governor-General appraising you of Parliament's action with regard to your application and a letter from England."

James determined that the letter was from his mother, but he set it aside without opening it, preferring to read it later in private. Quickly he opened the parcel from Governor McDonald.

Timothy popped the peeled *rambutan* into his mouth and extracted the big seed with his fingers. He plucked another piece of fruit from the bowl in front of him while he watched James anxiously read the document. He knew the essence of the contents and he knew James was certain to voice his disappointment.

After a few moments of silence, James tossed the document on the table. "Damn!" He leaned back in his chair, his face registering his frustration. "Parliament has only met me half way. They have affirmed that Brunei and Sarawak are within the realm of British influence as defined by the treaty with the Dutch, but because Sarawak is legally a vassal state to the Sultan of Brunei, they cannot grant a Protectorate to me specifically."

"It isn't all bad, Mister Brooke," Timothy offered. "Now that Britain has reaffirmed their suzerainty over Brunei and Sarawak, they have included this region in our regular naval patrols. The British Navy is now empowered to intercept and engage vessels suspected of smuggling and piracy along these coastal waters."

James brightened. "That's great news, Captain Irons. Does that include inland waters as well?"

"Only in pursuit of pirate craft encountered in coastal waters. Our orders prohibit us from searching inland waterways for pirates and, of course, we cannot pursue any craft into foreign territories."

"Like Marudu Bay?"

"Like Marudu Bay and any other lair considered a territory of another sovereign government," Timothy replied.

"Well, still that will be of great help to us," James said. "But I intend to resubmit an application for full and total protection. I am still an English citizen, you know."

Captain Irons nodded. "Certainly your decision to make, Mister Brooke and...Oh...I almost forgot, there's one other thing." Timothy handed James another document that he had kept on his lap. "Seems that news of your endeavor here has reached England and created quite a stir. The press there has made you out as some sort of hero and the King has granted you a knighthood."

"What?" James snatched the document and read it rapidly. It pleased him and alleviated some of the disappointment he felt for being denied a full Protectorate.

Although Arthur and Margaret had remained quiet during the conversation, when the announcement of James' knighthood was made, they both loudly exclaimed their congratulations. Kameja, not understanding what was being said was satisfied simply to notice that James' countenance had improved after he read the second document and received the praises of his friends.

"So, how is it that we commoners should address you now?" Arthur asked with a broad grin. "Will it be, James...Sir James...or Rajah James?"

"As you wish, Arthur. As far as I'm concerned any title is preferable to *lieutenant*," James said and pushed the documents aside. "Enough with these tiring affairs of State," he said with some magnanimity. "Tell me about yourselves Arthur, Margaret. When I last saw the two of you, you were bound for China. How is your mission going?"

Arthur shifted uncomfortably in his chair. He tossed a furtive glance to Margaret and cleared his throat. Although Margaret had given him every indication that she had recovered from her experience in China, he worried that a discussion about the mission might elicit a relapse. But before he could think of how to reply to James' question, Margaret surprised him by speaking up.

"The situation in China proved intolerable, James," she said, her voice steady and even. "The district war lord refused to cooperate in any manner with the mission or our efforts." She reached over and placed her thin fingers on Arthur's hand. "Although Arthur had some success healing the ailments of many of the villagers there, my efforts at education and teaching the Word of God were a most dismal failure."

"I'm sorry to hear that," James said.

"In fact," Margaret continued, "we were returning to England when Arthur happened to read about your, uh, adventures here in Sarawak."

"There was an article in the *Strait Times*," Arthur injected.

"Oh, what did it say? Did you happen to bring a copy with you?" James asked.

Arthur shook his head that he didn't have a copy with him and he didn't want James to be upset by the specific contents of the article either so he said, "The article simply made us aware of where you were and the success of your endeavor."

"That's why I persuaded Arthur to come to Sarawak rather than returning to England right away," Margaret chimed.

"I'm certainly glad you did." James noticed the two of them exchange a quick glance with one another.

Arthur cleared his throat. "What Margaret means to say, James is that she...uh...*we* are in hopes that we may be of assistance to you here in Sarawak. I'm still not a bad surgeon and Margaret is a most competent educator."

"You want to stay here...in Sarawak?"

"If you'll have us," Arthur spoke quickly. By the Grace of God, Margaret seemed fully recovered from her horrific experience, but Arthur feared that her mental health was still extremely fragile. If they were forced to return to England, the Anglican Mission Society would most certainly hold an inquiry which would force Margaret to reveal the events of that terrible day in China. Arthur would not let that happen. He had to convince James to allow them to stay.

"We have enough private funds to take care of our own living expenses and supply needed essentials for a clinic and a school. Even if the Mission would refuse to subsidize our endeavor here, we are confident that Margaret's father will find the means to provide us with necessary supplies as we may need them in the future." Arthur felt Margaret squeeze his hand as they awaited James' decision.

"Needless to say, Sarawak has a need for a doctor as well as a teacher, but you must understand that this is a primitive country, a dangerous one. I'm not sure that I—"

"We can be of great use to you," Arthur interjected. "A new country is in need of the skills we can provide. I also recall your personal feelings about missionary zeal, James, and I respect them. And I promise you, if you will give us this chance, we will make every effort to stay within whatever limitations you may see fit to impose."

James sensed a hint of desperation in Arthur's argument. He also sensed that there was something other than missionary fervor at the heart of his friend's request but he had enough respect for Arthur and his wife not to probe into the details of it.

"Very well," James said. "Sarawak will be delighted to have you both as residents and I will be happy to have a chess mate again."

"Praise the Lord, thank you, James, thank you!" Margaret and Arthur embraced and then Margaret extended her frail hand to James and grasped his palm, holding it as tightly as if it were a life buoy.

James had the feeling that he had done more than simply consent to their request and he was glad he made the decision he did.

## IV

### Sarawak River
### Near Sin Bok

"What do you think, *Datu*? Was the Chinaman telling the truth?" Si Tundok asked.

"He lies," the *Datu* Temanggong said without hesitation. "Loi Pek is a shrewd man and he has dealings with *Awang* Api. His words cannot be trusted."

Si Tundok nodded his agreement. "I think we should go back, *Datu*. I think we should take a closer look around and see if we can locate those gold mines he says he knows nothing about."

"In the daylight, it may be dangerous."

"True. Let's find a spot along the river just below the village and hide the *prau*. We will wait until the village sleeps and then we can look around. If the Chinaman has a mine, I suspect it's located somewhere in those hills behind Sin Bok."

The *Datu* agreed and gave the order and he, Si Tundok and the three Malay warriors accompanying them, feathered the *prau* in a tight circle and began paddling upstream toward Sin Bok once again.

# VII

*HMS Skimalong*
Sarawak River

Shortly before midnight, thick, ruptured clouds covered the waning moon and pelted the forest and river around Kuching with a torrential downpour. Like wet mermaids, mother and daughter, the *Skimalong* and the *Jolly Bachelor* rocked gently in the river harbor near one another and willingly accepted the rain while all hands on board, except the night watch, snored peacefully in the crew quarters below the two ships' forecastle decks.

The stern watchman aboard the *Skimalong* was the first to spot movement near the far bank of the river. "Mister Harris, ship off the stern!" he called. The watchman stepped closer to the railing, nearly slipping on a roll of rain-drenched hemp rope in the darkness. He strained his eyes to identify the fast craft sailing upriver on a course parallel to the sterns of the two anchored ships.

"What is it?" Harris asked, nearly tripping on the same coil of rope.

The watchman pointed toward the far bank. "Over there, sir," he said. "I can't quite make it out, but it appears several Malay triremes are heading upstream."

Harris pulled the brim of his hat lower onto his forehead, forcing the pool of water collecting in its brim to fall upon his shoulders. "Damnable weather," he muttered and squinted through the rain and darkness to where the watchman pointed. He saw the movement of the craft, but he couldn't distinguish any of the specific features of them.

"What do you think, sir? Shall I awaken Captain Irons?"

Since the boats seemed to be on a straight course upriver, Harris doubted they were a threat. "No, that won't be necessary. Probably just a fishing fleet that got caught at sea during the storm. It appears they're in a hurry to make their way back to their village somewhere upriver. Carry on."

"Aye, sir."

Harris turned and moved to a semi-sheltered position beneath the mainsail mast. He pulled his collar up against the rain falling on his neck and watched the Malay boats merge with the darkness beyond the British ships. "Damnable weather," he muttered once again and quickly forgot about the incident.

If anyone aboard the *Jolly Bachelor* saw Lutu's triremes race by them, they too, failed to report it.

VIII

Rajah's Palace
Kuching, Sarawak

The palace was quiet. James' long conversation with his guests had finally run its course for the evening and each of them had withdrawn for the evening; Captain Irons to his quarters aboard the *Skimalong*, Margaret and Arthur to a Malay *rumah* that Kameja had arranged for them, and Kameja to *Datu* Temanggong's former room in the palace.

Only James remained awake. Silently he lay on his cot with his forearms crossed over his eyes as if the pressure were enough to hold back any tears he might shed. But there were none.

The moon waned well past its zenith and his room was bathed in total darkness while heavily falling rain drummed a discordant tune on the palace roof. James didn't know how long he had lain there and he didn't care. He had read his mother's letter after his guests had departed from the palace and the contents were in sharp contrast to the pleasurable evening James had recently shared with his friends.

She had informed him about George Barton's efforts on James' behalf in securing the granting of his knighthood and she told him of how James was considered somewhat of a hero by the English press despite rumors circulated by the *Straits Times* to the contrary. She told him how much she missed him and how she prayed for his safety and how much she hoped he would return to England. His mother's letter also informed him of Elizabeth Wethington's suicide.

*...God only knows what Trial or Tribulation that sweet, dear young Lady must have experienced to drive her to such a Tragic Resolution. We both know that she had been Suffering from a lengthy Illness and perhaps her Agony was more than She could bear. Maybe We shall never know what compelled Elizabeth to take her Life. I can only hope that this terrible News does not Sadden you to the point of Despondency and I Pray that you will find Solace beyond the depths of your Grief. I know how much Elizabeth meant to You, James...*

His mother's written words swam through his mind and James felt himself reaching for them like a drowning man reaches for a gasp of air—hoping to grasp the words, rearrange them until their meaning changed and he would be rescued from his terrible sorrow.

James wouldn't sleep the remainder of that night, nor did he cry.

# VIII

## 11:30 PM
## June 20, 1826
## Near Sin Bok, Sarawak

The more Si Tundok thought about their earlier meeting with the Chinese *Kapitan* of Sin Bok, the more he was convinced the Chinaman had lied. Although Loi Pek had received them cordially enough, Si Tundok sensed the Chinaman deliberately withheld information from them. Of course the *Kapitan* was willing to comply with James' edict banning slavery in Sarawak. He concurred with the Rajah's sentiments concerning slavery. *Wasn't that why he had released Kameja to the custody of Rajah James?* Loi Pek had said.

When the matter of the gold mine was broached, Loi Pek adamantly denied their existence, using the argument that if mines existed, surely the former Rajah, Hasim would have been aware of it and demanded *serah* from it. Both Si Tundok and the *Datu* Temanggong observed that the apparent prosperity of the village was due to more than the cultivation of a few pepper fields and what little trade the Chinese conducted with the nearby Bidayuh tribes.

Just after nightfall, they maneuvered the *prau* into a large eddy some distance below Sin Bok and pulled it from the river. Within minutes, they had camouflaged the boat with *nippa* palms. Hidden in the jungle near the river, the five men ate some of the fish-stuffed rice balls Kameja had prepared for them and waited.

"It will storm soon, *Tuan* Si Tundok," the *Datu* said, gazing skyward. "We should leave soon."

"Let's wait a bit longer. I want to make certain that the village sleeps." Si Tundok located the haze penetrating the clouds and the night-blackened sky that was the moon and estimated the time by its position in the sky. "Another two hours or so and we will go."

Near midnight, the clouds erupted and sheets of rain pelted the small party. Beneath the shelter of a *sago* palm, they huddled together and waited for time and the storm to pass.

An hour later, one of the Malay warriors said. "Look there, on the river, boats."

The storm had eased and the moon had brightened and the men could clearly see the silhouettes of water craft moving rapidly up the Sarawak River.

"Fishermen?" Si Tundok questioned before he recognized the type of craft silently speeding by them.

"No, *Tuan*, Malay triremes," the *Datu* confirmed.

Both men knew that the large, speedy craft were seldom used for river travel and never used by the inland native fishermen.

"What do you suppose they are doing here at this time of night?" Si Tundok asked.

The *Datu* Temanggong frowned. "It is very peculiar, *Tuan*. Only the coastal Malay use the triremes...and pirates."

"I don't think any of the coastal Malay would have a reason to be here this late, do you, *Datu*?"

"No, *Tuan*."

"Where do you think they are heading?"

The *Datu* shook his head, perplexed. "I don't know, *Tuan*. The pirates very rarely raid the villages inland. And the only villages along the Sarawak River above Sin Bok are poor Bidayuh villages. I don't think they would waste their time with the Bidayuh."

"Wherever they are going it must be important," Si Tundok surmised. He considered that the triremes would have had to pass Kuching undetected, but given the dark night and the storm, it would be possible.

"Then we have another reason to take a closer look at Sin Bok," Si Tundok said. "We had better get started."

The five of them slogged through the jungle for nearly an hour before arriving at the perimeter of Sin Bok. The storm had passed and the partial moon glowed brightly in the night sky. "Look there," the *Datu* said, pointing to the riverside dock. "The triremes we saw earlier."

Si Tundok nodded. "And the only light in the entire village is coming from Loi Pek's shop," he said. "Something is going on, *Datu*."

"What would you have me do, *Tuan*?"

"Take your men down by the dock and see if you can find out who those triremes belong to. Be careful and stay out of sight. I'm going to see if I can find Loi Pek's mine. We'll meet at the back of Loi Pek's shop."

The two split up. The *Datu* Temanggong and his three warriors edged their way along the perimeter of the village toward the river's edge while Si Tundok circled the village in the opposite direction until he found what he expected-a wide, well-worn path which seemed to be an extension of the rock-surfaced road which bisected the village. The path snaked upward, toward the hills behind Sin Bok where Si Tundok suspected the mines to be.

The darkness was no obstacle for Si Tundok as the path, like a wide scar cutting through the dense forest on either side, sliced through the surrounding foliage and permitted a modicum of moonlight to bandage its surface, making it easy for Si Tundok to follow its upward climb.

Fifteen minutes later, Si Tundok found himself facing open ground littered with a mound of talus at the base of a hard rock outcropping below a sheer wall of exposed rock wearing a hood of trees and grass. The forest within fifty meters of the base of the outcropping had been entirely cleared. Rubble and mounds of crushed rock were silhouetted against the dim glow of the waning moonlight. *Bakuls* and *changkuls*, tools and wheelbarrows, were neatly stacked near the piles of rubble. Three black holes penetrated the face of the rock wall. Si Tundok carefully picked his way across the talus field toward the rock wall. He had found Loi Pek's mines.

He entered the center-most shaft and peered into the black abyss. Unable to discern its depth, he bent over and plucked up a hunk of rubble and tossed it into the hole. The stone hit with an echoing protest and signaled to Si Tundok that the shaft was very deep. Loi Pek had been mining for a very long time. How he managed to keep it a secret from the former Rajah, Si Tundok could not imagine.

Si Tundok did not bother to examine the other two shafts. Instead, he traced the face of the outcropping to his left and followed the sound of splashing water. There, at the far edge of the granite wall, was an elevated pipeline constructed of split bamboo. Water from a spring somewhere above the mine gushed from the ends of the wooden pipes and flowed evenly down a series of sluice gates. Loi Pek's mining operation was more sophisticated than Si Tundok originally suspected. He could only guess at the amount of gold taken from the mine. Whatever it was, it was more than enough to make Loi Pek a very wealthy man.

Satisfied that he had seen everything that he needed to confirm his suspicions, Si Tundok returned along the winding trail, circled the village once again and crept along the edge of the forest until he reached the rear of Loi Pek's shop. There was no sign of the *Datu* or his men.

"*Datu*," he whispered. He listened. Nothing. "*Datu!*" he called in a harsher whisper. Still nothing.

The light pouring from an open window at the side of Loi Pek's shop caught Si Tundok's attention. He could detect movement inside and heard voices. Like a huge cat, Si Tundok stepped from the cover of the forest and crept to the side of the shop and pressed himself against its rough exterior below the glassless window. Slowly, he straightened his knees and raised his head just enough to hear the conversation emanating from the room.

"We can't wait!" Api shouted and slammed his fist on the table and leaned menacingly into Loi Pek's face. We must attack Kuching tonight before the white Rajah sends a war party to look for the *Datu* Temanggong!"

*They have the Datu!* Si Tundok became aware that the new dawn was beginning to melt away the cover of darkness surrounding him. Before long, he would easily be seen by anyone coming to the side of the building. But the mention of an attack on Kuching and the knowledge that the *Datu* had been taken forced him to stay and learn what he could.

"But the Rajah's Malay who was with the *Datu* Temanggong when they visited earlier has not been found." Loi Pek pulled nervously on the long hairs growing from the mole on his chin. He was becoming less intimidated by Api than he was with the thought of participating in open rebellion against the new Rajah.

"All the more reason to act quickly," Api countered. "The Malay knows nothing of our plan to take Kuching, but he is sure to tell the white Rajah about your gold mines. The *Datu's* warriors have already told us that much, haven't they, Loi Pek?"

"True, but—"

"And you know what will happen when the white devil learns of your mines, don't you, old man? He won't be satisfied to take a small *serah* from you as I have done. No! He will take the mines from you and then you and your people will live like hungry dogs just like your Bidayuh neighbors."

Api snatched one of the heavily wrapped bundles of opium from the table and thrust it in Loi Pek's face. "How will you buy your precious powder then, old man?"

Api made his point. Without the mines, Loi Pek would lose his wealth, the source of his power and, most importantly, his ability to purchase opium, a substance he desperately needed to increase his wealth and ease the pain in his joints and temper his mood. He wouldn't be able to live long without the drug and he knew it.

"Very well, *Awang* Api, I will do as you say. We will join you against the white devil." He slumped wearily into the back of his chair and raised his defeated eyes to Api. "What would you have me do?"

"Good!" Api clasped the old Chinaman on his bony shoulder. "I knew you would see things my way," he said and patted Loi Pek's shoulder in mock affection. "And don't worry, Loi Pek. Once I have killed the white Rajah, I will then drive my cowardly brother from Brunei and assume my rightful place as Sultan. Your precious mines will be safe then and we can conduct our business with one another as we have in the past."

Api strutted to the far side of the table and sat down. He motioned for the others in the room to be seated. There were only four chairs so Geoff simply

300

stood behind Chin. He didn't understand what had been said, but he was anxious for the tall Malay to get on with it so that he and Chin could finish their deal with the old Chinaman. He could hardly wait to feel the weight of Loi Pek's gold in his pocket.

"It is almost dawn," Api said. "We will make our preparations and rest and then set out for Kuching late this evening. We will plan to arrive in Kuching and begin the attack at *pukal tiga jam malam*, three o'clock in the morning while the town sleeps." Api thrust a long finger towards Loi Pek. "Chinaman, your men will march on Kuching from the south. Arm your men with as many muskets as you have. It will be your task to disrupt things in Kuching, torch the buildings and keep the Malay from forming any resistance. Understood?"

Loi Pek nodded slowly. He dreaded the thought of the long march overland to Kuching. It meant leaving Sin Bok before noon with little opportunity to rest.

Api turned his flashing eyes to the pirate leader, Lutu. "Lutu, you will take your triremes down the Sarawak River and board the English ships—"

"Ships! There are English ships in Kuching?" Loi Pek was stupefied by the revelation. "But they will have cannons, and they will surely fire upon us," he said fearfully.

Lutu laughed. "Earlier my triremes sailed past these English ships without being detected. We will do the same tonight. We will be aboard the white devil's ships and have their throats cut before they awaken," he boasted.

Api confirmed Lutu's evaluation. "See, Loi Pek, there is nothing to worry about. As Lutu said, the white devils won't have time to fire their cannon. Lutu's men will be on them before they have the chance to open their eyes. Isn't that right, Lutu?" Api narrowed his eyes sinisterly and bored them into the pirate leader conveying the message that there would be consequences if Lutu didn't do exactly as he boasted he could do.

Lutu scowled, but then affirmed that he would stand by his word. Loi Pek wondered what Api had promised to pay the crass pirate leader for his part in the rebellion, but he didn't ask. Probably the English ships and cannon, he surmised. "And what about the palace and the Rajah?" Loi Pek asked.

"Leave the white devil to me!" Api spat. "The white devil is stupid! I am told he does not even post guards at the palace."

Geoff nudged Chin in the back. "When are they going to finish up? I want to get paid for the opium and get the hell out of here."

Chin ignored Geoff's interruption, but Api did not. "Your English friend has something he wants to contribute to the conversation, Chin?" Api asked sarcastically. Api didn't like the Englishman and he made it abundantly clear by tossing Geoff a deadly, unyielding stare.

Chin shrugged. He was also anxious to culminate their deal with Loi Pek, but not at the expense of irritating Api or Lutu, the two most dangerous men in the room. "He has a big mouth," Chin said in Malay, hoping no further explanation would be necessary.

Api tossed an arm casually over the back of his chair and leaned upon it. He smiled disarmingly at Geoff and asked Chin, "And what does his big English mouth have to say?"

Chin shifted nervously in his chair and scratched the long scar above his mutilated eye. "He only asks that we finish our business with the Chinaman. He is anxious to leave."

Api continued to stare at Geoff, but his smile thinned. "Ahh yes, the opium. He is eager for Loi Pek to part with some of his gold is he?"

Api reached to the center of the table where the bundles of opium bricks were set and picked one of them up. He pretended to study it for a time. "How fortunate for me that I happened to be with my friend Lutu in Marudu Bay the other day otherwise Loi Pek may have forgotten to inform me of his...uh...*transaction*." Api teased the Chinaman with a taunting grin and said, "You would not have forgotten to give me my share, my *serah*, would you have, Loi Pek?"

"No, *Awang* Api, of course not."

Api delighted in making the old Chinaman squirm. "I didn't think so," he said with a chuckle. "Well then," he announced. "Let's weigh the drug and lighten Loi Pek's stash of gold. Fetch your scales, old man."

As Loi Pek rose from his chair to procure the scales, Api directed his attention back to Chin. "Ask your English friend how he intends to leave after he has received his share of the Chinaman's gold."

Chin didn't like the implication of the question, but he was in no position to question it. What Lutu's men did with the captured Malay earlier was still fresh in his mind. He turned his blank eye up at Geoff and asked, "He wants to know how you will leave here after you have your gold."

"I'll walk or I'll hire one of these damned Chinese coolies to haul my ass out of here if I have to, not that it's any of his bloody business. One thing's for sure, Chin, I sure as hell won't hitch a ride with these bloody bastards again."

Chin told Api that Geoff planned to make his own way out of Sarawak. He also added, just to cover himself, that he planned to stay with Lutu and assist with the boarding of the English ships.

"You are a wise man, Chin," Api said with an ingratiating smile. "But tell the Englishman that there is only one way out of here and that is with me. I don't trust him to keep his mouth shut about what he has seen or heard."

Chin decided to make things simple. He turned back to Geoff and said, "Api says you are to go with Lutu. If you refuse, he will have you killed."

Geoff's mouth fell open and he started to voice his protest. But one look at Api's cold stare, forced him to shut his mouth. There was no bluff in the Malay's icy eyes, only deadly intent. Geoff shrugged his shoulders and managed a nervous smile. "All right, no offense meant. Tell him I'll do whatever he asks, Chin. Go ahead, tell him."

Si Tundok still could not put a face to the Englishman's guttural voice, but he was certain that he had heard it somewhere before. Dawn had already snatched away most of the dying night, exposing Si Tundok to the eyes of any early morning passerby and he knew he would need to make a decision about what to do and do it quickly. *Where are they holding the Datu Temanggong? Should I try to find and rescue him or return to Kuching and warn James that an attack was imminent?*

And the faceless voice of the Englishman gnawed at him. Cautiously, Si Tundok extended his head to the window for a quick glimpse inside. His timing could not have been worse.

# CHAPTER THIRTEEN

## I

4:35 A.M.
June 20, 1826
Sin Bok, Sarawak

Returning from the back of the shop with the brass balance scale in his hand, Loi Pek stepped through the inner doorway opposite the shop's lone window and caught the movement of Si Tundok's head directly across from him.

"The Rajah's Malay!" he shouted. He dropped the scale and threw his wrinkled arm towards the window. "There, at the window! The Rajah's Malay!"

Before Loi Pek had exposed him, Si Tundok managed to get a glimpse of the men in the room and he now knew who the guttural voice belonged to. It was Geoff, the man he and Henry had vowed to kill. But his only thought now was to reach the safety of the jungle and return to the *prau* they had hidden earlier and make his way to Kuching to warn James of the conspirator's plot. He almost made it.

While Api, Lutu and Geoff scrambled out the front door to sound the alarm and chase after Si Tundok, Chin shoved Loi Pek away from the shop's window and pulled his broad-bladed knife from his belt and hurled it at Si Tundok's back. End over end the deadly missile sliced through the air on its path to Chin's intended target.

"Arghhh!" Si Tundok straightened and then fell forward when Chin's knife blade penetrated his back, hitting him just below the right scapula. His hands reached behind him, trying to extract the knife from his back, but he couldn't reach it. Desperately, he pushed himself to his knees and tried to crawl into the jungle only a few meters away.

Api and the others caught up with him before he could reach the forest. They swarmed over Si Tundok's large body and forced him, face down, into the ground.

"So, we have caught the last of the Rajah's spies, have we?" Api spat.

Si Tundok strained to raise his head against the arms pressing him down, but Chin's knife, like a heavy, painful weight made it impossible to move.

Chin, having leaped through the window, dropped to one knee beside Si Tundok. He grabbed the hilt of his knife and pulled it from Si Tundok's back.

Si Tundok gasped in pain and then he felt the hands holding him begin to roll him onto his back.

"I'll be bloody damned!" Geoff exclaimed. "It's the black duffer who's been chasing after me!"

Si Tundok opened his eyes at the sound of the hated voice. Summoning all the strength he could muster, he shot his arms up to Geoff's throat, intent upon strangling him with his bare hands.

Instantly, Lutu, Chin and Api pounced on Si Tundok and forced his massive arms and chest back to the ground before he could lock his fingers around Geoff's neck. They held him spread-eagled until they felt his broad muscles weaken in submission.

"Duffer's a strong one," Geoff wheezed. He balled his fist into a tight mass of knuckles and slammed it into Si Tundok's face.

Si Tundok absorbed the blow without a hint of it phasing him. He grimaced and pulled his arms upward, almost tossing Chin and Api away from him.

"Still have some fight in you, do you, you black bastard!" Geoff sent another vicious blow into Si Tundok's face. Then another. And Another.

Si Tundok thrashed wildly and tried to extricate himself from the mass of bodies pinning him to the ground. He felt the blood pouring from his wound and fought to retain his precarious hold on consciousness but, like a drowning man, he sank into a sea of darkness.

"Your English friend, he knows this man?" Api asked of Chin.

Chin explained. When he finished, Api grinned wryly and looked at Geoff. "Chin, tell the white man that I give the Rajah's Malay to him to kill."

When Chin conveyed the message in English to Geoff, Geoff returned Api's wicked smile with one of his own.

"Give me your knife, Chin," Geoff said, his yellow teeth now fully exposed from the size of his grin. Geoff then straddled Si Tundok and took Si Tundok's head by the hair and pressed the blade to Si Tundok's throat.

"Kill him! Cut his throat!" Chin prompted when it appeared that Geoff was hesitating to draw the knife across Si Tundok's neck.

A deep throated-chuckle escaped Geoff's mouth. "No, not yet. Cutting his throat is too easy for this one. I've got me a better idea."

"You must kill him. *Awang* Api has ordered it," Chin cried. He glanced at Api who seemed to be watching the event with detached delight.

"Not to worry, Chin. I'll kill him all right. But not until he feels what it's like to be a cripple."

Geoff held up his maimed hand for all to see. "See this? This here is the bloody bastard that did this to me. Now I'm going to make him pay." Geoff released his grasp on Si Tundok's hair and Si Tundok's head crashed to the ground. Then he took Si Tundok's right arm and stretched it out, palm down, and held it fast against the ground. With Chin's knife, he pressed the blade against Si Tundok's thumb and pushed, severing the thumb from the joint.

Si Tundok stirred and cried out against the sudden intrusion of pain, but he was too weak to resist.

Still Geoff was not satisfied. One by one, he cut off each of the fingers of Si Tundok's right hand until the hand was no more than a bloody stump. "That ought to teach you to muck with me, you frigging half-breed."

Api was only mildly appalled by the brutality of the torture, but it didn't show. It simply confirmed what he believed about the white foreigners, they were all a barbaric lot. "Finish him," Api said in a soft but commanding tone of voice.

"Finish him," Chin chimed in English. "Cut his throat."

"Sure, I'll finish him," Geoff said, an evil grin pressed against his rotten teeth. "But he's going to suffer a bit more first. When I'm done with him, he won't even be decent fish food."

Geoff settled on his knees and bent over Si Tundok. He placed the tip of Chin's knife against the center of Si Tundok's bare chest and pushed it into his sternum. If Si Tundok felt the pain of the knife slicing his flesh, he gave no sign of it.

Slowly, Geoff drew the knife in a line through Si Tundok's chest from his sternum to his navel, making a surgical cut nearly a half inch deep. "I'm going to gut you, duffer," Geoff spewed. "But not so's you'll die right away."

When he finished with the cut, Geoff dropped the knife and with each of his hands, he peeled away the flesh from Si Tundok's abdomen so that his viscera was exposed to the morning light. Satisfied with his morbid surgery, Geoff stood up. "Give me a hand, Chin. We're going to feed what's left of him to the fish." Geoff grabbed Si Tundok by the shoulders while Chin reached down and took Si Tundok's legs and the two men carried him to the dock.

Swaying in the arms of his captors, Si Tundok momentarily regained consciousness. He felt a searing pain in his chest and abdomen and imagined reaching for it with the invisible fingers of his right hand, but he was too weak. His eyes rolled open in time to catch a fleeting glimpse of four bodies suspended by their feet from the branch of a tree. They were all headless.

Si Tundok knew then what happened to the *Datu* Temanggong and his warriors. Before he blacked out again, he caught sight of Lutu's pirates huddling around him and vociferously cheering on his captors. Si Tundok's last sensation was of being flung wildly through the air.

## II

11:50 A.M.
June 20, 1826
Kuching, Sarawak

"Rajah James, Rajah James, wake up." Kameja gently pushed on James' shoulder. She was surprised to find him fully clothed. Pages of a letter lay scattered at the side of his cot.

"Elizabeth?" James threw open his eyes and shot up in bed at the sound of the softly prodding feminine voice calling his name. Blankly, he stared at Kameja's puzzled face and realized he had been dreaming. Then he saw the pages of his mother's letter littering the floor and sadly understood that his nightmare had been real.

"*Tuan* Henry, the white man you spoke of is here to see you, Rajah James."

"Henry?" James rubbed at his face trying to massage the confusion from his mind. "What time is it?"

"Almost mid-day, Rajah. You must have been very tired," Kameja said and then helped James to his feet. "I will bring you clean clothing and carry water for your bath."

"Later, Kameja. Where is Henry?"

"Waiting for you in the kitchen. I gave him something to eat."

"Very good, thank you." James touched her affectionately on the cheek. "I'll see Henry, and then I'll clean up."

Henry was consuming the last of the meal Kameja had prepared for him when James entered the kitchen. "Henry, it is good to see you." James hadn't expected Henry to return from the Iban territory for at least another two weeks, the time they estimated it would take to complete construction of the outpost.

The two men shook hands and Henry surveyed James with mock disgust. "You look bloody awful for a king," he said through a mouthful of cold rice. "Has that pretty little wench who fixed lunch for me been wearing you out?"

James forced a smile and sat down at the table opposite Henry. "Just a bad night." He yawned and brushed his hands through his hair. "What about you? I hadn't expected you to return this early. Is the outpost finished already?"

Henry shook his head and pushed his now empty bowl of rice to the center of the table. "We're making progress on the fort, but it's still not finished.

But, I thought I'd better let you know what happened at Bintulu the other night."

James looked up with concern. "Kayan?"

"No, everything's quiet on the Barum and along the Bintulu River, but the Malay coastal village of Bintulu was razed by pirates the night before last."

"Pirates! Are you sure?"

Henry nodded. "We spotted the village burning the night it happened so I took a few of the Iban with me and we went downriver to check it out. By the time we got there, most of the village was burned to the ground."

"And the people?" James asked anxiously.

"A lot of them were killed. Many of the women and girls had been raped, but, fortunately, the majority of the villagers managed to escape into the jungle during the attack."

"Damn!" James exclaimed.

"That's not the worst of it, James," Henry said.

"Oh?"

"We interrogated a few of the survivors and they told us that Api was with the pirates."

"Api...with the pirates?" James thought about it for a moment knowing it made sense. He said, "They were probably right. I remember how angry Jau was that Api had misled him about our forces and he mentioned that Api had gone to Marudu Bay."

"Marudu Bay? That's the big pirate refuge in the Spanish zone of North Borneo, isn't it?"

"Yes, it is. And there's nothing we can do about it. And if Api's with the pirates, that can only signal more trouble."

Henry observed James for a moment and thought how much James had changed since coming to Sarawak. James was no longer the gallantly handsome and enthusiastically effusive man he once knew. Sarawak had transformed him. James had aged before his time; he was gaunt and drawn and whereas his flashing blue eyes previously radiated an eager confidence, they now appeared dull and haunted. Henry feared that Sarawak would eventually break James if it hadn't already.

"James, is it all worth it?" Henry asked, sincerely concerned.

"What do you mean, Henry?"

Henry shrugged and tossed his palms in the air. "I don't know James...it just seems that there's just one bloody problem after another. If it isn't the raids, it's the headhunting, if not the headhunting, it's Api or the pirates and on and on. I'm not sure there will ever be an end to it."

James nodded slowly and massaged his furrowed brow with his fingers. "I'll admit it's been more difficult than I initially thought it would be,

Henry," James confessed. "No doubt about it. But we are making some progress." James told Henry about Parliament's decision to provide partial naval protection on the coastal waters of Brunei and Sarawak and the arrival of the Claygates, but he didn't relate anything about his knighthood.

"Well, that's something, anyway, James," Henry said, referring to the Protectorate, but his doubts about ever taming this wild country still lingered. "But I fear you will never solve the pirate problem until you can figure out a way to destroy Marudu Bay."

"I'm afraid you're right, Henry," James sighed.

"By the way, James...the villagers we talked to at Bintulu said that when the pirates left, they may have been heading this way. Have you seen or heard anything of them?"

James shook his head. "No, but I don't think they would be foolish enough to sail into Kuching, not with the cannons of the *Skimalong* and the *Jolly Bachelor* sitting in the harbor.

Henry nodded. "You're probably right," he said. Then Henry brightened some and added, "It was good to see the *Skimalong*. I talked briefly with Captain Irons before I came over here. It was good to see him again." Then, somewhat of an afterthought, Henry asked, "Say, come to think of it, I haven't seen Si Tundok?"

James raised his eyebrows. "Damn, I almost forgot" he said.

"What's wrong, James?" Henry asked.

"I sent Si Tundok and the *Datu* Temanggong to Sin Bok yesterday morning." James explained the purpose of the trip to Henry. "I rather expected they would be back by now."

"Do you think they may have run into some sort of trouble?" the Welshman asked with sudden concern.

"I doubt it," James replied. "Things are generally always quiet upriver from Kuching." However, James recalled his uneasiness prior to the departure of the *Datu* Temanggong and Si Tundok the previous day and the same uncomfortable feeling returned. "But maybe we should check it out anyway, Henry."

Both men rose simultaneously from the table. Neither of them expressed it, but there was a sense of apprehension in the air—perhaps it was the discussion of the pirates or the mention of Api's name—in either case, both James and Henry felt it.

As James quickly stepped back to his private quarters to retrieve his muskets and sword, he called back to Henry. "Henry, you had best go back to the dock and send word to Captain Irons that there may be pirates in the vicinity. Have Captain Periweg put the crew of the *Jolly Bachelor* on alert too."

James emerged from his quarters fastening his leather girdle around his waist. "I'll gather up some Malay warriors and a few *praus* and meet you at the dock."

III

The Sarawak River
Below Sin Bok

Si Tundok's body sank into the depths of the murky river before being gripped by the cool currents and carried downstream and away from the boat dock at Sin Bok and the eyes of his tormentors.

Like a molecular masseuse, the cool water enveloped him, caressing his wounds and massaging his head until Si Tundok stirred from the depths of his unconsciousness. His head throbbed from the lack of oxygen, but the cold water and a bolt of pain shooting through his midsection revived him enough to realize he was drowning.

Si Tundok called upon whatever reserve of energy his battered body could find and began to kick his legs enough to fight the current that was carrying him away from one death and into the depths of another. Finally, his head bobbed through the surface of the river and his mouth opened and he swallowed gulp after gulp of precious air. Again he called upon the reservoir of his great strength and managed to stay afloat by lying on his back and flailing his legs. His mind struggled to ignore the pain in his hand, chest and back. As the cool water began to numb his wounds, Si Tundok slowly began to comprehend what his captors had done to him.

Gradually, deliberately, using every muscle his wavering mind could command, Si Tundok kicked against the river's current until he found himself sucked into a slow-moving eddy which swirled his floating body against a shallow mud bar near the shore. Exhausted, he only found enough strength to reach out with his good hand and pull his upper body onto the mud flat while his hips and legs dangled in the eddy. He shoved the stump of his right hand into the cool mud and packed it tightly to stop the bleeding. For a long while he lay there, sucking in huge gasps of moist air and gathering his strength.

The rising sun warmed his back and soon a swarm of mosquitoes nipped at his arms and shoulders, forcing Si Tundok to roll to his side and swipe at the pests with his good hand. He swallowed more air and slowly opened his eyes. His mind was a kaleidoscope of pain and confusion and he couldn't tell himself how long he had been lying on the mud flat. Tentatively, as if afraid to let his eyes confirm what his brain had already accepted, Si Tundok pulled his right arm from its muddy tomb and stared unbelievingly at the mud-caked stump of his hand. He flung his head backwards and moaned at the sight of his mutilation.

Weak, but still alive, his self pity turned to anger and with a supreme effort, Si Tundok rolled himself onto his back and exposed the long gash on his torso to the sun. With his good hand, he delicately touched the long wound. His viscera bulged through the slit in his abdomen, but strangely, he felt no pain from the wound. For a moment Si Tundok seemed transfixed by the sight of the wound and watched the movement of his internal organs rise and fall in rhythm to his heartbeat. Only the thin membranes which attached each of the organs to the inside of his muscles prevented them from spilling out across his waist.

Si Tundok believed he was a dead man, it was simply a matter of time. But as long as there was a pulse of life left in him, Si Tundok resolved to expend every effort to make his way to Kuching and warn James of the impending assault. Perhaps it was already too late. Maybe he had lain in the mud for more than a day? He didn't know, but to lie there and wait for death to grip him was not in Si Tundok's nature.

With his good hand, Si Tundok scraped away a handful of mud and packed it against the incision on his stomach, more to cover the wound from his own eyes than to stop the inconsequential bleeding slowly oozing from the wound. When he finished, he packed the stump of his severed right hand in the same manner. There was nothing he could do about the knife wound in his back. With his arm holding his internal organs in, he pushed himself to a sitting position. He moaned as he pulled his legs from the water and began to inch his way from the mud flat to the river bank.

When he reached a stand of dense grass by the bank, he rested a few minutes and glanced upward at the position of the sun in the sky and determined that it was nearly noon. Holding his arm tightly around his stomach, he pulled in his legs and forced himself to his knees. He gasped with pain and began to swoon, but still managed to stand upright and stagger to the edge of the forest. He examined a clump of *nippa* palms growing near the water and shuffled to one of the larger ones after seeing that its partially exposed roots had been eaten away by ants and beetles. He leaned his broad shoulders against the trunk of the palm and pushed with his legs. The pithy tree snapped at its rotten roots and toppled over with its palms crashing into the river.

Si Tundok stepped into the water next to the palm tree. With his stump, he held his innards while he pulled the downed tree into the eddy. Immediately, the tree bobbed along the surface of the water and began to float away from the bank. Si Tundok grabbed a handful of palm branches and hoisted himself onto the tree by straddling its stubby trunk with his legs and resting his chest and abdomen on the broad expanse of palm boughs. He kicked his feet until the tree gained momentum and floated beyond the eddy and into the river's swift current. He began to drift downriver, towards Kuching, but the effort had been too much. Already the water splashing against the *nippa* palm eroded away the mud he had packed around his abdomen and hand and his freshly exposed wounds began to throb with renewed vigor and Si Tundok again slipped into unconsciousness.

## IV

Kuching, Sarawak

Just as James and Henry were leaving the palace, a Malay warrior came running toward them. His chest heaved heavily when he reached them and he pointed excitedly towards the river. "The Bidayuh, *Tua* Endap, has *Tuan* Si Tundok in his *prau*. He is badly hurt!"

Together, the three of them sprinted to the dock. Endap had just finished tying off his *prau* when the three of them arrived and James and Henry spotted Si Tundok's body lying in the *prau* amidst the breadfruit and durian Endap was bringing to the Kuching market.

"Mother of God!" Henry wheezed when he caught sight of Si Tundok's mutilated body.

"My God!" James exclaimed. "Quickly, go fetch the white doctor!" he commanded of the Malay warrior.

Henry had already jumped into the *prau* and was examining Si Tundok. "He's still alive," he said.

James joined Henry in the *prau*. "Endap, give us a hand. We need to lift him out of the boat."

"Carefully..." James remanded as the three of them struggled to place Si Tundok on the dock. With as much care as they could muster, they laid Si Tundok down and both Henry and James knelt beside their broken friend. Si Tundok was unconscious and his breathing was shallow. Revulsion formed on Henry's face when he noticed the full extent of Si Tundok's wounds. "My God in Heaven, who could have done such a thing?" he breathed, unbelievingly.

James shook his head and looked to the Bidayuh leader for an explanation. "Do you know what happened, Endap?"

Endap shook his head that he didn't and related that he was on his way to Kuching to market his jungle produce when he found Si Tundok floating on a *nippa* palm.

Arthur arrived, followed by Margaret, Kameja and a contingent of Malay who had also been summoned. Arthur didn't ask for details. A single glance at the severed hand and the incision in Si Tundok's chest told him the man was near death. "Hurry, take him to my *rumah*." He called back to Margaret, "Boil some water, Margaret, and find some clean linens that we can make bandages out of. Quickly!"

Sensing the urgency in the doctor's voice, Kameja joined Margaret and the two of them raced back to the *rumah* to follow Arthur's instructions.

With the aid of Endap and a few of the Malay who had gathered, James and Henry gently hoisted their friend from the dock and carried him to Arthur's borrowed *rumah*. Arthur instructed them to place Si Tundok on his and Margaret's bed while he grabbed his medical bag and expeditiously examined the severity of Si Tundok's wounds.

"How bad is it, Arthur?" James asked, his voice still stunned by the event.

"Will he make it?" Henry asked on the heels of James' question,

"It's not good," Arthur replied. "We'll need to clean him up first, determine the extent of the injuries...then I'll have a better idea."

Margaret, carrying a bowl of hot water followed by Kameja carrying strips of clean linens, pushed by Henry and James. Margaret, used to the surgical process, told them, "Perhaps it would be better if you and your friend wait outside while we clean him up, James."

James and Henry didn't immediately leave. Both of them continued to stare blankly at Si Tundok, unable to accept the horrific site their eyes conveyed to them.

"Go on, James. You can't do anything for him now," Arthur said, rising and placing a gentle hand on James' shoulder. "I'll do everything I can for him."

James and Henry reluctantly left the room and walked mutely out the door. In shock, they sat on the steps of the *rumah* and pondered what could possibly have happened to Si Tundok and who could have inflicted such terrible wounds upon him.

James wrestled with an emerging sense of guilt for having sent Si Tundok and the *Datu* Temanggong to Sin Bok. He recalled the strange apprehension he had felt at the dock when they departed. *Why didn't I go with them? Why did I not insist that they take a larger force? Why had I sent them in the first place?* Si Tundok lay dying and James couldn't help but blame himself. In Singapore, he should not have encouraged Si Tundok and Henry to join him. After obtaining Sarawak from Hasim, he should have listened to Henry and looted the country instead of becoming involved in the internal affairs of Sarawak, he remanded himself. And now this had happened and it was all his fault. James held his head and eyes in the palms of his hands and fought back the tears of remorse welling in the corners of his eyes.

After a short while, Henry, deep in his own thoughts, withdrew from the porch of the *rumah* and sat against a palm tree removed from James. Unlike James, there were no tears for Henry, only a growing anger.

Both men maintained their private thoughts separate from one another as they waited for Arthur to report on Si Tundok's condition. Hours seemed to pass. Long shadows crept against the ground and grimly reaped away the fading sunlight when Arthur finally emerged from the *rumah*. Simultaneously, James and Henry rose to their feet and eyed the surgeon with quiescent apprehension.

Arthur's face was strained and had a dire cast to it. He wiped his blood stained hands on a piece of torn cloth and looked into James' and Henry's expectant faces. "I've done everything I can for him," he said in a hushed voice which offered no encouragement.

"He's dead?" James asked, his voice barely audible.

Arthur shook his head slowly. "Not yet," he sighed. "But he's lost so much blood and his wounds are extensive. He's very weak. I'm afraid it's just a matter of time...I'm very sorry."

James lowered his head and rubbed his forehead and eyes. He touched the railing along the side of the *rumah's* steps to steady himself. Henry approached the bottom of the steps. "Is he conscious, doctor?" he asked, hopeful that he could say all the things he thought about saying to his friend before it was too late.

Arthur shook his head. "No, he never awakened."

"Can we see him, Arthur?" James asked.

"Of course." Arthur stepped to the side of the doorway and ushered the two men into the *rumah*. Arthur had never met Si Tundok or Henry, but he remembered James' previous discussions of the men and knew they were both held in the highest regard by James. Arthur sighed deeply. *If only Si Tundok had been brought to him sooner, before he had lost so much blood. If only he were a better surgeon...if only...*

With trepidation and a grave sense of dread, James and Henry quietly approached the side of Si Tundok's bed. Kameja and Margaret had washed the mud and grime from Si Tundok and his chest and back were bandaged. His wrapped stump lay limp by his side. His breathing was barely perceptible.

James knelt near Si Tundok's head. He saw for the first time that Si Tundok's head had been bludgeoned. Tears welled in James' eyes and he reached out his hand and tenderly touched Si Tundok's swollen and battered face.

Henry stood at the side of the bed and stared incomprehensibly at each of his friend's wounds. Slowly, his sadness evolved into anger and then rage. He dropped to his knees by the side of the bed and grabbed Si Tundok's good hand and gripped it tightly. "Who did this to you, Si Tundok? For God's sake, say something. Tell me who did this thing to you. I swear, I'll find them...I promise you, I'll find them!"

James reached out and wrapped his arm around Henry's heaving shoulders to comfort him. "We'll find them, Henry, I promise you...and when we do—"

Henry slapped away James' arm and shot to his feet. "Leave me be!" he shouted vehemently. Henry's lips were drawn downward in an angry scowl and his tear-stained eyes, red and swollen, blazed in sudden anger. "You and your pathetic promises, where have they gotten us?" he spat. "Look at him, James! That's where your promises led!"

Henry turned abruptly and moved with enraged strides to the doorway. He grabbed the frame of the door with his hands and held himself motionless for a moment with his back towards James and his head lowered. He didn't turn, but in a cold slow voice said, "We should have never come here, James. You and your high-bred ideas about civilizing this damnable place. We should have walked out on you when we had the chance and left you on your own in this God forsaken land." Henry lifted his head and turned slightly. "None of this would have happened...Si Tundok would—" Unable to finish the outpouring of his emotions, Henry pounded against the frame of the door with his fists and ran from the room, leaving James alone with Si Tundok.

Henry's words sliced through James with the force of a cutlass. Stunned, he felt Henry's accusations pierce his heart and the pain that hurt the most was the pain of knowing that Henry spoke the truth. Why had he changed his original plans and then involved the two of them in it? It was vanity, he told himself. The title of a Rajah was too much for him to resist. It had almost led to Henry's death at Long Akar and it might well result in Si Tundok's death. James covered his eyes and sobbed. "Good God, what have I done?" He gently reached out and touched Si Tundok's face. "Forgive me, please... forgive me," he muttered through trembling lips.

But Si Tundok's sallow cheeks were cool to James' touch and James realized that his friend could never forgive him. Si Tundok was dead.

# V

### Rajah's Palace
### Kuching, Sarawak

James remained disconsolate behind the door of his private bedroom at the palace, refusing to receive condolences of Timothy Irons or the Claygates. Margaret brought by a freshly cooked curry and rice and although James had not eaten the entire day, he refused to acquiesce to Kameja's pleas and remained steadfastly alone within the confines of his room.

James preferred to deal with his grief alone, blanketed only by the solitary darkness which enveloped him. He sat on the edge of his cot and stared vacuously through the window and watched the blood-red moon stare accusingly down at him. He had made so many mistakes, he told himself. And all of them in the pursuit of a childish dream to find fortune at the edge of the Empire. He mentally tortured himself for his vanity and his foolhardiness. To think he could bring his own altruistic notions of justice and civilization to such a savage land. He had not only fooled himself, but more importantly, he had brought harm to others; Si Tundok, most likely the *Datu* Temanggong, the hundreds of warriors who had died at Long Akar, not to mention the men who were killed at Siniawan.

And there was Elizabeth too. In his self-deprecating mood, James also accepted blame and responsibility for being the cause of her death as well. Like grim reminders of his vanity, the multitude of dead marched through his head, deepening his grief and exacerbating his guilt.

James barely heard the soft rap of tiny knuckles against his bedroom door.

"Rajah James?" Kameja spoke softly. "Rajah, your friend, *Tuan* Henry wishes to speak with you."

"Send him away. I have no friends."

Undaunted by James' morose behavior since he returned from the Claygate's *rumah*, Kameja cracked open the door to James' bedroom and stepped into the dark interior. She stepped quietly to James' side, but he didn't acknowledge her presence. "*Tuan* Henry is still your friend, Rajah James. He shares your grief as we all do. Perhaps it would be good for you to speak with him." Kameja knelt at James' feet and tenderly placed her small hands on his.

"It's no use," James said. His voice sounded far, far away. "It's too late for talk now. Tell him to leave me be."

319

Kameja studied James with compassionate eyes. She knew how much Si Tundok meant to him and she remembered how distraught he was after returning from the slaughter at Long Akar. Here was a man who felt his grief deeply and his grief was for all the men whose deaths he felt responsible for. James was like no other man she had ever known; kind, sympathetic and gentle. She couldn't allow his depression to overwhelm him. Sarawak needed such a man—she needed such a man.

Kameja's voice was soft and tender when she next spoke. "I know in my heart that *Tuan* Henry is your friend, Rajah James. His heart feels the same pain as does yours. You must speak with him, share your grief with one another...it will make your heart heal itself sooner."

James slowly lifted his head and looked into Kameja's pretty face. The moonlight framed her head against the darkness of the room, forming an aura around her face and giving her a sensorial beauty that he had never noticed before. He reached out and touched her softly on the side of her face with the tips of his fingers. He thought of how much Kameja had given to him and he realized for the first time how much she meant to him. Her angelic face made him understand, that without him, she would still be a slave, bound forever to the wishes and desires of another human being. It made him think of Rentab and of Jau who had both agreed to stop their tribal feuds, giving new hope for the future of their small country. Maybe it had been for the better after all. Maybe something good would rise from the ashes of all the death, misery and pain.

James gazed tenderly at Kameja. Somehow she had made him understand so many elusive things by her very presence. Gently, he tilted her chin with his hand and pulled her to him. She didn't resist. He kissed her softly on the forehead. Kameja continued to raise her head toward him until her full lips touched his. He kissed her on the lips, this time passionately.

James knew then that he loved her. He loved Kameja for her innocence, her understanding and her vulnerability. He loved her in the same way that he loved this savage land and its primitive people. Reluctantly, he allowed his hands to fall away from Kameja's face. "Tell Henry that I will see him," he said. They exchanged a brief, knowing smile with one another before Kameja rose to her feet and exited the room.

Henry was pacing in a tight circle near the kitchen table when Kameja returned and announced that James would see him shortly.

"Thank God," Henry sighed as Kameja turned and disappeared just as James entered the room.

The two men stood silently facing one another for a long moment; James tall, lean and grim, Henry short, haggard and nervous. Henry broke the silence. "James, I...I came here to apologize." He drooped his head and shook it from side to side. "I had no call to speak to you the way I did. I'm truly sorry. I didn't mean what I said." His eyes looked up at James. They were sincere eyes and they begged for James' forgiveness.

James stepped forward and then stopped. "You had every right to say what you did, Henry. It was the truth. If I hadn't made the choices I made, none of this would have happened and Si Tundok would still be alive."

Henry peered steadily into James' sad blue eyes. "James," he said. "Si Tundok made his own choice to stay here, you didn't make it for him. I didn't understand that this afternoon when I said what I did, but I do now. Si Tundok didn't stay because of you, James, he stayed because of what you represented to him."

James tilted his head in puzzlement.

"These were his people, James. He was one of them. For the first time in his life, Si Tundok really felt as if he belonged somewhere. He believed in you and what you were trying to do." Henry shook his head emphatically from side to side. "No one could have guessed what was going to happen, not even Si Tundok. And I'm convinced that if Si Tundok were alive right now and was asked to make the choice all over again, he would make the same choice as he did then." Henry stared apologetically into James' eyes. "And so would I," he said with emphasis.

Henry extended his open hand to James. "Please accept my apology, James. I was bloody wrong to say the things I said."

James reached out and gratefully took Henry's hand and shook it. He smiled and drew Henry close to him and clasped Henry around his narrow shoulders and asked, "Friends?"

"Friends," Henry beamed. "Till the end."

# CHAPTER FOURTEEN

## I

2:15 A.M.
*The Jolly Bachelor*
Kuching, Sarawak

Following a lengthy conversation in which James and Henry reaffirmed that they would seek out and punish Si Tundok's murderers, Henry retired for the night aboard the *Jolly Bachelor*. Henry greeted the ship's two night watchmen and then went below the forecastle deck where the ship's skeleton crew slept. He found an empty bunk and without undressing, climbed into it. Henry lay there for a long time with his eyes open and listened to the snores of the sleeping crew and of the waves slapping rhythmically against the hull of the otherwise silent ship.

Henry reflected on his earlier conversation with James and the reaffirmation of their friendship with one another and of their vow to find Si Tundok's killers. "We'll find them, Si Tundok," Henry whispered in the darkness. "And we will make them pay for what they did to you."

Even as Henry lay on the cot confirming his vow of revenge, the man responsible for Si Tundok's death was aboard one of Lutu's triremes and was rapidly approaching the two ships anchored in the harbor.

II

The Jungle
Kuching, Sarawak

Api and Loi Pek led the well armed Hakkas overland from Sin Bok to the outskirts of Kuching. They had followed an obscure trail occasionally used by Bidayuh traders to reach Kuching during the monsoon season when the river was swelled with rain and unnavigable. From their position at the edge of the jungle, Api and Loi Pek could easily view the disorderly array of *rumahs* that comprised Kuching and the two ships nestled quietly in the harbor.

Kuching was silent. The two ships anchored in the harbor swayed gently near one another, rocked by the steady roll of waves cuffing their hulls. Lanterns fore and aft on each of the two ships were the only signs of life aboard them. To their left, slightly beyond the main community, was the Rajah's palace. It was totally dark.

"Remember, Loi Pek, it is up to you to burn Kuching and create confusion. But don't begin your attack until Lutu's men have taken the ships and disabled the guns, then rush the town and kill any who resist."

Loi Pek nodded wearily. Api had explained the plan many times and he was as tired of hearing it as was his aging body tired from the long and arduous overland march from Sin Bok to Kuching. Loi Pek still maintained reservations about participating in the coup. But, as Api had so convincingly stated, without his gold mines, Loi Pek had no power and he was willing to risk everything to keep hold of his precious mines and his power.

"There may be some white devils in the village," Api said. "When you find them, kill them. None of them must escape, is that clear, Chinaman?"

Lines of worry furrowed the old Chinaman's brow between the prominent folds of sagging skin and wrinkles along his forehead. Noting Loi Pek's dour expression, Api said, "Don't worry, old man, Kuching sleeps. By the time you torch the town and kill all the white devils, the Rajah will be dead and I will announce it to the *pangirins*. They will have no choice but to accept me as Rajah. It is our law.

Risking Api's displeasure, Loi Pek asked, "And if you fail to kill the white Rajah?"

Annoyed with the old man's reticence and constant complaints, Api grabbed Loi Pek's arm and squeezed. He looked down at the withered Chinaman and jerked him close to his face so that even in the shallow light of the moon, Loi Pek could read the anger on Api's face and hear the malice in his voice when he spoke. "The Rajah will not escape me, old man! Just do as you are told!"

Api eased his hold on the Chinaman's arm when he recognized that Loi Pek was sufficiently intimidated. His lips curled into a placating smile, but his eyes remained filled with fire. "This is the only way. Once I control Sarawak, it will be a simple matter to eliminate my pig of a brother. Without the English ships, Hasim is nothing. I will be Sultan within the month and things will return to the way they once were. That's what we all want, isn't it, Chinaman—a return to the old ways?"

Loi Pek nodded that it was.

"Very well," Api said, releasing the old Chinaman's arm. "Stay here where your men can't be seen and watch for Lutu's signal. I am going to the palace and kill the white devil. Are you clear on what must be done, Loi Pek?"

"Yes."

"Then see to it that it is done swiftly." Api turned away from Loi Pek and darted towards the palace carrying a war shield in one hand and a *parang* in the other.

III

Rajah's Palace
Kuching, Sarawak

James found himself filled with a new optimism about his role in the future of Sarawak following his earlier conversations with Kameja and Henry. Following Henry's departure, Kameja doused the oil lamps and joined James in his bedroom. They made love without a word being spoken, as if the act itself was an affirmation of James' renewed commitment to Sarawak and its people. And then James slept, untroubled by the events of the past and soothed by the hope of a new future.

It was Kameja who awakened at the sound of a muffled noise coming from the front of the palace. Thinking Henry had returned, she quietly rose from the bed, careful not to awaken James from his peaceful slumber and silently stepped across the small room. She eased open the door and listened again for the sound which had disturbed her. There was nothing.

Kameja stepped through the doorway and carefully closed the door behind her. She slowly picked her way along the corridor and approached the partition which separated the throne room from the other rooms in the palace. Soundless in her tiny bare feet, she reached the partition and stopped. She could hear the sound of heavy breathing. She pressed closer against the wall and slowly peeked her head around the side of the partition.

A man stood in the open doorway to the throne room, his dark outline silhouetted against the moonlight flooding through the entry way. His head slowly scanned the room from side to side as if he were allowing time for his eyes to adjust to the darkened interior. She saw that the man's muscular chest heaved as if he were catching his breath or trying to repress a growing excitement. He held a war shield in one hand and a *parang* in his other.

"Api!" Kameja gasped, then pushed her hands to her mouth to stifle her surprise.

Api's head snapped to the direction of the almost imperceptible sound that had escaped Kameja's lips. He raised his shield in front of him and gripped his *parang* tighter. With the stealth of a predator, he moved toward her.

## IV

*The Jolly Bachelor*
Kuching, Sarawak

Unable to sleep, Henry was distracted from his solitary thoughts by the sound of a hollow thump emanating near the quarter deck hatch. He rolled his head to the side and separated out the rasping noise of the ship's sleeping crew and listened for the sound of the thump to repeat itself. When it didn't, Henry relaxed and began to settle back down in his bunk.

But another sound reached his ears. It sounded like the footfalls of bare feet scampering along the main deck. Henry swung his legs from the bunk and stood in the narrow space between the row of double-decked cots and strained to hear a confirmation of the sound he was certain he heard. Again, the sound of running feet.

Henry quickly stepped to the stairs leading from the forecastle crew's quarters to the main deck. He climbed the stairs and eased open the hatch so that only his eyes peered between the overhead door and the hatch opening. Directly opposite the forecastle hatch was a closed cargo bay. A man lay face up, sprawled over the edge of it. A dark shaft protruded from the man's chest. It was Captain Periweg.

Henry's eyes didn't linger on the dead captain. Beyond the cargo hold, he spotted movement. Although barely discernible in the dark, the deck lanterns were enough for Henry to discern that many men, dark skinned and naked were pouring over the main deck railing and scattering along the ship's deck.

*Pirates! The ship's been boarded!* Henry shut the hatch and battened it from the inside and backed quickly down the steps to the crew bunks. As quietly as he could, he moved down the narrow isle between the bunks and roused the sleeping crew. He cautioned them to maintain their silence by pressing his finger to his lips and whispering, "Pirates! Grab whatever weapons you can find. The ship's been boarded."

# V

*HMS Skimalong*
Kuching, Sarawak

When Henry had arrived in Kuching the day before and had his short conversation with Captain Irons prior to going to the palace, he had mentioned what transpired at Bintulu and informed Timothy that there may be pirates in the area. As a precaution, Captain Irons had doubled the midnight watch aboard the *Skimalong* with Second Officer Harris in charge.

"Anything?" Harris asked the bridge watchman.

"As quiet as a church mouse, sir," came the reply.

"Keep a sharp eye out. There may be pirate craft in the vicinity."

"Aye, sir."

Second Officer Harris, his hands clasped together behind his back, rocked back and forth on the heels of his feet and scanned the dark river. He had volunteered to take the night watch, hoping that pirates would dare a night assault against the *Skimalong* or try to run by her guns. His brief initiation under fire with James at Siniawan had whetted his youthful appetite for glory and he wanted more. He didn't have long to wait.

A crewman from the aft deck trotted toward him and called to him in a course whisper, "Mister Harris! Mister Harris!"

"What is it, man? Did you see something?"

"There's movement along the deck of the *Jolly Bachelor*, sir. Better have yourself a look."

Harris followed the crewman beyond the mainsail mast to the ship's port side railing and together they peered across the expanse of blackness which separated the *Skimalong* from the Rajah's ship.

"It doesn't seem right that they would muster the crew at this time of night unless they were having trouble. What do you make of it, sir?"

"I don't like the looks of it," Harris concurred. He could discern the outlines of men moving rapidly along the Jolly Bachelor's decks, but he couldn't see any indications that the ship was in difficulty. There was no noise, no shouts of panic or any other signs to hint that the Jolly Bachelor was doing anything more than completing a night time deck drill. Still, it seemed peculiar that Captain Periweg would disrupt the sleep of his small crew for a drill at this time of the night.

Harris couldn't see Lutu's triremes huddled against the far side of the *Jolly Bachelor's* hull.

"Awaken Captain Irons," he ordered to the crewman.

"Shall I sound the alarm, Mister Harris?"

"No, let's have the captain take a look first."

"Aye, aye, sir!" The sailor darted down the deck and disappeared through the hatch which led to Timothy's cabin.

Meanwhile, Harris drew his cutlass from its scabbard. Something was wrong aboard the Rajah's ship, he was sure of it. The young officer sensed trouble as sure as he sensed his own eagerness for battle.

"What is it, Mister Harris?" Captain Irons asked as he suddenly appeared at the second officer's side. Timothy's dark locks of hair were mussed and he was hastily fastening a row of brass buttons on his tunic.

"Could be trouble aboard the *Jolly Bachelor*, Captain." He pointed across the void which separated the two ships. "Appears to be a lot of deck activity...maybe a drill, sir?"

It only took Timothy one glance to know that the *Jolly Bachelor* was not conducting a drill. He knew that she carried a skeleton crew and there were more shadows crossing her deck than the entire total of her ship's company. "She's been boarded!"

"Shall I sound the alarm, sir?"

"No. Wake up the crew. Issue cutlasses and muskets and get them to their topside stations and prepare to repel boarders, Mister Harris."

"Aye, Captain!"

Before Harris could sprint away, Timothy called him back. "And Mister Harris," he said. "Do it quietly. I want to surprise the bastards if we can."

# VI

## *The Jolly Bachelor*

Lutu planned his approach to the two sleeping ships with precision. His triremes simply drifted near the dark background of the jungle and then approached the port side of the Rajah's ship. Once his triremes were against the hull of the Rajah's ship, they could no longer be seen by the watchmen on the larger vessel. Stealthily, a small contingent of his cutthroats crawled topside and secured the deck of the *Jolly Bachelor* and took out the unsuspecting night watchmen without incident. He then ordered his triremes to swing away from the shelter of the Jolly Bachelor's hull and make for the bigger ship while the men aboard the *Jolly Bachelor* sought out and killed the remainder of the ship's crew.

Lutu knew that he would be exposed for the brief distance he had to propel his boats between the Rajah's ship and the British man-of-war, but even if his triremes were detected, the British would not be able to use their cannon for fear of hitting the Rajah's ship and he felt confident that his superior numbers would overwhelm any opposition once the British ship was boarded.

As Lutu's triremes narrowed the distance to the *Skimalong*, Lutu's confidence soared. He expected to hear the clamor of alarm by now, but even as his men held the Malay boats against the rolling hull of the *Skimalong* and began to board her, there was nothing to indicate that his force had been spotted. Taking the two ships was going to be easier than he initially anticipated.

# VII

## Kuching
## The Jungle

Loi Pek saw musket flashes in the harbor and heard the reports of the gunfire a fraction of a second later. He waved his Hakka irregulars forward to raze Kuching as Api had instructed him to do. Loi Pek stood at the edge of the jungle and sullenly watched his army of insurgents race toward the sleeping village. He saw them for what they were; miners, farmers and laborers. But they had obeyed him without question, knowing that if anything should happen to them, the *Kapitan* would care for their families. It was their way, a tradition forged through centuries of unquestioned obedience to authority.

Loi Pek watched his force of nearly one-hundred Chinese pour into the unsuspecting town. Although well armed, his men looked more like a mob than a trained army and he knew that if they encountered resistance, many would perish. Knowing that he could not contribute anything more to the success of the raid, he shuffled near a fallen *bilian* tree and sat down upon it. After shifting himself slightly to command a better view of Kuching and the harbor, he reached into his *baju* and extracted a small brass container. The long march from Sin Bok reminded Loi Pek of his age and exhaustion and his arthritic joints screamed for relief. He flipped open the lid of the container and took a large pinch of the white powder and placed it on the tip of his tongue. Long experience with the opium told him that he would not need to wait long before the drug soothed his painful joints and reduced his anxiety. Within a few short moments a rush of euphoria washed through the old Chinaman's body, cleansing away his fatigue and pain. Loi Pek lifted his aged face and watched the flashes of musket fire on the British ship in the harbor and smiled. To him, it was Chinese New Year and he had a ring-side seat for the celebration.

# VIII

## The *Jolly Bachelor*

Henry gathered the *Jolly Bachelor's* crew of eighteen men at the bottom of the quarter-hatch stairway. The men had armed themselves with whatever weapons they could find; knives, broadswords, cutlasses and belay pins. None of them had muskets. Quickly, Henry explained the situation.

"Pirates have boarded the ship. Our only chance is to get topside and make a fight of it. Down here, we don't stand a chance." Henry's eyes flitted from one anxious face to another. No one said a thing. They realized the predicament they were in.

"All right, mates, let's have a go!" Henry unbattened the hatch and threw it open and led the crew in an upward sprint to the main deck. Once topside, Henry dove behind the shelter of the cargo hold where Captain Periweg had fallen and slid his cutlass from its scabbard in time to cut down a pirate about to leap upon him from the top of the cargo hold.

"Fight for your lives, men!" Henry screamed as the battle was joined in deadly man-to-man combat. Henry jumped to the top of the cargo bay and slashed wildly at two Dayaks running on the deck below him. He felt his cutlass penetrate soft flesh and heard a man scream, but in the darkness and confusion, he couldn't tell where his cutlass had caught the pirate. Like angry wasps, the pirates swarmed over the outnumbered crew of the *Jolly Bachelor* and Henry realized they would soon be overwhelmed if he didn't think of something to do and do it quickly.

Henry spotted a deck lantern suspended from a ratline and had an idea. He made a dash for it and cut it loose from the rope with his cutlass. He tossed the lantern onto the main deck and when it hit, the lantern exploded in a line of flame, reaching its fiery tentacles upward to feed upon the halyards drooping from the mainsail mast. Within moments, the fire crawled up the halyards and spread along the tucked and wrapped mainsails and began to consume the mainsail mast itself.

The fire lit up the deck like a funeral pyre, its growing flame embracing the antagonists and casting the eerie shadows of mayhem against the ship like a violent puppet show. The fire grew rapidly and effectively blocked a number of pirates, located aft of the flames, from reaching the melee. Some were already backing away from the conflagration and leaping into the safety of the river.

Henry was about to yell to the surviving crew to make for the starboard railing and abandon ship when he caught sight of a man dressed in European clothing moving near the bridge, opposite the barrier of flames. At first glance, Henry assumed the man was one of the ship's watchmen who had somehow miraculously escaped the pirate's initial assault.

Henry made a move toward the wall of flame and yelled for the man to jump overboard to save himself when he caught sight of a burly Chinaman near the man in European clothing. The rising flames illuminated the Chinaman's mutilated face and the thick scar which bisected his eyeball. Henry's eyes darted to the European. *Geoff!*

## IX

### *HMS Skimalong*

Captain Irons' bluejackets huddled against the *Skimalong's* port railing and waited for Timothy's signal. They could feel the hollow bumps of the Malay triremes brushing against the *Skimalong's* hull and knew that the pirates were crawling up the side of the ship.

Timothy waited until the first unsuspecting head appeared above the railing. "Now!" he yelled. He fired his musket pistol directly into the face of the surprised corsair, sending his body in a downward spiral to crash on one of Lutu's triremes below. As a unit, the bluejackets stood up and fired their muskets point blank into the startled faces of the boarding Dayaks. The bluejacket's first volley of fire cleared the hull of climbing pirates.

"Away the lines!" Timothy shouted while his bluejackets primed and packed their weapons. Upon hearing Timothy's command, seamen tossed ropes over the railing and stood with their broadswords and cutlasses at the ready, awaiting Timothy's next command. Timothy peered over the side of the ship. The Dayaks aboard the triremes were hastily trying to disengage. "Second volley...take aim...fire!" he commanded and a thunderous volley of shot dropped more of the scrambling Dayaks aboard Lutu's triremes. "Boarding party...forward!" Timothy commanded, and half of the Skimalong's crew climbed down the ropes and dropped themselves onto the decks of the pirate boats to engage the enemy.

From above, Second Officer Harris, directed the discretionary fire of the bluejackets who continued to pummel the Malay boats with lead pellets of death.

Timothy released his grip on the rope and dropped the last few feet to the deck of a trireme and rushed to the side of two of his men who were parrying with three Dayaks. The pirates, unnerved by the sudden swarm of Timothy's men, began to shrink away from the assault. Many panicked and abandoned the triremes altogether, others chose to fight to the death.

"Press to them, men!" Timothy yelled above the clamor. "Don't let them escape!" Timothy dashed toward an older Dayak warrior who had just hacked a sailor to death with his *parang* and was preparing to escape by diving into the river.

Lutu knew the situation was hopeless and he quickly searched for an opening amidst the confusion so he could hurl himself from the trireme and escape the onslaught, but an English officer had blocked his escape route. He searched for an alternative, but there was none. Lutu faced Timothy and screamed a bone-chilling war whoop and charged.

Timothy crouched and stood his ground, meeting Lutu's attack with a swipe of his cutlass. Like a cat, Lutu dodged the blade of Timothy's sword and slashed at Timothy's head with his *parang*. Timothy ducked the blow and stabbed at Lutu with his cutlass. Lutu jumped back, avoiding Timothy's blade, but he momentarily lost his balance. Before he could recover, Timothy swung his cutlass in an upward arc and the blade caught Lutu on the shoulder, severing it to the bone. Timothy followed up his attack with another swipe of his cutlass and this time his blade found Lutu's neck, severing his vocal cords and arteries. Lutu dropped his *parang* and slumped to his knees. He clutched at his throat and stared unbelievingly at his assailant as his life's blood streamed between his fingers. It was only then that Timothy recognized Lutu as the savage who had slaughtered the crew of the *Cecilia*. Without a moment of thought, he raised his cutlass above his head for the final killing blow.

"No! No!" Lutu's mind screamed. But the only sound that could be heard was the gurgle of blood from his severed throat.

As if splitting a stubborn block of oak, Timothy brought his cutlass down with all the force he could muster. The blade ripped through the top of Lutu's head, splitting it like a ripe melon. When Timothy pulled his blade from Lutu's skull, the pirate slumped backwards and fell, spilling the gore from the inside of his head to the trireme's deck.

Timothy, his chest heaving and his eyes blazing, quickly surveyed the action around him. Immediately he determined that his counter-attack had been successful and already his men were clearing the last of the Dayaks from the triremes as the bluejackets aboard the *Skimalong* picked off those who had jumped into the river.

"Captain Irons! Captain Irons!"

Timothy looked upward. "What is it, Mister Harris?"

"Kuching and the *Jolly Bachelor* are afire!"

## X

### Kuching, Sarawak

Loi Pek's mob of Hakkas raced through the uneven corridors between the Malay houses and set them afire. They fired their muskets indiscriminately into the houses and tossed torches onto the thatched roofs as they ran by. Malay, awakening in time to escape their burning houses, were descended upon by the mob and hacked to death with knives, scythes and garden hoes. Like an army of locusts, the Chinese moved as a single unit, surrounding each of the hapless Malay and cutting them down before moving on to torch the next house and falling upon its fleeing inhabitants.

Margaret heard the commotion and awakened with a start. "Arthur! Arthur!" She pushed her husband's shoulders and he began to stir. "Arthur, wake up! Something is happening!"

Arthur bolted upright in the bed. Shouts from the frenzied mob reached his ears and he leaped out of bed and ran to the window. "My God!" Arthur saw the flames of the burning *rumahs* illuminating the night sky and caught sight of the swarm of Chinese brandishing weapons and torches moving their way.

"Arthur, what is it? What is happening?" Margaret held a thin cotton blanket to her bosom. Her eyes were filled with fear.

Arthur, bare chested and wearing only his long flannel undergarment stepped away from the window. "I don't know," he said. "But we've got to get out of here!" He threw a blanket around his wife and pulled her from the bed. He wrapped an arm around her narrow waist and half-pushed and half-drug her to the rear of the *rumah*. He knocked open the shutters to the back wall's lone window and said. "Follow me, we'll have to jump!"

Arthur extended his legs out the window and pushed himself off the ledge. He dropped easily to the soft ground below and scrambled to his feet. He reached his arms out and shouted in a harsh whisper, "Jump, Margaret! I'll catch you!"

Margaret clutched the blanket tightly around her and climbed onto the window sill as she had seen Arthur do. She only hesitated a moment before she pushed herself away from the window and dropped into Arthur's waiting arms.

"Are you all right?" Arthur placed Margaret on the ground and ducked his head to peer under the stilts supporting the house to see how close the mob had come.

"Yes, I'm fine, Arthur, but what is happening?"

The mob was already approaching their *rumah*. Frantically Arthur surveyed their surroundings. The jungle was too far. Margaret would never make it. "Quick, in here!" Arthur lifted the lid to a huge clay water vessel used to collect rainwater from the roof of the *rumah*. It was only partially filled with water.

Margaret started to protest, but before she could voice her concern, Arthur had picked her up and hoisted her into the jar. "Whatever you do, stay put and stay quiet! I'll try to lead them away!" He pushed Margaret's head lower into the jar and quickly replaced the lid.

"Here I am you bloody heathens!" Arthur yelled and then he took off in a sprint towards the jungle.

Margaret heard Arthur and then she heard musket fire and the shout of the mob as they rushed by her hiding place in pursuit of her husband. She squeezed her hands over her mouth to silence her fear, closed her eyes and silently began to recite the Lord's Prayer.

Arthur ran as fast as his rotund body could carry him. There were more than fifty meters of open ground between himself and the safety of the jungle, but if he could reach the forest, he had a chance. He heard the whine of a lead musket ball breeze by his ear. Instinctively, he pulled his head in like a tortoise and kept running. A second musket ball grazed his shoulder and knocked him sideways but he didn't fall. He regained his stride without considering the extent of his wound and continued his sprint to the forest.

Arthur didn't stop when he reached the wall of the jungle. He crashed headlong into it, letting his momentum carry him through its leading edge until the dense foliage slowed his progress. Branches grabbed at his arms and face, thorns clawed at his bare feet and legs and creeping vines tried to trip him. Arthur stumbled, but he didn't fall. He pushed and tumbled against the thick jungle until the only sound he could hear was his own heavy breathing. The mob had not pursued him into the forest.

He collapsed beneath a *sago* palm and tried to refrain from breathing while he listened for confirmation that he had escaped. There was only the distant sound of burning thatch and bamboo, the shouts of the mob and sporadic gunfire. He breathed heavily and wiped the sweat from his face and eyes. He examined the wound on his shoulder and knew that it was not serious.

*Margaret!* Arthur pushed himself to his feet and made his way back to the edge of the forest. The *rumah* from which he fled was on fire and the mob was beginning to move on. He could clearly see the water vessel where Margaret was hidden. It had been tipped over but he couldn't tell if the lid was still on it. *Oh God, had they found her?* He wanted to bolt from the cover of the forest and race back to rescue her, but the situation demanded that he wait until the mob was diverted elsewhere and moved away from the burning building.

# XI

## The Jolly Bachelor

The fire aboard the deck of the *Jolly Bachelor* widened, consuming everything in its path. Already the surviving members of the ship's crew and the pirates were disengaging from the foray and saving themselves by leaping overboard to the river below.

Henry watched Chin and Geoff retreat aft of the ship as they tried to escape the conflagration. He glanced about, trying to think of some way to delay their escape. Henry caught sight of Captain Periweg's body and ran to it. With one foot holding the body to the cargo hold, he wrapped his hands around the shaft of the spear that had impaled the captain and jerked the spear from the captain's body. He sprinted toward the creeping wall of flame and hurled the spear through the fire and towards the fleeing pair.

Already Chin had reached the aft railing and had one leg straddled over it, preparing to jump. Geoff was right behind him when Henry's spear whistled by his head and plunged into Chin's back with a sickening thud. Chin screamed and slumped beside the railing, clutching the railing as if it were life itself. He rolled his head inward toward Geoff, his mutilated eye searching vacantly to discover the source of his death. Chin's hand released its grip on the railing and he dropped to the deck while a stream of blood from his torn lungs gurgled from the hole in his chest.

Henry grabbed a burning ratline hanging from the ship's main mast. With his feet straddling the port rail and his body leaning outward supported by the burning rope, he cat-walked the railing and swung around the wall of flame separating him from Geoff. "Geoff!" he screamed. With cutlass in hand, Henry now stood on the bridge to face the man who had eluded him and Si Tundok for so long.

Geoff swung around to the challenging call of his name. The light from the fire danced upon Henry's grim face and he looked like a banshee from hell itself.

Geoff studied the challenger for a moment, then suddenly recognized Henry. "You!" he spat in surprise. But Geoff's surprise melted and was quickly replaced by a mask of malevolent hatred. He squared himself to meet Henry and ripped a musket pistol from his trousers. He fired.

Henry dropped to the deck of the bridge and Geoff's errant shot whistled through the air where Henry had stood only a fraction of a second earlier. Henry jumped to his feet and charged forward.

339

Geoff barely had time to pull his saber from its scabbard before Henry was upon him. Geoff blocked Henry's first slashing blow with his saber, steel clanging against steel, and stepped sideways. The two men crouched and slowly circled one another, each seeking an opening. Geoff sensed his advantage. His sword was longer and lighter than Henry's cutlass, making it an easier weapon to wield. And he was bigger, with longer arms. He thrust his weapon forward in a succession of quick jabs, driving Henry backwards. He curled his lips into a sinister grin and taunted Henry.

"So, mate, we meet again." Geoff faked a thrust at Henry's chest, forcing Henry to leap further backwards. Geoff chuckled wickedly. "It's going to be the last time..." He circled the tip of his sword in front of Henry and then made a quick thrust at Henry's throat. Henry barely managed to block the blade with his cutlass and backed up a few more steps. "I'm going to slice you into little pieces, just like I did to your big, black friend. And then I'm going to feed you to the fish," Geoff spewed.

Henry's eyes flashed with furry. "You! It was you who killed Si Tundok!"

"Just like I'm about to do to you!" Geoff spat through his yellow teeth. He shot his arm forward in a lightning thrust.

Henry narrowly parried the blow to his chest, but Geoff's blade managed to slice the flesh of Henry's shoulder in the exchange. Henry winced. Geoff attacked again. But this time Henry dodged it by rolling to the side and Geoff's blade only caught air. Before Geoff could mount another attack, Henry began a slashing attack of his own.

"You bloody bastard!" Henry screamed. As if possessed by a demonic force, Henry swung the cutlass wildly, up and down, right and left, forcing Geoff to back away and defend himself from Henry's fury with quick parries of his sword.

But Henry pressed the attack. With little regard for protecting himself, Henry swung his cutlass from all angles, keeping Geoff on the defensive. Geoff continued to back up until he reached the top of the stairs which led from the bridge to the main deck below. Propelled by his anger and hate, Henry savagely moved forward, forcing Geoff to take a hesitant step to secure his foothold on the stair behind him.

Metal clanked against metal with the rapidity of a blacksmith pounding hot iron as Henry backed the bigger man down the stairway and toward the encroaching fire. Furiously, Henry chopped and hacked with his cutlass until Geoff was forced to grab the stair railing with his free hand to steady his downward retreat. Still Henry came forward, moving down the steps as rapidly as Geoff backed away from him.

His free hand sliding along the railing to steady himself, Geoff took the last step onto the main deck, but unaware that he had reached it, he stumbled with his trailing foot. Blindly he grabbed at the railing which was no longer there and for an instant, he was off balance and dipped the tip of his saber.

It was all the opening that Henry needed. He swung the heavy blade of his cutlass around in a tight sideways arc over the top of Geoff's lowered weapon. Henry's curved blade landed with a sickening crunch to the side of Geoff's head. The blade sliced Geoff's left ear and tore through the side of his skull, ripping through his eye socket and severing the top of his skull cleanly from the rest of his body. In a spasm of death, Geoff's body twitched spastically and tumbled backwards into the encroaching fire.

Henry stood on the lower step of the bridge and leaned against the railing. He breathed heavily and felt exhaustion course through his body. He stared at Geoff's corpse until it was thoroughly consumed by the fire. "For Si Tundok," he whispered before retreating aft and diving into the safety of the river.

XII

*HMS Skimalong*

Back aboard the *Skimalong*, Captain Irons quickly ordered the lowering of boats to rescue the survivors of the *Jolly Bachelor* and to dispatch any Dayaks they might find in the river trying to escape and then he turned his attention to Kuching. "Fetch my eyeglass," he commanded. "Mister Harris, come with me." They hurried to the stern of the ship and gazed across the river to the burning town. Timothy quickly ascertained that nearly one-half of Kuching was on fire, but the palace where he assumed James was residing, was still intact.

"Your eyeglass, Captain."

Timothy snatched the eyeglass and hoisted it to his eye. He scanned the burning town and saw the Chinese mob swarming through the streets tossing torches to the roofs of the buildings and massacring their inhabitants.

"Mister Harris, man the forward canon," he ordered.

"Aye, Aye, Captain!" Harris called for the forward gun crew and with a flurry of precise and well-trained movements, the bluejackets loaded and primed the two eight pound guns in the bow of the man-of-war and awaited further orders.

"Mister Harris, I want a volley of fire right in the midst of that mob. Can your crew do it?"

"Aye, Captain. We can do it."

"Very well then, fire when ready," Captain Irons said, coolly.

Harris estimated the elevation and instructed the gun crew. When they finished elevating the canon, he yelled, "Fire!"

Timothy watched through his eyeglass as the two balls of steel exploded short of the mob of Chinese. "Elevate the guns two degrees, Mister Harris and fire when ready."

No sooner had Timothy adjusted the focusing ring on the eyeglass than the crew fired a second volley of shot. Timothy watched the explosions fall near the center of the tightly packed mob. When the smoke and earth settled, he saw that the mob was scattering in a headlong flight toward the jungle.

"Elevate the guns another two degrees, Mister Harris," Timothy calmly said. "One more volley along the edge of the jungle should keep them running."

Loi Pek heard the whine of the plummeting cannon balls screeching towards him like a diving bird of prey. In his drug induced stupor, the old

342

Chinaman remained immutably fixed to the *bilian* log. Lok Pek only had time to lift his head skyward and touch at the long hairs protruding from his chin as if to ponder why it was that the Chinese New Years' celebration had suddenly turned upon him. Then, shrapnel from the *Skimalong's* final volley ripped through his shriveled flesh and killed him instantly.

# XIII

## Rajah's Palace

Kameja screamed and pulled the bedroom door closed behind her. James bolted upright in the cot. He heard the sound of commotion and gunfire and realized he was no longer dreaming. He tossed off the blanket covering his legs and leaped from the bed. "Kameja! What is it?"

"Api!" she screamed, her voice broken by terror. "He is here, in the palace!" She slammed the weight of her small body protectively against the lockless door.

James scrambled to pull on his breeches, his mind racing to grasp what it all meant. He heard the chaos of exploding guns and the shouts and screams of confusion coming from the Malay village and the river harbor and he saw flashes of light dart through the window and slam against the floor and walls of the room signaling that Kuching was on fire.

Api slammed his shoulder into the bedroom door and Kameja tumbled away from the door and rolled against the far wall. Api stood dark and tall in the doorway, his deadly eyes glued to the white Rajah.

James' leather girdle containing his sword and muskets dangled from a peg near the head of his bed. He reached for it, but he was too late.

Api lunged across the room, piercing the darkness with an ear-shattering war cry. With his shield held in his left hand and his *parang* raised over his head in his right hand, Api charged, prepared to deliver a single, deadly blow to James.

James was momentarily frozen by the sound of Api's war cry and the suddenness of the attack, but Kameja still dazed from her crash against the wall, managed to extend her leg out in time to trip Api. Api fell forward and tumbled towards James.

James ducked Api's errant blow and pivoted away from him just before Api's *parang* crashed harmlessly into the edge of James' cot. James didn't hesitate. He reached for the hilt of his saber and pulled it from the scabbard. No sooner had he grasped his weapon than Api had regained his balance and had wheeled to face James. Again he swung his *parang* at James.

James parried Api's blow and ducked sideways, near a side wall and delivered a thrust with his own sword. Api easily deflected James' thrust with his war shield and attacked James again. Kameja reached out to try to grab the Malay prince by his ankle, but Api saw her with his peripheral vision and

344

swung his war shield around and smashed it into the side of her face, knocking her unconscious.

Api bent his knees in a crouch and prepared himself for another lunging attack at James. His eyes blazed with the same hate and defiance James had seen on the Malay lord's face when they encountered one another at Siniawan. From the corner of his eye James could see Kameja lying slumped against the wall behind Api. He didn't know if she were dead or alive.

"Why?" he breathed as he prepared himself for Api's assault.

"Sarawak!" Api screamed. "It is mine by right of birth. I will bury you for it, white devil!" Api bolted forward as quick as a lunging leopard and whooped a loud war cry. He brought his *parang* down hard with a crushing blow.

James raised his sword in time to parry the heavy *parang*, but the force of Api's stroke knocked James' sword from his hand. But before Api could raise his *parang* to strike again, James lowered his head and charged Api's midsection. James' shoulders blasted against Api's war shield and drove him backwards. James wrapped his arms around Api's waist and continued to drive his legs across the small room, carrying the two men into the cot and tumbling them over it. The small bed collapsed under their weight and sent them crashing to the floor.

James kept his body pressed against Api's shield and grabbed Api's hand holding the *parang* before Api could bring it down on James' head. The two men grappled, Api trying to dislodge the taller man and James fighting with all his strength to prevent Api from breaking lose.

James held tightly to Api's wrist, preventing the Malay from using his *parang*. He kept his chest buried against Api's war shield while his other hand grabbed for Api's throat. James pounded Api's wrist holding the *parang* against the broken frame of the bed, but Api held tenaciously to his weapon. James' other hand dug and clawed into Api's throat until Api released his grasp on his war shield and pulled James' hand away from his neck.

Unable to wrest James' grip from his wrist, Api drove his free fist into the side of James' head. James' grip on Api's wrist slackened. Api pulled back his arm and delivered a violent blow with the heel of his hand into James' jaw. James' hand fell away from Api's wrist and when it did, Api twisted sideways and pushed with his knees and free hand and tossed James away from him.

James rolled over the top of the broken bed, dazed from Api's vicious blow. Before James could push himself from the floor, Api leaped to his feet and was bringing his *parang* down on James' neck in a final, culminating stroke of death.

Meanwhile, Arthur, having rescued Margaret from her hiding place in the water vase, sprinted to the perceived safety of the palace and reached the doorway to James' room in time to see a flash and hear the sound of a musket pistol being fired. In the half-light of the room, Arthur saw a tall Malay waiver unsteadily above James who was sprawled on the floor at the Malay's feet. A *parang* fell from the Malay's hand and bounced harmlessly on the floor at James' side. The Malay staggered and turned around slowly. His lips curled into a tight grimace of pain and hate and his frenzied eyes, like dying embers, sparked one final time with rancor before they rolled upwards in their sockets. Api reached out, his fingers arched like claws and extended his arms towards the far wall before he crashed to the floor.

Kameja, tears flowing down the sides of her smooth cheeks, held James' expended musket pistol in her trembling hands.

## EPILOGUE

### 1832
### Long Selah'at

Batu sat shoulder to shoulder in a tight circle with the Kayan, Jau and members of the Punan clan. The Punan listened silently and attentively to the words being exchanged between Batu and the Kayan Headman.

Both Batu and Jau chewed beetle nut which Jau had provided. Jau spat a stream of red liquid to the ground and said reflectively, "The old ways have changed, things are no longer the same as they once were."

Batu concurred with a nod of his head. He looked beyond Jau, to the village of Long Selah'at which had been rebuilt over the years. It wasn't as large or as prosperous as it once had been, but Batu felt grateful to still have the opportunity to trade the pygmy rhinoceros horns and the honey bear bladders for the much prized steel blades and spear tips Jau gave to them in exchange for their jungle products.

"There were signs even before the coming of the white Rajah," Batu said. "My people saw them and we feared it was the end of the world."

Jau wiped beetle nut juice from the corner of his mouth. He slowly lifted his head and his eyes drifted far into the jungle as if he were trying to recall a dream. "When the *Pengulu* Rentab told me of *Awang* Api's attack against the white Rajah, I traveled to Kuching with the Iban to see for myself." Jau shook his head slowly and sighed, "Many had been buried when we arrived...Chinese, Malay, Sulu, Dayaks and others. But it was not the same as when the Malay were the Rajahs of this land."

Batu tilted his head and looked questioningly at Jau.

"The Malay in those days would bury the shadows of the dead and afterward, things would never change. Sarawak always remained the same." Jau sighed pensively.

"How have things changed, Jau?" Batu inquired.

"There were many people gathered in Kuching on that day. Many who had once been enemies came there; Iban and Kayan, Bidayuh and Milanau, Kedayan and Chinese, even a few of the white people were there." With his finger, Jau removed the spent nut and leaf from his mouth and flicked it to the ground before he continued relating his story. "And there was peace among these people," he said.

Batu, unable to comprehend the lack of bitterness in Jau's voice since it was the coming of the white Rajah years earlier that had brought about the destruction of Long Selah'at asked, "Is this a good thing, Jau. Is it a good thing that Sarawak has a white Rajah?"

Jau shrugged. "Things have changed," he offered solemnly. "Whether it is for good or bad, I cannot say."

Batu reflected a moment and then said, "It is a difficult thing to bury a man with such a long shadow."

Jau and the Punan clan murmured their agreement.

**The End**

## AUTHOR'S NOTE

James Brooke (1803-1868) was the first of three successive Brooke's to rule as white Rajah's of Sarawak. In 1946, Sarawak was annexed to the British Crown. In 1963, Sarawak become one of fourteen states to form the Federation of Malaysia.

# GLOSSARY

| | |
|---|---|
| Amah | Maid |
| Api | Fire |
| Areca | Jungle wild nut |
| Awang | Youngest male of royal line |
| Baju | Shirt |
| Bakul | Basket |
| Banyak | Many |
| Batu | Rock or stone |
| Bao | Steamed and filled bun |
| Bidayuh | Dominant tribe of western Sarawak |
| Bilek | Room |
| Bilian | A hardwood tree |
| Borak | Bitter fermented rice beer |
| Brunei | Territory in northern Borneo |
| Bukit | Hill or mountain |
| Bulan sa'tinga | Midnight |
| Changkul | Hoe |
| Chawat | Loin cloth |
| Dapor | Kitchen |
| Datu | Male title of distinction |
| Dayak | Indigenous tribes native to Sarawak |
| Dayang | Feminine title of distinction |
| Durian | Sweet tasting but foul smelling fruit |
| Gadong | Climbing plant whose tubers are narcotic |
| Gawai | Celebration |
| Hantu | Ghost or spirit |
| Hutan | Jungle |
| Iban | Dominant tribe of central Sarawak |
| Ipoh | Poisonous tree |
| Jaga-Jaga | Take care as a warning |
| Jilangtan | A wild rubber tree |
| Jumbo Biji | Yellowish fruit |
| Kalapa Mudah | Green coconut |
| Kati | Unit of measurement |
| Kapitan | Leader of Chinese community |
| Kayan | Dominant tribe of eastern Sarawak |
| Kedai | Shop |

| | |
|---|---|
| Kongsi | Chinese community |
| Kris | Wavy bladed dagger |
| Kueh | Cake |
| Lalang | Long, course grass |
| Landas | Monsoon rains |
| Longan | Small, round fruit |
| Lychee | Fruit similar to a grape in texture |
| Mudah | Young |
| Nanjat | Native dance performed by males |
| Niap | Iban mating ritual |
| Nibong | Tall tufted palm used for flooring |
| Nipa | Palm used for thatching |
| Orang | Person |
| Orang-hutan | Literally, jungle person |
| Orang Puteh | White Person |
| Padi | Rice |
| Parang | Thick bladed sword |
| Pangirin | A title for princes and nobles |
| Pengulu | District headman |
| Prau | Dug-out canoe |
| Pukul | To strike |
| Punan | Tribe indigenous to Sarawak |
| Rambutan | Sweet, hairy fruit |
| Ruii | Covered verandah |
| Rumah | House |
| Rumah Tidor | Bedroom |
| Rusa | Miniature forest deer |
| Sago | Pithy palm tree |
| Sarawak | Territory in northwestern Borneo |
| Selamat Datang | Welcome |
| Selamat Pagi | Goodbye |
| Seperti Perempuan | Effeminate |
| Serah | System of taxation |
| Sireh | Betel vine |
| Sultan Mudah | Sultan's son |
| Tanju | Exposed open verandah |
| Terima Kaseh | Thank you |
| Tuan | Lord |
| Tuan Besar | Great Lord |
| Tuak | Thick, sweet rice wine |
| Tua | Old, elderly |
| Tua Kampong | Headman |